"Olivia."

Ben stepped close, too close. His shoulders blocked her view of the parking lot. They were secluded beneath a low willow tree. No one could see them.

She had time to change her mind. As she'd paid the bill and picked up her files, she could have changed her mind. But now, outside the restaurant, it wasn't fear or uncertainty skittering over her skin.

It was arousal. Arousal that this man had followed her outside. That this man had backed her up against her car, his big body blocking out the world.

She wanted his touch. Wanted his hands on her, wanted his mouth.

Wanted to lose herself in the taste and touch and feel of him.

His lips hovered a breath from hers. Heat radiated from his skin. His breath mingled with hers but neither of them moved. A twisting, writhing dance of almost touches, of the barest caresses.

She dared to lift her gaze from that strong mouth that so often wore an easy grin to his eyes, those dark, laughing eyes.

They weren't laughing now. They were desperately serious, dark, and hungry...

BACK TO YOU

"Touchingly sincere…Scott's prose is witty and sharp, and her delightful cast of characters keeps this delectable page-turner vibrant throughout."

—*Publishers Weekly* (starred review)

"A story with genuine honesty…This is a very real story about a marriage with all the good, the bad, and the things in between. The military aspect is realistic and well written. This novel will pull at your heartstrings and make the happy ending worth it."   —*RT Book Reviews*

"*Back to You* is a moving story with rich, layered characters and real, heartfelt emotion. Don't miss this fabulous read!"

—Brenda Novak, *New York Times*
bestselling author

"This is a great novel which combines a fantastic love story with harrowing realism about the cost being paid constantly for participating in war, and if I could give it more than five stars, I would."   —NightOwlReviews.com

JESSICA SCOTT

It's Always Been You

FOREVER

NEW YORK   BOSTON

Copyright © 2014 by Jessica Dawson
Excerpt from *Back to You* copyright © 2014 by Jessica Dawson
All rights reserved. In accordance with the U.S. Copyright Act of 1976, the scanning, uploading, and electronic sharing of any part of this book without the permission of the publisher constitute unlawful piracy and theft of the author's intellectual property. If you would like to use material from the book (other than for review purposes), prior written permission must be obtained by contacting the publisher at permissions@hbgusa.com. Thank you for your support of the author's rights.

Forever
Hachette Book Group
1290 Avenue of the Americas
New York, NY 10104

www.HachetteBookGroup.com

Printed in the United States of America

Originally published as an ebook

First mass-market edition: March 2015
10 9 8 7 6 5 4 3 2 1

OPM

Forever is an imprint of Grand Central Publishing.
The Forever name and logo are trademarks of Hachette Book Group, Inc.

The Hachette Speakers Bureau provides a wide range of authors for speaking events. To find out more, go to www.hachettespeakersbureau.com or call (866) 376-6591.

The publisher is not responsible for websites (or their content) that are not owned by the publisher.

To Michele
Thanks for going the distance with me

Acknowledgments

No matter how far we go in this world, we don't go it alone. I have to thank my husband and kids who put up with cereal for dinner and far too many cranky mommy mornings when I stayed up too late working. My fabulous agent, Donna Bagdasarian, who takes freak-out phone calls in the middle of the night and repeatedly talks me off the ledge. Dana Weinberg, you are a true mentor and friend. Thanks for letting me lean on you. Nick, thanks for letting me use your trucker hat story. It is now forever immortalized in a romance novel. Patty Collins, you told me once that feelings were real, they weren't necessarily true. Glad I listened to that and a lot more of your sage advice. Thanks for giving me the honor of command. And perhaps most importantly my talented editor, Michele Bidelspach. Thanks for not giving up on me with this one and for taking the time to help me get it right. We cut it close to the wire on this one but I'm truly grateful to have you in my corner.

It's Always Been You

Prologue

Is this hell? Because it feels like hell." Second Lieutenant Ben Teague swiped his sleeve across his forehead and accomplished absolutely nothing. Sweat still dripped steadily down his forehead as he walked the perimeter of their tiny combat outpost with his platoon sergeant.

"Don't start complaining about the air conditioner again." Next to him, SFC Escoberra scowled at him.

Ben smirked and patted Sarn't Escoberra on his shoulder. It was so easy to get his platoon sergeant irritated. "I was not going to mention the a/c. What makes you think I'd do such a thing?"

"Fuck off, LT." Escoberra looked down the alley toward the city that hated them. It was a shit position, as shit positions went. Nothing quite like being alone and unafraid on the battlefield.

"Easy there, big fella. Didn't mean to get your PTSD all riled up."

Escoberra snarled and Ben grinned. "You're in a lovely mood. Don't tell me you're cranky about this lovely little mission, too?"

"Don't start, LT."

"What? We can barely defend our position, we don't have enough ammo, and we're not serving any purpose other than to hold some piece of real estate down. The commander can't even give me a good reason for us to be out here."

Beside him, Escoberra sighed heavily and lifted his weapon, checking the field of fire. "LT, you need to quit pissing and moaning about this. The men are going to hear you."

Ben sobered and snapped his mouth closed. His platoon sergeant was right. It wasn't good to let the boys hear the leadership arguing about the mission. "Let's change the subject to something less depressing. How's the family?"

Escoberra's eyes crinkled at the edges. "My wife seems to think our almost twelve-year-old daughter needs a personal trainer."

Ben coughed, trying to hide a laugh. "Yeah, 'cause that's all you need is to think about your daughter getting smoking hot while you're deployed."

"Not funny. I'm not ready for her to grow up yet and she's not even mine," Escoberra said quietly. "I love that little kid. I swear to God if some raging hard-on hurts her…"

"No boy is going to dare come around with you there."

"That's the problem. I'm not there," Escoberra said. "I'm stuck here."

Ben adjusted the strap on his weapon then toed the concertina wire strung across a low concrete barrier. "Does her dad ever come into the picture?"

"Nah. He's out of the picture. I'm not complaining, though. She might not be mine by blood but she's family in every other way that matters." Escoberra glanced down the road. "And speaking of the commander, guess who's coming to the family dinner for a site visit later tonight?"

Ben rubbed his eyes beneath his sunglasses and let out a hard sigh of frustration. "I don't want to deal with the fucking commander. I'd rather deal with my mother."

Escoberra snorted. "What's wrong with your mother now?"

"The Almighty Colonel Diane Teague called the battalion commander and tried to get me moved to go take an executive officer job. Fuck that, man. I don't want to count pens and toilet paper." Ben wiped his gloved hand over his forehead, looking out over the edge of the barrier on the roof. Their single building stronghold wasn't exactly an impenetrable fortress but at least it provided a nice view of the city. When things weren't getting blown all to hell around them.

"She's just trying to look out for your career."

"My mom needs to worry about her part of the war and let me worry about mine." Grit scraped over his skin. "Fuck, man, moms are supposed to bake cookies and kiss your boo-boo when it hurts. Mine eats napalm and pisses razor wire."

"You never struck me as the kind of guy who had mommy issues," Escoberra said.

"Screw you, man. I don't. I was just saying I'd rather deal with her than the commander. The commander is a pain in my ass that can get me killed as opposed to just a pain in the ass. See the difference?" Ben spat into the dirt, not actually wanting to delve into talking about his mother. He shouldn't have brought it up. "We need to get ready to head out on patrol. Maybe I can avoid the commander if I'm too busy getting shot at."

"Play nice, LT. I'm tired of the first sergeant running a wire brush over my ass because you're constantly fighting with the commander. You're a lieutenant, he's your boss. You don't get to tell him how you really feel about things," Escoberra said. His words were mild but beneath the calm was a temper. Ben knew this firsthand, and as much as he liked screwing with Escoberra, he also knew his limits.

He wasn't entirely sure that Escoberra wouldn't take his head off if given the right provocation. "Think of it as an exfoliation treatment," Ben said after a while.

After an impossible silence, Escoberra finally glanced at him, then looked back out toward the endless, dusty city. It was too quiet out there. "The sun is getting to you. You should drink water."

Ben bit his bottom lip where it had split some time during their last firefight. It opened again with the movement and warm, coppery blood coated his tongue. He spat into the dirt. "It's a hundred and twenty-six degrees. Of course the sun is getting to me." He adjusted his body armor, itching to go out on patrol and *do* something. "Tell me again why we're hanging out here?"

"Waiting for the bad guys to drive right by." Escoberra pointed at a white pickup that zipped by the end of the road, then stopped. Two faces peered out at them.

Ben's stomach flipped beneath his ribs. His heart started racing in his chest. "You're really fucking scary sometimes with that warrior intuition shit you've got going on."

Escoberra palmed the butt stock of his weapon. "Call it in. Get air support en route. This could get ugly."

But Ben didn't get the chance. A brilliant flash of heat seared across his skin a second before the boom knocked him on his ass.

And then all hell broke loose.

Chapter One

Fort Hood, 2009

Four years later

Captain Ben Teague prayed to the caffeine gods and waited for the espresso machine to dispense the morning sacrifice. He'd never really considered why an infantry battalion had an espresso machine in the middle of the battalion operations office but right then, he wanted to kiss the man who'd had the foresight to buy it and keep it well-stocked with beans.

Somehow, he didn't think that Sergeant Major Cox would appreciate the gesture.

It was four-thirty in the morning on a Monday and someone had had the good idea to call an alert. Which meant that instead of getting to sleep like a normal person, Ben and everyone else in this clusterfuck of a battalion had dragged their carcasses on post at the ass crack of dawn.

Ben was liable to stab someone if he didn't get coffee stat.

Funny, he'd actually thought he was going to finally get some sleep when he'd actually nodded off. But as usual, it had all been a tease. The phone had yanked him out of that fog between sleep and waking. Damn it, he was getting caffeine before the morning briefing.

He kicked his New Kids on the Block trucker hat higher up on his head and counted to ten while the espresso machine ground the beans, then dispensed the precious liquid.

The warning light flashed red and the steady stream of espresso dripped to a halt. Ben wanted to cry.

"It needs water, sir."

"Thank you, Captain Obvious." Ben shot Sergeant Dean Foster a baleful look then jerked his thumb toward the espresso machine, saying nothing further. He wasn't in the mood to deal with Foster's smart-ass comments this morning. Not when Ben's sense of irony was still hung over from the night before.

"Did someone wake up on the wrong side of the bed?" Foster asked, taking the lid off the reservoir. "Do you need a hug?"

"No jokes before caffeine. Off with you, minion." Ben narrowed his eyes then waved his hands. "Now to figure out why the hell we're here at this ungodly hour," Ben muttered.

Not that it mattered. Ben had long ago given up trying to change things. And to think, once upon a time, he'd thought he could make a difference.

What a miserable joke.

"Teague, I don't give a flying fuck how much you were abused as a child, if you don't get that goddamned hat off in my building..."

"Good morning to you, too, sunshine," Ben said to the battalion sergeant major. Any day he could get the sergeant major's goat was a good day. It was one of life's few pleasures.

"Teague, one of these days..."

Someday, that would backfire on him. Until then, though..."We'll go take a long hot shower together and you can tell me your childhood traumas?"

Sarn't Major swung at him but Teague ducked. His hat wasn't so lucky. Cox grabbed it and tore the thin white mesh in half. Sarn't Major Cox was five and a half feet tall and about as wide, and none of it was fat.

"Oh come on!" Ben threw his arms up in mock disgust. "It took me at least four hours of surfing the Internet to find that hat."

Cox held up a single finger then balled his hand into a fist around Ben's hat. Cox balled up the hat and threw it at Ben's chest. "We've got brothers and sisters who died in this uniform. How about you start treating it with some fucking honor?" he growled as he stormed by. "Get your sorry ass in the conference room. You've got a meeting with the boss in twenty minutes."

Ben ground his teeth looking down at the rank on his gray uniform. Honor?

Ben knew all about it. It didn't get you anywhere.

Foster walked back in, carefully carrying the water. "Mission accomplished?"

"Yep. Right on target. And I even did it before coffee." Ben sighed. "What's going on?"

Foster shrugged. "No clue but there's a line of dudes outside the battalion commander's office right now."

Ben frowned. "Huh?"

"'Bout fifteen dudes lined up in the hallway." Foster said, jerking his thumb over his shoulder.

"No shit?"

Ben walked out of the office and turned down the hall toward the conference room. Foster wasn't kidding. There were sergeants and officers from every company in the battalion. Ben couldn't remember the last time he'd seen a line like this outside the boss's office.

Ben stopped short, his breath caught in his throat. Escoberra stood near the front. His arms were folded at parade rest, his palms resting at the small of his back. He stood solid and unmoving. Ben stood there, frozen. Escoberra shifted. For a moment their eyes locked and for the briefest flicker, Ben saw the warrior he'd admired and looked up to when he'd been a scrappy, smart-assed lieutenant. Before he'd failed to defend a man he'd have followed to hell and back again.

Escoberra was still a warrior. It was Ben who had changed. Ben who had let the time and the bad memories drive him away from a man who'd been as close to a father figure as Ben could have asked for.

There were shadows in his former platoon sergeant's eyes now. Deep and dark.

Ben took a deep breath. A single step toward a man he admired and looked up to. Heat crawled up the back of Ben's neck. He wanted to speak, to say something to the man who'd saved his ass more times than he could remember.

"Escoberra!" The sergeant major's voice rang out. Escoberra ground his teeth and looked away, before he snapped to the position of attention and disappeared into the sergeant major's office.

It took everything Ben had to stand there while Escoberra walked away. He wanted to ask how the family was. How he was doing since the last deployment.

But Ben let him go. Because to say anything would be to acknowledge that the man in that hallway had changed. Ben didn't know if it was the war, if it was some fucked-up trauma, but the war had changed him, changed them all.

And Ben no longer knew the man in that hallway. Shame burned on his neck, the weight of his failure heavy around his shoulders.

Ben broke into a wide grin as he walked into the conference room and saw an old familiar face. "Holy shitballs!"

Captain Sean Nichols looked up from his BlackBerry, his

dark expression going from guarded to grinning the moment he recognized Ben. "Holy shit, you're not in jail?"

"Very funny." Ben gripped his old friend's hand and pulled him into a one-armed man hug. "Some things never change. What are you doing here?"

"Looking for a job, apparently," Sean said.

Ben frowned. "Huh?"

"Supposedly there's some command positions opening up soon." Nichols ran his hand over the back of his neck. "I'm supposed to interview today but there's some massive shitstorm going on."

"Yeah, I saw that. Where have you been?"

"Iraq, Afghanistan, and back again." Sean nodded toward the other officers in the room. There was a big dude in one corner who looked like a professional wrestler, talking with one of the first sergeants. "These all your guys?"

"Nope. Never seen any of them before," Ben said.

The battalion commander, Lieutenant Colonel Gilliad, walked in, followed by Sarn't Major Cox and a small brunette major Ben had never seen before. She walked stiff and straight, and her hair was pulled back sharply from her face. Her right sleeve was missing a combat patch. Ben found himself wondering how she had been in the army long enough to be a major but had somehow managed to miss the war.

He didn't look away as she scanned the room, her eyes cool and appraising.

Ben wasn't fooled. He'd seen that look far too many times.

She was a woman on a mission. Just what they needed: a lawyer on crusade. Ben didn't do crusades.

They all snapped to attention as the commander walked to the center of the room.

"Gentlemen, welcome to Death Dealer Battalion. Congratulations. Every one of you in this room will take command in less than a month," Gilliad said.

Silence hung in the heavens for half a moment. No one moved. No one spoke.

Ben breathed in deep and slow, keeping the ragged edge of his emotions in check. "Uh, sir, I think there's a mistake."

Gilliad pinned him with a hard look. Next to him, the major looked down at her paperwork, shaking her head, disapproval written on her pretty face.

"Teague, I'll see you in my office." Gilliad turned back to the other captains. "Bello, you and First Sarn't Delgado have Diablo Company. Martini, you and First Sarn't Tellhouse have Assassin Company. Teague, your first sergeant will be here before the week is out. You're taking Bandit Company. Navarro, you and First Sarn't Sagarian are taking Headquarters Company. Nichols, you and First Sarn't Morgan are taking Chaos Company."

"Sir—"

"Let the commander finish, Captain Teague," Sarn't Major Cox warned quietly.

Ben ground his teeth and fought the anxiety twisting in his guts.

Gilliad cleared his throat. "Every company command team in this battalion has been relieved of their duties effective immediately. You all are the new team. Major Hale is going to help with transition on the legal side of the house. We have our hands full, gentlemen, and I expect you to clean house and get this unit back to fully mission ready."

Ben blew out a low whistle. He'd never heard of something like this. Not in his entire life as a military brat or his own career. One commander, maybe two in rapid succession, but an entire battalion worth of company leadership fired on the spot?

And Gilliad expected Ben to be one of the new commanders? Not in this lifetime.

Gilliad continued. "The forward support company leadership is changing out as well. That new command team will be on the ground shortly as soon as the support battalion figures out who that will be." He glanced over at the small major. "Major Hale has my guidance. Your number one priority for the next forty-five days is getting rid of the shitbag soldiers running this unit into the ground. I want the druggies gone. I want the dealers and the gangbangers gone. I want the fucking criminals out of my army. Am I clear?"

A murmured *hooah* went through the gathered men.

Ben couldn't speak.

His lungs had stopped working.

Command.

He didn't want this. He couldn't do it.

There had to be a mistake. The boss could find someone else.

He had to.

Because to command, you still had to believe what you did mattered. He released a shuddering breath.

And Ben hadn't believed that in a long, long time.

Major Olivia Hale watched the captain at the edge of the room. His back was stiff and straight and he radiated unspent fury. She wondered at the tired lines beneath his eyes, the hard set of his jaw.

He was so furious at being told he was taking command. The rest of the men had stiffened with awareness. Excitement. Command was the greatest reward for an officer's hard work—a chance to lead soldiers and make a difference. Olivia would command in a heartbeat if she could. Successful commanders made their units better places.

Why didn't this dark and angry captain want the job?

She lifted her chin. Whether or not the pissed off captain took the job wasn't her problem. Her job was to help clean up this unit. She'd been asked personally to assist by the division commander—she'd been on his staff many moons ago when she'd been a brand new shiny lieutenant and she'd loved working for him. He'd been decisive. He'd been a mentor.

She hadn't been able to say no when he'd asked her to help this battalion.

"Gentlemen, I need time with each of you to go over the current status of your legal situations." She pointed to the stacks of folders in front of her. "I've got each company's information here. Please take your files and look them over before you come see me."

Gilliad nodded once in her direction. "Olivia is the best at what she does. We are going to clean this battalion up."

The angry captain shifted and she saw his nametag. Teague.

"Motherfucker," he muttered, loud enough for the entire room to hear.

"Teague!" Sarn't Major Cox exploded but LTC Gilliad held up his hand.

"In my office. Now, captain."

Teague shoved off the wall and stalked out of the conference room, followed closely by the battalion commander.

She watched him go, her gaze hanging on the man struggling with such fierce resentment at being given a great honor. What kind of man interrupted his battalion commander?

What kind of man was so angry at the chance to be a leader?

She pushed her thoughts away. He was not her problem. She focused on the men in front of her as they stopped by the conference room table.

A tall, lean captain with dark hair and green eyes stopped near the table. "Sean Nichols, ma'am. Do we have any discretion in these cases?"

"What kind of discretion are you talking about, Captain Nichols?"

"In general. Do we get to say this kid did a dumb thing and he deserves a second chance?"

There was nothing Olivia could say. She knew there was a difference between the right answer and the legal answer, and even the army answer. "That's going to be a conversation between you and the battalion commander."

The tall captain nodded once and left, and after another moment, Olivia was alone in the conference room with the sergeant major.

She didn't quite know what to think of Sergeant Major Cox. He was her height but stocky and he looked mean as hell. She definitely wasn't used to his kind outside of the hospital headquarters where she used to work.

"Things are going to get rough around here, ma'am," he said after a long silence. His voice sounded like gravel and rocks.

"I'm not sure I understand what you mean."

"You start taking away people's livelihoods and things start getting tense. So while I have no doubt that the new command teams can handle things, just watch yourself around here. Don't hesitate to let me know if you're having problems with any soldier."

"Thank you for the warning," she said, not wanting to alienate the command sergeant major. "I've seen the misconduct you have down in this battalion, Sergeant Major. The quantity doesn't even come close to some of the terrible things I've seen."

"I hope you're right." Cox rubbed his hand over his mouth. "One more thing. You see that?"

He pointed toward a black cowboy hat with gold cord wrapped around the base that he'd carried in with him. "Yes?"

"Get one. You can't be assigned here without it."

She smiled flatly. "I'll add it to my to-do list."

She couldn't care less about the silly hat, but she just smiled and nodded and headed to her next meeting.

She was here to do a job, not buy a hat and the swagger that went along with it.

Chapter Two

"There really needs to be a good reason my phone is ringing at four a.m. on a Tuesday." Ben leaned his head into his palm and held the phone to his ear. He'd just fallen asleep a half hour before and right then, he felt like committing murder and mayhem.

"I'm at the hospital."

Ben sat up, instantly awake at the familiar voice. "Escoberra?"

"Yeah."

Ben blinked rapidly, trying to clear his brain and think about why Escoberra would be calling him this early. Or at all.

Then he remembered. He was the commander.

"Are you okay?" he asked.

"No. Just. I need my commander here—and that happens to be you. As soon as you can get here." His voice broke and the line went dead.

Cold slithered down Ben's spine as he sat for a moment. His hands shook as bitter, angry memories crashed over him, none of them good. He sat and breathed deeply, trying to let them go as opposed to stuffing them back down again.

But they were relentless, pounding away on the inside

of his skull like the thundering of artillery on a distant battlefield.

His lungs ached but the memory came anyway. Once again, he was standing at the position of attention in front of his commander.

"Sir, I gave the order."

"You were flat on your ass getting your guts stitched up." His battalion commander looked at him. *"The enemy broke through six t-wall barriers, killed four of your men, and you're telling me you gave the order to pursue in direct defiance of my orders."*

Ben exhaled sharply, the memory as raw as it had been four years ago.

Funny how therapy never worked outside the office.

But after a minute, he stopped thinking about when things had started fraying at the edges and focused on the here and now. And that meant getting his ass up and on post. He pulled on a pair of sweatpants and an old sweatshirt. The jagged scar on his belly itched and he rubbed it absently before he rinsed his mouth then headed out the door.

It didn't bother him so much anymore. Except when it did.

Fifteen minutes later, he flashed his ID card at the emergency room entrance and asked at the desk for Escoberra.

He was not prepared to see two young MPs guarding him. "Jesus, what happened?"

Escoberra looked up, his eyes red and watery—from drinking or crying, Ben couldn't tell. "Hailey. They said I beat Hailey."

Time froze as Ben looked at a man he'd worshiped and saw now as a broken, beaten man. "Is she okay?"

Jesus, how old was Hailey now? Fifteen? Sixteen? Ben couldn't remember. It had been so long since he'd seen her.

"They're checking her out now." Escoberra covered his face with his hands. "I don't know."

Ben sucked in a deep breath, his brain racing. What the hell was he supposed to do? He scrubbed his hand over his mouth. "I'll go see if I can find anything out," he said quietly.

He stepped outside the small room and leaned back against the wall, closing his eyes against the unexpected sting.

"Hey, you okay?"

He opened his eyes at the familiar voice. Captain Emily Lindberg stood near his shoulder, looking neat and prim in a white lab coat.

Emily had started dating Sergeant First Class Reza Iaconelli, one of Ben's good friends, a few months ago. Despite their being from completely different worlds, she and Reza worked together. Luckily for Ben, his best friend's significant other was a resident shrink at the hospital.

"You look far too awake right now," he said by way of greeting.

"I've been here since last night," Emily said. "I've been mainlining coffee since about nine p.m." She folded her arms over her chest. "What's got you in here?"

Ben breathed out hard. "Apparently I'm a company commander now."

She made a sympathetic noise. "Reza mentioned that."

"I have a soldier who may have put his—" Ben stopped, his throat blocked. There was a long pause before he cleared his throat roughly. "His daughter's being examined. Can you help me find out any info?"

He liked Emily, but for a brief second he thought she was going to grip his shoulder or show some sympathy. Ben wasn't sure he could hold himself together. Not for that.

"Sure. What's her name?"

"Hailey Escoberra."

"Give me a few."

Ben went back into the room with the two military police and Escoberra and stared at the cops. "Do you two really need to be here?"

He shouldn't be a dick but he didn't like what their presence implied.

He couldn't wrap his brain around what it all meant.

"Are you taking custody of him, sir?" the little female private asked.

"Yes," was all he said. It might have been true, it might not have. Ben didn't know and he didn't care. But he damn sure wasn't going to let them continue to sit there and treat Escoberra like a criminal.

"We're going to need him to be brought to CID tomorrow," the private said.

"Call my ops tomorrow. Later today. Whatever." Ben nudged a small black stool out from beneath the stainless steel sink.

For a moment Ben thought they were going to argue but then, mercifully, they left.

"What happened?" he finally said when he was sure he could speak.

"I don't know." Escoberra leaned back against the wall, his face a mask of misery and guilt. "Hailey was arguing with her little brother and the next thing I know, we're here."

Ben looked away. Down at his hands, clenched into useless fists in his lap. He wanted to ask but was terrified of the answer. If Escoberra was so drunk he didn't remember doing it...Jesus, he couldn't even think it.

"I didn't do it."

Ben opened his mouth to speak, then snapped it closed again. The door opened and Escoberra's wife Carmen walked in. Her eyes were red, her jaw set. She smiled sadly when she saw Ben. "Hey, stranger."

Ben stood and hugged the woman he'd asked to adopt

him once upon a time when he'd been a renegade lieutenant and Carmen had love and giving and kindness to spare.

She was everything his own mother wasn't.

"How's Hailey?" he asked, wondering where Emily was.

"She's fine. Three stitches on her shoulder." Carmen slipped from his arms and moved to Escoberra. She knelt in front of him, cupping his face. "She's fine," she whispered to her husband. "She wants to see you."

A sob ripped from Escoberra's throat, violent and torn. He collapsed against his wife who knelt there, her arms tight around his neck.

Ben slipped from the room, wishing he hadn't been such a shit to let his friendship with Escoberra and his family lapse.

"Hey?"

Emily motioned for him to follow her. She closed the door in a separate exam room behind them.

"This doesn't bode well," he said dryly.

She didn't smile. "The entire family is shutting down. No one will talk but the hospital has triggered a Child Protective Services case anyway."

Ben's heart pounded in his throat. "I don't know what that means."

"It means you need to call Olivia and get legal advice about what to do next."

Ben frowned. "Olivia?"

"Major Olivia Hale. She's a good friend of mine. Didn't she just start working in your unit?"

Ben thought of the rigid female major he'd seen in the conference room, what, yesterday? "Somehow, I don't think she's going to be up for a four—" he glanced at his watch. "Five a.m. phone call."

Emily moved then, sliding her fingers over his shoulder. His scars throbbed where she touched him. It took everything he had not to flinch. To stand straight and steady and hide his reaction from her.

Because if what Reza said was true, Emily was pretty damn perceptive; and Ben wasn't really up for sitting on her couch and spilling his guts.

And he damn sure wasn't about to call the lawyer.

Bad things always happened when lawyers got involved. Like hell was he going to call her.

Olivia walked into the emergency room a half hour later. Her stomach wrenched with an all too familiar anxiety.

Teague hadn't called her. She was there only because Emily had given her a heads-up about the platoon sergeant in the hospital with his daughter.

Granted, Emily had given Teague the benefit of the doubt but Olivia had her own suspicions about what was going on. She'd seen too many soldiers shielded by commanders, soldiers who had done terrible things.

She hoped she was wrong, that a friend of Emily's wouldn't do something like that, but the fact that Emily had called her and not Teague didn't bode well.

Olivia was braced for a fight—not exactly high on her to-do list first thing in the morning, but it was her job.

She walked into the back and found Emily talking to the tall, angry captain from the conference room.

He wasn't angry this morning. He looked wrecked, as if part of his soul had been taken outside and stomped. Her heart slammed against her ribs.

She knew that look, etched into the lines around his dark eyes—the look of someone devastated by a doctor's words. Old memories collided with the sterile reality of the emergency room and she shoved aside the churning emotions she saw on his face to focus on the facts.

She walked up, palming her keys, ID card, and cell

phone in one hand while she extended the other. "Captain Teague?"

He accepted her offered hand. Olivia wished she didn't notice the strength in his fingers, the heat in his touch.

She didn't want to notice. She couldn't.

"Yes, ma'am."

"What's going on here?" she asked, keeping her voice mild. She looked between Emily and Teague.

"I'll let him fill you in," Emily said. "I've got to go make my rounds." She glanced over at Teague. "Are you going to be okay?"

It was one of the things that Olivia loved about Emily— her endless compassion. Teague looked at her, his eyes bleak. The compassion Olivia had felt earlier was back, stronger, urging her to offer comfort where she knew it would do little good.

She deliberately took a step back, needing personal and professional distance from the torment she saw in his eyes.

"I don't really have a choice now, do I," he said to Emily. There was irony in his voice, a deep-seated anger below the surface.

She wondered why Emily didn't call him on his response. But then she remembered that Emily had said Teague was a friend of Emily's other half, Reza.

That would explain things.

Olivia folded her arms across her chest. "So what's the story?"

"Supposedly, there's a Child Protective Services thing being triggered?" He sounded unsure. "The family wants him to come home. What do I do?"

"Why is CPS involved?"

"I don't know." He refused to look up at her, staring instead at his feet.

She had the distinct sense that he was hiding something

but she couldn't get a read on what it could be. "Why is the daughter in the hospital?"

"Three stitches."

Olivia took a deep breath. They could be here all day if this was how he answered questions, one at a time and excruciatingly slowly. "There's a mandatory three-day cooling off period. You have to order him into the barracks and give him a no-contact order."

He looked up sharply at that information. "His wife wants him to come home."

"His wife doesn't get a vote," Olivia said simply. She'd seen this movie one too many times. The wife loved her husband, loved him enough to bring him home after an incident of domestic violence.

The story too often ended the same way—with a dead wife.

It was worse, so much worse, when there were kids involved. Her heart ached as memories unfurled inside her. Memories of a time long past that, try though she might, she couldn't forget.

People were counting on her not to forget what it felt like to be that little girl in the exam room.

Olivia took a deep breath and focused on the here and now, shoving away the bad memories. *Judge each case on its own merit.*

Teague straightened. "What do you mean, his wife doesn't get a vote?"

"You don't have a choice in giving him the no-contact order and putting him in the barracks for the cooling off period," Olivia said. "That's dictated by higher headquarters."

She watched his eyes darken as the meaning of her words sank in.

She braced for the argument. She narrowed her eyes, studying him, trying to get a read on the man in front of her as she listed the other formalities.

"Okay," he said simply after a pause.

"You don't look too happy about it," she said softly.

The muscle in his jaw pulsed; his neck was tight and tense. He looked away, down the shiny hallway. "I'm not."

Olivia let the silence hang on for a moment. "The first ninety days in command are always the roughest," she said quietly.

He grunted in response. "Thanks for the encouragement."

He pushed away from the wall and headed down the hallway. Olivia watched him go. He was hiding something.

But for the life of her, she couldn't figure out what.

She'd have ample opportunity, though, in the coming months. She signed out of the emergency room and headed to her car, making a note of the case information for her spreadsheet.

She'd never lose track of another case. Ever again.

"Captain Teague!"

Ben stiffened behind his company formation. He wasn't in the mood to deal with Sarn't Major Cox, not after spending the last two hours getting Escoberra and his family out of the hospital. He didn't want to be the one responsible for keeping Escoberra away from his family.

He knew, *knew,* that Escoberra hadn't hurt Hailey.

Major Hale's recommendations chafed. There was no way he was going to restrict his old platoon sergeant from going home—not when his wife wanted him there.

Ben didn't know what the hell had happened to get Hailey put in the hospital but he damn sure wasn't going to add to the stress.

He owed Escoberra too much.

Ben sighed and headed toward the sergeant major, crossing the quad toward him. Cox saluted sharply and Ben returned the salute.

"What happened this morning at the hospital?" Cox asked.

Ben ground his teeth. If he told Cox, the old man was going to find out, and once the battalion commander knew, it was going to be out of Ben's hands. Hell, it might already be out of his hands.

"One of my platoon sergeant's kids ended up in the hospital. Fighting or something."

The lie felt awkward and thick on his tongue.

Cox rocked back on his heels. "Was she admitted?"

"No."

The cannon went off and the entire formation shifted. One of the platoon sergeants called "present, arms" and as one the formation saluted, rendering honors to the flag. Reveille ended and Ben dropped his salute, turning back to the sergeant major.

"I could really use my first sergeant down here, Sarn't Major," Ben said. It was as close as he could come to asking Cox for help.

He had some pride, after all.

"He'll be here in the next day or so. We asked him to sign in early." Cox spat into the dirt. "So there's nothing else I need to know about this morning at the hospital?"

Ben bit the inside of his lip and shook his head, hating the job that put him in this position, where he had to lie to the leadership in the battalion or betray one of his own.

Of the two, betrayal was the worse sin. He could sleep at night with the lie—well, if he slept, that is. He and sleep weren't exactly BFFs.

Beside him, Cox grunted and toed the dirt. "I hope there's nothing the boss needs to know, Teague," Cox said quietly.

"Or what, Sarn't Major? I'll get fired?" He tried to look hopeful and failed. He was just too damn tired.

"You wish. You're not getting fired, Teague. You can just get that out of your damn mind once and for all."

"Shit," Teague muttered.

Cox shook his head. "I don't know what the hell is wrong with you. Most officers would jump at the chance to command."

"Yeah, well, I'm not most officers. I'm not up for throwing my soldiers under the bus to save my own ass."

Cox stared at him, hard, and Teague wondered if he was getting ready to snap. The old man wasn't known for his sanity. "There's more to command than saving your own ass. If you're too stupid to figure that out, then maybe you don't deserve this damn job."

Cox walked away, leaving Ben alone, trying to figure out what the hell had just happened.

Cox knew he was lying. He wasn't sure if Cox knew the specifics but that didn't matter. He knew.

And he hadn't called Ben on it.

Ben scrubbed his hand across his mouth, wondering how to read between the lines.

"You look grumpy. Did the coffee pot break again?"

Ben turned to see Sergeant First Class Reza Iaconelli approaching from the Headquarters Company formation.

"I saw Emily this morning," Ben said, falling into step with Reza. They were both in PTs for first formation. Good a time as any to go for a long, therapeutic run.

"Yeah, she told me. How's Escoberra's kid?"

Ben swallowed the lump in his throat. "She's okay."

"What happened?"

"I'm going running. You coming?"

Reza nodded. "Sure. How far you going?"

"I was thinking the water tower across post."

"Someone's in a mood," Reza said.

"Just because your old ass . . ."

"Don't start with the rehab jokes," Reza growled.

"What?" They fell into step, weaving through the masses

of formations and bodies running on Battalion Avenue. The sun was just creeping over the corps headquarters across post and the sound of five thousand feet running in formation beat a rhythm into Ben's chest.

It was a comfortable rhythm.

"How're things with Emily?" Ben asked.

He glanced over and saw Reza's face break into a slow grin. "She's good."

"Look at you, going all soft and mushy over a woman." Ben rolled his eyes. "You've got it bad, don't you?"

"Yeah."

A simple statement but one he'd never thought he'd hear from his longtime friend. Reza was always going to struggle with alcohol but he'd found someone to stand with him.

It was a fucking miracle and damn if Reza wasn't a guy who deserved some good luck.

"I'm happy for you," Ben said after a long silence.

"Thanks."

They ran in silence, the only sound the rhythmic shuffle of their feet on the pavement. Ben lost himself in the beat, falling into the rhythm and letting it take over every conscious thought.

"What are you going to do about Escoberra?" Reza asked when they reached the tower.

Ben turned around, heading back toward Cav country.

"I don't know. I don't believe Carmen would let him back into the house if he beat up Hailey. She wouldn't put up with his shit." Ben smiled. The one time Ben had gone out drinking with Escoberra and they'd gone back to the house drunk and needing a place to crash, she'd put him to bed and then given him hell the next morning, all while cooking him breakfast.

"The lawyer was in the headquarters this morning, talking about it with the battalion commander," Reza said quietly. "If you're planning on telling him, you might need to go see him when we get back."

"Goddamn it," Ben muttered. "She has no business telling the boss this shit."

"She sure as hell didn't see it that way."

Heat that had nothing to do with the run scorched through his veins. He picked up the pace until his lungs burned and his thighs screamed.

He figured running some of the aggression in his blood out *before* he got a hold of that major was going to be a good thing. Maybe then he'd be able to hold on to a trace of his military bearing.

He wasn't exactly known for his tact.

They turned into the battalion footprint and lo and behold, there was the target of his frustration.

Ben started across the field, ready to throttle Major Hale.

"Whoa." Reza grabbed his shoulder, stopping him before he could leave. "Calm the hell down."

"No. No goddamned staff officer is going to do my job for me."

"You weren't going to tell him," Reza pointed out.

"That's not the point," Ben snapped. "Escoberra was like a father to me and goddamn it—"

"Goddamn it what, Captain?"

Ben turned to see the little major suddenly standing behind him. Great, she was a ninja, too.

He refused to salute. "Goddamn it, *ma'am*, you have no business briefing the battalion commander about my soldiers."

Major Hale lifted her chin. "That's where you're wrong, Captain Teague," she said quietly. "It's in my duty description to make sure you're doing your job." She tipped her head and smiled sweetly. "And since you didn't opt to inform your commander that one of your NCOs put one of his children in the hospital last night, I did it for you."

"He didn't do it," Ben said, barely restraining the violent anger in his voice.

"That's not for you to decide," she said quietly.

"It's not for you to decide, either," Ben spat. He took a step closer, not giving a damn who saw. "You might be down here to clean up the battalion, but don't get your responsibilities confused with my goddamned job."

She lifted her chin, refusing to back down. A part of him admired her willingness to go toe to toe with him. "Maybe if you did your job, *Captain,* I wouldn't have to," she hissed.

"Captain Teague! Major Hale!"

Ben stiffened as the battalion commander's voice interrupted the anger throbbing in his temples.

He took a single step backward.

"What the ever-loving hell is going on that I've got two officers getting into a pissing contest in front of the troops?" Gilliad pinned Ben with a hard look. "And who the hell do you think you are to talk to one of my majors that way?"

Out of the corner of his eye, he saw Major Hale stiffen and straighten to the position of attention.

Ben did the same, searching for a way out of the hole he'd just dug himself into with his boss.

"We were just having a heated debate, sir," Major Hale said before he could speak.

"That debate wouldn't happen to involve Sarn't First Class Escoberra, would it?"

Ben stiffened. "Sir, I was coming to brief you on that situation after formation." Not really a lie, not completely the truth, but Ben wondered if LTC Gilliad could appreciate his desire not to crucify someone he'd bled with.

"I'm already aware of it. Major Hale has told me that you're doing the required paperwork?"

Ben sucked in a deep breath and barely avoided glancing at Olivia. "Roger, sir. I was going to take care of it this morning, then talk to Child Protective Services and see what direction this was going to go."

LTC Gilliad nodded sharply. "Next time, *commander*, make sure I hear about these things from you first."

Ben saluted as the old man turned away. "Roger, sir." He stood for a moment, letting the realization that she'd covered for him sink in.

He pivoted to face Major Hale, noticing for the first time that her hair framed her face and clung to the side of her neck. Seeing *her* and not the woman in the uniform. He opened his mouth to speak but she cut him off.

"Do your job, Captain Teague, so that I can do mine," she said quietly. She left before he could say anything else.

He watched her go, breathing deeply as his heart rate slowed to something approaching normal. She'd held her ground against the worst of his temper. Ben almost smiled. That was something most grown men wouldn't do.

She lifted her arms, retying her hair into some twisted mass at the base of her neck to keep it from falling out of regulations. He caught himself wondering how long it was.

He watched her until she was out of sight.

She hadn't narc'd on him. She didn't know him from Adam but she had just covered for him. People didn't just do things like that, not out of the blue.

So why had she?

Chapter Three

Olivia set the last folder on a smaller pile and paused, looking down at the stack of files in front of her. Then she gave up and lowered her face into her hands, replaying the conversation with the battalion commander and Captain Teague in her head.

Over and over again. She couldn't explain why she'd covered for Teague with the battalion commander. But the more she replayed the scene in her head, the more she kept circling back to the man she'd seen at the hospital that morning.

So he'd gotten the benefit of the doubt. Not that she'd ever tell him that. She doubted he'd appreciate that the trouble she saw brewing in his dark eyes did something to her insides that she wanted to ignore. It made her feel something, and feelings got her in trouble.

They clouded her judgment.

There was a quiet knock on her door. "You look like hell, ma'am."

She looked up to see Sarn't Major Cox standing in the doorway. "Interpersonal hostility is always a fun way to start off the morning," she said dryly.

Cox grunted. Sometimes she wondered if he spoke in

more than single sentences. Still, she noticed the way the young troopers looked up to him. They worshipped him. And the battalion commander trusted him. He was not a man to make an enemy of.

"It'll get easier once everyone gets on board and all these guys figure out they can't save everyone."

She looked down at the files on her desk. She knew that. She knew that all too well.

"How long will it take them?"

Cox shrugged, chomping on the end of his unlit cigar. "I think the A Co commander will get it quickly. He doesn't strike me as a guy who believes in second chances. A couple of the others, though? They look hardheaded."

"Which ones?" she asked, interested in his read on the new command teams.

"Pretty much all of the rest of them," he said roughly.

She groaned. "That's going to be so much fun," she muttered.

He closed the door behind him, stepping fully into her office. He bumped into the scales on her desk. The cracked plate rattled in its swing. "What happened with Escoberra this morning?" he asked, his voice low.

"He was at the hospital with his daughter," she said, wondering why he was here asking about this since he'd been present when she'd told the battalion commander about it. "Child Protective Services is investigating."

"What's your gut tell you?" he asked.

Her gut? "My gut says there's more to this story than we're seeing, Sarn't Major," Olivia said quietly. "And I don't think that Teague is going to be objective about this."

"Probably not. He and Escoberra go way back." Cox wrapped his index finger around the cigar. "Keep me posted if you hear anything else."

He was gone before she could get another word in edgewise. Amazing how a man so big could move so quickly. But that wasn't what stuck with her. There were politics at work down here and she had no idea about the lay of the land, especially considering the cases against the previous key leaders in the battalion.

Once upon a time, she wouldn't have cared about the politics. Once upon a time, she would have charged headlong into the fray and damn the politics.

Once upon a time, she would have told her battalion commander exactly what she thought and she damn sure wouldn't have cared what one of the company commanders thought. But she was a little bit older and a lot wiser now and a hell of a lot more cynical. She had learned some hard lessons about rank and its privileges.

Now she knew she needed to figure out the power players in her new unit. Now she knew she needed to choose her battles more wisely.

It was going to be a long day. She glanced at her water bottle and wished she'd managed to find more of the dehydrated lemon packets for it. She didn't think she would ever get used to the taste of the water here. She'd meant to get a filter but it was on her unending list of things to do.

She took a sip and grimaced as the taste coated the inside of her mouth. She was going to have to rethink moving that filter up to the top of her priorities list.

"It only lasts until the rain comes."

She lowered the bottle. Teague. She should have been expecting him to show up. But no matter how much she saw him, she couldn't get used to seeing the haunted look in his eyes.

She took a deep breath, hoping to *not* have another replay of their showdown at PT this morning. "I'll keep that in mind, thanks." She motioned for him to have a seat in the chair in front of her desk and moved the packets until she found the ones that belonged to him.

He scrubbed his hand over his mouth, looking at the mountain of manila folders in front of her. "So this is what company command is? Chasing around legal packets and problem soldiers?"

The silence stretched between them. There was a vulnerability in his eyes. A loneliness, she realized.

She wasn't supposed to care. And yet, she found herself wondering about this captain—the one who'd been furious when he'd been told he was taking command. She had the sudden urge to run her fingers over the lines at the edge of his mouth, to soothe away the hardness there.

"It's only that way if you let it be that way," she said softly. "Once you clean up your unit, you'll be able to focus on the important things."

He looked up at her, his eyes dark. "And what's that?"

She frowned. "I'm not sure I understand what your question is, Captain Teague."

"What are the important things? Cleaning up my unit or having loyalty to men I've bled with? What really matters?"

She didn't hesitate. "What matters is training your men to go back downrange."

"Are you always this prickly or is it just me?" he asked abruptly.

"It's just you," she said without missing a beat. "You bring out my charming side."

"Why?"

She set the water bottle down hard. "Because you don't seem to care that this job isn't about taking care of your buddies."

Ben leaned over the table. "You don't even know me."

"I know you were going to keep the boss from finding out about Escoberra."

He leaned back sharply, shifted, his jaw grinding hard. "You don't know what I was going to do."

"Doesn't matter what I think I know—I know what you didn't do. But you *are* the chain of command now, Captain Teague, and you can't protect someone who's beating his children." She tipped her chin at him.

"What the hell is your problem?"

She should have made him use her rank but he'd crawled under her skin and gotten her temper going. Again. She ground her teeth a moment, searching for her words. She decided on honesty, no matter how jagged the blade.

"My problem is commanders like you who won't do their jobs. Who take advantage of their positions to protect their buddies, to keep them safe. My problem, Captain Teague, is officers like you, who don't utilize the power of their rank and position to make things better for the soldiers who work for them."

"Looks like you've got all the answers." Ben's smile was humorless and flat.

"Well, now that we got that out of the way, shall we get to work?" she asked.

She wasn't prepared for his total lack of response. He sat there, rolling a pen on the table in front of him, the silence stretching into the realm of uncomfortable. She blinked rapidly a couple of times then picked up her pen. He'd done the same thing in the hospital—walking away instead of standing his ground and arguing. Suspicion tickled down her spine. "Yes, let's."

Ben couldn't remember a time when he'd been more off kilter than he was at that moment. He was used to sniping at the uptight dickheads he worked around whenever he got the chance but Olivia Hale took uptight to a whole new level.

He hadn't realized she was going to be overseeing his work. He'd seen the previous commanders have a hard enough time dealing with the battalion executive officer and the operations officers. Now he had to watch his back with the lawyer, too?

She had no real authority but she had access to the boss and that gave her power. Power he was confident she would use. She seemed so serious, so driven. He watched her fiddling with the lid of her water bottle. He still didn't know what to say. Didn't know how to bridge the chasm he was at least partially responsible for and ask for help. Because God knew he was going to need it.

Olivia Hale was a woman who wore the word *cause* tattooed on her forehead.

He didn't do causes. But he didn't do command, either, and look how that had turned out. Goddamn it, why couldn't Gilliad find someone else for this job?

He was going to be working with Olivia Hale, and he'd have to be dead not to be intrigued by a woman like her. A woman who was reserved. Withdrawn. Not cold.

And that made him curious. Deeply so. She wore the rules and regulations like a shield.

And seeing how Ben felt about the rules and regulations, that didn't exactly set them up to be buddies.

But right then? He had the strange and sudden urge to know if she ever laughed. Something dark simmered in his belly. Something deeply inappropriate at work. But that didn't stop him from noticing her dark hair tied up neatly at the base of her neck. He blamed his interest on lack of sleep. There was no way he could be attracted to someone as... driven as Olivia was.

He had no idea what to say. What to ask for from the lawyer who would now be responsible for keeping his ass walking the straight and narrow. He didn't want the job. He didn't want anything to do with sending soldiers on missions approved by commanders too removed from the fight to care about the kids on the front line. He'd kick a door in any day

of the week with his old team. But that was a world of difference away from being a commander ordering said door to
be kicked in.

Now he was judge, jury, and executioner over men he'd
served with. A power he didn't want and a power he'd done
his best to avoid.

"Fuck," he muttered.

Olivia raised one eyebrow. "Yes, that about sums things
up," she said dryly. She slid a packet toward him. "Here's the
paperwork on Escoberra, opening the investigation at Child
Protective Services."

Ben leaned forward, wishing he had something to do with
his hands. He closed his eyes, seeing Carmen kneeling in
front of her husband. "There's no way Escoberra did this.
He'd never hurt his kid."

"The initial report says otherwise," Olivia said cautiously.

He looked up at her, barely reining in his temper. "The
initial report is wrong. First reports often are. He's a goddamned warrior and a damn fine senior NCO."

The muscles in her neck tightened. Oh yes, Olivia Hale
had a temper. "Rank shouldn't matter," Olivia said quietly.

"You're a major." Ben's smile was merciless. "You
should've been around long enough to know better."

"Rank matters more than it should."

Ben leaned forward, bracing his elbows on the table.
"Maybe, maybe not. But rank matters less than the fact that
Escoberra didn't do this. He wouldn't." He met her gaze.

Olivia pinned him with a hard look. "You're awful certain about a situation when you weren't there."

"I know my NCO." At least he had, once upon a time. But
the war and different missions and a hundred unsaid things
had drifted between them. And Ben had let the drift widen
until he could no longer see across the chasm.

"How close to Escoberra would you say you are, Captain

Teague? Close enough that it's going to keep you from doing your duty?"

Ben looked away, down at his hands. Not as close as he should be. The distance had grown over the last couple of years. They'd been at opposite ends of the city on this last deployment.

Ben looked at her then and carefully chose his words. "The only people who care about the separation between officer and enlisted are people who've never bled together." He glanced at her empty right shoulder. "The rank on your chest doesn't matter."

Her throat moved as she swallowed. He could almost see her pulse hammering against her throat. "You're talking about ignoring regulations that are the foundation of our service." She pinned him with a hard look. "Are you telling me the rules don't matter?"

Ben met her gaze clearly, refusing to back down. "They don't."

There was more to this story but Olivia had no idea what it was. Watching him right then, she caught a glimpse of the man she'd seen just a hint of at the hospital that morning. A man who'd been to war and back again and come home changed.

Because the man in front of her was tense, had been ever since the subject of Escoberra had come up. "How can you protect a man who put his daughter in the hospital?" she asked softly.

"He didn't do it. You don't know him." Teague's expression shuttered closed.

"You can't be friends with your men," she said quietly.

"I know that," he snapped. He sighed and dragged his hand over his mouth. "So what do I do?"

She sighed heavily. "We talked about this at the hospital this morning. You flag him until the CPS investigation is complete. You give him a no-contact order and put him in the barracks and you get him to mental health to get checked out."

He ground his teeth but wrote silently. His neck was tight. The veins on the back of his hands stood out in stark contrast against his skin.

He shifted then and looked up. Their gazes collided. Silence hung in the air, thick and filled with stubborn anger. Time slowed. His throat moved and he swallowed.

Olivia blinked and the spell was broken, if it had ever even been there to begin with. "I know this is going to be difficult," she said quietly.

"Thanks," he said. He reached for the packet and put it to one side. Something snapped between them and he was back to business, the tension gone. "Okay, what's next?"

She took a deep breath. "The clear-cut misconduct. The drinking and driving, the Article Fifteens for minor offenses. You can get a big chunk of these knocked out within a week, a month tops, then focus on the more serious incidents."

Ben frowned across the desk at her. "How many serious incidents am I dealing with?"

"You don't know?"

He shook his head and angled his chair so he was leaning across the table and angled the files so he could see them better. "I haven't even been to my new office yet and supposedly, I'm without a first sergeant."

She lifted her gaze to meet his. "Alone and unafraid, huh?"

He offered a cocky half grin and for a moment, the lines on his face relaxed and she caught a glimpse of the man beneath the tired warrior. There was so much more to this man than the tired warrior sitting across from her. "Something like that."

Olivia looked away. The first packet was heavy in her

hand. "The quick summary is that you have five drinking and driving, two assaults, three hot urinalysis tests, and five soldiers caught with other intoxicating substances."

"Define 'other intoxicating substances'? What the hell does that mean?"

"Huffing, spice, bath salts."

"Bath salts? What the hell are bath salts?"

Olivia pulled out her phone and opened up a website explaining the drug. "They're really new but we're starting to see more of them. They're meant to be a synthetic drug that mimics cocaine and ecstasy but they're really bad stuff. Some of them are variants of plant food."

Ben reached for her phone and angled it so he could see. His hand was big and rough against hers. Hot where their skin met. If he noticed, he didn't give any indication. "Plant food?"

Olivia tried to ignore how his hand felt against hers. Because, oh yes, she'd noticed. Heat spread across her skin, sliding up her forearm and tingling down her spine. "Soldiers will smoke anything these days," she said quietly.

"Why?"

"That's a whole 'nother discussion," she said, easing her hand out of his. "The short version is that intoxicating substances are prohibited by regulation and I advise you to do two things with these kids: send a strong message that this behavior won't be tolerated but also enroll them into drug abuse counseling to send a message that you'll help those who want it."

Ben studied the paperwork in front of him. Tormented emotions flickered over his face and it was everything she could do not to ask him what was on his mind. She didn't have time or reason to go crawling around Ben Teague's head but that didn't stop the want pulsing warmly over her skin.

"I know this kid," Ben said quietly. "I served with him

downrange last deployment but ever since he's come home, he's been nothing but trouble to the old commander. Zittoro has three previous drug charges," he said.

"Private Zittoro is a different case. I recommend you separate him from the military under a chapter nine, rehab failure."

She heard his quick intake of breath. Saw the conflict flicker over his sharp features.

He cleared his throat roughly in the awkward silence. "Zittoro... he's got nowhere to go. He's got a deadbeat dad and his mom is... well, she's not winning any parent of the year awards." His fist clenched on the table in front of her. "If I throw him out of the army, what happens to him? He's an addict."

She flinched at the pain in his words. Ben had only been a commander for a couple of hours but the strain was already obvious in his voice.

"You can't save everyone," she whispered. She waited until his eyes met hers. "You know that, right?"

"Yeah. Sure."

There was no comfort she could offer. This was the burden of command: to balance the needs of the army over the needs of the individual. A tightrope he had to walk alone.

All she could do was give him the facts and her opinion. But in that moment, she had the sudden urge to save him from this. "If you keep him, do you have the manpower to keep going to his room and making sure he hasn't overdosed every night? Do you trust him enough to give him a weapon and believe he'll do his job?"

Ben's throat moved as he swallowed. "Guess not," he said quietly. He leaned back and it was as if a wall of glass crystallized between them. "What other fun things do you have in there for me?"

Olivia wasn't convinced by the sudden shift in Ben's

mood but now wasn't the time or the place for digging any deeper. She reviewed the rest of the drug packets, watching him tense more with each one. She stopped after the last driving under the influence.

"Why is this bothering you so much?"

He offered a half-assed cocky grimace that failed to mimic the smile he was going for. A pretty shitty attempt to cover the darkness twisting beneath the surface. He took a deep breath. "I'm a big boy. I'll do what has to be done."

"I didn't imply that you wouldn't. But that doesn't mean it's not bothering you."

He drummed his fingers on the table. "Let's finish this up. I've got to get down to my company and start digging out from the mountain of crap that my predecessor left me."

He brushed her off. The action was as insignificant as a paper cut.

She leaned back and picked up the next packet and wished it didn't sting like it did. Then she made the mistake of meeting his gaze. There was such a dark lack of hope in his eyes. A bleak resignation to the things he was forced to confront. She almost reached for his hand. It would have been a simple gesture of support. But he looked at her as though a single touch might have shattered him.

He was not her problem. She didn't do damaged and introspective.

Because there were people counting on her not to get distracted.

But looking at him now, she wondered about the glimpse of the tired warrior she saw behind those tormented brown eyes.

Chapter Four

Ben walked into the Bandit Company ops—his company—
and noticed that everyone stilled as he walked through. No
one approached. No one said anything but there was an
undercurrent to the watchfulness. Almost as though they
were waiting for the other boot to hit the floor.

This week was one for the record books. An entire battalion's worth of commanders fired. Soldiers in jail, friends
accused of horrible things.

Ben didn't want this job. He never had. He never wanted
to balance the scales of his friends' actions.

And yet, here he was.

Good times.

He stopped in the orderly room. All activity came to a
grinding halt.

"It occurs to me that maybe the company probably should
be called to attention?" Ben said. The ops sergeant glanced
toward the commander's office. Lights on. Looked like
someone was home—oh joy. The former commander was
there.

"That explains things," Ben muttered.

Captain James P. Marshall the Third himself. Ben had

to remind himself that Marshall was just another man, and not a good one at that. He was a bully and he was cruel.

The banality of Marshall's cruelty, though, had permeated everything around him. None of the higher ups had a clue that Marshall had been poisoning the atmosphere across the entire battalion from the time he'd been a platoon leader through his time as a commander. That alone led Ben to wonder what the environment really was in this battalion for the soldiers who'd had to suffer under the yoke of Marshall's shitty leadership.

Now? Karma had finally come through for him. Ben might not want to command but damn it, if doing so took Marshall's power away from him? Oh, it was a beautiful thing. And this was a target of opportunity, one that did wonders for Ben's shitty mood.

He walked into what was now his office and there was Marshall sitting behind Ben's desk. As if he was still in charge.

"I guess you didn't get the memo about needing a new job?"

Marshall looked up, his jaw tense. "I'm here to brief you on the legal stuff."

Ben smiled and it lit up the shadows around his heart. He'd been waiting for years for Marshall to get what he deserved, ever since Marshall had tried to get Escoberra and Ben fired after their outpost had been overrun. "So yeah, I'm gonna need you to clear out your desk." He paused for dramatic effect. "And get the hell out of my company."

The words felt strange and foreign on Ben's tongue. His company. Words he once would have embraced. Words that now tasted bitter.

But seeing Marshall's expression twitch made it all better.

"Do you want to know about these cases or not?"

"Not really much you can tell me, seeing how you haven't done jack shit about them." Ben folded his arms over his chest and leaned against the door. "You know, if it wasn't for me having to clean up your mess, I would be exceptionally happy that you've been relieved." He rubbed his hand over his jaw. "Couldn't have happened to a nicer guy."

"You always were a cowboy, Teague. Too idealistic to do what needed to be done. You should have fired Escoberra after your base got blown up, but instead you sacrificed your career for him."

"Didn't make a damn bit of difference, now did it," Ben said mildly. As badly as he wanted to throw Marshall—physically—from his office, he figured he should probably refrain. Especially after the pissing contest with Major Hale in front of the battalion commander. "Looks like I get a chance to command after all."

Marshall snorted. "You're just going to fuck this up, too. You couldn't make a hard decision to save your own ass back then; you think you're going to be able to do this?"

Ben smiled. "I'll do a better job than you. And I'll do it without betraying everyone around me to save my own ass."

"Mistakes were made on that mission," Marshall snapped.

"Indeed they were. And I thought we were supposed to be responsible for our subordinates' actions?"

"You don't know the meaning of the word 'responsible,'" Marshall said quietly.

"And you don't know the meaning of the word 'loyalty.'" He brushed a piece of lint from Marshall's shoulder. "Now, get the fuck out of my office and go mourn the end of your career."

Marshall's smile was ice cold as he stood, an inch from Ben's face. The peppermint sting of Copenhagen snuff filled Ben's nose and he fought the urge to gag. "You think this fiasco matters? Do you know who my father is? I'm going to be reassigned to the Infantry Center at Fort Benning and I'll be commanding a real infantry unit in less than six months and all of this heavy armored Cav bullshit can kiss my ass."

Ben patted Marshall's collar down. "Jimmy, Jimmy,

what's the weather on your world like? Because where I'm standing, you've been flagged by *division headquarters*. That means you're stuck here at The Great Place until the investigations are complete. Which means that unless you've been giving the chief of staff of the army hand jobs in your spare time, you're not going anywhere until this is over. And these things tend to take a very, very long time."

Marshall's face turned an unhealthy shade of purple. "Fuck you, Teague."

"You're really not my type. Oh, and let's not forget how many future high-powered officers come out of Cav. You can call it bullshit all day long but your ticket is punched, sport. Daddy can't save you. You might want to brush up on that résumé. I hear they need check-out boys at Walmart."

Marshall's nostrils flared. He was getting ready to start screaming. Ben could see it in the vein pounding in Marshall's forehead. Good. It would give him an excuse to throw his sorry ass out of the office.

"Before you blow a gasket, can I remind you of something?" Ben leaned close, close enough to see the five hairs on the edge of Marshall's jaw that the other man had missed when he shaved this morning. "You're in my office now. So get the fuck out."

Marshall grabbed his headgear off the desk and slammed the door against the concrete wall as he stalked from the small office.

The stink of Marshall's snuff hung in the air after he left. Ben badly needed some air freshener. Maybe a scented candle or something. He sighed and glanced at the chaos on his desk. He didn't even have time to look at his e-mail, which was probably just as well—his inbox had probably already exploded with pointless garrison stuff that meant little in the grand scheme of more important things. *Like the war.*

It was probably just as well that the formal passing of the

BlackBerry hadn't occurred. It meant that Ben wasn't tied to his e-mail. Yet.

He lifted one stack of files and skimmed the names written neatly on side tabs. Fifteen names. He'd be damned if he'd ask Marshall a single question about any of them. The soldiers and NCOs would help him figure it out.

Wouldn't they? The way everyone had appeared incredibly busy when he'd walked through gave him pause. How bad were things down here in Bandit country?

He was going to have his work cut out for him. He'd never taken over for someone who'd destroyed the utter soul of an organization.

Fifteen soldiers out of a company of one hundred plus facing pending legal actions. That didn't even count those already under investigation for a myriad of offenses, or the ones Ben didn't even know about yet.

Ben sighed and sat down at his computer and laid his head on his desk.

Escoberra. Zittoro. Dear God, what the hell had happened to the warriors he'd known?

He needed to call Escoberra's wife and check on her. Carmen Escoberra had put up with a lot over the years but something had to have changed.

The woman who'd sent them care packages every week to make sure they had food couldn't have changed so much that she would have called Child Protective Services.

Why hadn't she called Ben?

He sat up, rubbing his hands over his face. Because Ben hadn't been part of their lives for years now. Not since the army had held Escoberra responsible for a bad attack and Ben had failed to defend him.

Ben stared into the distance. Escoberra would never put his hands on his family. That much Ben knew.

So what the hell had happened?

Grabbing his hat, he knew there was only one way to find out.

He hoped Carmen was home.

"Ma'am?"

Olivia looked up from the pile of paperwork on her desk and saw a young woman standing in her doorway. Definitely not a soldier, judging by the civilian clothes and the youthful fullness of her cheeks. "Can I help you?"

Her eyes were wary. Guarded. "My name is Hailey Escoberra, ma'am. I was wondering if you were the person I needed to talk to about my dad?"

Olivia noticed Hailey favored her left arm, cradling it against her abdomen in a very subtle movement that Olivia might have missed if she hadn't been paying attention.

"Sure. Come in and have a seat."

On the spectrum of strange things, a visit from a soldier's family member wasn't unusual—except that it wasn't normally kids that came to visit her. Usually she met with spouses, begging for their husbands.

Sometimes, things ended up working out. Other times, far too often, they ended badly. Olivia blinked rapidly; the sight of this young woman in front of her mixed with memories of a little girl. They were not the same.

She took a deep breath, centering herself. "What can I do for you?"

"I want you to leave my dad alone," Hailey said quietly. Her voice was soft yet filled with iron.

What had made this little girl so strong? Hell, she wasn't a little girl. She was fifteen, if Olivia remembered the reports correctly.

She gripped the pen on her desk. "I'm not doing anything to your dad," Olivia said quietly. There was never a good response to something like this.

Never.

Because no matter what she did or said, the person in the seat across from her would want something Olivia could not give them.

"He didn't mean to hurt me. It was an accident and he's sorry. Just leave him alone so he can go back to work and do his job." Her voice wavered a little, just a little. Nothing more.

"Sometimes, the people in our lives don't mean to hurt us," Olivia said. "But that doesn't make the pain any less real."

Hailey's dark eyes flashed. "I'm not stupid. Who do I need to tell to get the army to leave my dad alone?" Her voice edged up a notch. Just a little, but it was enough to make Olivia's stomach twist with nerves.

"Hailey, maybe you should talk to someone about your dad? I'm not really the right person…"

"They said you were the lawyer. They said you could make this go away."

Olivia clicked the pen cap off. "I'm not sure who this 'they' is but they gave you wrong information."

Hailey stood, still cradling her arm. "I don't want any trouble for my dad. I thought the army was supposed to care about families."

"We do care."

"Then leave my dad alone," she said.

She didn't stomp from the office but it was a close thing.

The part of Olivia that wasn't jaded and cynical admired Hailey's love and devotion for her father.

The part of Olivia that had already seen this movie a time or two knew how it was likely to end.

All of the love in the world couldn't save Hailey's dad if he was hitting her.

Love betrayed was a terrible, terrible thing.

She wished she was wrong. She wished she had more

faith in the power of love to heal men like Escoberra, who hurt everyone around them.

But she didn't.

Because she'd seen the worst of it too many times.

And she'd be damned if she would leave Hailey to face this alone. Because Olivia knew all about facing these things alone.

She'd lived it.

Ben had never considered himself a hero but he'd never thought he was a coward, either.

But as he sat in Escoberra's driveway in front of the little house in the Comanche III housing area, his stomach writhed and knotted. As he listened to some stupid shit on the radio, he struggled to find the courage to go and knock on that front door.

It was the second longest walk of his life.

Part of him hoped that Carmen wasn't home. That he could absolve himself of his sense of guilt and say that he'd tried.

But she opened the door.

Her eyes went wide when she saw him.

Then she opened her arms and Ben stepped into her loving embrace. She wasn't much older than he was but she was more a mother to him than his own had been.

"You've been away too long," she whispered, patting his back.

He squeezed her tightly. "I know," he said. "I'm sorry."

She released him, patting his cheek. "Don't let it happen again. We missed you. Come in. Have something to drink?"

"Water's fine."

The house was impeccably neat, just like it always was. It smelled warm, like home.

But there was a shadow here now. And that shadow was the reason Ben was there.

"I suppose you want to talk about what happened?" Carmen asked, handing him a glass.

"No point in delaying the obvious," he said. "What happened?"

"I don't know. I had gone to sleep because I was supposed to be at work early. The next thing I know I hear screaming and crying. Hailey is on the floor and Jose is holding a towel to her shoulder." Carmen busied her hands in the sink, washing dishes Ben was reasonably certain were already clean. "Neither of them will tell me what happened." She looked over at him, her eyes hard. "I won't talk to the police, Ben. Don't ask me to."

"I wasn't going to. I just... I wanted to know what happened. If he—"

"Is it true you're his commander now?" Carmen asked, stacking a plate in the drying rack.

"I am. I don't want to be, but I am."

"Then you can fix this," she said.

"I'm going to try," he said softly. Because it was the truth.

He didn't know what had happened but if Carmen still had faith in her husband, then damn it, Ben would believe in him, too.

He didn't know how he was going to protect his former platoon sergeant but he was damn sure going to try.

Nine o'clock and Olivia was finally ready to call it a night. She'd made decent progress on the packets today after Hailey had left the office. Despite that, she was running on an empty stomach and the tension in her neck had finally reached the point where she had to stop and take some Motrin.

All she had left to do was organize the files for tomorrow and she could head home. She still had more work but she could do that on her couch.

She pulled out the first file and sucked in a deep breath. Escoberra.

She paused, breathing hard. She hadn't shown Ben the pictures. She could have. Maybe she should have. Maybe confronting him with the reality of his sergeant's actions would make him less reluctant to do what needed to be done.

It had been so hard reconciling the photographs from the hospital with the brave young girl who'd come to her office today. She'd worn makeup to cover the bruises and had favored her damaged arm but that young woman had gone through hell that night.

She needed to follow up with Teague to make sure he'd done everything he was supposed to do to protect Hailey and her family. Too many victims were left to fend for themselves because commanders refused to believe their men were capable of this kind of violence.

She wanted to get more aggressive. She wanted to tell commanders what they *would* do instead of what they *should* do.

But she'd learned her lesson. She would follow the letter of the law exactly.

She would never lose another case because of her own zealousness.

No matter how much she believed in Escoberra's guilt, she couldn't push beyond her legal responsibilities.

She closed the folder and made notes for the next day then headed out. The first five cases were all from Ben's company. She set a calendar reminder to follow up on the packets she'd given Ben.

She'd seen commanders "lose" packets before.

She'd developed tricks for that, too. She knew how to force the system to work. There were few things she hadn't seen.

She stepped into the hallway. The headquarters were all but abandoned at this late hour.

The last thing she expected to see was Ben Teague, stepping out of the battalion commander's office.

She didn't want to notice the breadth of his shoulders or the rough edge of his jaw. She might not want to notice but her body did. Her blood warmed as he approached.

"You're here late," he said mildly.

She didn't miss the fatigue in his eyes and damn it, she didn't like the way it pulled at her. The way it made her fingers twitch to smooth those tired lines away.

"Pretty standard night for me, all things considered," she said, accepting the tentative peace offering.

What the hell was she doing? She didn't even like Ben Teague, and now she was suddenly making trite conversation in the hall?

"No family waiting at home for you?" he asked, falling into step with her as she headed out the door.

"Nah. Not with these hours," she said. "You?"

"Same." He held the door for her. "Are we really having a normal conversation right now?"

She almost smiled. "Looks that way."

"Huh. Miracles will never cease."

She said nothing in response. It was too easy to take his point of view, to forget why she did what she did, in order to be accepted as one of them.

But part of her lot in life was to remain on the outside. Fighting the good fight.

She'd never counted on that meaning she would always be alone but there you had it.

She couldn't let sympathy or any other emotion she might feel for Ben get in the way of doing her job.

Or making sure he did his.

Because command was a marathon, not a sprint. And so was being the lawyer in a brigade combat team. But that didn't soothe the ache pulsing through her blood as she stood a little too close. She caught a hint of something clean and crisp and warm.

"Why are you here so late?" she asked after a while.

"Had to brief the boss on some stuff."

"Life of a commander, huh?"

"Something like that," he said. "Wish I could remember if I have food in my fridge. I think I have cookies."

She laughed at the unexpected comment. "Cookies? What are you, twelve?"

"Don't underestimate the power of cookies to soothe a bad day," he said. His mouth curled at the edges and she noticed the creases at the corners of his lips. His mouth was wide, his bottom lip fuller than any man's should be.

"Do you always make jokes?" she asked.

His smile crooked up on one side. "Much cheaper than therapy," he said lightly. "Though I know a therapist now so..."

"Emily speaks highly of you," Olivia said. This easy conversation was the first normal conversation she'd had since reporting to the unit. It was nice.

It was something deeply human.

It was something she missed.

"I can't imagine why," Ben said.

She grinned. "I have more faith in her judgment than that."

"Is that a tacit vote of confidence?"

"It's only day two," she said softly. "Let's save any votes of confidence until I know you better."

Ben laughed. "That's probably a good call. I don't tend to live up to expectations often."

She tipped her chin, studying him in the fading light. "That's an odd thing to say."

He shrugged, stuffing his hands in his pockets. He jerked his chin toward her briefcase. "Taking work home with you?"

"You don't?"

"I'm planning on showering and not sleeping."

She frowned as he looked out over the parade field across the road. The lights overhead glinted across the freshly watered grass. A single beam of light glittered over the Cav Memorial. He sniffed and looked away.

"You don't sleep?" she asked.

"Not much."

Silence lingered after his comment, heavy and thick with awareness of this man. She wanted to ask more, to delve into his reasons for not sleeping, but instead, she said nothing. She didn't know what to say or how to deal with this personal side of Ben Teague.

This side of Ben that was warm and solid and infinitely male. There was an easy tension about him just then. A tension that drew her closer when she should be going the other way.

Her job was hard enough without having to overcome personal bias.

"So listen." He palmed his keys, looking edgy. Wary. His voice was deep and thick as he spoke. "I went by the Escoberras' today."

Her breath caught in her throat. "That's interesting, because Hailey Escoberra came by my office today."

He raised both eyebrows. "How was she?"

"She seemed to be doing fine. She wanted us to leave her dad alone." She folded her arms over her chest. "How is his wife?"

"Shaky but okay. She wants her husband home." He met her gaze then, his eyes dark and filled with an unspoken torment that she could only guess at.

"You can't. You have to maintain the restraining order."

The muscles in his neck tensed. "What's the point? They want him home."

"This is one of those rare cases where what the family wants doesn't trump what the army says, Ben." She caught herself a moment too late. His first name slipped from her lips, crossing a boundary she'd set for herself with these men.

There could be no first name basis with him. Or any of them, for that matter.

But especially not Ben.

He looked away, avoiding her eyes. She studied him closely. "What are you hiding?" she whispered, more to herself than him.

"Nothing." He palmed his keys. "I'll talk to you later."

She expected him to fight. She expected the anger and defiance she'd seen earlier.

So when he met her gaze, her heart did an unexpected flip in her throat. She stood there in the silence—searching, probing, seeking answers in his eyes that he would not trust her with. It was the lack of trust she saw looking back at her that nearly broke her.

Who had crushed this man's faith in those around him?

She almost reached for him. Almost asked him who had broken him.

But Ben turned away before she could summon the courage to span the chasm between them, breaking the spell and leaving her there alone in the nearly dark parking lot.

She watched him walk away, fading into the night before he climbed into his truck. The truck didn't move for the longest time and she wondered if he was watching her.

She headed toward her own car and the empty, quiet house that awaited her. Being close to other people had never been her strong point. She told herself it was because she was too busy worrying about work to unwind and relax in the bedroom, but the truth was darker. It always had been. Maybe it was because she'd been overweight and awkward as a teen, but that was a comfortable lie she told herself to avoid the painful memories lurking in the shadows of her dreams. They were always there, always threatening to twist into a too familiar nightmare if she gave them a chance. But none of that knowledge could shake the loneliness that snuck up on her at moments like this—moments when there was a spark of connection, a hint of something *more*.

Something more that she could never have. She sighed heavily.

Maybe she could get a cat. Maybe a fish.

But that felt a little too melodramatic. She smiled thinking of Emily, who finally had Reza back from rehab. God, but she was happy for her friend. If anyone deserved happiness, it was those two. They were such an odd couple but she'd never seen Emily happier than when she was with the big sergeant.

She entered the quiet house, turning the radio on to a quiet country song as she left her files in the kitchen. She turned on the shower, letting steam fog up the mirror.

She didn't look down at her body as she stripped off the weight of the day and left her uniform in a pile near the sink. She didn't look in the mirror.

She didn't need to see the scars on her body to know they were there. They would always be there, a constant reminder that people would always let you down.

The scars tracing over her ribs no longer ached but the memories threatened to morph into something darker as she thought of Escoberra and his daughter.

Hailey thought she wanted her father home. What she needed, though, was an advocate: someone to stand for her when she couldn't stand for herself. Olivia breathed deeply as painful memories crashed over her, her scars throbbing as she saw again that lost little girl standing in the flashing lights of the ambulance.

No one had stood up for Olivia when her own father had tripped the final line.

No one had believed her when she'd first gone to the police. The officer had told her she shouldn't put marks on herself like that. She hadn't gone back a second time.

She should have been happy when her father had finally left her alone. But she wasn't.

Because it meant that she was alone.

Always alone.

He'd loved her. She knew that, just as Hailey knew her dad loved her.

But love wasn't enough when the rage exploded.

She stepped into the shower, letting the heat sluice over her body, washing the memories from her flesh.

The house was silent when she stepped out of the shower some time later.

Always silent.

She dressed and padded to her kitchen, ignoring the lingering ache in her ribs. Funny, she'd once thought the pain would eventually stop.

But it hadn't. And in the silence, the scars on her ribs throbbed as old memories surfaced and reminded her that no, she could not fail.

Ben watched her walk away, her directive to keep Escoberra away from his family echoing in his ears.

She didn't know he'd told Escoberra to go home.

And she didn't need to know.

He knew in his soul that Escoberra hadn't hurt Hailey.

Keeping him away from his family was the worst thing right then and his meeting earlier with Carmen had confirmed his decision. So was hearing that Hailey had gone to see Olivia.

The army was wrong on this one. The restraining order

was meant to give people a chance to calm down. Escoberra was calm.

His family wanted him home, and what the hell was the point of this job if Ben couldn't make that happen? He'd take the ass chewing if the battalion commander found out. But he wasn't going to.

Ben hadn't been able to keep Escoberra out of trouble when their base had gotten overrun, but if he could help him now, that's exactly what he was going to do.

If Ben was going to command, damn it, he was going to make some decisions.

Chapter Five

Ben pulled into the commander's parking spot the next morning, grateful at least that he no longer had to worry about finding a place to put his truck in the mass confusion that was PT traffic on Fort Hood.

It had been so long since he'd actually come to a PT formation, he was a little thrown off by the fact that it was 5:50 a.m. and he was conscious *and* at work. He was usually one but not the other. Now? Now responsibility dogged his every waking hour. He'd used his insomniac powers for good last night, getting all his required policy letters and other requisite paperwork updated.

Because nothing said "cover your ass" like a good set of policy letters.

He wasn't sure why he was even doing all this work. He didn't want the job and he was confident that any day now, LTC Gilliad was going to figure out that he'd made a huge mistake and tell him he could go find himself another job.

Ben could only hope.

His phone vibrated on the seat next to him.

He let that sink in for a moment.

It was 5:50 in the morning and his phone was *already vibrating*. He parked the truck and looked at the text message.

Sir, this is PFC Walsh. The new first sergeant is here to meet you.

"Huh, how 'bout that." Yesterday had been absolute chaos. He was reasonably certain that every soldier in the company, half their wives, and at least three ex-girlfriends had stood outside his office, looking to either piss on his leg, whine about the previous commander, or kiss his ass.

He didn't have a lot of patience for any of that. Especially the ass-kissing part. He'd been overwhelmed by the sheer volume of people parading through his office and all he'd been able to do was take notes and try to put faces to names. His lieutenants hadn't been anywhere to be found, either. The *last* thing he was going to do was walk into his boss's office and cry about too many people. Ben wasn't a religious man but damn if he hadn't prayed that the gods of war would send him a first sergeant.

Someone he could count on. Someone like Escoberra or Reza.

Because if God had meant for captains to run companies by themselves, he wouldn't have made NCOs.

He grinned in the darkness at the phone. It looked like the gods had decided to answer his prayers. He killed the engine and headed into his company ops.

Five minutes later, Ben wasn't sure where the army had dusted off his new first sergeant, but he was more than a little impressed.

He'd heard of people described as six feet tall and bullet-proof but they rarely were. First Sarn't Gale Sorren was built like a bear—a big one. Six and a half minutes into their conversation, Ben suspected that Sorren might be the myth turned reality.

His hand swallowed Ben's and Ben was reasonably certain he'd felt bone break.

"Glad you're here," Ben said.

"Damn glad to be here, sir." Sorren's voice was deep, rumbling from some dark abyss that produced born leaders. Hell, Ben wanted to follow the guy's orders. But that wasn't how this relationship was supposed to work.

"Where are you coming from?" Ben motioned for his first sergeant to sit and took his own seat across from him at the conference table in the middle of the company ops.

"Fort Lewis," Sorren said. "Just got the word that this job was open so I jumped at the chance."

"They got you here for this job that fast?" The army never moved people that quickly. Ever.

Sorren grinned and the smile creased his entire face, from the corners of his mouth to his nearly black eyes. "I was already on my way here. Sarn't Major asked me to sign in from leave early. Said something about keeping you from fucking things up too badly."

"Sergeant Major Cox is the president of my fan club." Ben laughed out loud and leaned back in his chair. Some of the fatigue from his not-sleeping habit receded. Just a little but enough to be noticeable. "I'm glad to see my reputation precedes me."

"I've heard your name before." Sorren snapped his fingers. "You were Escoberra's platoon leader."

Ben nodded, picking at a ragged nail. Just like that, a wave of crushing uncertainty and anxiety washed over him. "Yeah." He frowned. "You know Escoberra is here now?"

"No shit. I'll have to look him up."

"Here's the thing." Ben sighed heavily and folded his arms over his chest. "He's kind of in our company. But he's in trouble."

Sorren scowled. "What kind of trouble?"

"The kind involving Child Protective Services."

"What the hell happened to him?" Sorren muttered. "All right; well, we'll deal with that later. The family is safe?"

"Yeah. Escoberra stayed in the barracks all day yesterday." That part was the truth. He didn't know Sorren from Adam and he wasn't going to start off by letting him know that Ben was playing fast and loose with the rules right then.

"That really sucks. Escoberra was a good dude." Sorren rubbed the back of his neck. "Guess we'll have to take the paperwork and get this ball rolling."

"I already did the paperwork." Not entirely true. He'd *meant* to do the paperwork; he just hadn't gotten around to it because every time he thought about it, his lungs tightened until he couldn't breathe. "It doesn't bother you?"

Sorren tipped his chin and looked at Ben, his expression hard and unreadable. "We have a job to do, sir. Whether it bothers me or not is irrelevant." He sighed, then stood. "I guess that's enough with the warm jaunt down Memory Lane. I'll need your help getting the lay of the land, sir."

"That eager for the bad news?"

"Oh yes. There's nothing you can throw at me I haven't seen before." Sorren grinned, a gleam of anticipation burning in his dark eyes. He glanced at the clock over Ben's head. "But first we've got to hold formation and do some PT. You a runner, sir?"

"Yeah, I run." Who in the infantry—hell, the army—didn't run?

"Good. I figure we'll put in a good six miles this morning. Give us a good assessment of where the formation stands."

Ben took a deep breath, glad he hadn't been drinking last night. There was nothing quite as terrible as puking the remains of a good night up onto Battalion Avenue and then getting back in formation, stinking of stale alcohol, sweat, and vomit, and finishing the run anyway.

"Good times," Ben muttered, following the massive first sergeant out of the company ops.

Olivia loved running. She didn't care that she had to drag her dead ass out of bed long before the sun came up; she loved the feel of her feet pounding on the pavement and the sound of formations around her.

It was something sublime, like being part of a whole.

She stretched with a couple of the other staff officers and saluted the flag when the cannon went off at the corps headquarters.

She wanted to run at least five miles today. It wasn't like the battalion commander expected her in her office, so she had the time. He'd instituted a new policy that staff officers *would* do PT. She'd heard that he'd caught a couple of captains in the operations office skipping PT in order to get a briefing done about a week ago.

It had not been pretty.

She turned down Battalion Avenue and started running, soon losing herself among the blur of gray and black-clad bodies, the rhythmic sound of feet in formation pounding on the pavement. A mile into her run, she crossed over Clear Creek and headed toward the golf course.

A formation ran by, singing something bawdy and loud that probably contained fifteen EO complaints.

Then the silence and the darkness ran together, bleeding into one another until the only thing she could hear were the sounds of her own hard breathing and her shoes crunching on the leaves of the PT trail. She didn't usually encounter many formations out here on the trails behind the golf course. A few pairs of runners now and again but it was much less crowded. It was peaceful, a different kind of being than out on Battalion.

"Come on, Zittoro. Stay with me, man."

She knew that voice, knew it all too well. She rounded the corner on the trail. Ben walked with a skinny kid who couldn't be more than a hundred and twenty pounds soaking wet. He looked up when she ground to a halt nearby.

Ben met her gaze, grim determination in his eyes. He quickly looked away and focused back on Zittoro, who seemed to be having trouble breathing. "Come on, man, you got this. Let's finish strong."

Zittoro's lungs heaved. "Just leave me, sir."

"Not gonna happen. The way I see it, we got two options. You can walk in or you can run in, but whatever you choose I'm doing, too."

"You just took command. You can't walk during PT," Zittoro said.

"Then do we have our option?" Ben grinned. "And I'm sure Major Hale would love to finish the run with us." He looked at her, the dare clear in his eyes.

"Sure would," Olivia said. She had no idea what was going on in Ben's head but right then, if he wanted her help to motivate the kid, then so be it. It had been a long time since she'd run PT with soldiers. She missed it sometimes.

Zittoro looked between the two of them, then spat onto the dried out leaves. "All right, let's do this."

Ben looked at her, held her gaze a moment too long. Then she fell into step with the two men and they were off.

Zittoro was not a strong runner. Not by a long shot. Olivia probably could have walked faster, but a look at Ben was all she needed to see that there was more to this than just making sure the kid finished the run. His name was familiar, too, but at the moment she was drawing a complete blank.

In the end, she didn't get in her five miles. She probably got closer to three, but by the time they made it back to the headquarters parking lot, the sun was already creeping over the corps headquarters. Olivia swiped her forehead on her

PT uniform sleeve as Ben gripped Zittoro's shoulder. "Good job today."

Zittoro shrugged Ben's hand off and looked sheepish. "Nah, you and I both know you're blowing smoke up my ass," Zittoro said.

"Well, we all need a little something now and again to lift us up. Don't be late for work call."

"Whatever, sir," he said with a grin. He paused then looked back at Olivia and smiled. "Thanks for finishing the run with me, ma'am."

Olivia smiled. "No problem." And then she was alone with Ben. "So you want to tell me what that was all about?"

Ben stuffed his hands into the waistband of his PT shorts. Olivia didn't miss the way his sweat-soaked shirt outlined the lean, hard muscles on his chest or the way the uniform stretched tight across his shoulders. There was a hint of a tattoo beneath the edge of his short sleeve PT shirt. It drew her gaze like a compulsion. She had the deep, driving urge to push his sleeve slowly up that smooth, muscled skin and look more closely at the intricate design.

She gave herself a mental shake. Since when did she like tattooed men?

She breathed out deeply, thoroughly distracted by the idea of tracing her fingers over his forearm, then lower, to thread with his.

"Zittoro's one of the kids we talked about yesterday," Ben said.

Just like that, the name connected with the memory. It was always harder to put a name with a face. "He's the kid I recommend immediately separating." Her voice fell with the realization.

And there was something deeper here, something heavy beneath the way Ben had encouraged the kid, refusing to leave him.

Any other commander wouldn't have tried to keep the druggie kid in the formation. Another commander would have left him, treated him like shit.

Despite Olivia knowing what the norm sadly was, to her there was something admirable in the way that Ben had stuck with Zittoro. Her mouth went dry as she studied him.

She licked her bottom lip, seeing something in Ben Teague she hadn't expected. There was something deeper beneath the sensual, dark exterior. Heat radiated off him from the run and she caught a hint of his scent, something spicy and warm that made her want to step closer than she should. "Yeah." His voice was thick, throaty.

He met her gaze then, watching her watching him. The world fell away until it was just her, just him, and she was tempted, far too tempted, to take a single step toward him. To feel the heat from his body wrap around her and draw her closer. To feel his heart beat beneath her cheek and feel his arms surround her. The need was strong, so strong.

She inhaled deeply as her heart slowed, blinked to break the thrall that held her there. "I'm sorry, Ben. I know you want to help him but I just don't think you can." She wiped her forehead again and took a single step backward. "I highly doubt the brigade commander is going to let you retain him, even if you wanted to. There are too many soldiers testing positive these days."

"I know that," he said. "Doesn't mean I have to like it." Ben pulled his t-shirt out of his shorts and wiped his face. Olivia tried and failed not to notice the narrow band of hair on his belly or the deep golden tone of his skin against the black of his shorts. But it was the ragged scar running down the center of his abdomen that drew her attention.

Time stood still, moments ticking by with painful slowness. Deep pink against the tan skin of his belly, the scar traced down his stomach and curved along the top of his hip bone. She hesitated, curling her fingers into her palms to keep from reaching out to touch it with the tip of her finger. She looked up and knew in an instant that she'd been caught staring.

His eyes darkened but he didn't look away. His throat moved as he swallowed. His lips twitched at the edges. Just a hint.

"You know, if you keep undressing me with your eyes, I'm going to need to file a sexual harassment complaint." He lowered the shirt with deliberate slowness. It hung at his sides, untucked and out of regulation. "I feel violated," he whispered.

"Ben." His name caught in her throat. She swallowed, badly needing space from this man that made her lose her composure. "That looks like it hurt," she said simply, trying to catch her breath.

He didn't move. He stood a little too close. Her skin was a little too warm, craving that human connection that she missed. "It still itches sometimes."

"How did it happen?"

There was a darkness in his eyes now, a tension tightening the muscles in his neck. One fist bunched by his side. "Shrapnel when our base was overrun."

"Our?"

"Me and Escoberra," he said softly. His eyes darkened, his mouth a flat line.

"That explains a lot," she whispered.

"You have no idea," he said. "He's like family to me."

"I'm sorry you have to do this," she said simply. Because she was. She'd never faced something like this—she'd never had to process actions on someone she cared about.

"Thank you," he said. He studied her quietly. "You haven't deployed, right?"

"I have," she said softly.

He frowned, folding his arms over his chest. His uniform

stretched over his chest, drawing Olivia's gaze to the raw power of the man in front of her. "I thought you didn't have a combat patch."

"I was in Kuwait. I don't feel right wearing a combat patch when I wasn't in harm's way."

He frowned then, studying her carefully. "That's an unusual attitude," he admitted. "You know you've opened yourself up to problems down here by not wearing your patch, right?"

She lifted a single shoulder. "When I earn a combat patch for going to combat, I'll wear one," she said quietly. "I'm not going to wear it just for the sake of it."

He lifted one eyebrow. "That's either really brave, or really stupid," he said easily.

Her own grin caught her off guard. "I'll let you know how it turns out," she said, folding her arms over her chest. What was it about this man who could so easily disarm all her defenses?

"Thanks for helping me out with Zittoro. He has too much pride to fall out around a female."

She swallowed, tipping her chin to study him. "Why did you do that with him?"

Ben scrubbed his hand over his mouth. "Because he's had a rough time of things. He's a good kid who has problems. He's still a soldier."

Her heart caught in her throat at the raw determination in his eyes. "You want to save him."

His mouth pressed into a flat line. "There are worse things for a commander to want," he said roughly.

She took a single step toward him. It was stupid for him to care this much, this deeply about a soldier he couldn't save.

"You have to know you can't," she whispered. The urge to curl her fingers over his heart, to reach out to him, was damn near overwhelming.

He swallowed, his movement violent and filled with hurt. "Maybe I have to try," he whispered. "Otherwise, what's the point of all this power and responsibility?"

There were so many things she could say to that. So many things that would make this harder, not easier.

Instead she said nothing.

She looked away, her gaze landing on a couple of soldiers walking by, sporting their Stetsons. Something about those things made the troopers down here walk taller.

"Did you get yours yet?"

"You mean the black cowboy hat everyone wears here?" She shook her head, grateful for the reprieve from a painful subject. "Sarn't Major Cox mentioned it."

"Stetson," Ben corrected. "You're an officer. You need one before next Friday."

She frowned, wishing she had her phone with her calendar on it. "What happens next Friday?"

"We wear them instead of our regular headgear to Stable Call. It's tradition."

"Stable Call. I'll assume you didn't just speak a foreign language." She smiled and it was warmer than it should have been toward Ben Teague.

"Mandatory fun. We all go to Legends Sports Bar and listen to our fearless leaders pontificate on the meaning of life, the universe, and everything."

Olivia smiled, grateful for the easy subject for once. Funny, she never would have thought talking about a silly hat would make her feel more at ease with him. "Thanks for the warning. I'll add it to my to-do list. Where do I get one?"

"The Cav Museum or there's a place off post off Stan Schlueter Loop."

Her throat moved as she swallowed. Ben's gaze fell to the soft line of her neck. He cleared his throat roughly. "They'll

take care of you at either place. Just tell them you need officer cords."

"I have no idea what that means but I'm sure I'll figure
it out."

She met his gaze, unsteady in this strange truce between
them. But Ben's kindness was something out of the ordinary.
And it stood in stark contrast to how he'd been that first day.

Ben swiped his cheek against his shoulder. "Thanks for
running with me and Zittoro, Olivia," he murmured.

"You already said that," she said softly, undone by the
quiet ease in his voice. "You did a kind thing. Kindness
these days is in short supply."

His smile was warm. "I'll try to remember that."

He stood a little too close. She could smell the heady mixture of soap and sweat, of man, primal and raw.

This man called to her. This man, who'd been kind to a
soldier who'd fallen out of a run, tempted her to step out of
her comfort zone.

This man, she needed to get far, far away from.

Ben walked into the company ops—into his company ops—
to see a pissed-off first sergeant pacing the orderly room.
It was just after eight a.m. and Ben had just come from the
gym and a cold shower because the gym's hot water had
been out.

Because the universe was screwing with him.

"You know you can't do that again," Sorren said.

"Who pissed in your corn flakes?" Ben asked.

"You did, sir."

Ben stopped short. "Sorry?"

"You can't leave the entire formation to go back for one
guy, sir. That's what we have NCOs for."

Ben breathed deeply. "I didn't see any NCOs heading
back to scoop him up."

"Yeah, well, I'll deal with them at first formation 'cause that is going to be the one and only time something like that happens." Sorren downed his cup of coffee and Ben wondered if it had been hot when the big man had gulped it down. "Now take me through our problem children."

Forty minutes later, Ben thought about offering Sorren a beer.

"I honestly didn't think that was possible," Sorren said after his fifth cup of coffee. He glanced mournfully at his mug then at the ancient coffee pot, that looked like it was about to die at any moment. "I think it's going to take a lot more than coffee to get through all this."

"We've got our work cut out for us, that's for sure." Sorren scrubbed a big hand over his jaw. He was the kind of guy who needed to shave three times a day. "We need a better coffee pot than this fucking relic. Where the hell did that thing even come from?"

"A twelve-dollar one from the Goodwill, most likely." Ben thought longingly of the espresso machine in the battalion headquarters. Maybe he'd start a coffee fund and get one for the company ops. Maybe he'd lead a stealth mission to steal the espresso machine. "New generation doesn't believe in caffeine. They're all about the energy drinks and soda."

Sorren made a disgusted face. "What the hell is wrong with kids these days?"

Ben kicked his feet up on the table. One of the legal packets slipped over the edge and onto the floor. Ben just sat there looking at it for a long time.

Zittoro, Anthony. The name written in neat block letters. Ben stared at it over the edge of his coffee cup, resting his elbows on his knees. The packet would end the career of a once solid infantryman who hadn't been able to beat his addiction and could no longer stay in the fight.

And Ben had to put him out of the army *knowing* the kid had nowhere to go.

Ben looked into his own coffee cup and wished he could find some smart-ass comment to lighten the weight around his heart.

He looked up to find Sorren watching him.

"You don't want this job, do you, sir."

It wasn't a question.

Instead, he said nothing. Because there were no words to describe the fierce tension rioting inside him.

"What makes you say that?" was all he said after the silence hung on too long.

Sorren shoved Ben's boots off the table, then leaned down to pick up the folder. He tossed it onto the table and sat back down.

"Why don't we clear the air on this right now," Sorren said. He leaned forward and Ben leaned back.

Right then, his first sergeant was pissed and it was all directed straight at Ben. Once upon a time, he might have been intimidated. Now? Now he was just tired. Far too burned out and cynical for his age.

"We've got eight months to get ready to head back downrange. Whether or not you go with us is up for discussion." Sorren jabbed a thumb at his own chest. "I've got a job to do but to do that, I need you to do yours. So whatever angst or teenage drama or unresolved trauma you need to overcome to do your fucking job, I need you to get over it. I've buried enough soldiers. I'm not going to let another petulant captain ruin my men."

Ben rocked slowly in his chair, contemplating the myriad of things he could say. His first sarn't was like most senior NCOs, wary of the officer corps that led them. Far too many officers had thrown their senior enlisted man under the bus to save their own asses.

His throat constricted with a wave of guilt. Escoberra had taken the hit when their base had gotten overrun, despite Ben trying to shield him.

Goddamn it, he was going to take care of Escoberra this time. He wouldn't fail a second time.

But Sorren's words hit home with an accuracy born from experience. Ben wondered just how much beer it would take to get Sorren to open up.

There would be time for that some other day.

"I'll do my job, First Sarn't." He had no idea how he was going to do that, but he'd figure it out. Maybe start drinking at lunch or some other self-destructive habit. Get Emily to give him some free therapy.

"I hope so, sir," Sorren said roughly.

Instead, Ben set the coffee cup on the conference room table and stretched. "Well, I'm glad we got that out of the way. Want to go take a warm shower together and sing "Kumbayah"?"

Sorren just looked at him for a minute. A tick at the corner of his left eye jumped. Ben seriously wondered if he'd be able to move fast enough if Sorren tried to take a swing at him.

Sorren's sudden laugh surprised him. "All right then, sir." He stood and slapped Ben's shoulder and damn near knocked it out of joint. "Let's go to the motor pool and get some work done."

Ben turned around in his chair to see Sarn't Major Cox standing in his orderly room. Sorren moved to his feet quickly and called, "At ease!"

Ben frowned. "Has hell frozen over?"

As usual, Cox didn't appreciate the joke. "I need a few minutes of your time, Commander."

"I'm sorry? I don't think I heard you correctly." Olivia reached for her water bottle, hoping to push the lump down in her throat.

There was a fellow major sitting across from her. He was a thin man—wiry would be an apt description—and his eyes shifted constantly, darting around the office she had yet to claim as her own.

There was a meanness about Major Denis that had her backbone up. There was something lethal about him that had nothing to do with the bad things in this battalion, but everything to do with the man himself. She'd decided she didn't like the Death Dealer Battalion executive officer the minute she'd met him. Five minutes was all it had taken to turn that dislike into active loathing.

"I need the files on Captain Marshall."

"Again, Major Denis, I'm not sure how you think this works but I deal with your battalion commander on these things."

He cleared his throat, shifting in his chair. "I'm working legal actions for the battalion commander. I'm trying to get caught up on the legal situation before the briefing."

Olivia felt the anger start to simmer someplace deep inside of her. "I'm under specific orders to deal only with commanders on several of these cases. This is one of them. So while I appreciate your desire to get caught up—" and she made air quotes around "caught up" to emphasize her point just in case he missed it—"I'm not giving you those files."

Denis's face darkened as a flush crept up his neck. "Fine. We'll see what the boss says about this. I'm sure he'll be thrilled to know how you're negatively impacting the processing of legal actions."

Olivia set the water bottle down roughly and stood. "Don't threaten me," she said quietly. "I'm the very last person you're going to swell up on and try to intimidate. And if you don't like the way I'm doing my job, go find someone who gives a damn, because I'm not the one."

Denis stood and leaned over her desk, trying to force her to either sit down or step back. She did neither. "You think you can come down here and just run things the way you want? We do things differently down here. You'd better learn that."

She stood her ground, refusing to back down. She glanced over his shoulder at the man who'd just stepped into the doorway. "Captain Teague, did you need something?"

Ben stared hard at Denis quietly, but Olivia could see the barely restrained violence in his stillness. Without taking his eyes off Denis, he pulled his cell phone out of his jacket pocket. "Just need a few minutes of your time, ma'am."

"What are you doing here, Teague?" Denis asked. "You're supposed to be in the motor pool conducting inventories."

Ben's smile was ice cold, his fingers tight around a dinged-up water bottle as he slipped his phone back into his pocket with his other hand. "Commander business," he said quietly.

The tension between the two men was palpable. Something physical and something real.

She wondered at the history between them. But this wasn't the time to ask. Ben didn't take his eyes off the skinny major as Denis shuffled out of the office, leaving a trail of grease hanging in the air after him.

"Nice timing," she said, gesturing toward the chair recently vacated by her new BFF. "What's the story there?"

"That would take a hell of a lot longer than we've got right now." Ben glanced over his shoulder and halfway out of the office to make sure Denis was gone. "He was my commander, once upon a war. Between us girls, you might want to watch your back with that one. He's a nasty little fucker."

Olivia chewed on Ben's words for a moment. "Oh, I already figured that out."

Ben shook his head as he sat and folded his hands in his lap. "No, I don't think you're following. He's well connected and he could easily start something at echelons well above your pay grade that could get you into a world of shit."

Olivia's skin went cold. She tucked that little piece of information away someplace safe. Maybe she'd need it, maybe she wouldn't, but she wasn't one to brush off advice. She reached for her water bottle.

"Well, I guess I'll just have to watch my back. I appreciate the warning." She twisted the lid off her water bottle. "What can I help you with?"

He tapped his finger against the lip of his bottle. "I have a problem."

She waited for him to continue, not wanting to poison the well by jumping to conclusions. Warmth spread over her skin as she sat with him. Recollection of that morning's earlier conversation hung in the air between them. A jagged scar that she'd wanted to trace with her fingers. Her gaze dropped to his belly, covered now by his uniform. Scars like that changed a man. What had he been like before his body had been broken by the war?

What had *he* been like?

She looked up to find him watching her. Heat rose inside her, heat that she had no business feeling toward this man. She licked her bottom lip, wishing that things were simpler. That she wasn't a bundle of screwed up everything, and that he wasn't as dark and wounded as she suspected he was.

She couldn't save him.

No matter how much she might want to take away his pain, his memories were his own.

Still, that knowledge didn't stop her from wanting to soothe some of the jagged pain she saw in his eyes.

She needed some distance, and some perspective on the complicated man in front of her.

She let the silence stand between them until he found the words he needed.

"Sergeant First Class Escoberra."

Olivia swallowed but stayed quiet. Cold washed over her skin. She couldn't afford to jump to conclusions but damn it was hard. "What about him?"

He turned the cap on his bottle. On. Off. "Is there any way to speed this thing up?"

Olivia sank back in her chair. He wasn't asking her to break the rules. At least she didn't think he was. "What's going on?"

Ben's eyes flashed darkly. Just a moment before he looked away, down at his hands. "I can't go into that with you," he said quietly. "But it would mean a hell of a lot to me if we could get his case wrapped up. I don't care how it ends but we can't have this one dragging out forever and a day."

There was a warning there. A plea. "There's little we can do until Child Protective Services finishes their investigation," she said quietly.

Ben studied the water bottle in his hands.

"You still want to defend him?" Olivia couldn't keep the incredulity from her voice.

Ben met her gaze. "You know why," he whispered.

Frustration clawed at her. How could she get him to see that the man he was defending was not the man he knew? Or maybe he was.

But Ben needed to see the truth before he made any more decisions. He needed to understand what his platoon sergeant had done to his daughter—a man he defended so willingly.

She searched through the stack of files until she found Escoberra's. Flipped it open and tossed it onto her desk. "Before you say another word, explain to me how this happened. Then we'll have this conversation again."

Ben looked at the pictures, then looked away. "Jesus Christ."

Hailey—Escoberra's stepdaughter—oh God, Hailey. Her back. Black and blue bruises covered her back in the photos. Ben could see knuckle marks embedded in her pale skin, the open slash in her shoulder.

Ben covered his mouth, feeling sick, his brain rioting denial even as his eyes remained glued to the pictures.

Slowly, Ben shook his head. "There's got to be something we're missing."

"Does that excuse his action if we are?"

Ben's gaze collided with hers. "I can't believe this man did this to his little girl. He loves that kid. He loves his family."

But the sickness churned in his guts, doubt twisting like a knife.

"All the love in the world doesn't explain this," she said quietly. Olivia crossed her arms over her chest. Ben had never seen her angry before. Her pale skin flushed. He wished he didn't notice. "Stop looking for ways to break the rules," she said.

"I'm not. I asked if we could speed this up at all. There's a mile of difference between the two."

"Not in my world," she said.

"Well, this isn't your world," he said, standing and leaning over the desk. She didn't even flinch. "It's mine."

"That's not true." She stood, anger radiating off her. "You want to know about trauma? How about having a young woman sit across from your desk, begging you to let her husband come home? Pleading that he didn't mean it, that things were going to change?"

Ben leaned back, blown away by the force of her anger.

"You want to know trauma, Captain Teague? How

about that young woman dead less than a week later? And the man she loved so…damned…much? He killed her." She slammed Escoberra's packet on the desk. "So don't sit there and defend this and expect me to sit back and believe that man is a hero." She jammed her finger against the packet. "Because I've seen heroes do some terrible fucking things."

Ben folded his arms over his chest, anger ripping at him. He'd come here to ask for help and instead, she'd torn into him. "Escoberra isn't that man," Ben said, his voice cold.

"You don't know that," she said.

"And neither do you," Ben snapped.

"I know what I see in that packet. I see a man who is capable of incredible violence."

"And I know a man capable of incredible love."

"The opposite side of love is hate," Olivia said. "They're not mutually exclusive."

She stepped back, her features hard, the anger a tangible thing in the room. "I need his mental health evaluation done ASAP."

Ben ground his teeth, hating that he had to do that to Escoberra. But those pictures planted a seed of doubt now, and it nagged at the base of his skull, whispering that he might be wrong. "We've got the appointment in two weeks."

"They can't see him sooner?"

Ben shook his head. "You obviously don't know how things work around here."

"I just came from working at the hospital. Things weren't that slow there."

Ben snorted and swiped his water bottle off the desk. "You really have no idea how the rest of the army works, do you? You've spent your entire career safe and sound up in some headquarters while the rest of us have been getting our asses handed to us."

Something dark flickered over her expression. A haunted memory, something bent and gnarled.

Something that hurt.

She shut it down as quickly as it appeared but not before Ben saw it and wondered at its source. What had hurt her so deeply that it could sneak out like that?

Ben knew all about being hurt. About memories that haunted the darkness, memories that kept him from sleeping.

But he'd be damned if he was going to ask about hers.

"Don't sit there and think you know me, Ben," she whispered. "Because you don't know me at all."

He twisted the top off his bottle. "You're right. I don't."

Ben stalked out of the office, wishing he hadn't seen that moment of vulnerability in her eyes. Wishing he hadn't seen the pictures of Hailey.

Wishing he didn't have to deal with any of this.

But he did. And goddamn it, Escoberra owed him some answers.

Chapter Six

"Are you ready for this, sir?"

Ben stared at the packet in his hand, wanting to be anywhere else but there at the moment. "Did I ever tell you about the time our base got overrun?"

Sorren watched him silently.

"Zittoro manned the fifty cal for thirty-six hours straight. Never took a break for chow, nothing. Just kept watch over his sector and kept the enemy from exploiting a weakness in our perimeter." He looked up at Sorren. "The kid's a fucking hero and now I've got to throw him out of the army?"

Sorren folded his arms over his chest and leaned against the doorframe. "We can't keep him in, sir," he said after a moment.

"I know that. Realistically, I know that." He flipped open the packet and read the first page, bitterness surrounding his heart. "It doesn't make it suck any less."

Sorren let the silence hang. Finally Ben leaned forward, setting the folder down. "Bring him in, Top."

The warrior Ben had known was long gone, replaced by the skinny, burned-out addict in front of him. Zittoro's hands trembled as Ben continued reading the separation packet.

His face flushed. A single bead of sweat ran down his temple. His entire body shook now.

First Sergeant Sorren put his hand on Zittoro's shoulder. Zittoro flinched at the touch, then looked up at the big first sergeant. "It's going to be okay, son," he said softly.

Zittoro nodded, blinking rapidly. The contact steadied him. Enough so that Ben could clear his throat and finish reading. He turned the packet toward Zittoro for him to sign. Zittoro's hand shook so badly he dragged the pen off the edge of the paper.

Ben signed after him. His heart was a lead weight in his chest.

And then there was the silence.

Until Zittoro spoke. "Can I ask a favor, sir?"

Ben glanced at Sorren then back at his soldier. "Yeah, what's up?"

Zittoro cleared his throat. "I'm... I hit thirty-six months in three weeks. Could, could I stay until then? So I can qualify for my GI Bill?"

His hands shook as he spoke, his throat jumping with each word.

Ben would be breaking the rules. He was supposed to process the packet within a certain amount of time. If he didn't, the process was supposed to start all over again. The battalion commander had given him clear guidance to get these guys gone—guys like Zittoro that took time away from training the rest of the team for the next deployment.

But Ben looked at Zittoro right then, the decision weighing on him. He could do the right thing... or he could do what the army wanted him to do.

Ben had never been a company man. It wasn't time to start now, just because he was a commander.

Ben gripped his shoulder. "Yeah. I can do that. But you've

got to promise me you'll stay clean. You can't use or you'll
tie my hands."

Zittoro's eyes widened and filled with tears. As though
he'd expected Ben to say no.

Because any other commander would have.

"Thank you, sir. I-I won't let you down." His voice shook
violently.

"I know." Ben swallowed the lump in his throat. His eyes
stung with frustration. The kid had nothing. Nowhere to go.
No family. And the goddamned army was throwing him out.

Ben was throwing him out.

He felt dirty.

He wanted to hit something.

At that moment, he hated. Hated the fucking rules. Hated
that Zittoro looked at him and *knew* that Ben knew he had
nowhere to go.

Ben cleared his throat.

Zittoro looked like he would crumble with relief beneath
the news. He licked his lips quickly. "I—thank you, sir. First
Sarn't."

Ben stood and circled his desk, gripping the younger
man's shoulder lightly. He didn't squeeze. He was afraid Zittoro's bones would snap from the pressure. "Just . . . you need
to figure out how to get clean, man. This shit is going to kill
you," Ben said quietly. It was a terrible thing to say to an
addict. He couldn't stop himself from using any more than
Ben could stop himself from breathing.

Being an addict meant he couldn't be a soldier. Zittoro
wasn't like Reza—Reza had finally managed to get himself
clean. Zittoro? He couldn't quit the monkey that drove him
to use. Ben wished it were otherwise, but wishes weren't all
that useful against addiction.

Zittoro hadn't managed to kick his addiction. But that didn't
mean that Ben had to treat him like he was a piece of shit.

It wasn't going to do a damn thing to make Ben feel less dirty than he did right then. Like he was betraying a kid who'd counted on him, on the army, not to break him.

Ben felt sick.

Sorren closed the door behind him. "You know he's going to use, don't you, sir?"

Ben leaned back against his desk and folded his arms over his chest. "Probably."

"But you're willing to risk it?" Sorren's expression was carefully blank, leaving Ben to guess whether or not his first sergeant approved of his decision.

"He might make it. And maybe someday he'll get clean and be able to use the benefits he earned." Ben swallowed roughly. "It doesn't cost the army a damn thing to let him finish out this month. If he manages to ever use the benefits, he's earned them. If he doesn't, so be it." But it was a chance. A chance Zittoro hadn't had five minutes before.

Sorren grunted and said nothing. He shifted and mirrored Ben's stance, folding his arms over his chest. "For what it's worth, sir, I think that took some balls. The battalion commander isn't going to be happy when he finds out."

Ben held out his hand for the packet. Sorren handed it back. "If he finds out. Just tell the sergeant major that I'm being a pain in the ass about processing things."

Sorren scrubbed a big hand over the back of his neck. "You did the right thing."

Ben said nothing. Because it was a line of bullshit.

He'd done the army thing because Zittoro was still going home. Nothing Ben did could change that.

And that was not the same in his book.

He stalked out of the office, needing some fresh air.

"I'm sorry, Captain Marshall, but you're no longer the company commander and therefore, I'm not required to tell you anything." Olivia stood in the small office that had become her workspace, ready to do battle with the arrogant bastard in front of her. She rounded her desk, her wrist bumping into the cracked side of the scales of justice on her desk. The broken plate creaked on the chain.

Olivia felt the split against the heel of her hand. Reminding her of her purpose. Her task.

Marshall was oblivious. Guys like him always were. Guys who let the power of command go to their heads. Who thought they were above the law.

"I have a right to know what the charges are against me." Marshall was not a small man. He was built like Ben, only leaner and with a whole lot more mean layered over that muscle.

"Actually, you haven't been charged with anything yet, Captain," Olivia said, putting mild emphasis on his rank. Olivia had dealt with men like Marshall more than once. It chafed that she didn't have the means to put him in his place...yet. There was no desk between them but she'd be damned if she was going to back down against this son of a bitch. If he hit her, he'd only do it once.

And she'd add assault to the charge sheet that she hadn't written yet.

"You're hiding information. I have a right to face my accusers."

"Once you've been accused." She lifted her chin. "I can't help you. And I'll thank you to remember your military bearing, Captain Marshall."

Ben rounded the corner of her office door and Olivia was never so glad for a distraction as she was at that exact moment.

The fact that it was Ben was an added bonus but she kept that fact to herself.

Ben stepped between her and Marshall. Olivia wasn't

foolish enough to argue. She didn't actually *want* to get punched today.

And his willingness to step into the fray...She stopped the mental detour she'd just taken. She didn't want to see Ben Teague for anything more than he professed to be, no matter how much the shadows in his eyes made her want to know more about the man she suspected he was hiding from the world.

"Take it up with the battalion commander, shit for brains." Ben tossed a stack of packets on a chair and squared off with Marshall.

Marshall took a step closer until his face was an inch from Ben's. "Get the fuck out of my face, Teague."

"You want to do this, I'm fine with that," Ben snarled.

"Mind your own fucking business."

Ben slipped his hands into the collar of Marshall's uniform top and shoved him backward out of Olivia's office. Marshall went down with a crack that sounded like a bone had broken.

"Out."

Marshall got to his feet and looked as if he was about to lunge at Ben, but then thought better of it. "This isn't over, Teague. You think you're hot shit because you're taking over my sloppy seconds again."

Ben stepped forward. Marshall didn't back down. Neither did Ben. "Not the first time. Won't be the last. Might want to go put some ice on your pride."

Marshall stalked out. Ben turned and Olivia held up Marshall's patrol cap. "He's going to be back for this," she said, dangling it off her index finger.

Ben grabbed it and threw it out into the adjutant's office. "Not back in here."

"Wow, you're going all caveman. I'm not sure if I should swoon or wring out my panties."

"Did you just make a joke?" Ben froze and frowned. His nostrils flared from the mix of too much adrenaline and the sudden lack of an appropriate place to put it. "When did we reach the joke-making phase of this relationship? I thought we were still at the swiping hostility phase."

"Nervous tension," she said, waving a hand. "I don't know what I'm saying." For a moment, all her shields fell away and she stood there, grinning up at him. As though he was a normal man and she was a normal woman. Her breath caught in her throat when he met her gaze, his quiet laugh filling the space. The joke had felt good, too good. She shifted her focus back on the job. "You two worked together before?"

"He tried to have my platoon sergeant court-martialed back in '05. Let's just say we're not taking warm showers together anytime soon." He looked at her then and his eyes softened. Olivia's insides twinged at the unexpected concern. "You okay?" A concern she hadn't counted on. It slipped behind her shields and warmed her in a way that she knew she shouldn't be warmed.

She nodded, folding her arms across her chest to hide her shaking hands. She had been willing to fight but now that the threat had passed, she had nothing to do with the adrenaline that still pumped through her veins.

Ben pushed her back into her office and closed the door behind them. "You would have gotten your ass whipped. You know that, right?"

"I was banking on him not actually hitting me."

"Based on what?"

"Pure stupidity," she mumbled, admitting it before he forced her to swallow the bitter pill. It *had* been stupid antagonizing Marshall, but the more she learned about him and his minions, the more she wanted—badly—to see him punished for abusing his power. Half the packets on her desk were there because Marshall hadn't been doing his job.

She backed up against her desk and knocked Ben's Stetson to the floor. "Ugh, I still haven't gone to the store."

"You didn't get one yet?" Ben leaned down and scooped up his Stetson, set it on top of the files, then looked down at his watch. "What are you doing for lunch?"

"Working."

"Not anymore. Come on. I'll buy you lunch at McDonald's or something equally romantic but you can't walk around tomorrow without a Stetson."

She didn't move. "Why are you doing this?" she asked abruptly. "One minute, we're arguing, the next you're taking me to buy a silly hat."

"Bite your tongue and never repeat that." His lips twitched at the edges, reminding her of that first smile the other morning. "Besides, maybe I find interpersonal hostility deeply sexy." He picked up his Stetson from the top of the pile of folders.

Her lips twitched. "Do you?"

"Maybe." His mouth crooked at one corner. He stood a little too close. His shoulders were a little too broad.

"You're a complicated man," she whispered.

"So are you," he said. "Woman, I mean." A flush crawled up his neck.

She laughed out loud, covering her mouth at the unexpected sensation. It was such a rare thing for her to laugh with someone. To feel this easiness.

Like something she might start to crave if she wasn't careful.

"A Stetson is tradition," he said, his voice rough. "And you want to fit in, right?"

"You don't strike me as a traditional kind of guy," she said.

"Depends on the tradition." He tapped the patch on his right shoulder. "Like this one. Why is it so important?"

"I already told you that," she said softly, not liking where this line of questioning was heading.

"No, you told me why you wouldn't wear your patch from Kuwait, not why wearing one you earned was important to you. There's a difference."

Olivia's skin prickled at the question. Her breath caught in her throat. She retreated against her desk, rubbing her hand over her face. He'd struck a sore spot with that comment. A direct hit at the aching feelings of always being on the outside. Striking at the heart of her insecurity. "The Stetson is as serious as a combat patch?"

"Yes," Ben said simply.

Olivia sighed, grateful that her hands had stopped shaking now that the threat from Captain Marshall had passed, both in its proximity and from her body's reaction. "Fine."

Ben frowned then narrowed his eyes. "You're not going to argue anymore?"

"Are you going to stop pestering me?" He folded his arms over his chest and looked every bit the belligerent warrior. "See? It's not a good use of my energy."

She could see him calculating. She wasn't entirely sure why she agreed to go with him. Maybe the situation with Marshall had unnerved her a little more than she was willing to admit. Ben's timing had been perfect.

And beneath the swagger of male egos, she'd seen something intriguing. Beneath the smart mouth and wisecracks, there was something deeper.

Something serious that Ben Teague tried to hide from the world. But she kept catching glimpses of it and the more she saw, the more curious she became. What else was there to this man who rejected the idea of command and leadership and all the things army officers were supposed to grow up to be?

"Whose files did you drop off?" she asked as they drove out of Fort Hood's main gate.

He couldn't quite figure out what he was doing with the lawyer. She sat next to him in his truck, her hands twisting in her lap. She was nervous, that much he could tell. She was usually always so confident, so strict and businesslike.

To see her a little nervous? A little vulnerable? It did something to his insides. Made him a little bit hungry for something he couldn't have.

He fiddled with the radio, needing something to fill the silence and derail his thoughts from the dangerous direction they were taking. "Remis, Bisco, and Hooch. Why?"

"I want to mark them off on my tracker." She pulled out a tiny notepad from her shoulder pocket and jotted down the names.

"Tracker?"

"I'm keeping tabs on every file that I've pushed out to commanders and how long they've had it."

Ben glanced at her. Her eyes were hidden beneath brown Wiley-X glasses. "That seems a little..."

"Anal?"

Ben lifted an eyebrow and suddenly found the leather of his steering wheel fascinating. "You said it, not me."

Olivia turned her head toward the passing traffic. The muscles in her neck tensed. "I've had problems with packets disappearing," she said quietly. "Commanders not turning them in, sergeants not getting the required paperwork. Then I'm stuck answering for them and bad soldiers are still here. There was one time a commander decided to retain an NCO..."

Her words faded. There was a memory there. A subtle undercurrent to her words. A tension beyond her usual stiffness. It filled the cab of his old truck, an insidious thing.

"It still bothers you." He turned toward the country-and-western store where she could get her Stetson.

She clenched her jaw. It was a long time before she answered. "It doesn't matter now."

He glanced over at her. "Must have been a big deal for you to be upset about it after all this time."

"I don't think I'll ever get over it completely," she admitted. She lifted one shoulder and dropped it. She looked over at him, her mouth pressed into a flat, cynical line. "I failed to protect a family. The boss didn't listen to me." A deep breath, filled with regret. "A week later, the sergeant's entire family was dead in a murder–suicide." She paused and he heard her sharp intake of breath. "It still hurts. I wish it didn't but it does." A painful admission.

"That was the case you told me about." He didn't bother to hide the sympathy in his voice.

Her fingers tightened in her lap, her eyes dark with emotions as raw today as they must have been the day it happened. She hadn't dealt with their deaths. Not at all. He could see that in the bleak emptiness looking back at him. "It's all said and done now. Not much I can do about it except learn from my mistakes."

"Why do you do that?" he asked suddenly.

"Do what?"

"Brush things off." He rolled to a stop at a light. "You get so fired up about things, so passionate, but when something hurts, you brush it off."

"I don't like remembering painful things," she said quietly. "It doesn't help anything."

"Neither does running from the memories," he said. He looked over at her, surprised by the vulnerability in her voice. "Everyone makes mistakes, Olivia."

Her smile was sad and filled her eyes. "My mistakes got someone killed," she whispered.

"You didn't make the choice to go home to an abuser," he said.

"It's so much more complicated than that," she said. "The army protected him when they should have protected her." She paused, looking away. "I could have done more."

She looked so lost, so alone. He reached for her then, because he couldn't stop himself. He brushed his thumb over her cheek. A gentle touch. Something he shouldn't have done but something he wouldn't regret. "You can keep telling yourself that," he whispered. "But it won't make it so."

Silence wound between them. Her skin was warm beneath his touch. Her breath huffed over his knuckles. Her lips were parted, a tiny space that he had a sudden longing to taste.

He searched her eyes, looking for what, he didn't know.

A horn blared behind him, jolting him out of the moment.

She looked away, but not before he noticed the flush creeping over her skin.

"Do you have a first sergeant now?" Olivia asked. The obvious change of subject wasn't lost on Ben.

He let it ride for now. Her admission revealed a complex woman beneath the hard adherence to the rules and regulations, and suddenly Ben found himself wanting to know more about the very real, very complicated person that she worked so hard to hide.

There was more to this woman, so much more.

And Ben wanted to know all of it. She pulled at him in a way that a woman hadn't pulled at him in a long, long time.

He parked outside the Western wear store and led her into the depths. A bell jangled over the door. The smell of leather permeated the air, thick and heavy and clean. Boots were stacked on boxes, displaying every style under the sun.

At the counter an old man was steaming a Stetson. "Be with you in a second," he said without looking up.

Olivia looked up at Ben who shrugged. "Need some cowboy boots while you're here? Embrace your inner Texan?"

She shook her head. "I don't have an inner Texan."

"Everyone has an inner Texan. Most folks just don't figure it out until it's too late."

"Too late?"

"Yeah. They find out they really did have an inner Texan while they're—oh, I don't know—freezing their asses off in Alaska or South Korea." Ben pulled a tan hat off one of the racks. "Think the sergeant major would like my substitution?"

"Aren't you the guy who wears the trucker hats just to piss him off?" Olivia asked, fighting the urge to grin.

Ben grinned wickedly even as a flush crept up his neck. "You heard about that, huh?"

"Everyone has heard about it. The clerks in the adjutant's office were trying to figure out if Sergeant Major Cox had really kicked you in the tail on the way out of the ops."

Ben lifted both eyebrows, putting the hat back on the rack. "The sarn't major might be grumpy but he'll have to get up a lot earlier than that to take me out."

The old man behind the counter finished what he was doing and planted himself at the edge of the counter. "What kind of cord do you need?"

Olivia looked at the wizened old cowboy like he'd lost his mind. "Um…"

It took everything Ben had not to point out the obvious officer rank in the middle of Olivia's chest. The old man took in Olivia's confusion and grunted, "Officer," before turning away to pluck the black and gold braided cord from a hook. "Here."

He handed her a Stetson and started fiddling with the cord while Olivia tried to figure out the two leather straps on the inside of the hat.

Ben tugged it from her hands. "Like this." He loosened the straps and put the hat on her head, tugging the leather straps over the bun at the base of her skull.

She adjusted it. "It's tight."

"It's supposed to fit snug. Otherwise, it'll blow off in the first gust of wind."

She glanced at his Stetson. "What are the knots on the front of yours?"

Ben picked his own Stetson up. On the front of the cord were two knots on either side of the center loop. "Combat knots." Olivia's gaze flicked to Ben's right shoulder. "Why does this matter so much to you?" he asked.

"Because I haven't earned a combat patch." Olivia lifted the Stetson from her head and smoothed her hair back into place. She looked down at her new Stetson, gleaming black and unformed. "You earn your place in the world," she said softly.

She was lost, he realized. Adrift in the newness of being in the Cav, a new unit and one where she was utterly alone. But there was more to this than simply being in a new place. He stepped closer to her, close enough to see the blue streaks in her eyes, and gave in to the urge to tilt her face up to meet his gaze. "Who let you down, Olivia?" he whispered.

Her throat moved as she swallowed. But she didn't pull away from his touch. "It doesn't matter anymore."

But it did. Oh, but it did. She mattered, but now was neither the time nor the place. He slipped her Stetson from her hands and handed it to the old cowboy. "Shape it up?"

"No problem, boyo."

Olivia wandered off, clearly trying to avoid the rest of the conversation. Ben was tempted to follow her, to find out what was so damned important about earning the big horsehead patch, but something about the way she stared aimlessly at the wall of boots on display had him holding back.

There was a strange truce between them now. She tugged at him.

And despite everything that happened between them, he

savored the delicious pull toward this complicated, driven woman. He wanted. He could admit that to himself, at least. He wanted to see if the passion he saw when she was at work carried over to the rest of her life.

He watched her then and saw the damaged woman she tried to conceal behind a cool professional façade.

And he let himself wonder what if.

Chapter Seven

Olivia was silent on the ride back to post. She felt rude but she couldn't explain to Ben why wearing a combat patch was important to her. Why buying the Stetson felt pretentious and fake—because she didn't feel like she belonged and the Stetson only accentuated that feeling.

It wasn't about fitting in. It was about legitimacy, about being good enough to deserve to wear the combat patch. It was about being part of a team that would stand with you when things went to shit. She was tired of pretending to fit in, only to find herself alone when things went a little nuts.

The combat patch was important to her, more so than the Stetson that seemed so important to everyone. There were cases—too many cases—of officers flying to Kuwait and staying for thirty days, just so they could wear a combat patch. Their duplicity tainted the entire system and cut away at their credibility. Such cases might be just an urban legend but it planted a seed of fear. Fear that she would not be taken seriously.

And Olivia needed her credibility. It was the most important thing she had. But trying to explain that to a man who wore his confidence with casual arrogance? Ben Teague had probably never had a hard day fitting in in his life.

No matter how hard Olivia worked, she would never feel

like it was enough. She would never trust that she would have someone standing next to her.

And so she said nothing. Because it was better than opening her mouth and sounding like an insecure idiot.

Ben pulled into the parking lot and parked his truck. Silence was heavy and thick and awkward between them. "You're being quiet," he said.

"Just thinking about work," she said, trying to brush off his concern. She wasn't ready to do deep and introspective with him.

Some things were better left alone.

"You keep running away every time I ask a personal question." His voice sounded off. She glanced back at him. "If you keep it up, I might think you don't like me or something. Male egos are notoriously easy to bruise."

She blinked at his remark: offhanded but serious beneath the light comment. "You keep asking questions about something that isn't there."

"What, you're a Cylon? No human feelings? 'Cause that would be pretty awesome."

Her lip twitched. "I love *Battlestar Galactica*."

Ben lifted his sunglasses and peered at her. "Really? You lawyer types don't like *CSI* and stuff?"

She shook her head. "They get so much wrong, I can't watch." She sniffed. "I don't get to watch much TV at any rate." She glanced down at her watch. "I'll send you a note later on the rest of the packets I need back. Zittoro's should have been processed already?"

If she hadn't been watching him, she might have missed the slight tightening of his grip on the steering wheel.

"Zittoro's on emergency leave," he said, avoiding her gaze. "I'll have it completed when he gets back."

Olivia stilled, watching him. "When did he go on leave?" She didn't bother to hide the suspicion in her voice.

"Today. Emergency at home."

More lies. Olivia's chest tightened. It was the same old song and dance. Commanders hiding their soldiers' misconduct. Keeping bad soldiers in the army.

Hiding the crimes that the "good soldiers" never committed.

The anger rose from a bottomless pit inside her. Her breath was tight in her chest. "I'll make a note of that for the battalion commander," she said, trying to keep her voice normal. It sounded harsh and ragged to her ears.

"Don't do that."

She fought to keep the rage out of her voice. Fought for calm. "Why not?"

"Because I haven't briefed him on it yet. And that's something a commander should tell a commander."

Olivia felt the leash on her temper snap. "You're lying to me," she said through clenched teeth. "Stop. Lying to me."

"This isn't about *you*," he said. "This is about me taking care of one of my soldiers."

Olivia's hands shook. The cold plastic of the door handle burned her skin. She shoved open the door and slammed it shut, rounding the truck. She yanked open his door and jammed a finger in his direction. "You're sitting on a packet. That soldier needs to be out of the army uniform and you're sitting on it. You have no right—"

"I have every right!" Ben stepped out of the truck, forcing her to back up or fall. "You met Zittoro. You saw the kind of kid he is. How can you push all of that aside and say he needs to be out of the army when he has *nothing* to fall back on?"

"Because I've seen how this movie ends, Ben," she whispered. "And it's not going to have a happily ever after. Addiction doesn't just go away with a little magical thinking."

"You don't know that. He could get clean."

"He could." Her voice caught on the ragged edge that threatened to choke her. "But you don't have the right to keep him on active duty to take that risk." She swallowed the bitter sadness of her words. "I wish it were otherwise but it's not."

"Don't tell me what I have the right to do or not do." Ben radiated quiet, unspent fury. His eyes flashed, his mouth was a hard line, his words filled with quiet anger. "I'm a company commander or so everyone keeps telling me. If I want to sit on this kid's packet so that he can get some goddamned college money, I'm allowed to do that."

"The packet is complete," she said. "And you're sitting on it. The battalion commander charged me with cleaning up this battalion. That means this soldier has to go home." She tried to take a deep breath. Tried to fight the rage that burned behind her eyes and threatened to embarrass her.

"And he will go home," Ben said quietly, his voice low and filled with frustration and something else. Sadness lined with regret. It was killing him to put this soldier out of the army. This was a side of Ben Teague she'd never seen. Her heart broke for him even as she stood there and argued with him. "When he's back off leave."

"Why are you protecting this soldier?" she whispered. The man who'd tried to make her laugh was long gone. In his place was this commander, this man who looked like he carried the weight of the world on his shoulders.

An aching pity rose inside her. Raw and powerful. But she shut it down. She did not want to feel pity for this man.

She'd been an army lawyer for years now. She'd seen the terrible things that soldiers did to one another. She'd seen the worst of the army and what that did to commanders who cared about their soldiers.

Some took it as a personal failing that their soldiers had gotten into trouble. Others made it a crusade to throw as many soldiers out as they could.

But all of them were worn down beneath the weight of the guidon.

It hadn't even been a week but she could see the change in him since they'd met.

"It's the right thing to do," she whispered.

He shook his head. "How? How is throwing him out of the army the right thing to do?"

"Because he's an addict. And we don't have the resources to treat him if he doesn't want to get clean. And even if he does want to, that's no guarantee. Addiction is a powerful thing." She took a deep breath, remembering the lost kid she'd run with the other day. Ben couldn't save him. Didn't he see that? "You have to prepare this team to deploy into combat. You can't do that if you're chasing around after all the kids you refuse to send home."

He looked at her then, his eyes hard and flat. "Have you ever done this? Have you ever had to look in someone's eyes and tell them they were going home when you know they've been through some horrific shit downrange?"

"That's not an excuse for doing drugs."

"I know that. Damn it, I know that." He sighed roughly. "That doesn't mean I can't understand it. That doesn't mean it doesn't fucking burn to put him out *knowing* he's got problems that are bigger than what he's capable of dealing with."

"How does that make this the army's problem?" she demanded, irritated at his recalcitrance to do his job.

She could see him breathing hard. His breath forcing its way in and out of his lungs as he just stood there.

His gaze flicked to her right shoulder, bereft of the patch she craved.

"You wouldn't understand," he said quietly. He looked away, the veins in his neck standing out in stark relief against his skin. "He needs this. It's one tiny bit of hope and if I can't do something good for one of my guys, then nothing I do matters."

Jessica Scott

* * *

Ben didn't usually pick fights he couldn't win. He didn't usually fight at all. But that argument with Olivia played over and over in his head. She was going to ruin the one chance he had to do something good for one of his boys.

Zittoro's packet was not a little thing.

Ben had no idea if Zittoro would ever use the college money. There was no crystal ball that said the kid would clean himself up and use it to make his life better. But he'd served, damn it. He'd served his country at war when so many others had abdicated that responsibility.

He'd volunteered to go out on the roads when they were the most deadly place in Iraq. He'd volunteered to man the guns in the turret.

If Zittoro was a hero, he was the epitome of a tragic hero. The war was going to kill him yet.

But if Ben could do one thing—even one small thing, like keep him in the army long enough to earn his college benefits—then damn it, Ben would do that.

And if that meant that Ben had to sit on his packet for a half a year, he didn't rightly care. Because there was a chance, even if it was a small chance, that Zittoro might clean himself up. He might stop using and find a good training program. Or maybe he'd use his college money to send one of the kids that he didn't have yet to college.

Ben had no idea.

All he knew was that he couldn't throw a combat veteran who'd done something as harmless as abusing drugs out on his ass. It was a victimless crime. The only person Zittoro hurt was himself.

He'd asked Ben to stay long enough for the college money.

And Olivia Hale was about to fuck that up because she was on her high horse about throwing "bad" soldiers out of the army.

Ben stalked into his company ops and into his office without saying a word to anyone. He threw his hat onto his desk and seriously considered the need for a flask in his desk drawer.

He'd be damned if the lawyer was going to tell him how to run his company.

"You look annoyed." First Sergeant Sorren stood in the doorway, filling it.

"What gave it away?"

"The sulking? Maybe the thrown hat?" Sorren shrugged. "Not sure. Either way, what put the sand in your panties?"

Ben didn't smile. "Lawyer caught me about Zittoro's packet."

Sorren took a sip of his coffee, saying nothing.

"We argued. She's going to dime me out to the battalion commander. Tell him I'm sitting on packets."

Sorren lowered his mug. "Technically, you *are* sitting on a packet."

"Yeah, but it's for a good reason. It's not like I'm defending a hardened criminal." Ben leaned back in his chair, kicking his feet up onto the desk and folding his hands behind his head.

Sorren glanced at Ben's feet. "Some people think doing drugs is a crime."

Ben looked up at his first sergeant and deliberately crossed one foot over the other. It was his desk, damn it; if he wanted to put his feet on it, he'd do it. He was feeling peevish. He needed a good fight to release all the pent up anger and frustration tearing up his insides.

He needed to clear his head.

He waited for Sorren to say something but his first sergeant didn't rise to the bait. Ben was a little disappointed. "What do you think?"

Sorren was silent for a long time. "I think drugs are pretty horrible. I've seen what they can do to people. To families. So I'm not exactly unbiased when it comes to these things."

"You think I made the wrong choice with Zittoro's packet," Ben said flatly.

"I think you made the *hard* choice, sir." Sorren lifted his mug in mock salute. "Too many commanders I've served with wouldn't go out on a limb to do something good like this."

Ben stared at his boots. "Doesn't feel like it's going to make a difference," he said.

"Maybe it will, maybe it won't. But you took a chance to do a good thing. And I can advise you all day long but at the end of the day, this is your company. You're going to run it how you see fit." Sorren took a sip of his coffee. "That's what the army pays you the big bucks to do."

"And people wonder why I didn't want this job," Ben muttered. He unlocked his fingers from behind his head and drummed them on one thigh. He was bone tired and he hadn't even made it through his first week in the job yet. Funny, he'd thought command would make him tired enough to actually sleep. Too bad it had only made his insomnia worse.

"The XO is here to brief you on the inventory schedule," Sorren said.

Entire days spent counting wrenches and radios and parts and pieces of tanks and Bradleys. He couldn't wait. "Lovely."

It was going to be a long day.

Olivia was irritated. Five hours had passed and her blood pressure had ticked higher with each passing minute at Ben's failure to accept his responsibility and do his job.

Her emotions migrated from irritated to highly pissed to irrational inside of that passing time.

It was usually much harder to piss her off. Damn it, she was even swearing. Which meant she was really pissed.

She closed her eyes, seeing again the fear in Ben's eyes when he'd realized she'd caught him about Zittoro's packet.

Memories rose to the surface, like snakes rising from an abyss.

The stench of piss and shit and rotten food scorched the inside of her nose. It was as if she was standing in that room again, surrounded by death.

There was never a good age to find your father dead from an overdose.

It didn't matter that he'd beaten her three days before. It didn't matter that her body would bear his scars forever.

Her heart had broken that day.

She hated the drugs. Hated the addiction that had taken him from her, that had destroyed the man she'd worshiped once upon a time. Hated the men who'd looked at her with disdain and told her she was making things up. She lowered her head to her desk.

Goddamn Ben Teague for bringing back those twisting, writhing memories.

"To hell with this," she mumbled. She shuffled the files into her briefcase and headed out. Across post to her friend Emily's office, where there was a sympathetic ear and a stash of emergency chocolate.

Emily looked up when Olivia knocked on the door. Her friend's expression softened immediately.

"You look like you're having a rough day," Emily said by way of greeting.

"I could say the same to you. What happened to your hair?"

Emily's hair was never messy. Emily's cheeks flushed. "Reza stopped by," she said, her words soft.

Olivia laughed and some of the anger and the hurt and the sadness that had been squeezing off the air in her lungs evaporated as she twisted the top on her water bottle.

"Which doesn't explain why your hair is a mess at three in the afternoo—oh, you dirty girl."

Emily's flush deepened. "He missed me."

"Apparently." The laugh felt good. Really good. Her eyes burned with tears. Too much in one day. She swiped her fingers beneath her eyes. "That's hysterical. How did you manage to not get caught?"

Olivia removed the top of her water bottle and lifted it to her lips. Emily flicked the cap on and off her pen. "We were really quiet."

Olivia choked on her drink and barely avoided snorting water out her nose. "I'm impressed. You've embraced your wild side. Did you do it in the office?"

Emily tried to lie but her eyes gave her away.

"I'm speechless," Olivia said. "I'm so glad I came by. You've made my afternoon."

"You're welcome." Emily cupped her chin in one palm. "Why are you having such a rough day?"

Olivia tipped her water bottle toward Emily. "That, m'dear, is a conversation to be had over wine. Or chocolate."

Emily opened her top desk drawer and pulled out a box of Godiva truffles. "I keep these here just for you."

"You're a goddess. You know that, right?" Olivia took a dark ball from the container.

"Spill. What's wrong? New job worse than you thought?"

"You have no idea. There's so much. I could work all day every day and not get caught up because new work comes in faster than I can process the old stuff."

"But that's not what's bothering you," Emily said.

Olivia nibbled on the truffle and considered her words carefully.

"Ben Teague is the problem," she said quietly. She was less angry than she'd been when she came in but Emily's question brought all the emotions churning back to the surface. Olivia took a deep breath. "He's sitting on a separation packet. He's refusing to throw a kid out of the army."

"And this matters because?"

"Because the battalion commander wants the bad soldiers cleaned up."

"I know Ben. He's not really a dishonest guy." Emily raised both eyebrows. "So what's really going on?"

"I—" Olivia took a deep breath. "Remember when we first met?"

"Yeah. You were talking to some full bird colonel in the hallway."

Olivia smiled bitterly. "That colonel was my first battalion commander many, many moons ago." She looked down at her hands, the memories from earlier rising up and threatening to tumble free. "I'd advised him to court-martial a sergeant. The sergeant had been arrested five times for assaulting his wife." She looked up at her friend, her voice cracking. Again. Goddamn it, she was so tired of crying over things she couldn't change. The chocolate had lost its flavor. It melted on her fingertips. "My commander opted not to court-martial him. He opted not to do anything. He didn't want to ruin the sergeant's career. A week later, the sergeant and his wife were dead."

She hadn't realized Emily had moved until her friend's arms came around her shoulders. She thought about resisting, about pulling away, but instead she leaned. Just for a moment.

"I'm sorry," Emily whispered.

"Me, too." She sucked in a deep breath and reached for a tissue for the chocolate. She no longer wanted it. She didn't want to talk about her father or the men who hadn't believed her then but every single time one of these files turned up missing, it was like she was that sixteen-year-old girl, being ignored all over again. "So yeah, I get a little prickly when these guys hide packets and try to protect some of these men."

"Why do you think Ben's hiding this?"

Olivia looked down at the smeared mess in her hands. She sucked her thumb clean. The chocolate was bitter on her tongue. "I don't know why he's hiding the packet," she admitted softly.

She hadn't thought to ask.

"I'm going to say this because you're my friend and I love you."

Olivia squished the chocolate in the tissue. "But this is going to chafe, isn't it?"

Emily lifted one shoulder apologetically, her grin sheepish. "I think you're letting your past cloud this. These soldiers aren't your responsibility to save or punish. You're there to make the system work, just like I am."

"Part of me knows that." Olivia's lungs tightened again with Emily's words. It was suddenly so hard to breathe. "But what if there isn't some altruistic motive? If he sits on this one, how many others will he sit on?"

"A very wise friend of mine told me once that feelings are real, they're just not always true. So while your fear is real, it may not be justified. Why is he sitting on the packet?"

"Does it matter?"

"Maybe? Maybe he's got a really good reason for sitting on it." Emily stood to put the chocolate away. "Ben is good friends with Reza. And I'm confident that Reza would not have that man as a friend if he wasn't trustworthy."

She hated that her temper had clouded her vision so completely. She turned Emily's comment over in her head but couldn't come up with a reason for Ben to sit on the packet. "Being trustworthy in a firefight isn't the same thing as doing the right thing back home," Olivia said dryly.

Emily slid the box of chocolates back in her desk. "I

get that. On a rational level, I get that, but we're not talking about someone he went to church with every week." She paused. "Combat forges some powerful bonds."

"Reza taught you that," Olivia said softly.

"Yeah. Among other things. He's taught me a lot."

Olivia smiled, desperately needing something to lighten the oppressive pressure in her chest. "Including how to have a quickie at lunch without getting caught."

Emily choked and covered her mouth with her hand as she laughed. "That was sneaky," she said.

"My job here is done."

Later, Olivia sat in her car a long time, letting the conversation tumble over in her head, staring at the Stetson in her passenger's seat. Emily was right. Olivia swiped at her eyes. The tightness in her chest eased back, enough that she could breathe again.

On a gut level, she knew it. But Ben hadn't come clean with her. He could have told her the truth.

Then again, she hadn't given him any reason to.

But if he lied to protect this soldier, what would happen when they got to the serious misconduct cases? To Escoberra and the others? Would Ben still fail to act?

How far would he go to protect the men under his command?

Chapter Eight

Ben was used to not sleeping well. He supposed it had started in Iraq, after their base had gotten blown all to hell and nearly taken Ben with it. But it had worsened with a vengeance when he'd been in the hospital after having his stomach stitched up and with the burns on his shoulder itching and driving him crazy. He'd drift into that foggy space between consciousness and unconsciousness, unsure whether he'd ever really fallen asleep.

He supposed it had been around the same time that he'd started to let things drift apart between him and Escoberra. He was too ashamed that he hadn't been able to keep the commander from lighting Escoberra's ass up over the attack. He'd given up sleeping much after that and developed a strong affection for caffeine.

But he'd also learned to appreciate the little bits of sleep he did get. So when the phone started ringing at the ass crack of dawn, it really ruined any chance of him actually sleeping.

He squinted at the blurred number.

"Sir, it's First Sarn't. We've got guys in Bell County jail."

Ben sat up, cradling his head in his hand, and waited for the words to connect to actual thoughts in his brain. "Who?"

"Sarn't Foster and Wookie."

"Ah fuck." Ben frowned, surprised to hear First Sarn't call one of their boys by his nickname so soon after arriving to the unit. Of course, Wookie *was* exceptionally hairy. The kind of hairy where you could see the thick carpet outlined through a combat t-shirt.

Ben had once bet him a three-day pass that he wouldn't wax his chest.

He'd waxed it. He'd bled while he did it, but he'd waxed it. At the time, Ben had been a lowly platoon leader who had not yet had his faith in the men around him destroyed by malfeasance.

And now Wookie was in jail. With Foster. Awesome.

Ben was going to kick both their asses. Foster's especially.

"What'd they do?" he asked First Sarn't.

"Public intox with a possibility of a bar fight still being considered. I talked to the arresting officer. Sounds like our boys were in the wrong place at the wrong time." Sorren sounded far too alert for this early in the morning.

Ben scrubbed his hand over his face. "Can we send someone to pick them up?"

"You sure about that?"

"Why wouldn't I be?"

"Because the battalion commander has a policy that if our boys go to jail, they'll post their own bail."

Ben stared into the darkness. "Were they actually arrested or are the police just holding them at the police station?"

"What else would they be doing at the police station?"

He scrubbed his hand over his face again. He was going to kill Foster. Damn it, Foster knew better than to do this shit. "The cops here sometimes just take our boys in without arresting them. Which means we need to send someone to go pick those two knuckleheads up before they *do* get arrested and hit the blotter."

"Got it. But you're going to need to call it in."

"Sure thing, Top." Ben clicked off the phone and cradled his head in his hands. He wanted to crawl into bed and wake up in the middle of the afternoon like he'd done when he was a lieutenant.

First Sarn't expected him to follow the rules and call the incident with the police in to the battalion commander. Except that they hadn't really been arrested so there really wasn't anything to tell. Ben wasn't about to wake the old man up for something that could easily wait two more hours.

It wasn't as if they'd killed someone. Then the police would have actually arrested them and then they'd have had to do a lot more than just call the first sergeant.

Anger pulsed in his veins. He wanted to whip Foster's sorry ass for being dumb enough to get into trouble. Damn it, Ben didn't need this shit right now. There was another reason he didn't want to be a commander. He didn't want to have to bail his boys out of jail. He wasn't cut out for responsibility. He looked at the phone. He probably should call the boss. But a little piece of his soul died at the thought.

It felt too much like narc'ing on his boys.

His to-do list ran through his head as he sat there and he debated heading into the gym or not. He still had to inventory all his property. He had to counsel his lieutenants on what he expected of them. All the administrative tasks that responsible commanders were supposed to do.

He didn't want to be a good commander. He wanted to be a good friend. It was infinitely more important to him at that moment to take care of Escoberra and Zittoro and even Foster's stupid ass.

He scrubbed his hand over his face. It was easier to think of the tasks than the people. His mother would tell him he was being weak. That he was there to accomplish the mission, not coddle soldiers.

She certainly hadn't coddled him after his dad had died. And her coldness had left an emptiness in Ben that he'd given up trying to fill with anything other than the war and his boys. Because those things never let you down.

Everyone else always did.

Except that now Ben was in charge, so he had to be the guy that didn't let people down.

And that just wasn't how he was wired. He hated letting people down.

Ben sat up, frustrated that he couldn't sleep. He was going to pay for this later. And by later, he meant about three in the afternoon when he'd want to curl up beneath his desk and hide from the world, and try to catch a fifteen-minute nap to sustain him for the rest of however long the day was.

Funny how he'd learned to nap over the years when he'd realized that insomnia was going to be a permanent companion.

He shuffled into the kitchen and made a pot of coffee. It was going to be one of those days—the kind that required chewing on coffee beans straight up instead of just drinking coffee.

All he could do was get up and get after it.

Maybe a good workout before he faced the day would help. He glanced at his watch. He could get into the gym at the division headquarters. It was open twenty-four hours. Ben packed a bag.

He wasn't going back to sleep. Might as well do something useful with the time.

Olivia made a habit of working out every morning. She tended toward cranky when she didn't get in her morning run, a fact that more than one of her subordinates had pointed out on more than one occasion.

So when she got to her regular gym that morning and it

was closed for maintenance, her temper sparked. She had a routine for a reason.

She didn't want to work out in the division headquarters but it was the closest building to her new office and she could shower there and walk across the street to her office after, thereby avoiding the morning traffic jams.

She hoped it wasn't busy. One of the reasons she preferred her usual gym was because she timed her morning workout so she'd be showering by the time everyone else was first arriving. She always managed to avoid the crowds that way. She didn't enjoy pressing up against towel-draped bodies in the female locker room. It closed her in and threatened to suffocate her.

It was early but not so early that the division headquarters wasn't already filling up. She walked to the back and headed into the locker room, changed and secured her bag in one of the lockers, then made her way toward the small but functional gym.

She checked her e-mail as she walked toward the gym. Music blasted in her ears from her iPod.

So it was a complete surprise to run into a solid wall of man.

She braced her hand on his chest to keep from stumbling.

And then looked up.

Ben. God but her life was such a cliché.

His fingers gripped her upper arm where she'd collided with him. His t-shirt was wet, his hair spiked with sweat. The smell of man and soap mingled in her senses and crashed over her.

Her eyes met his. A silent look passed between them. A silence that alternated between a fragile truce and a terrible anger. It was all there, thick and heavy.

She should move.

But neither one of them did.

And then she felt it. A slight caress. The barest of gestures. His thumb brushed over her exposed upper arm.

Her breath caught in her throat. Her skin came alive beneath the strength and power in his grip. His lips parted and she could see the tiny lines at the edge of his mouth.

It was Ben who moved, releasing her arm and taking a step back.

And just like that, the spell was broken.

"Sorry," he mumbled.

"No problem." She had to work with him. She didn't have to run around pissed off and angry. She could be civil despite their last argument. Right? "Is the gym busy?"

He ran his tongue over his teeth, making an irritated sound. "Just two guys lifting. Cardio is clear."

"Thanks." *And that, ladies and gentlemen, is what interpersonal hostility feels like at five o'clock in the morning.* But she didn't say that.

Ben moved out of the way and she pushed open the door to the gym, needing the workout now more than ever. She made a beeline for the stair stepper, her preferred torture method, and popped her headphones back into her ears. Cranking up whatever came on, she hit the start button and started climbing.

She was not going to spend the entire day pissed off. She refused. She was going to listen to music and find her happy place and go to work and do what the army paid her to do.

She was not going to fume over Ben Teague's refusal to do his job. And she damn sure was not going to think about the feel of his skin on hers or the smell of his skin...

She took a deep breath and cranked up the speed on the StairMaster. If her brain was working overtime, it meant her legs were not.

She closed her eyes and let the music pulse over her. Her feet fell into step with the beat.

She climbed, leaving behind the anger. Leaving behind the frustration.

Leaving behind too many bad memories, dragged to the surface by Ben protecting his men.

She breathed deeply, forcing her legs to work harder. Forcing her body to comply.

She was never going to be weak again. She would never again fail to act.

She could have gone over her commander's head all those years ago. Should have gotten the lawyers at division involved. She should have done *something* other than stand there when her commander had decided to protect his sergeant.

But she hadn't. And a family was dead because she'd failed to act.

But Emily was right. All night, she'd wrestled with Emily's words. Ben hadn't said he wasn't going to process the packet; he'd only said he wasn't processing it right now. She could give Ben the benefit of the doubt. But she was not going to forget about that packet.

There were too many good soldiers doing the right thing that deserved an army focused on how to bring them home from war. They deserved leaders not distracted by bad seeds who took time, effort, and energy away from training for the next deployment.

They deserved officers worthy of being called leader.

The anger crept back in over her ineffectiveness, her inability to argue her case better. If she closed her eyes, she could still see Mrs. Hellman the day she'd come to battalion. The bruise blackened her left cheek. She'd made eye contact with Olivia and slipped her hand into the hand that had put the bruise there in the first place. Olivia knew the feeling so well.

She knew what it was to put your hand in your abuser's and hope that your love was enough to make him change.

Even if Olivia had managed to get her commander to act, Mrs. Hellman had already decided to stay with her husband.

The futility of it burned. Olivia climbed harder, trying to outpace the demons from her past. She kept going even as the haunting echo of her failure stung behind her eyes.

She needed to stop before she imploded. She'd hit a wall before. When frustration and anger and hurt had overwhelmed her and she'd been unable to act.

She was terrified that if she stopped she'd never get started again. She hated that fear. Hated that weakness. She should be better than that.

But she wasn't.

Her feet moved in time with the beat. Climbing. Climbing. Trying to leave the past behind. Trying to forget how she'd failed. Trying to stop blaming herself for someone else's decisions.

The StairMaster slowed. She glanced down. Her workout was over.

But the blame, the residual flame of anger was still there.

And so was Ben Teague.

Ben was a firm believer in the magical powers of a hard workout to cure even the shittiest of bad days but considering this one hadn't even started, he was more than a little shocked that Olivia's day was as bad as her workout indicated.

Her skin was slick with sweat. Her hair clung to her face, her clothes to her body.

But it was the torment etched into her features that gave him pause.

He'd showered and started to leave the headquarters. But instead, he'd detoured down the corridor and headed back to the gym.

He'd planned on telling her why he hadn't processed Zittoro's packet. He didn't want her telling the battalion commander. He didn't want his boss breathing down his neck, micromanaging him, limiting his ability to command.

If he was going to do this, he was going to do it right. And that meant doing something good for his soldiers when he could.

But getting Zittoro his GI Bill benefits would only happen if Olivia didn't tell the commander. And as much as he resented the hell out of her threatening to go over his head, he couldn't discount the chance that she might actually listen to him if he tried to explain.

He didn't have to do this. But there was some part of him that needed someone to acknowledge that this was the right thing to do. Ben was doing the best he could but he didn't know how to do this.

He needed an anchor. Someone to make sure he didn't lose his soul in this job fighting the demons.

But Olivia had her own demons. Watching her then, seeing the violent, haunted emotion on her features as she worked out, shutting down the world and lost in her own thoughts, something else pushed aside his selfish need. Concern.

Olivia Hale was running from some powerful memories.

Ben didn't know what they were, but he recognized the feeling as she lost herself in that workout.

He looked up at her now, her skin flushed and wet, her cheeks flaming red—either from exertion or embarrassment, he couldn't tell.

"Sorry to interrupt your workout," he said after an uncomfortable silence stretched between them for too long.

Her lips were parted as she struggled to catch her breath.

Uncertainty flickered over her expression. "I was done anyway."

Forced civility.

She stepped off the machine, palming her iPod. Waiting

silently for him to step into the breach and say whatever it was that he was going to say.

Ben breathed out. "I wanted to explain about Zittoro's packet."

A slight crease appeared between her brows but other than that, her expression remained impassive. "I'm listening."

"Zittoro's got problems. And I get that the army can't fix those problems." Ben clenched his fists, fighting for the right words. "I'm sitting on his packet to make sure he hits his thirty-six months' time in service so he can qualify for his GI Bill." Ben ground his teeth, wishing she would say something, do something. Show some sign of a human fucking heart. "He may never use it but we owe him that." He cleared his throat. Met her gaze and hoped—prayed—that she would hear him out. "And I'm asking you not to tell the battalion commander."

The words were hard for him. She could see the strain written in the tense muscles of his neck, the rigidity of his stance, that she wanted to smooth beneath her fingers. It was tempting, so tempting to reach for him.

She looked into his dark eyes and saw the quiet hope, the faith that it took for him to trust her enough to talk to her.

Ben Teague was not a man who trusted easily. She could see that now. And she wanted to know why.

He stood a little too close. His body was a little too warm. With that simple request, Ben had turned her damning indictment of commanders—of him—upside down.

She had judged him harshly. Unfairly.

All because of her own bias. She was supposed to be better than that. She'd based her opinion of him on another commander's behavior in another unit in another time.

He stood there asking for her help, and she was at a loss.

She wanted to cross that divide, to bridge the chasm

between them. She wanted to trust him. More, she wanted him to trust her.

Because she was so tired of being alone. Of standing and fighting the good fight with no one by her side.

Ben dragged his hand over his mouth, breaking the spell. "Look, never mind."

"Wait," she said quickly. She reached for him. Her hand closed over his upper arm, over the leading edge of that intricate black ink only hinted at beneath the cuff of his army t-shirt. "I was trying to think of what to say."

He looked at her hand on his skin. He didn't have his uniform jacket on yet. A simple omission but where their skin touched, heat radiated through her palm. She yanked back, releasing him quickly.

"A simple yes or no would have worked," he said mildly.

Her hand tingled where she'd touched him. She rubbed her thumb against her palm. "But it's not a yes or no answer."

The muscles in his neck tensed. His eyes searched her face. "I thought it was a pretty simple request."

"It was. But there's more to it than just that." She took a deep breath and hoped she wouldn't screw this up. Met his gaze and summoned every ounce of her courage to step into the breach and ask this man's forgiveness.

Ben frowned, his brown eyes locked on hers. Her pulse throbbed in her temple. Nerves tightened in her belly. "What does that mean?"

"It means that I made assumptions about what you were doing." Olivia swallowed the bitter pill. "I owe you an apology." It choked her but she swallowed it anyway, the biting realization that she'd been so flat out wrong. "I won't say anything to the battalion commander."

He didn't relax. He didn't say anything. His eyes searched hers. His lips were parted, just a little. And then she felt it. The sigh of relief. A slight sensation of air brushing over her skin as he breathed out deeply. That simple movement released every ounce of tension. The lines around his brown eyes lessened. His mouth softened.

He shifted then. His hand moved before she could realize what he'd done. His palm cradled her cheek, his touch soft, his hand gentle.

It was something so simple yet it rocked the foundation of the world beneath her feet.

"Thank you," he said. His throat moved as he swallowed and lowered his hand.

She didn't know if he'd meant to do it or not but her skin cooled without his touch.

She nodded in acknowledgment. "Next time? Next time just tell me what you're doing?"

He offered a wry grin. "Maybe next time, you don't jump to conclusions?"

"Yeah, that would be a good place to start." Deep breath. "I've had bad experiences with commanders hiding things. I judged you based on my past experiences and I'm sorry."

Ben lifted a single eyebrow, his lips quirking at one corner in that ridiculously sexy way of his. "You're not wrong often, are you?"

"I try not to be," she said, swiping her palm across her forehead. "When I'm wrong, bad things happen."

He cocked his head at her. "Like what?"

She shook her head slightly, looking away, not wanting him to see the truth of the failure she could never atone for. "It doesn't matter. But I made a mistake and when I make mistakes, I own up to them and try not to repeat them." She draped her earphones around her neck and offered him a tentative smile. "Next time? Let's confer properly without me jumping to conclusions."

"I doubt there will be a next time. Not for something like this," he said. A shadow flickered across his face. He licked his lower lip and her gaze locked on that simple, reflexive movement. "I've been looking through my packets. There are a lot of straight-up criminals that need to go home."

"We're scheduled for a legal sync meeting this afternoon with the battalion commander. We can do a quick huddle afterward to set up the next priority of your packets to start tackling some of them."

Ben nodded and shifted his assault pack to the opposite shoulder. "Sounds like a plan. I appreciate it."

There was cool formality between them now, but beneath the professional veneer something simmered. Something dark and hungry that made her want to lean in, to feel his touch again.

To let his fingers trace over her skin.

He held the door open for her as they walked out of the gym and started down the hall. "Thank you," he said after a moment. "For letting me do this for Zittoro." Something in his voice cracked and she was tempted, so tempted to reach for him.

She stopped near the locker room door. He stood a little too close and for once, she didn't take a step away from the heat radiating off his body. She lifted her chin to meet his gaze. "It's not the by-the-book right thing to do but I understand why you're doing it."

"You do?"

"Yeah." She paused. Terrified that she was giving in to something unprofessional, that she was doing this because she was starting to look at Ben like he was someone who could be more than a coworker. Her own motives made her suspicious. Still, she stood too close. And made the leap of faith. "Giving him something tangible like his GI Bill to hold on to, even if he probably won't use it, is hope. Maybe he can kick his addiction, maybe he can't. But you're giving him hope if nothing else." She paused. She reached for him then, because to do otherwise was to admit to herself that she was a coward. She cupped the soft skin on his neck. Felt the prickle of stubble against her palm, the heat sear through her skin. "It's a kind thing to do," she whispered.

A strange emotion flickered across his face. "There's not a lot of room for kindness in command," he said softly.

She slid her hand down his shoulder, her fingers brushing over the cool fabric of his uniform. It was crisp beneath her fingertips, his muscles solid beneath her touch. She squeezed his forearm gently, then released him. Because it would have been too tempting to linger.

"Command is difficult. But there's room for being just. And it's sometimes more difficult to be just and easier to be cruel."

Ben opened his mouth to say something then snapped it closed.

"What?" she urged. There was something in the way he looked, the flicker of fear in a confident man that drew her to push past her own barriers and misconceptions.

"I worry about that," he said.

"What, being unjust?"

His jaw tensed and he looked away, down the empty hall-way. "About being cruel."

Olivia wiped her neck with the towel. She took a single step forward, her palm resting on his upper arm. "The fact that you're worried about it is a good sign."

Silence. Awkward and heavy. His arm was solid and warm beneath her touch.

He glanced at her then, his eyes dark with uncertainty and shaded in doubt. "This is the part where I'd normally have a snappy comeback. But I seem to lose my stride around you."

She dropped her hand, because to leave it in place would take this conversation to a place she wasn't ready to go. Not with Ben, not with anyone.

She smiled, grasping for something light and flip to ease some of the want pounding in her veins. The space between them crackled with heat, with electric energy. "That's good. It means I'm keeping you on your toes."

"You think so?"

She backed up, one hand on the locker room door. "I'm leaving now."

"Hey." She paused and turned back. He stood where she'd left him, his assault pack thrown over one shoulder. His eyes were dark, his mouth wide and far too beautiful. "Thank you, Olivia."

She offered a light smile, knowing it was a mistake and making it anyway. There wasn't room for her to feel this way. Not for Ben Teague. She had to work with him. "You're welcome," was all she said instead.

He left her there, holding on to the fleeting connection for as long as she could.

Chapter Nine

"Am I correct in understanding that you had two soldiers picked up from the police this morning?" Major Denis asked.

Later that morning, Ben stood in the XO's office, biting the inside of his lip to keep from smarting off at the field grade officer. He had absolutely zero business questioning Ben about his company. Zero.

But First Sergeant Sorren had told him to play nice so he was trying to play nice. At least that's what he kept telling himself. First Sergeant had threatened to lay his hands on Ben if he didn't keep his smart mouth in check and Ben was reasonably certain that he did not mean it in a "heal his immortal soul" kind of way.

"Roger, sir."

"Why didn't you complete the proper paperwork?"

Ben fought down a smart-ass remark. "Because they weren't arrested. They didn't meet the requirements for the serious incident report."

"That's no excuse for not informing battalion."

Ben sucked on his teeth and considered how to play this. He didn't really need a confrontational relationship with the battalion executive officer but then again, what did he care what Major Denis thought? Denis had lost Ben's respect a long time ago.

Ben wasn't here to kiss his ass, or anyone else's for that matter, and while his soldiers were guilty of going out and drinking and generally making asses of themselves, they hadn't done anything wrong. Maybe in the lily white pure world of Major Denis, who'd never bothered to descend out of his ivory tower to the mud and muck and grime where the soldiers lived and worked and played. Denis had never lived with the men; he'd never walked patrols.

He'd spent his first deployment avoiding the war, hiding out on the FOB and always finding some excuse not to go out in sector. Now he was in charge of a combined arms battalion, trying to lead sergeants and officers who knew the truth about the kind of man he was and called him on it.

Ben had never judged anyone too harshly for what they did on a deployment but damn it, the war had been going on for eight years now and Ben was reasonably certain the only time Denis had fired his weapon was on a range. How the hell did that happen *as an infantry officer?*

"I'm waiting for your answer, Captain Teague," Denis demanded, interrupting Ben's mental gymnastics.

"I informed the battalion commander, sir."

"You think you should have thought about who else needed to know?"

"Yep, and I made sure my first sergeant told the sergeant major."

Denis spit into the bottle on his desk. "You're pushing your luck, Teague."

"I'm doing nothing of the sort. I'm pushing you out of commander's business, sir. You're responsible for maintenance and supply, not my soldiers' actions, adverse or otherwise," Ben snapped.

He was going to have to go for another run before the day was over to get his temper reined in.

"Did it ever occur to you that if I'm asking you for information, the boss has already given me my marching orders?" Denis asked.

"And did it ever occur to you that if you step into commander's business, that I would ignore you?" Ben said.

"Remember who you're talking to, Captain."

"Yeah, yeah, I got it, *sir*. Are you done pissing on my leg? I've got soldiers I need to take care of. Unless you need me to fill out paperwork for that?"

Denis slammed his hand onto his desk, scattering papers and knocking over the dip bottle. "Goddamn it, Teague, watch your fucking mouth."

Ben offered a two-fingered mock salute as Sorren appeared in the doorway. "I've got to go."

"Get your ass back here, Captain. I'm not done with you."

"Sir, you're not allowed to do anything with my ass. That would be a violation of Don't Ask, Don't Tell."

Ben walked out, falling into step with his first sergeant as they walked down the hallway and out of the headquarters. He could hear Denis still yelling as they left the building.

"Did you have to go out of your way to piss him off?" Sorren asked after a while.

"I make a special effort with him."

"Any particular reason why?"

"Our history is long and distinguished, but primarily because he takes pleasure in being a pretentious asshole and I just like to remind him that he's not all that special."

"That seems to be a trait common in the officer corps these days. Something about pinning on field grade makes all y'all's brains turn to mush."

Ben slapped Sorren's shoulder with a grin. "Don't worry, the same thing will happen to you when you pin sergeant major."

"Nah, not me." Sorren shook his head. "I'm probably retiring after this tour."

Ben glanced over at his first sergeant, not bothering to hide his shock. "Why?"

They started walking back toward the company ops. "The army's not the place for me anymore."

Ben frowned and stuffed his hands in his pockets until Sorren glared at him and he pulled them back out. "Why do you say that?"

"I think I've reached max effectiveness as a first sergeant. I don't think I'll politic well enough to make sergeant major."

"I'm sure if you hold your nose, you can kiss the right hairy ass to get picked up."

Sorren grunted, clearly unamused. "It's not about politicking. It's about bringing our boys home from combat. And I don't think I can do that at any higher level. If they'd let me stay a first sergeant forever, I'd do it."

"The army's changing, that's for sure." Ben cleared his throat.

"So I've got some bad news," Sorren said as they entered the company. "Foster ended up getting himself arrested."

"Ah hell." Ben scrubbed his hand over his mouth. "For what?"

"He decided to get lippy with the cop. Who happened to be the father of the girl Foster's seeing. That girl was the reason Foster got into a bar fight in the first place."

"Lovely," Ben muttered. "Well, let's go get him."

Sorren shook his head. "We can't do that, sir." He toed the door to Ben's office shut behind him. "We've got to let him make his own bail."

A warning tickled in the back of Ben's neck. "We can't just leave him there."

"We can and we will. I've played this game before. When the civilians have them, we leave them there until the civilians either turn them over to us or they make bail."

Ben couldn't shake the unease that settled in his guts. It was nerves. He knew it was nerves and still, he couldn't rein it in.

He couldn't leave Foster in jail.

"I'm going to go visit him at least," Ben said quietly.

Sorren studied him, his eyes filled with weariness and resignation. "I figured you'd say that."

An hour later, Sorren pulled up to a traffic light, slowing his vehicle to turn into the Bell County parking lot. "We're just going to make sure he's not being mistreated, if there's anything we can bring him and all that stuff."

Ben nodded, not saying anything.

He'd done a lot of stupid shit over the years. Hell, a lot of it had been done with Foster in their wilder days.

But he'd never had to visit Foster in jail.

A thousand emotions rioted inside him, unspent anger and shame that he'd left his friend behind when Ben had taken up the mantle of command.

And now, when he had all the power in the world, there was nothing he could do. They pulled up to Bell County jail and went through the check-in procedures. Foster was brought out into one of the visiting areas. He was gaunt, his eyes sunken and hollow. His bones cut harsh lines beneath his skin. His fingernails were dirty and crusted and there were harsh black smudges beneath his eyes.

He looked nothing like the smart-mouthed gunner Ben had served with. Panic twisted in Ben's guts. "What the hell happened to you?"

"Couldn't really sleep last night, worrying about my virtue," Foster said, trying to grin. "For a county lockup, there are some horny bastards in here."

Ben rolled his eyes. "That's not funny."

"It's a little funny." Foster grinned but it didn't reach his eyes. "Nice of you to finally come by," Foster muttered.

"Sir. You will remember your military bearing," Sorren corrected.

Foster jerked a thumb toward Sorren. "Where'd you dig this guy up?"

Sorren took a step toward Foster, who took a corresponding step backward, hands held up in supplication. "Whoa, there, big fella." Foster glanced at Ben with a grin. "Someone needs a hug."

Sorren made a noise deep in his throat and Ben laughed. "Stop picking at him, Foster. Jeez, I need you two to play nice together."

"Did you come to bail me out?" Foster asked.

Ben sucked in a deep breath. "I can't, man."

"Nice," Foster said. "The only reason I'm in here is because Monica's dad doesn't like me."

"Maybe you should have made more of an effort to get along with her dad," Sorren said gruffly.

Foster leaned forward, cupping his chin in one palm. "Sounds like someone is an angst-y dad. Someone's daughter start dating?"

Ben glanced at Sorren. "You have a kid?"

The muscle in Sorren's jaw pulsed, tight and tense. "Yeah. She lives around here with her mom."

A slow smile spread across Ben's mouth. "Oh, really?"

"Now is neither the time nor the place for this conversation," Sorren said roughly. "And you need to mind your own damn business, smart ass," he said to Foster.

"Oh, I can't wait to post bail," Foster said. "Life around the company is going to be so much more interesting now. You really can't spot me the bail money?" he said to Ben.

The comment was light but beneath it was a seriousness. A very real edge. Being in jail wasn't fun, no matter how much Foster was trying to make light of the situation.

Ben swallowed, the words bitter in his throat. "I can't."

"I'm not sleeping. I want to come home."

"Do you have any family or anything to help with your bail?" Ben asked, memories twisting inside him, like a knife beneath his ribs. Seeing his soldier in jail—no matter how stupid the charges—grated on his last nerve.

And there was nothing he could do.

Foster shook his head. "I'll see if I can't line something up with one of the bail bondsmen," he said. He looked up at Ben sheepishly. "Sorry if this got you in trouble with your boss."

Ben shrugged. "It's not my boss I'm worried about."

Foster stood as one of the guards came in. "Time's up. Hopefully, I can post bail soon." He looked up at Sorren. "Nice to meet you," he said with a grin.

"Oh, I can see you're going to be incredibly fun to have around," Sorren said roughly.

"I shall aim to please," Foster said.

He shuffled to the door where the guard waited. Ben didn't move, hating himself for leaving Foster there.

Foster paused, looking back.

And Ben saw it. The very real fear of going back into lockup. He swallowed the sudden dryness in his throat.

He hadn't even been in command a week and he was already turning his back on the soldiers who depended on him. Foster tried to play it off but Ben could see the look of betrayal on Foster's face as they left. It burned, deeply, that he wasn't supposed to do shit like bail his buddies out of jail anymore. It felt like betrayal—because that's what it was. It penetrated Ben's sense of self and ate away at who he thought he was.

Already he was becoming what he feared. A man more concerned about accomplishing the mission than taking care of his soldiers.

And Foster was the first victim on that sacrificial altar.

He followed Sorren out of the county jail, his thoughts a million miles and a half a war away.

Which is why he ran straight into Olivia Hale.

"I'm noticing a pattern," Olivia said dryly.

"Sorry," Ben mumbled.

He was distracted, deeply so. There were dark shadows beneath his eyes and his mouth was pressed into a humorless, flat line. "I'm actually glad you're here," she said.

He frowned, glancing at his first sergeant. "That is a really strange thing to say in front of the county jail," he said wryly.

She grinned. "Not if I need you to take custody of one of your soldiers."

Relief washed over his face, raw and primitive. "Really?"

"Yeah. Bell County doesn't want to hold Foster. They want to turn him over to us to deal with his case."

"You realize there's no case there, right?" Ben asked.

She lifted one shoulder. "I figured you'd say that," she said. "But we'll get all the paperwork together and see about getting him out."

Ben licked his lips, pressing his mouth flat. "What's the catch?"

Olivia exhaled deeply. "You'll have to make the decision of whether to go forward with charges, for him getting into trouble off post." She studied him carefully, watching his expression closely. "Think you can handle that?"

His throat moved as he swallowed. "Yeah, I can do that."

It was a ridiculously long process to get a soldier out of jail but she was reasonably certain she'd never seen Ben relax more visibly than when Foster walked out a free man. She sat on one of the waiting room plastic chairs, reviewing paperwork while they waited.

Escoberra's packet was on her lap. God, but this case was such a disaster. CPS hadn't managed to get anything done.

It was going to drag out forever.

She glanced over at Ben. She knew how badly he wanted to believe in his platoon sergeant but the paperwork simply didn't match up with Ben's version of reality.

Escoberra *had* put Hailey in the hospital.

She turned the page, double-checking all the paperwork in the packet. She frowned. An awards citation. Tucked into the very back of the folder. Army Commendation Medal with V device for valor. Awards weren't usually part of military justice packets. Not like this.

Olivia read the citation carefully, then turned the page for the awards form. Second Lieutenant Ben Teague had written the award.

Escoberra had been wounded in combat and Ben had been the officer who'd put him in for an award. An award for valor was a very big deal. Those didn't happen often.

She read the write-up then turned it over.

It had been downgraded.

Sir, a talented soldier but valorous action occurs every day. This is not worthy of a Bronze Star.

Olivia frowned at the summary rejection of Ben's recommendation. She read the award again and the captain's remarks on the back. Captain Paul Denis. She frowned. Surely this couldn't be the same Denis as the executive officer in Ben's battalion?

That would explain a lot of the interpersonal hostility she sensed whenever Denis and Ben were in the same room.

She knew Ben and Escoberra had served together, but this? This said there was more to this story than she knew. She looked up at Ben, where he stood talking to Sorren and Foster, waiting on the final paperwork.

Would he tell her if she asked? She had her doubts.

She read the comment on the back of the award again. Something about it struck her as cold. Uncaring. Escoberra had received three bullet wounds—luckily none life-threatening—and his commander had, with the stroke of a pen, said his actions weren't enough to warrant a higher award.

What kind of man thought like that?

Was this what Ben was afraid of becoming?

Suddenly, some of his reluctance to take command made sense. If this was the kind of man Ben had served with, no wonder he was worried about what the power of the job would do to him.

And what had that downgrade done to Escoberra? More, what had it done to Ben?

She looked at the date of the firefight and wondered if she could find out anything else about it. There was something here. Something that nagged at her. A missing piece to the mystery that was Ben Teague.

She didn't think that Ben would defend Escoberra on a whim—it should be a no-brainer with the man's being charged with that kind of violence against a child.

But his slap at her the other day when he'd told her she wouldn't understand what combat did to someone stung, not because he was wrong but because he was right: she didn't know.

She watched him laugh with Foster.

And reading the award citation, she wanted to know, badly, how that incident had shaped and changed the man now in charge of Bandit Company.

She should just stop being a coward and ask Ben. But despite their awkward truce, she wasn't sure he would talk to her about it.

Maybe he would.

Whatever had happened during that firefight was personal. One, if not more, of his soldiers had gotten wounded. She remembered the scar she'd seen on his stomach. Had that happened during the same battle? How could it be anything but personal?

She stood and approached the three men. "Captain Teague," she said. "I was wondering if you'd like to ride back to Fort Hood so we can get caught up on some of the legal packets." God, but the words sounded awkward and painful to her—she could only imagine how they sounded to him.

Ben glanced over at his first sergeant. "You two promise not to kill each other?" Ben asked.

Sorren flipped Ben off before grabbing Foster by the neck and shoving him playfully out the front door.

"That seems like a healthy relationship," Olivia said, watching them go.

Ben grinned. "It's the start of one. Foster's a pain in the ass but he's a good soldier."

She fell into step with him as they headed outside toward her car. "So the first week in command is almost over. How does it feel?" she said when he climbed in beside her.

He didn't answer for an eternity. "Like I'm the biggest hypocrite on the planet," he said finally.

"Why do you say that?" she asked.

"You see him? Foster? I've been in more trouble than that kid can even imagine and yet, I'm getting rewarded. It's going to take every ounce of persuasion I've got to keep the boss from stepping on my neck about him to keep him out of trouble."

Olivia watched him silently. "Maybe he should just stop getting into trouble," she said softly. "I mean at some point, doesn't he have to grow up?"

Ben leaned forward. "Funny thing about growing up," he said. "It's never as fun as you think it's going to be when you're a kid."

"You couldn't wait to grow up?"

His smile was humorless. "I wanted to get away from the ghost of my father and out of my mother's shadow. Of course, I joined the army so that didn't help much."

She wanted to ask about his mother but she kept her question to herself. She figured if he wanted to talk about her, he'd bring it up. "I'm sorry about your dad," she said quietly.

He looked over at her, the sunlight glinting across his cheek, cutting a hard line across his cheekbone. "Thanks, but it wasn't a big deal. He died when I was little and my mom decided to become superwoman without any corresponding superemotions."

Olivia said nothing for a long while, letting Ben's words sink in. There was more there, more she wanted to know, more she wanted to ask but she couldn't. Not yet. After a moment, she changed the subject. "You don't like being in command, do you, Ben?" she whispered. The air was thick between them, heavy with unsaid things.

He shook his head. "It's too much responsibility for other people's problems. I'm not qualified to judge someone else's screwups," he said.

He shifted so he could face her, his body angled toward hers. A shadow partially concealed his face, casting it in hard lines and a dozen shades of gray.

"You're not supposed to be perfect to be a leader," she whispered. Her voice cracked, hung on the tension in her neck from sitting a little too close.

Silence filled the space between them. Heavy and warm and crackling with latent energy.

He licked his bottom lip, his gaze locked with hers. "I don't want to be either," he said. His voice was a husky whisper filled with need.

Her breath caught in her throat. A hesitant movement. A breath closer. This was monumentally stupid. Infinitely so.

And yet she parted her lips, her entire body trembling in anticipation of the faintest touch of his. He was there, just there. A breath separated them. Nothing more.

It was a hesitant kiss. A light, teasing brush of his top lip against hers. Her breath mingled with his, threading between them and urging her closer. She met his eyes, waiting. Wanting. Needing more of this deeply sensual man who made her *feel* so many writhing, hungry things.

It was forever before either of them moved. Her breath was locked in her throat. Then she felt it. His palm slid over her cheek, his fingers rough on her skin. Warmth penetrated her, wound its way over the surface to slide beneath her skin and stroke something long dormant to life.

Need. It was need that made her lean toward him. Need that made her part her lips and trace his mouth with her tongue. Need that made her nip his bottom lip and thread her fingers in the short hair on the back of his neck.

Need that made her gasp in pleasure as his tongue slid against hers, twining in that sensuous dance that brought her blood to life. Heat pounded between her thighs, an aching, pulsing want that scorched her like nothing she'd ever felt.

She gave herself over to the sensation, to the pleasure of his touch. Knowing it was a mistake and far past caring as her breath finally released, mixing with the heated strokes of his tongue.

She eased back after a moment, before she did something monumentally stupid, like crawling into his lap in broad daylight.

"We really should talk about those legal packets," she said against his mouth.

His smile was unexpected. "Wow, you are hell on a man's ego," he said.

The laugh caught her off guard and she rested her forehead against his as she struggled to regain her composure.

Something opened against her heart, something unexpected and warm.

Something complicated.

For a brief moment, it was tempting to throw caution to the curb, to nuzzle his mouth with hers, to absorb his taste and warmth.

And then reality kicked in.

"We really should head back. We've got that meeting in two hours," she said.

He smiled. "Always responsible and focused."

He brushed his thumb over her lip as he said it. This was something nice.

Unexpected.

It was going to be an interesting legal briefing, that was for damn sure.

Chapter Ten

"Want a cookie?"

"Do I look like someone who enjoys cookies?" Sorren asked.

"What? Cookies make everything better. Not as better as, say, vodka, but hey, it's a start."

"You sound like a woman who needs chocolate," Sorren said.

Ben felt his chest and his groin, making sure all his man parts were still intact. He needed something to take his mind off that mind-blowing kiss with Olivia earlier.

"Nope, still a guy. And that's a pretty sexist thing to say. Seriously? I offer you cookies and you insult my manhood. Fine. Go to the legal meeting pissed off and cranky."

"Sir, I'm really not in the mood."

"You're never in the mood."

"You should be a little more somber after getting your soldier out of jail this morning."

"Just because I'm burying my feelings in cookies doesn't mean it's not bothering me." Ben chewed on that for a moment, along with a chocolate chip cookie that practically melted in his mouth. "Foster's out of jail, it's fine." The cookie dried out in his mouth.

"It's stupid shit like this that's going to take away from training our boys for war," Sorren said quietly.

Ben's temper snapped, shoving aside the lighter mood he'd been bullshitting anyway. "Foster is a damn good soldier. So what if he's blowing off steam on the weekends?"

"That kind of thing is contagious—first you have a guy getting arrested for partying, then it gets worse and worse until you've got a goddamn gang running your company."

Ben pointed the sleeve of cookies at him. "Already took care of the gang. They're already being court-martialed or separated from the military. Next problem?"

"You think this is a joke?"

"It's not a goddamned joke, Top, but I can't condemn Foster when I've done the same damn thing more than once."

Neither he nor Sorren moved for a long time. Ben continued to eat his sleeve of cookies.

"I know." Sorren scrubbed his hands over his face, breaking the silence. "This place is a goddamned disaster."

Ben chewed on his cookie. "Yeah, well, get ready because we're about to go into the happy fun times of the legal sync." Sorren looked mildly horrified and Ben pushed away from the table, dropping the cookies on his desk and picking up his headgear and the rest of his folders.

Ben had made light of it but silently, he was worried. Olivia had said she wasn't going to dime him out about Zittoro's packet and he trusted that. Still.

But he'd take the ass-chewing for not having Zittoro's packet done.

Someone shouted at the back of the orderly room. Ben glanced at Sorren and they both sprinted to the back of the company where the platoon offices were.

LT Gillis and Sergeant First Class Lazarus were squared off toe to toe, screaming at each other.

Ben didn't know whether to be pissed or impressed. Gil-

lis was a hundred pounds soaking wet and Lazarus was built
like a pit bull.

Ben grabbed his lieutenant, yanking him backward before
Lazarus could put him in intensive care. Now wouldn't that
be fun to explain to the battalion commander?

"What the hell is going on back here?" Ben demanded.
Sorren shoved Lazarus back.

"The goddamned lieutenant doesn't listen," Lazarus
shouted.

Sorren stuck his finger in Lazarus's face. "Watch it," he
said quietly.

Lazarus swore. "Top, I told him I'd take care of the range
planning. He went and did it himself without me checking it
and now we don't have the right range for next week."

Ben looked at Gillis. "He's never at work," Gillis said, his
face flushed. "I can't get him to answer his damn phone. So
yeah, I did the damn paperwork myself."

"What range do we have next week?" Ben asked.

"Mark nineteen range," Sorren said.

"Not anymore," Lazarus said. "Now we've got a nine mil
range."

Ben sighed. "Then we go shoot a nine mil range. Get
with the company ops and try to find another mark nineteen
range to piggyback off." He patted Gillis's shoulders. "See?
Problem solved. Another happy day in Bandit Company."

Sorren looked at Lazarus. "Answer your damn phone
when your lieutenant calls you," he said. Ben wondered if he
ever shouted.

"You two have to stay together for the kids," Ben said. All
three men looked at him like he was crazy. "You've never
heard of the relationship between a platoon sergeant and platoon leader or commander and first sergeant as an arranged
marriage?"

"I'm positive I have never heard of that," Sorren said as he followed Ben out of the company. "I think you need to get a handle on your LTs quickly. Their old commander probably rubbed off on them and not in a good way, more in a need-a-shower-with-bleach kind of way."

Ben cleared his throat. "Did you just make a joke?"

Sorren grunted. "Maybe you're rubbing off on me."

"But not in a need-a-shower kind of way?"

"Fuck you, sir."

They walked in silence for a little bit. Ben was a pragmatist but that didn't mean he wanted to spend the next year chasing down the bad seeds. He agreed with Sorren. They needed to find the bad actors and get them gone.

Meanwhile they had a war to prepare to fight. A fact conveniently forgotten by the staff, who kept having meeting after meeting.

Meetings like the impending legal sync. He wondered if he could get the commander to change this to once a month. It would clear up some time on their Friday afternoons. But that would only give the sergeant major an excuse to hold a longer formation and Ben...Ben hated formations with a loathing that he usually reserved for spiders, snakes, and hamsters.

He shuddered. He had no idea why people liked hamsters. Evil-looking little bastards.

Now that was a holdover from childhood trauma. He'd have to remember to break that one out the next time Sorren got sand in his panties. The big first sergeant didn't seem like he'd be afraid of anything.

Ben would have to be on the lookout. It was the big guys who were terrified of the strangest things. He'd found out Iaconelli was afraid of geese on their last tour. Geese? Who the hell was afraid of geese?

He scrubbed his hand across his jaw as they walked into the headquarters and down the hall to the conference room.

Chapter Eleven

The silence in the battalion conference room was thick and awkward. The kind of awkward that came from being the only female and the only non-combat veteran in a room full of combat veterans and from being the person to tell them they had another soldier in jail.

The new command teams sat around the table. It was a toss-up who looked more uncomfortable: the commanders or the first sergeants. Legal meetings were painful for all parties involved.

"Teague, how many soldiers are you sending to trial defense tomorrow?" Gilliad asked.

Olivia glanced over at Ben, doing her best to keep a neutral expression. It was hard, so damn hard when the memory of his kiss still tingled on her lips.

Ben met her gaze briefly, then looked down at his notes. "Five, sir."

"Which ones?"

Ben rattled off the names and his battalion commander flipped his glasses to the top of his head. Gilliad read over paperwork silently.

"Where's Zittoro's packet?" He tapped the sheet with the tip of his pen. "It's on the list that you received it on Monday."

Ben glanced up at her quickly. Just a glance but it was filled with questions. Damn it, she hadn't updated the slides.

Ben opened his mouth to speak. "Sir, Zittoro—"

Olivia cut him off. "Sir, Zittoro's packet had errors on it. I found them this morning and didn't have time to update the slides before the meeting."

Gilliad nodded but Major Denis leaned forward, his shoulders bunched, his expression hostile. "Next time, make sure you all have accurate statuses before you brief the battalion commander," he said with a pointed look at Olivia.

She ran her tongue over her teeth. She didn't answer to Major Denis but she opted not to pick the fight just then.

Not here and not now. But there was nothing she could say because he had her on the slides not being updated. She knew he was looking for an opening, any opening, to skewer her in front of the battalion commander and she wasn't going to give him one.

She said nothing, daring him to push for an acknowledgment. Everyone stood and saluted sharply when the battalion commander left, then started filtering out of the room when he'd gone. Ben said something to his first sergeant but Olivia didn't stick around to chat.

She slipped out of the conference room and down the hall to her office at the back of the adjutant's area. It was private and she had her own space where she could secure the more sensitive files.

She had less than an hour to clear up everything for the day before she had to head out to Stable Call. She had no idea what to expect at this event. She glanced at her new Stetson. At least she'd have an excuse to wear it.

A quiet knock on her door broke her stride. She turned from where she'd been putting files in a drawer.

Ben stood in the doorway.

"Hey," she said quietly.

The memory of that kiss made him crave another taste of her. He'd thought she was fire and passion and so damned determined before. Now he knew that quiet energy she directed toward work was merely a hint of the passion concealed beneath that cool exterior.

It was a passion he wanted to feel beneath his fingertips. That he wanted to slide against.

"Hey." He swallowed, about to cross a line from professional to . . . something else.

And damned if he wasn't afraid to cross that line. That kiss earlier was nothing compared to what she'd just given him.

She'd lied for him today. Ben had been about to make something up that would get his battalion commander off his back and Olivia had stepped in with a smooth story that had deflected Gilliad's attention with no one the wiser.

She'd agreed not to tell the boss. He hadn't expected her to all-out lie for him. And now that she had? He didn't quite know how to broach the subject with her. Not at all.

She straightened and leaned against her desk. The broken scale tray swayed as she bumped it with her hip. He grasped at it for a distraction from his racing thoughts. "You know one of these is broken?"

She nodded. "It's supposed to be."

He studied her quietly. "What like broken justice?"

"Exactly."

Ben paused, studying the soft bun at the nape of her neck. Her skin was exposed. Her neck was long and lean. He had the sudden image in his head of dragging his tongue down that tender flesh. Would she gasp? Would she tip her head and grant him access to more of her secret places?

He cleared his throat roughly. "You lied for me today."

She stilled, guilt flashing over her face. "Yeah, about that…"

"Thank you," he said quickly.

She lifted one brow. "For lying?"

"For giving me the benefit of the doubt. That doesn't happen very often," he said quietly.

"Really? But you're such a charmer."

Ben shifted until he stood a little too close. Until he could see her eyes darken the way they had in the car when he'd given in to the temptation to kiss her. "Are you teasing me? Because if you are, I think I need to make a note on my calendar that yes, you do officially have a sense of humor."

A smile crossed her lips. It took everything he had not to slide his thumb over that soft skin. He wanted to see her lips close over the tip. To feel her warm mouth encircle him and…Jesus, he still had to go back to work.

"I do have a sense of humor. I just don't get to break it out very often because the only thing I see at work is the seedy underbelly of the army. There's not much humor in what I do."

"Maybe you need to relax a little more." Ben shifted until he could nudge the door shut behind him. He didn't want anyone to see. Didn't want to give anyone a hint of something that was private and intimate and deeply compelling. Were they flirting? This felt like flirting. And with this woman, he had absolutely no basis to say either way what this really was.

"I don't know what this 'relax' is that you speak of," she said.

He felt a long-forgotten twinge deep in his belly. It was something so foreign, he'd forgotten it was something he was capable of. In all his casual encounters, he'd forgotten what real attraction felt like.

He swallowed the dryness in his mouth. He didn't know what to do with this realization that Olivia Hale was someone he wanted to...someone he wanted. It was one thing to flirt with someone at a bar, to take them home for a few hours of mindless sex.

This? This was something entirely different.

Something more than wanting a few hours of sheets sliding over skin, of warm bodies slipping together. This was something darker. Something warmer.

Something infinitely more valuable.

"Maybe I'll ply you with alcohol tonight at Stable Call. We'll see if we can't get you to unwind a little bit." His voice was low, grating on his ears.

"Good luck with that. I only drink socially. There will be no drunken pictures of me immortalized on the Internet." She stepped toward him then, closing the last distance between them. She reached up and slid her hand over his cheek. Ben went very still as her palm slid over his skin. Her palm was cool against his face. Gentle. It took everything he had to let her slip out of reach again.

He captured her palm before she could slip away. Held it there against his cheek. "Thank you," he whispered. "For Zittoro."

Her lips parted. He could feel the slight huff of breath on his skin. "Thank you for trusting me with the truth." She slipped her fingers from his, her eyes sparkling. "Just don't make me come after you for that packet."

Ben caught her hand before he thought about it. His hand closed over hers, her index finger captured in a gentle loop between his thumb and forefinger.

He had the sudden wild idea to put her finger to his lips. He pressed it gently to his mouth. Felt the pad of her finger on his bottom lip. A single bolt of electricity snapped over his skin.

A simple touch. Nothing more.

They were at work. It was the single stupidest thing he could have done.

He released her quickly, before anyone could see. Before he could do something stupid like pull her close and kiss her again. The want inside him was powerful. Raw and needy.

"Sorry," he mumbled.

A pink flush crept up her cheeks. Her bottom lip parted from her top and a tiny gap appeared. A tiny gap he wanted to slide his thumb into to feel her tongue run along the pad.

He needed to get the hell out of there. What the hell was wrong with him? Nothing said "sexy" like sexual harassment at the office.

"I have officially lost my fucking mind," he said, reaching for the doorknob and angling his body toward the narrow hall. "I'm going to leave now before I do something else really dumb."

Ben felt awkward. Tense. He didn't know what had possessed him to do that. Hell, they weren't even on friendly terms and he'd gone and done something...something he would have done with a date. Something he would have done to a woman he'd been flirting with.

At least he was when they weren't sniping at each other over legal packets.

That was the only thing that could describe the moment of pure insanity that had him pressing his lips to her finger.

Ben took a step into the hallway, unable to break the silence, hardly able to move. Olivia followed him and paused in her doorway, a breath of a distance between their bodies.

Time froze, silent and heavy between them.

Her lips parted, her tongue darting over her bottom lip.

"I'll see you tonight, Ben," she said quietly.

Chapter Twelve

Ben handed each of his lieutenants a beer and took careful note of how many each of them had had to drink. Ben was the last person to nag at someone about how much they drank but then again, he was a commander now.

It was implied that he act like a damned grown-up and that meant buying his officers *a* drink, not multiple drinks. Every one of them would be driving away from here in an hour or two and they damn sure better be sober before they did.

Jesus, he was responsible for how they turned out. What a terrifying thought. Sergeant majors all over the army would be tearing up trucker hats in no time. He grinned over the edge of his beer and listened to what they were saying.

"Sir, Captain Marshall didn't like us pissing on his leg about things we could solve at our level," Gillis said.

Ben took a deep pull off his beer at that comment. It was exactly what he'd been afraid of. "Okay, so let's clear up a couple of things. First, I'm not Marshall. If you have questions, come ask me. I'm not going to rip your face off for asking me a question. I am, however, going to get pissed that you've got guys in the motor pool at seventeen hundred on a Friday night when you're off drinking a beer, though. So whatever problem you thought you were going to solve, you're going to have to wait until Monday."

"But sir—"

"No 'but sir,' LT. Next time, you'll come get some guidance first. Your platoon sergeants thought this was a good idea?" Ben looked between his two platoon leaders and his executive officer.

"Sir," Vitiliano finally found his voice. Either that or his balls had just dropped and he was finally able to talk. "Captain Marshall told us to tell our platoon sergeants what to do. We outrank them; we're supposed to be in charge."

Ben choked on the sip of beer he'd just taken. He covered his mouth with his fist and barely avoided spewing the remains all over his lieutenants. "Okay. We've got much bigger problems than I realized. Check it out, LT. Brace yourself, I'm about to break your little heart." He took a pull off his beer to ease the sensation of nearly choking to death. "Yes, you outrank your platoon sergeant. But nowhere on the good Lord's green earth are we going to let you run off and take all that vast knowledge you acquired in officer basic course or ROTC and actually start running things. This is not to say that you're incapable of doing it but there's a lot to be said for experience. The only one in the half of your relationship who has that experience is your platoon sergeant."

Ben took a deep breath. He could not wait to tell Sorren about this zinger. He'd have to wait until Sorren took a drink of his own beer. "Listen. You and your platoon sergeant are a marriage. And you don't get a vote over your life partner here. Which means you two need to start attacking problems together. There is no other way. Get me?"

The lieutenants glanced at each other like he'd just imparted some vast unknowable wisdom to them. Ben shook his head. "Seriously? You guys thought you were running things?"

Vitiliano spoke again. "Sir, it's just the way it was. Officers run shit, according to Marshall."

"Okay, so new rule: the next time you start to do something Marshall told you to do, punch yourself."

"Sir?" This from Gillis, who looked like he might take Ben's advice far too seriously.

"It's a joke." Ben sighed. Obviously his lieutenants had had their senses of humor corrupted while working for that shitbird Marshall. "Look, just—if you catch yourself doing something the way Marshall wanted, I want you to step back and question why you're doing it. And then go find your platoon sergeant and ask him what the best way to attack the problem is." He pointed at Gillis. "Right now, you need to send your people home. You can figure out what's going on with your platoon sergeant over the weekend."

"Roger, sir." Gillis pulled out his phone and stepped away from the noise.

Ben listened as Redding and Vitiliano talked about something one of the soldiers had done earlier that week involving a box of grid squares and keys to the drop zone. He scanned the bar, looking for one particular face.

And stopped when he saw her in a corner, talking to Reza. Iaconelli met his gaze, then lifted a glass in mock salute. That was water, right? Had to be. Reza was serious about getting sober this time and Ben had faith in him. He had something to live for, something other than the war and the constant deployments.

With Emily standing with him, Reza was going to pull this off.

But Ben was curious now as to just what Olivia was doing with Reza. He couldn't see her face beneath the rim of her Stetson but the shadows caressed the back of her neck beneath her bun. A single tendril of hair escaped, resting beneath her ear.

The Stetson looked good on her. Too good. Added bonus that he'd get a chance to tease Olivia about it. Oh yes, his lieutenants were about to get a reprieve.

Because he just couldn't stay away from Olivia Hale.

Legends was far too small to have this many people crowded into it. Olivia was fairly certain that every inch of floor space was now filled with dusty boots, and some people were wearing actual spurs.

She couldn't get used to the feel of the Stetson on her head. The strap pressed tight against her bun, which in turn tightened the band against her forehead.

But everyone else was wearing their headgear inside so she figured she needed to keep hers on. When in Rome and all that.

She enjoyed watching the room. Seeing the new lieutenant in the signal section laugh a little too loud. Or seeing the ops officer, Captain Loehr, stand a little too close to his significant other Captain Montoya. Olivia was going to have to make an effort to get to know Claire. She'd heard so much about her from the soldiers.

But right then, she wasn't in the mood to go crowd surfing. It had been a long week and she was comfortable, standing off to one side, talking to Reza. He was a known good quantity, a person she trusted simply by virtue of being Emily's other half. And the fact that he was talking to her and keeping her from standing alone in a corner of a room full of virtual strangers spoke volumes about the man himself.

She glanced at his glass, then flushed when he caught her looking at it.

"Fun new side effect of being sober," he said quietly. "I'm always hydrated."

Olivia smiled, wishing some of the heat in her cheeks would cool. "I wasn't going to say anything."

He offered a lopsided shrug, taking a sip. "I know that but you were thinking it. Everyone who knows thinks it. I figure I can argue and be pissed about it or acknowledge it and move on. I'm choosing course of action B."

"Greetings, shitbag," said a familiar voice.

Olivia turned to see Ben weaving around a fat major and entering their small space.

Reza lifted his glass in greeting. "Nice to see you, too. I take it you haven't managed to get relieved your first week on the job?"

Olivia raised both eyebrows and Ben shot Reza a dirty look before he turned to Olivia to explain. "I may have considered trying to get fired when I first took command," Ben admitted.

"Oh, really?"

Ben took a deep breath and Olivia tried not to notice the rise and fall of his chest. Heat unfurled in her belly, stretching like a cat after a long sleep. She found herself wondering about the glimpse of the tattoo she'd seen. How far up his arm did it go?

"I've been avoiding command for a long time," Ben said. "For a lot of reasons."

"You seem to be doing okay so far." The memory of his mouth against hers teased her. Made her want to stand a little too close. Want a little too much. His lips were far too soft for a man.

Reza laughed quietly, distracting her from the distinct detour her thoughts had taken. "I threatened to whip his ass if he got himself fired."

"On purpose," Ben clarified, holding up one finger. His lips curled into an easy grin. She'd never seen Ben this relaxed. Maybe it was because she'd only seen him since he'd taken command and command took so much out of everyone. This new side of him was intriguing and deeply, deeply sexy. "It only counts if I do it on purpose."

They were an odd little group. A senior NCO talking with a captain and a major. Most of the smaller clusters of people were wearing the same ranks. The lieutenants ran with the lieutenants, the majors with the majors. But Olivia was comfortable.

She looked up at Ben. Her fingers tingled at the memory of his mouth on her. A little too comfortable.

God, but her body ached.

"So Major Hale was just asking about your history with Foster and Escoberra and the gang," Reza said. "I told her Escoberra saved your sorry ass when you'd gone and gotten yourself blown up."

Ben looked down into his beer. "Yeah, Escoberra saved my ass in that fiasco," he said quietly. He took a sip from his beer but Olivia didn't miss the tightening of the muscles in his neck at Reza's comment. He looked down at the bottle in his hand, rubbing his thumb absently along the lip. "And how did we repay him? By damn near ruining his career over that attack," Ben said. His words were packed with bitterness, his eyes filled with an old, painful memory.

"Someone put Escoberra's awards citation in the legal folder," Olivia said. Relief pulsed through her, giving her the opening she'd hoped for to ask about the award. "I was curious because your name was on it. Unless there's some other Ben Teague running around."

Ben smiled but it didn't reach his eyes and it took everything she had not to reach for him, to squeeze his hand in sympathy. To let him know he wasn't alone. "Nope, I'm the one and only as far as I know." He looked at his beer. "This tastes like watered-down piss," he muttered.

Reza laughed. "Because you know what watered-down piss tastes like?"

"No, but I suppose you would."

Reza held up his glass. "Finely brewed H_2O."

Ben smirked. "Good. I'd hate to have to tell Emily you weren't behaving. And Sergeant Major would likely have your balls if you get in any more trouble."

Reza sniffed. "I'm not getting in any more trouble. I can't if I want to go on this next deployment."

Olivia frowned slightly. "You're volunteering to go?" Unspoken was the question of whether Emily knew or not. It wasn't her place to ask but she wanted to. Oh, but she wanted to.

"It's not that I'm volunteering," Reza said. "I'm just making sure I'm in the eligible pool of soldiers they can take." He took another sip of his water. "But yes, to answer your question, I would volunteer. Emily understands that," he said softly.

Olivia felt the emptiness on her right shoulder. These men both had multiple deployments under their belts and they would willingly go back. She had no deployment—not a real one anyway—and fear of the unknown was a powerful thing.

"I'm glad she supports you," Ben said softly. Olivia watched the unspoken bond between the two men. "You're lucky."

There was something there, beneath his flippant words. An echo of a memory. An old hurt. She looked up at his words and found him watching her, his dark eyes intense and shadowed even for the dim light inside the bar. And in his eyes, the shadows she'd heard in his voice.

"She's too good for me," Reza said. His throat moved as he swallowed roughly. "And I'll spend the rest of my life trying to be good enough for her."

Ben pulled his gaze away and sniffed, swiping a finger beneath his eyes. "That's so romantic."

"Fuck you, Teague." Reza tipped two fingers to the brim of his Stetson. "On that note, I'm out of here. I've been seen. My mandatory fun is over."

Ben shifted to give Reza room to maneuver through the crowd.

Olivia watched him go, keenly aware of the man standing beside her. Standing too close, so that she could smell the lingering scent of his skin. It was a powerful lure, urging her to stand closer. She wanted to bury her face in his neck and inhale, breathing him in.

He shifted after a moment, leaning close enough that the edge of his Stetson bumped hers. His voice whispered over her ear, sending a chill down her spine. God, but this man was doing something to her, something that made her hungry and needy and achingly aroused.

"I hear you were asking about me?"

Ben watched a hundred emotions flicker across her face at his question. He stood too close on purpose. He couldn't span the distance completely, not where they were, but he didn't need to. Just watching her eyes darken, her lips part. The woman was on fire and she had no idea what her response was doing to his insides.

It did something funny inside his chest to find out she'd been asking about him.

"Don't get excited. It was purely professional," she said dryly. Her voice was thick. On edge.

He leaned down, closer to her ear. The temptation to nibble on that soft exposed skin beneath her ear was too much. Instead, he blew a quick breath over her skin. Saw, rather than felt her shiver. "Oh, you're talking dirty now?"

This was foreplay without touching, the forbidden fantasy of not getting caught that added power to their erotic dance.

She looked at him as if he'd gone crazy, her eyes crackling

with dark, sexual energy. Maybe he had. That was the only reason to explain why he was standing here flirting with the sexy lawyer. But he felt something around her, something he hadn't felt in a long, long time. Maybe never.

There was more to this woman than just passion for the job.

And he wanted to curl around her, embracing her spark for life, for energy. Just one touch of something real.

"There's something wrong with you," she said. But there was laughter, deep and sensual, in her voice.

There was something deeply sexy about the way she leaned against the wall, her mouth relaxed, her shoulders easy.

It was like she'd finally found her bearings. Like she was finally starting to find her place.

"What did you want to know about the award?" he asked. He had to lean close to be able to hear her. It was tempting to be that close to her neck and not be able to nibble on the spot just below her ear.

"I was curious about your relationship with Escoberra. You have so much loyalty to him."

"You could have asked me," he said mildly. The scar on his belly ached. She hadn't asked him. Even after that kiss earlier, she could have asked but she hadn't. Then again, even though he was standing there wanting to nibble on the soft flesh beneath her ear, they hadn't exactly been friendly until very, very recently.

And he couldn't stay mad when she angled her body toward his.

"I could have but we've been prickly enough without me asking a question you could misinterpret."

He smiled down at her, trying to yank his mind out of the gutter before she figured out the direction of his thoughts. "Aww. You were thinking of my sensitive feelings?"

"Something like that," she said. She had to lean a little too close for him to hear her without shouting. It was disconcerting, getting close enough that he could catch the scent of her hair. Something clean and soft and female.

Her face was cast in soft shadows. He had the sudden urge to kiss her. Not right then, not surrounded by uniforms and Stetsons and curious eyes. But if they were alone? Maybe out at Talarico's. Maybe on the patio overlooking Lake Belton. He'd feel her breath between them. Her tongue would dance against his, their clothes a barrier to getting any closer.

In his fantasy, she'd lean into him. She'd curl her hand into his neck.

He'd invite her back to his place.

Fantasies crashed over him, slamming into him, taunting him with soft, sensual promises. He was attracted to this woman. More than he'd been willing to admit.

"Are you flirting with me, ma'am?" he asked quietly.

Was she? She looked up at him, and he felt the dark promise in her eyes, the lingering taste of her lips on his. He was hungry for this woman in a way that stunned him with its power.

"I think maybe I am." A husky admission.

That simple sentence slammed into him, rocking his world on its axis. He was chained, unable to move, unable to act on the opening that presented itself.

In a million years, he had never expected . . . what? A little harmless flirting? But his brain had already detoured to a dark quiet place heavy and thick with sensual gasps and the slide of warm bodies.

Jesus, he was about to embarrass himself.

He cleared his throat, yanking his brain back from the edge where it tormented him. "What did you want to know?" he asked, leaning close. He saw the tiny curl of hair near her ear that had come free from the severe hairstyle she wore at work.

"Escoberra's award was downgraded," she said. "Do you know why?"

The scar on his belly itched. He rubbed it absently. How to explain the politics at play during the war back then. The power plays that had left Ben still standing while Escoberra paid the price.

"When our base was overrun," he said softly, painful, burning memories slamming into him. "I got blown up pretty bad. It was Escoberra who coordinated the defense until air support arrived." He looked down into his beer, fighting to lock the memories back down where they'd lain dormant. "My commander blamed him because he pursued the enemy instead of holding our position. I tried to have that award pushed through but they weren't hearing it." He met her gaze. "He saved my life. Escoberra is the reason I'm alive and the army tried to fry him over violating an order in the heat of battle."

He watched the emotions flicker over her face. Her eyes darkened, no longer with arousal but with sympathy. He held his breath, waiting for the pity that never failed to infuriate him.

But it didn't come.

Instead her fingers slipped over his. Hidden from prying eyes, her touch was a warm reminder of their shared humanity. "I'm sorry, Ben," she whispered.

"It says something about me," he said, unable, unwilling to move away from her touch. "That I wasn't able to defend him."

Olivia shook her head. "I don't think that says something about you, Ben." She leaned closer, her hand colliding with his chest as she lifted on her toes to get closer to his ear. "You blame yourself, don't you?" she said after a moment.

He sipped his beer. "Somewhat."

She wanted to say more. He could see it. That was the Olivia he was coming to know. He almost smiled at her but the memories swirling around his chest were too tight, too painful.

"I can't hear myself think in here," Olivia said, letting her fingers slip from his. "How long do we have to stay?"

"Have you been seen?" Ben asked, leaning down so he didn't have to shout.

"Yeah."

"Then you're good. You can sneak out any time."

"Are you staying?"

Ben shook his head. "I haven't slept well all week. I want to go home, have a beer and crash." He paused. "I'm starting to think I'll never sleep well again."

She smiled and it was filled with sympathy. "You'll sleep again. After you change command," she said.

He offered a wry grin, wishing that she wasn't telling the truth that he'd already started to suspect. "That's not encouraging." He set his half-finished beer on one of the tables then motioned toward the door. "I'll walk you out?"

"You're not expected to stay because you're a commander?"

"Nope. Or, if I am, I'll just make some emergency up if the boss asks."

Olivia laughed quietly as she followed him out.

Outside, he walked her to her car. They were alone, around a corner and away from prying eyes. The temptation to kiss her, to continue what they'd started only hours earlier was strong, too strong.

It was something he needed to walk away from. Fast, before he did something stupid like ask her to come home with him. He knocked the brim of her Stetson with the tip of his finger. "Your Stetson looks nice."

"Thanks," she said.

He left her there because the temptation to surrender to the invitation he saw in her eyes was too strong, too compelling.

He wanted. More than he had in a long, long time, he wanted Olivia Hale.

Chapter Thirteen

Working on Saturdays was nothing new but her first one in her new job ended with a whimper, and that whimper involved a lack of food. Olivia realized there was no food in her house only after she'd driven by the HEB grocery store, the super Walmart, and any other shot she'd had at foraging for sustenance on her way home. She didn't feel like cooking anyway. Not at all.

She was mentally exhausted. All she wanted to do was curl up with a glass of wine and continue to dig into the files in her briefcase in the vain hope that she could make a dent in the massive pile of work that kept breeding in the dark when she wasn't looking.

She turned the corner and the answer to her dinner prayers stared at her from its perch overlooking Belton Lake. Talarico's was relatively new, designed by some big shot architect in Austin. Tuscan and completely upscale, it served the best seafood around. It was her favorite place to hang out—before she'd gone to work in this new brigade and all the fun in her life had died.

There was a small crowd gathered outside—older folks dressed in business casual and talking about a local football team. She walked in and snagged a seat at the bar. She was hungry but suddenly, nothing sounded good. She ordered stuffed mushrooms and a glass of wine, then pulled out a file to start reading.

It wasn't easy going through some of these backlogged cases. There were three incidents of child abuse in this brigade alone. She strongly suspected there were others that hadn't been uncovered yet.

Her phone vibrated on the bar and she opened her e-mail. Child Protective Services wasn't making any progress. Sergeant First Class Escoberra was refusing to talk to investigators without a lawyer.

Christ, what a shit show. She closed her eyes, rubbing her glass against her forehead. It was so hard to reconcile the man Ben spoke about with the man who could have done what he did to his daughter.

She took a long pull off her glass as she read through the initial incident report again. Hailey had come home from school and she and Escoberra had argued about television. The report said Escoberra had just snapped.

And Hailey had borne the brunt of his temper.

And now no one was talking. CPS was getting ready to close the investigation. Olivia's heart ached for the family. They obviously loved Escoberra. That kind of love was powerful—but it wasn't powerful enough to overcome the beast inside of the man who was tormenting them.

Olivia asked the waiter for another drink and wondered if she was going to have nightmares tonight.

Olivia dragged her hand through her hair, hating this part of her job. The daily confrontation with evil that seemed to eat away at any sense of human decency left in the world. Sometimes it felt like there was a poison, a rotten, creeping poison in the belly of their society. Who could do this to a child and think it was okay? And how could anyone defend it?

How could Ben? How could he ignore what Escoberra had done? Even if Escoberra had saved Ben's life, how could he ignore what he was capable of?

She scrubbed her hands over her face as her emotions threatened to snap free from their moorings. She was tired. She needed to take a break from the constant work but there was no time. There were people counting on her. She couldn't rest, couldn't take time for herself when there were people who needed an advocate, who needed someone to stand up for them.

There was no room in her life for personal things. Escoberra's case file mocked her from the bar.

This was just another case. One more family, broken by the war.

It wasn't simply another case, damn it. It was a family. A mother and children.

She didn't want to let justice run its course. She knew in her heart she was supposed to uphold the procedures, to make sure that the process worked, but sometimes that wasn't good enough. She let the anger come, let the rage seep into her fingertips as she started writing out the charges against the sergeant. The minute the investigation was complete, she wanted his packet on Colonel Horace's desk. She wanted Escoberra away from the family who loved him too much to push him out of their lives.

That love could kill them. God, she wanted to be wrong but she'd seen it too many times.

She caught herself breathing hard and forced herself to take a deep, quieting breath. Then another. Then she took another sip of her wine and slowly started writing again, focusing on the clarity of her argument, writing the charge specifications neatly so her clerk could type them up tomorrow. Pushing aside the writhing emotions and holding on to the rational side of her brain that demanded perfection.

She needed to take the anger and the hate out of it and focus on the legal argument. She could get as passionate as she wanted but if she lost her temper, she would lose the case and the monster would walk free into the light once more.

A monster wearing the smiling, charming face of a decorated war veteran.

The only lead they had right now was the school nurse who had spoken with investigators the day after Hailey had been treated at the hospital.

It didn't matter. None of it did.

The world fell away as she continued to write, losing herself in the smooth rhythm of her pen scratching against the paper. She imagined it was carving the charges into the monster's skin, rendering him powerless.

"You look ready to snap that pencil in half."

Olivia looked up at the familiar voice, the heat rushing along her skin as she met Ben Teague's eyes.

He'd watched her, contemplating the fluid movements of her hand over the paper. But it was the torment in her eyes that had finally compelled him to move, to breach the divide between them and approach her. Cautiously, the riot of emotions twisting across her face as much a warning as they were compelling.

He'd seen her like this before. The other day at the tiny gym in the headquarters, she'd been lost in the memories. The anger and the sadness had radiated off her, shoved aside by sheer force of will, as though she could save the world simply by ordering it to be done.

"I get a little wound up when I'm working," she said, setting the pencil down carefully. Her movements were too guarded. Too stiff. As though she was afraid she might snap.

She speared a mushroom with a fork but Ben wasn't fooled by the sudden ease of her movements. He'd stood by the door watching her for a few good minutes and could have sworn he'd seen smoke pouring from that pencil as she'd scribbled furiously.

She'd been focused. In the zone. Writing hard and fast and utterly unaware of the world around her.

There was something rough about the way she'd tackled the paperwork. Something fierce in the strokes of her pencil.

She was a woman on a mission. Dedicated. Focused. For a fleeting moment, Ben wished he could have that kind of dedication to his job. That sense of purpose that motivated him to get out of bed every day.

But command came with so much power. Power that was so easy to abuse.

He didn't want this job. But now that he had it? He hated to admit it but his first sergeant was right—Ben had a job to do and it was a job that came with a huge responsibility. He was slipping into his role as commander slowly. Easing the heavy weight of responsibility around his soldiers. Keeping the fear of the power he wielded at bay.

Because it was fear. Fear that he would become like his mother, a woman who wielded power and authority like it was her personal right to lead soldiers.

She was wrong about that. Command was a privilege, not a right, and the power that came with the guidon was not something to be toyed with.

Ben didn't want to forget that. "Are you okay?" he asked when she didn't say anything.

"Fancy meeting you here," she said, slipping her fingers around the stem of her wine glass.

He didn't miss the slight tremble of the glass as she raised it to her lips or the way she avoided his question. There was something dark and tormented in her eyes, something that called out to him, beckoning to him in the setting sun that glinted across the bar from the bay windows that overlooked the lake.

And Ben wanted to know why.

* * *

She looked up when he'd said nothing for a long time and found him watching her. "What?"

The need inside her morphed into something yearning, something demanding a human touch.

Ben's touch.

She very much wanted to slide closer to him right then. To feel his arms curl around her shoulders and feel the beat of his heart against her palm. She wanted to slip into his embrace and let the darkness fall away from the warmth of his touch. She wanted this man. She wanted the dark, needful things that made her body ache with long-denied demands.

The work she did was an ugly thing. A necessary thing but so dark and filled with hate and hurt.

She wanted to push away that ugly darkness for just a moment. She wanted the gasps in dusky light, the sensual slide of his body against hers.

She licked her bottom lip, the want thick and heavy in her veins.

"You're very intense when you're working," he said. He stepped close enough that she could see the faint stubble along his jaw. "Do you always work on weekends?"

She nodded toward his own uniform. "I could ask you the same question."

His lips quirked at the edges. "Some shithead got a DUI and the commander called all of us in to yell at us."

"Sounds fun," Olivia said dryly.

"It was a hoot." He tipped his chin and studied her quietly. "Are you always this intense?" A husky whisper, filled with innuendo.

"Depends on what we're talking about." She lifted one brow. His lips curled at the edges. Up close, she could see a thin scar at the edge of his mouth. She hadn't noticed it before and she had the unexpected urge to trace the tip of her finger over the pale, raised flesh.

"Are we back to flirting again?" His voice was deep. Teasing. Sensual.

She laughed and it broke apart the block of ice in her chest. "Maybe."

He leaned closer then and she caught the scent of his skin, warm and male. It wrapped around her, that teasing warmth. It sparked hungry needs inside her and turned her thoughts away from the legalese in her files to something darker and infinitely more sensual.

"You don't do this very often, do you, Olivia?"

She couldn't look away from the intensity in his eyes. From the heat in his gaze that made her want to strip away every barrier between them. "Do what?"

"I think you know what."

His lips curled slightly as his dark gaze fell to her lips. A night with Ben would push away all the darkness and let her forget the evil she was fighting. It was tempting, so tempting. She could lean a little bit closer. Slide her fingers over his wrist. Feel the heat from his skin. Trace her fingers over the designs etched into his flesh.

"This could get complicated," she murmured, watching his mouth as he took a drink.

"It's already complicated." He set the glass down. A flicker of moisture beaded on his bottom lip. "How much worse could it get?"

"A lot worse," she said. She reached for him then, sliding her thumb across his bottom lip. The drop of water was warmed by his skin. It penetrated the pad on her fingertip, warm and wet and smooth.

He leaned closer. "Considering I'm not avoiding you like the last lawyer, yeah, it's complicated."

"You avoided the last lawyer?" This casual flirting was . . .

nice. It felt surreal, like time had stopped and they were two normal, well-adjusted adults with all their shots and . . .

She could not get involved with one of the company commanders. She tried to remind herself of that but sitting there right then, seeing the sunlight glint off the edge of his cheek, she wanted. Oh, but she wanted. Something hard and fast in the darkness. Something wild and intense that would let her forget—for just a little while—all the evil that she confronted on a daily basis.

His eyes darkened as he watched her. One gesture. One whispered word and she could cross the line.

She watched his mouth move as he talked, her gaze locked on that wide, full bottom lip.

"Oh yeah. You have no idea how I avoided the brigade lawyers at all costs. They made my life miserable every time I was responsible for investigating missing property. This one time, I was chasing down a wrench—"

"Wait, did you say a wrench?" She covered his hand to stop him. His gaze dropped to their hands. But neither of them moved. "Why would you have to conduct an investigation on a wrench?"

Ben grinned. "It was a really expensive wrench."

Olivia laughed quietly before she took a sip of her water. "And what happened to said wrench?"

"A contractor had sold it to an Iraqi for a hard drive full of porn."

She choked and barely managed to cover her mouth to avoid spitting water at him. "You're joking."

He lifted two fingers into the air. The cool night air kissed her skin where the heat from his touch evaporated. "Scout's honor. The platoon leader still had to buy the damn thing."

"Why?"

"Because in that particular unit, the battalion commander found negligence in every single case so he could charge the commanders the full amount for missing property. I saw another guy get hemmed up for two months' base pay for combat-lost equipment."

She sobered and the budding desire aching through her veins faded just a little. "Really?"

"Yeah."

"The lawyer should have objected."

"You're kidding, right?"

She narrowed her eyes. "No."

Ben's smile faded. "Let's just say that commander got what he wanted out of that lawyer and leave it at that."

"That's not how it's supposed to work," she whispered.

He covered her hand with his. "It's not a perfect world down here in the brigade combat teams. It's gritty and raw and deeply flawed. The commander is king and if you don't acknowledge that right off the bat, you're going to be in a world of trouble." She opened her mouth to argue and he squeezed her hand. "I'm not telling you this just for shits and giggles, Olivia."

"You're telling me something that conflicts with everything that I believe in."

"Look, it's really easy to try and fall on your sword. The only one who ends up hurt by that is you." He removed his hand from hers and the kiss of cool air sent a chill racing down over his palm. "Your convictions are going to get the better of you if you don't temper them. The brigade commander isn't interested in all the bad shit you're going to see. You can't recommend that he court-martial everyone. Pick your battles."

He reached for her, his hand swallowing the thin bones of her wrist. Ben's hand closed over her forearm. Heat penetrated her skin, pulsing through her blood. "I'm not telling you not to recommend prosecution. I'm telling you to pick your battles carefully or you'll lose all of them."

She pulled her arm free. "What battles did you lose?" she whispered, and her words struck him dead in the chest. She wanted to ask what happened to Escoberra after he'd been held responsible for the attack on their base. She wanted to know the things that kept him up at night.

She wanted to know Ben, the man in front of her. Not the commander. Not the man in the uniform.

The man behind the uniform.

"The wrong ones," he said simply. He looked away, down at his glass. Just like that, the mood between them was once again filled with the dark ugliness of the war.

She swallowed a hard breath. "I can't walk away from this, Ben. I can't be strategic and try to figure out how to play this. Not this case. Not cases like it. I can't."

Ben studied her quietly. "Why is this so important to you?"

Her temper snapped. "Because someone has to do the right thing. Everyone always cares about the soldier. No one cares about the families." Her voice was thick.

"You're wrong," he whispered.

He knew she thought he was protecting Escoberra out of blind loyalty. He knew what she saw when she looked at him—just another commander, playing fast and loose with the rules. But that wasn't the case. It wasn't.

But everything was so complicated.

Olivia deserved to know the truth, no matter how hard it was for him to resurrect enough to put into words. It was a truth he'd been avoiding for years, just like he'd been avoiding Escoberra.

"I resigned my commission after they hemmed Escoberra up for the attack," he said quietly.

He closed his eyes against the physical pain of the memories. He did not expect her fingers to slide over his. In the cool evening light, her touch was a beacon of warmth, of human connection.

"I was lying in the hospital when my battalion commander came and visited me. He told me what they were doing—that they were considering court-martialing Escoberra for the base attack. All because he pursued the enemy instead of holding his position."

His body tensed involuntarily. Her fingers slid over his knuckles, a soothing gesture. So simple. So powerful.

"They said Escoberra failed to disseminate information about the attack. That they were holding him responsible for it." He swallowed the bitterness that tightened at the back of his throat. "I told my commander if they did that, I would resign." He couldn't lift his gaze to look at her. He was terrified of what he might see.

"But you're still here," she whispered.

"Because after I resigned, my mother pulled in every favor she could to keep me in."

"Your mother is in the army?"

He nodded. "Colonel Diane Teague is currently somewhere in the Pentagon's puzzle palace."

"She's a colonel?"

"Yeah. A colonel with a lot of powerful friends in the right places. Which is how I'm still in the army."

Finally he dared to meet her gaze. "I tried to resign in protest. Mom squashed that plan," he said. "And now, here I am."

"And now you're staying," she said.

He looked down at her hand where it covered his. Twisted his palm until it was flat beneath hers. His fingertips brushed the inside of her wrist.

"Escoberra adopted Hailey when she was nine." He smiled warmly at the memory. "He used to bring her into the office when she was a little kid." He rubbed his hand over his mouth, stunned by how long ago that had really been.

He glanced over at Olivia and found her watching him silently. "I know you think he did this," he said quietly. "But there's got to be something else there. He loves that little girl. He wouldn't do this, Olivia."

Olivia looked away, her fingers drumming on the bar. Finally she slid the folder toward him. "I don't know how to reconcile the man who did this with the man you describe."

Cool fingers slid over his wrist. He looked down at her hand resting against his skin. Such a simple, loaded gesture.

It was a long time before Ben met her gaze.

"I'm sorry, Ben," she whispered. "I know you believe in him but there's no other explanation for what happened. You can't let this go, no matter how much he means to you."

"I can't do it, Olivia." He looked down at their hands where hers still rested against his. "Maybe that makes me weak, maybe that makes me a horrible person, but I can't believe he did this." He bit his lips. "I've seen the pictures but there's got to be something else that explains this. There has to be."

"And what if there's no other explanation," she whispered. "What then, Ben?"

He met her gaze then, unable to look away from the quiet resolution in her eyes. The lack of judgment stunned him. "I don't know," he whispered.

The sun sank into the lake, casting pale shadows over his cheek. Her fingers rested against his wrist.

He sat still, completely motionless.

But when he moved, he stunned her.

He turned his palm over, threading his fingers with hers. Nothing more. Palm to palm, their skin connected in a way their bodies and souls never could be.

His hand was big. There were calluses on his palm and his fingertips were rough. But there was a gentleness in that touch.

She bent her fingers into his. A hesitant gesture.

She met his gaze.

"It hurts so fucking much to think this happened." His big hand closed over hers. "But don't mistake my silence for not caring," he whispered. "Please don't do that."

She was so used to commanders not caring, so used to them doing whatever it took to win. The honest pain she saw in his eyes melted her defenses. Heated her blood and drove the longing in her blood to a fevered need.

She didn't think. She lifted her hand to cup his cheek. The stubble from his five o'clock shadow was a soft scrape against her palm. "You're an admirable person, you know that?" she whispered.

He scoffed gently. "Not quite." He didn't look away. "But thank you for saying so."

She took a shuddering breath and released it before she looked down at the packet, at the bleak and empty night she faced writing up the charges against a man who might never see the inside of a jail for what he'd done.

Everything was so fucking corrupted and dark. When she looked at Ben and saw him watching her, she felt like she'd brushed up against something…something good.

"This is probably going to make me the biggest fool in the world," she whispered. "But I'd very much like to go somewhere else. With you."

Ben went very still. His eyes darkened. His bottom lip parted from his top. "Why?" he whispered. His voice was rough and thick.

"Maybe I need to remember something good in the world tonight," she said. "Will you come home with me?"

"Olivia."

He stepped close, too close. His shoulders blocked her view of the parking lot. They were secluded beneath a low willow tree. No one could see them.

She had time to change her mind. As she'd paid the bill and picked up her files, she could have changed her mind. But now, outside the restaurant, it wasn't fear or uncertainty skittering over her skin.

It was arousal. Arousal that this man had followed her outside. That this man had backed her up against her car, his big body blocking out the world.

She wanted his touch. Wanted his hands on her, wanted his mouth.

Wanted to lose herself in the taste and touch and feel of him.

His lips hovered a breath from hers. Heat radiated from his skin. His breath mingled with hers but neither of them moved. A twisting, writhing dance of almost touches, of the barest caresses.

She dared to lift her gaze from that strong mouth that so often wore an easy grin to his eyes, those dark, laughing eyes.

They weren't laughing now. They were desperately serious, dark, and hungry.

Now the barest space between them felt like an impassable chasm.

His fingertips brushed her cheek. The faintest touch. A kiss of sensation that traced pure electricity over her skin. Her breath caught in her throat. She swallowed and his gaze dropped to her neck. She was sensitive there. She almost closed her eyes and tipped her chin toward him. Almost.

For the life of her, she couldn't say who moved first but between one moment and the next her top lip brushed against his. A whisper of sensation. A delicate gesture.

Those fingertips curled into her cheek.

"I want to kiss you so fucking bad," he whispered.

His words vibrated over her lips. A wicked sensation that promised pleasure with every stroke of his tongue.

It was Olivia who moved then. Olivia who opened her mouth and slid her tongue over his bottom lip to taste him.

As if waiting for her permission, he slanted his mouth over hers. This, this was what she had been waiting for. This, the tacit feel of his touch, of the powerful man who held her in both hands as though she was something precious. This man was what she craved, what she needed to push away the darkness of her job and the evil she fought. His tongue danced with hers but it was his body that pressed into her, his body that overwhelmed her.

Her arms slid around his neck and she arched against him, just a little. A hint of what she needed. A taste of what she wanted.

But common sense was an ugly reality that would not be ignored.

It was Olivia who leaned back. "Do you have condoms?"

He made a soft sound against her neck. His breath was hot on the exposed skin and then the cool night air licked at the damp trail he traced with his tongue. "It's part of my BII."

She smiled, nudging his lips with hers again. "BII?"

"Basic Issue Items. I brought a box of them into my orderly room for my joes to grab before they go out on the weekends." He tugged her closer, his hands dancing on her hips, his lips sucking gently on her ear. His voice whispered over her skin until she wasn't sure where he ended and she began. "You should have seen my first sergeant's face."

"Priceless?"

"I think he almost had a heart attack." He shifted until his hands were on either side of her neck. The car was cold against her back. "Can we please stop talking about work?" He caught her earlobe between his teeth, nipping gently.

"Yes please." Her fingers spasmed against his sides.

He burned her then, branded her with a fierce kiss that rocked her to her very center, chasing away the last vestige of the darkness that had haunted her for the majority of the afternoon. Sucking, sipping kisses as he rocked gently against her, showing her with his body what he wanted. What she wanted.

What she craved.

She wanted mindless abandon. Passion and fury.

She felt him everywhere, his body hard where she was soft, demanding where she was a needy, hungry thing.

"Ben." His name was a plea on her lips. A sensual demand.

He lifted his mouth from her neck. Cupped her cheeks in both hands. "Tell me what you want," he whispered against her mouth.

Last chance, her brain whispered. Last chance to reclaim her sanity and walk away from making a huge mistake with this man.

Instead, she curled her fingers around his neck. Pulled his mouth down to hers.

"You," she whispered. "I want you."

Chapter Fourteen

The door closed behind him. In the part of his brain that was still functioning, he heard the deadbolt click in the lock. Heard her keys hit the entryway table.

He'd followed her to her place. Letting her go, letting her get into her own vehicle had been fucking torture.

Because the riot he saw in her eyes made him step back from the ledge. He wanted her to be sure. Needed her to take that step toward him. Needed her to thread her fingers through his hair and kiss him. To remind him that this was okay. That it was okay for them to steal this quick moment of pleasure when everything was going to shit around them. He knew she was running from those packets, from work, from the cases that stood between them...

He wanted the same escape. Needed the human connection that would let him escape from the torment, the weight of the decisions he was supposed to make every single day.

The normalcy he felt right then was something he hadn't felt since he'd been pulled into the commander's office two weeks ago.

At that moment, he felt real and whole and alive.

There was no threat of abusing his power. No way to screw this up unless he underperformed.

He bit his lip, hard, needing the reminder that he could not screw this up. Something about her had drawn him to her, from that moment when he'd first plowed into her at the office.

She was fierce. She was loyal.

She was scarred.

The door closing was a finality. She could still change her mind. Still ask him to leave and keep her secrets, her scars to herself.

But Ben had trusted her. Tonight, it was her turn to trust him.

Fear slithered, cold and prickly, up her spine. She shivered, afraid to show him the physical reminders of her failure.

She hugged her arms around her waist, summoning her courage, shoving aside the doubt and the fear and the lingering insecurity that he would recoil from the marks on her body.

She felt the air stir as he stepped in front of her. Heat radiated off his body.

And then he cupped her face gently.

Urged her to open her eyes.

She tried to hide the fear, the uncertainty.

But one look in Ben's eyes and she knew it was futile. Because he saw the truth she struggled so desperately to hide.

He didn't know who had put the scars on Olivia Hale but they were there. He saw the ache in her eyes, saw the pain. He wanted to smooth that pain away but not if this wasn't what she wanted.

Her lips curled as she stepped into his space, hooking her index finger beneath his uniform jacket and into his belt. His stomach jerked beneath her touch.

"You're not getting cold feet, are you?" She lifted her face to his, rising up to press her lips to the edge of his. He nuzzled her lips gently.

"Wouldn't dream of it," he murmured against her mouth. He sucked on her bottom lip, cradling her face in his palms. Absently, he traced her temple with one thumb.

Her eyes fluttered closed. "That feels so good," she said.

Her voice whispered across his skin. His mouth went dry. He wondered when the last time was that she relaxed. Really relaxed.

And he had an idea. A way to get his hands on her beautiful body. A way to make her squirm beneath his touch. He pressed his lips to her forehead. "Where's your bedroom?"

"Down the hall. First door on the left."

He lifted her then, a single movement that pulled her flush against him, bringing her into intimate contact. Her breath was a gasp as she wrapped her thighs around his waist. She didn't protest when he padded across her carpet with his boots on. She simply nibbled along the edge of his jaw as he walked, her body sliding against his. Her teeth pinched the edge of his earlobe and sent an erotic thrill through his blood.

He crawled over her bed, lowering her to the gray and royal purple coverlet before he captured her mouth again. Her tongue danced with his, sliding along his and doing something that twisted up his insides.

She pushed up then, until he knelt over her. His breath caught in his throat when she slid her hands beneath his t-shirt and jacket, pulling his clothes free from his uniform trousers. "Olivia—"

She reached up, unzipping his jacket. Lifted his shirt to

reveal the dark edges of the black ink that started at the seam
of a wicked-looking scar. She wanted to ask. About the scar,
about the intricate tattoos that wound over his shoulder and
down his chest and the scars that looked like burns beneath
the black ink. He could see those questions in her eyes and
braced for them.

But she didn't. And he was grateful because he didn't
know what he'd say. Instead she pressed her lips to his stomach, just above the waist of his pants. Next to the narrow scar
on his abdomen. Her breath stirred the hair on his belly. It
tickled her lips and she nuzzled him there.

His stomach tightened and he tensed at the tenderness of
the gesture. Still, he didn't move as she lifted her lips away
from the sensitive skin near the scar and the ink. He couldn't
breathe as she unhooked his belt and flipped it open. Then
the buttons. One by one, she opened his pants, pressing her
lips to his skin, close to that damned scar that he hated and
resented and wished he could carve from his skin.

She ran her fingers over the hard edges of his hip bones
and Ben's control nearly snapped. He eased back, out of
reach of her hands and her teasing lips.

"We're going to have a stunning disappointment to this
evening if you don't stop," he said, taking her hands and lifting them over her head as he laid her back on the bed.

"Coward," she whispered, but there was nothing but sensual heat in her words as she surrendered to his touch.

"Yep." There was no shame in his answer. "My ego really
couldn't handle having a misfire right now."

"As opposed to some other, more opportune time?"

He laughed and pulled her jacket open. The zipper made
a rasping sound as he slid it open, revealing the concave hollow of her belly beneath the same tan t-shirt he wore. "There
really isn't a good time for that," he said.

He framed her stomach with his palms, sliding them higher,

higher, pushing her shirt up, exposing the edge of her bra. It was functional, pale beige in soft, soft cotton and he'd never seen anything sexier. He tugged and she shifted, rocking and twisting until she'd shrugged out of her uniform top and t-shirt.

And waited.

Time was a frozen, shimmering thing as his eyes traced over the scars on her body, clearly visible now that she was stripped bare.

Her breath locked in her throat and it took everything she had to keep from crossing her arms over her stomach.

He dropped to his knees in front of her.

Cradled her ribs gently in his hands.

"Tell me about these," he whispered.

She pressed her lips together in a flat line, her eyes stinging as the memories struggled to escape.

"My father," she said. "He died from a mixture of painkillers and alcohol." She looked away.

"He hit you," Ben whispered. She closed her eyes, unwilling to see the pity in his eyes at her painful admission.

The silence was heavy and thick and filled with so many questions. Neither of them moved.

Then she felt it. The gentle slide of his thumb over the largest scar on her rib. A gentle kiss where his thumb had been. A shiver ran through her as he traced the scar with the tip of his tongue.

She summoned her courage and looked down.

Her gaze collided with his and the patient desire she saw looking back at her slammed into her. Her breath shook in her lungs. Trembled before it escaped.

"That's nice," she whispered when she could speak. She scraped her fingernails through his scalp. She tugged and urged his mouth to hers. And she lost herself in the powerful arousal in that kiss.

*   *   *

When she kissed him, he forgot his own name. "Those pants have got to go," she said, using her boots to push them down his hips.

He wanted them gone, wanted to feel the sensual slide of skin on skin. Wanted to feel her thighs wrap around his waist as he slid inside her and watch her face as he started to move.

The waist of his underwear caught on his erection. "Ow, stop!" he said with a laugh. He lurched backward, his body missing the heat from her skin. "I'll do it. Before you unman me."

She sat up and laughed, unlacing her own boots and shucking her own uniform pants. It was strange sitting on her bed, pulling his boots off as she stripped off her own uniform. Everything about this felt surreal. Strangely rational and sexual all at once.

He'd never imagined he would see her relax or that it would be his touch that pushed away her stiff exterior to reveal the sensual woman underneath. She was a live wire, complex and sinfully erotic standing there in her panties and bra. He had the sudden urge to see her in his t-shirt. He wanted to see the edge of the fabric brushing against her upper thighs. He wanted to push it higher, to reveal the sweetness at the center of her.

Instead he simply sat for a moment, reveling in this soft and sexy side of Olivia Hale that unlocked something he'd thought he'd put away for good.

This was something secret. Something special. This was something she would deny in the harsh light of day because it didn't fit into her personal save-the-world narrative. But right then, Ben could live with being something secret.

He wanted this woman.

He leaned down to shuck his own boots. Her arms slid around his waist from behind. Her palms folded against his heart, beating its fierce, wild rhythm beneath her hands. His skin burned him where she touched him over the black tattoos that covered his heart, and he braced for the questions.

They didn't come. The intimate gesture was nothing more than a simple touch. A touch from one lover to another.

Ben paused for a moment. Savored the feel of her breath on his back. The softness of her hair on his spine. The casual weight of her arms around his waist was an erotic comfort. There was a warmth in that touch that unnerved him.

This was something powerful. And he'd be damned if he was going to screw it up.

His back was smooth and hard against her exposed skin, his skin hot against hers. She folded her hands together over his heart and rested her cheek against the solid wall of his back. He stilled. Then his hands came up to close over hers. It was a quiet gesture. A connection in the midst of casual sex that spoke of something deeper.

Something she wasn't ready to acknowledge.

She pressed her lips along the edge of the black art that ran the entire line of his spine. Felt him stop breathing as her tongue flicked over a spot. She scraped her teeth over his back and his hands tightened over hers. A surge of power rocked through her as the man trembled beneath her touch. She licked again.

He dropped his head back, exposing his throat. She pushed up onto her knees, licking his throat. She sucked gently at the edge of his jaw, then ran her tongue along the sensitive tip of his ear. A gentle tasting. He let her take the lead, let her set the pace, and she fell a little harder for the man in her bed.

Monday at work would be awkward but she'd deal with that then.

He released her hands as she slid around his body and

into his lap. His hands scooped her bottom and pulled her closer.

"No regrets, Olivia?" he whispered.

She traced her fingertips over his cheeks. "No." She bussed her lips against his. "I need this," she breathed.

He stood and crawled onto the bed, lowering her beneath him. He braced himself on his elbows. "I want to make this good for you."

Her lips curled of their own accord. "As opposed to just bending me over and having your way with me?"

He closed his eyes and dropped his forehead to hers. The laugh tore out of him and shook through his big body. "I cannot believe you just said that," he said when he could breathe again.

"You're not the only one who can make jokes," she said.

"I like your sense of humor when you're mostly naked," he whispered. "It's so fucking sexy."

She closed her eyes, savoring the feel of his fingers tracing her cheeks. It made her feel cherished. Protected.

Valued.

"It's better for me at work if people are wary of me."

"I think you're scary at work." He brushed his nose against hers. "But after tonight, I'm just going to picture you like this."

"As long as you don't tell anyone." She licked his bottom lip then captured it in her teeth with a gentle tug. "Can we stop talking?"

He traced tiny kisses over her lips, her jaw. He captured her hands, sliding them up over her head. Held them with one of his hands while he explored her body with slow, languid strokes.

Who would have known Ben Teague was a thoughtful lover? But somewhere along the line, thoughtful transformed to heat and heat to passion. Her blood sang with his touch.

Arched beneath his lips as his fingertips slid down her arms and over her ribs.

He slipped her bra free and lifted it away from her body.

And watched his eyes darken when he saw the scars tracing over her ribs and down her right side.

Her mouth went dry as his gaze took in the damage to her body. "I've thought about getting a tattoo to cover them," she whispered.

His fingers danced over the mottled flesh, the gnarled ramifications of a failed decision.

"Tell me," he said. His voice was deadly calm, steel beneath ice.

She cradled his face in her hands. "It's not important," she whispered.

He opened his mouth to protest and she kissed him. Claimed his tongue, his mouth, his breath. Stole coherent thought and the rage that she saw building in his eyes.

They were new lovers. The anger in his eyes shouldn't have been there. Not this quickly.

But Ben had a strange sense of justice. He was the kind of man who would lie to let a kid get a benefit he'd been a few weeks from earning. It might have been wrong to the letter of the law but in Ben's world, it was just.

In Olivia's, it was enough that he cared. For his men. For his unit.

For her.

There was care in his touch now as his fingers slid down her body, hooking in her panties and sliding them down her hips.

He urged her onto her back, using teeth and tongue and fingers to coax her body to heights she'd never flown. And when he kissed her where she ached for him, she nearly came off the bed. He held her, his hands on her hips as he feasted on her body.

It was only when she shuddered and tried to scoot away

that he relented, a satisfied male smile on his lips even as he continued to stroke her slick, swollen heat. "Like that?"

"Oh, you definitely know how to make someone forget a bad day," she said, shivering when he slid one finger inside her. "Oh!"

He kissed her as he stroked her body. Kissed away the darkness, the sadness, the sense of feeling nothing she ever did would be good enough.

He wanted this to be good for her. He'd known that when he'd agreed to follow her home. But as he slipped between her thighs, capturing her hands, threading her fingers with his as he found her center and slowly filled her, he realized he wanted more than just a casual encounter.

She made sexy noises in her throat. He kissed away the pain she caused when she bit down on her lip to keep from crying out. And he urged her to ride the pleasure. "Don't fight it," he whispered. "Let go."

She did. And it stunned him and dragged him under with her.

It was the tipping of the bed that woke her.

Her body hummed with latent arousal as she came fully awake. The sheets were warm on her skin where they wrapped around her body.

But it was the emptiness of the bed beside her that caught her attention.

Ben sat on the edge. She didn't have to see his hands to see that he was pulling his boots on.

He glanced over at her when she sat up. He leaned into her and pressed his mouth to hers. No hurt. No acrimony.

But something less than what they'd just shared.

"I can't sleep," he confessed against her mouth. He lowered his forehead to hers. "I didn't want to wake you."

"It's okay," she said. She lifted her hand to let it rest on his opposite shoulder. Where the black ink bordered on clean, hot skin. "Do you always have trouble sleeping?" she asked.

He looked away. "Yeah."

"I think I can cure your insomnia," she said.

He glanced back over at her. "Oh yeah?"

Her breath caught in her throat as she let the sheet slip low over the swell of her breast. Her nipples peaked at the sensation. They were sensitive and sore from his mouth, his touch, but still she wanted more.

He lifted one finger. Traced the outline of her nipple over the sheet warmed from her body heat.

His gaze locked on hers as he continued to stroke her gently. He tugged the sheet down, down over the stiff flesh.

She had never done this. Never looked into a man's eyes with his hands on her body. Never watched his eyes darken and his breath catch as he touched her.

He slid his thumb over the bottom swell of her breast. A teasing touch, meant to torment.

It was Olivia who moved.

Who crawled into his lap and straddled his uniform-covered hips.

"Don't go," she whispered against his mouth.

And then there was no further thought.

Chapter Fifteen

Olivia looked at the packets on her passenger seat and sighed heavily. It was going to be a long week. Maybe if she could get notes done up on all the cases, she could make a dent in the work. She didn't know why she kept lying to herself. She was never going to get caught up. Wasn't that what her old boss always said? Work will always be there.

She smiled. She certainly didn't have time for any more distractions named Ben Teague.

He'd left later that night. For a little while, she'd forgotten—at least until long after he'd gone—the darkness she'd been hoping to avoid. He'd made her laugh. Who laughed during sex?

Ben Teague, apparently. And now she did. She had no idea how he'd done it but he'd erased all of the darkness from her life with his tender, skilled fingers.

And she'd enjoyed every minute of it. It had been a hard thing not calling him over the weekend. A terrible temptation she struggled to contain.

And now she had to hide the sexual energy that prickled over her skin just thinking about him. She might as well wear a neon sign over her head that announced she and Ben Teague were lovers.

As she walked into his motor pool, needing to touch base with him about Foster and a few of the other packets, she put the stunning night she'd spent with him in a box and locked it away. She could meet up with all of the commanders and catch up with any actions from over the weekend.

She scooped up her packets and grabbed her hat as reality crowded out the memories of Saturday night and pushed away the lingering goodness of the memories.

It hadn't taken long after Ben had left for the hard reality of her job to come crashing back. She'd awakened Sunday morning, her sheets soaked with sweat from the fear that she might fail to convince the commander to act. Her scars throbbed with the memory. She focused and tried to not let her emotions get the better of her.

She wasn't usually nervous about cases but Ben's words had haunted her into the night as she tried to chase elusive sleep. She took a deep breath and pushed away the memories of the nightmares and the anxiety. Olivia needed to get to work on the rest of the caseload stacking up in her office. She would not fail this time.

She wondered about the woman's child, the only survivor from that hellish nightmare years ago that Olivia had tried and failed to end. The little girl with huge brown eyes and a sadness that had shattered Olivia's heart into broken, jagged pieces. Ultimately, these decisions weren't hers. She wasn't a commander; she was an *advisor* to the commanders, and there was a distinct difference.

She built the cases and made recommendations. Guys like Ben had to make the decisions.

But Ben had planted a seed of doubt and it wormed into her brain and nestled up to her ear, whispering insidious things.

What if she was wrong about Escoberra? God, but she wanted to be. For Ben's sake. For Hailey. God, she wanted to be wrong.

She took a deep breath and wove through the vehicles in the motor pool until she found Bandit Company's guidon.

And in front of the company was Bandit Company's commander.

She had to admit that Ben, standing in front of his forma-tion, presented a powerful figure. But it wasn't just the power of his position that attracted her to him. There were scars on his body, scars on his soul that he hid with a quick smile and an easy grin.

She'd wanted to ask but she hadn't wanted to break the mood with a troubled jaunt down memory lane.

And he'd let her dodge the painful questions, too. Ben was a good man. A smart ass, but the kind of man who couldn't stand to see people around him hurting. She'd seen that side of him when he'd asked her not to turn him in about Zittoro's packet.

That took audacity, especially in the face of a battalion commander who wanted to clean out his formation. Ben was willing to stand on principle.

Men like him were rare, too rare.

She didn't know what it said about her that she'd willingly fallen into bed with him just two short weeks after he'd first tried coaxing a smile out of her.

She wondered at the man beneath the jokes, though. Standing in front of that formation, she saw him cracking comments to the skinny kid next to him. She smiled and shook her head. He never stopped.

She wanted to know more, though, about the man who'd avoided responsibility but now seemed to be stepping into his new role well enough.

"You're staring, ma'am," a deep voice said.

She cocked a grin at Reza. "I thought you were with Emily today?"

"I had an appointment earlier. Emily went with me.

Now I'm at work, trying to get my feet back under me," Reza said. He folded his arms over his chest as formation continued.

"How's that going?" she asked.

"Slower than I'd like." He sniffed. "I'll get through it, though. You, on the other hand, might want to stop looking like you're undressing Teague with your eyes. You're so fucking obvious."

She pressed her lips to hide the smile that spread slowly across her mouth as embarrassed heat crept up her neck. She was at ease with this man because of his relationship with her friend.

"That obvious?" she asked.

"Pretty much," Reza said lightly. "I've known Teague a long time. He's a strange one but he's also a man I'd have in a firefight with me any time. I trust him."

She looked up at the big man next to her, amazed that a man like him had managed to find happiness with her friend. Amazed at her own comfort around him.

"He's a good guy," she said softly. "Command is going to be hard on him."

"If you're doing it right, command is hard for everyone." Reza reached for her, squeezing her shoulder gently. "And I suspect Teague is going to do it right, no matter how much he may protest to the contrary."

Ben was having a hell of a time concentrating on the standard Monday morning briefings. He stood in formation listening to the sergeant major drone on and on about some ruck march up some mountain somewhere. There was beer involved but Ben couldn't really see how that was a good thing. Dehydration and mountain climbing seemed to be a combination that never ended well, but hey, Ben wasn't about to judge.

He just wasn't interested in participating.

No, his mind was definitely circling back to last Saturday evening when he'd curled around the beautiful Olivia Hale.

He'd wanted to press her on those vicious scars running down her ribs but she'd been determined to brush off his concern.

He'd let it go in the name of keeping the peace but Ben wasn't easily dissuaded.

Somehow he'd managed not to call her after leaving her place. He'd thought about it. Several times. And each time he'd considered picking up his phone, he'd set it back down again. He was suddenly as inept as a thirteen-year-old boy. He had no idea if he should call her, or if he should wait.

Dear Lord in Heaven, when had he lost his balls? Had he left them at her place that night? What was it about this woman that drove him to distraction to the point that the following night, he'd been trying to get some paperwork done and all he could think about was what she might have been doing at the same time.

Damn.

A tap on his shoulder made him turn around. Olivia was in his motor pool. Standing between two tanks, she looked positively tiny. Her hair was pinned up. Her uniform neat.

Not a hint of the woman he'd made gasp and cry out his name through clenched teeth as he'd touched her.

Her expression was polished glass. Once he would have been intimidated by the cool, distant expression but he caught the glint of awareness in her eyes. Just a hint, and if he hadn't been looking for it, he might have missed it. "Captain Teague, do you have a moment?"

Captain Teague. He wasn't a moron. He knew they were around a thousand pairs of prying eyes. Still, he wanted to hear his name on her lips again.

Damn it, he needed to figure out what the hell he'd done with his balls. He cleared his throat. "Sure, ma'am."

It felt strange calling her "ma'am," but he'd be damned if he'd give away what had happened between them the other night. It was nobody's business what the two of them did on their off-duty time.

Ben wanted to do it again. He had a sudden dark and vibrant fantasy of taking her inside his Bradley and stripping that stiff uniform off her body.

"What's up?" he said when they'd moved away from the mass of humanity.

He watched her closely as she pulled out the files she needed.

"Child Protective Services called." It was a long moment before she looked up. "They want to know if we're going to follow up on the Escoberra case."

Ben swallowed the sudden lump in his throat. "Can you try that in English? Small words, maybe, no more than four syllables each?"

His joke felt flat and listless.

She smiled and it was more than just a grin at his crack. It was sympathy. She knew this was a tough choice for him, but she asked him about it anyway.

He took a deliberate step backward. She was asking him to do his job and right then? It involved prosecuting someone he was close to. Someone who'd saved his ass on more than one occasion. "What does that mean?"

"It means we can prosecute him under military law instead of waiting for the civilians to do it," she said. She took a step closer, needing to offer comfort despite the harsh reality of her recommendation.

Ben shoved his hands in his pockets. "Do I want to do that?"

"Normally, I would say no. But here?" She hesitated. "If CPS closes their investigation, there's no case," she said.

Ben rubbed his hand over his mouth, his heart pounding in his chest.

"It means you don't have to prosecute."

He looked down at her then, her eyes hidden beneath dark sunglasses. "I wouldn't think you'd be happy about this," he said. His words were thick. Rough.

"I'm not." She swallowed. "But I trust you to make the right decision about your men."

Ben took a deep breath, meeting her gaze. A quiet nod passed between them, tacit acknowledgment of things better left unsaid. They'd talk later. Away from prying eyes.

"Thank you," he said when he could speak. It was more trust than he deserved.

God, but he hoped he was right about Escoberra. Because that night at the hospital was haunting him. Tormenting him with what ifs.

What if he was wrong? What if Carmen was simply protecting her husband instead of loving him too much?

Olivia trusted him to make the right decision.

So why did he no longer trust himself?

Ben was in his office, wading through three hundred and twelve unread e-mails. He seriously considered doing a control-a, delete and emptying all of them in the trash but somehow he didn't think that the XO or the ops officer would approve of his actions.

There was nothing in his office that made it officially his. He hadn't made time to move things in and honestly, he wasn't sure when he'd get time to do that.

It wasn't important, except that the space didn't feel like his.

He still felt out of place and unsettled sitting behind the commander's desk. He stared at an e-mail that embodied everything about this job that he'd hated and feared. It was a request from Major Denis for an update on all of his legal actions.

How was he supposed to do his job when he'd deployed with half the guys in the company? It wasn't even that he didn't want to believe they could do bad things—some of the guys like Foster did stupid things but they were just that— stupid. It didn't mean they should lose their careers over them.

It was acknowledging that any loyalty he'd had to his men was now gone and that the rank he'd always said didn't matter now stood between him and his longtime friends.

On the list of things he was worried about, that was at the top, right along with returning to combat in less than eight months with barely sixty percent of the soldiers he needed. About half of the soldiers he did have were brand new troopers—either folks finally forced out of Korea or out of hiding from other posts, or brand new kids straight out of boot camp.

And he still had to clean up the non-deployers he did have. Starting with Foster and going downhill from there.

He clicked through, filing the e-mails where they belonged, unable to actually concentrate.

There was a quiet knock on his door. He looked up as Reza sat down on the couch, kicking his feet up on Ben's desk. "Rough day, huh?"

Reza tossed a sleeve of chocolate chip cookies onto Ben's desk. Ben shot him a wry look and opened the package. "You're going to enable me now?" he asked.

Reza grinned. "I've found them to be a deeply therapeutic substitute for alcohol."

Ben stopped chewing. "Really?"

"No not really. At this rate, I'm going to bust height and weight standards if I keep gaining weight." Reza looked at him silently. "Want to tell me what's prompted this cookie bender?"

Ben stared down at the sleeve, then set it on his desk. "Escoberra's at the hospital getting his mental health evaluation." There was deep wariness in Ben's words.

"That was fast," Reza said.

"Emily helped get him in sooner." He took a deep breath, looking up at his long time friend. "I still can't wrap my brain around him doing this to Hailey."

Reza was quiet for a long time. "I haven't seen too many cases where Child Protective Services gets involved when there isn't something going on."

"How many cases have you been involved with?"

"A few over the years." Reza shifted on the couch that Marshall hadn't taken with him, dropping his feet to the floor in front of him. "They're not perfect by a long shot, but they're people doing the best they can."

"When did you become so forgiving of the bureaucracy?"

"Remember Tag?"

"Tagalogue? Sure." Tag was a heavy kid from somewhere deep in Louisiana. He'd married his high school sweetheart who Ben and Reza had suspected was related to him in a not-too-distant way.

"Well, it turned out that her uncle was coming to visit a little too often. He would watch their kids when they'd go out on dates or whatever. Tag started to feel like something wasn't right but didn't want to piss off his wife. He got a call from the on-post daycare that sparked an investigation."

The cookie in Ben's mouth suddenly tasted like cardboard. He spit it into the trash. "Tell me their kid is okay. He was a little bit older, wasn't he?"

"Tag's kid was six when it happened. The uncle hadn't done any permanent damage but he'd been working up to it." Reza cleared his throat roughly, rubbing the back of his neck as if to scrub away the memories. "I guess my point is that maybe CPS isn't blowing smoke up your ass."

"Fuck man, but Escoberra?" Ben covered his mouth with his hands. "There's got to be a piece of this that's missing. CPS dropped the case. Nothing makes any damn sense."

Reza shrugged. "I don't know what to tell you. I don't want to believe our boyo could do that but I don't know."

"I was there. At the hospital that night when Hailey was there. I saw Escoberra." The pictures of Hailey's back would haunt Ben forever. He'd seen some terrible things over the years but this? This was somehow worse. "I've never seen a man look more devastated," Ben said softly. His heart threatened to break in his chest.

Reza shifted again, his eyes darkening. "No man should hurt a child like that," he said softly.

"I know," Ben admitted.

"War changes people."

"But this? Whipping a kid that he loves like his own daughter?" Ben scrubbed his hands over his face.

"When you're presented with the facts, you'll have to deal with them. Whatever they are." Reza looked up at him. "Because you're not just another soldier now, Ben. You're a commander and these decisions come with the job."

Silence stretched between them. Uncomfortable and filled with terrible choices and ugly truths.

Finally Reza cleared his throat. "And you have to figure out what you can live with."

Chapter Sixteen

Sorren walked into Ben's office a bit later and closed the door behind him. "We're going to have problems, sir."

Ben closed his laptop and gave Sorren his undivided attention. "What kind of problems?"

"Monica Glass has been calling Foster since he got out of jail."

Ben took a deep breath and folded his hands in front of him. "Isn't this the woman who had him arrested in the first place?"

"Yep." Sorren sat down on the couch, draping his arm across the back. His fingers drummed angrily on the back.

"Shit." Ben pulled out the limited information he had on the night Foster had been arrested. The serious incident report had remarkably little detail. "She's the damn reason he's been in jail to begin with. Didn't she call the police when her father and Foster started fighting?"

"Yep. And now Foster's out of jail so she's blowing up his phone and mine," Sorren said. "She keeps calling and telling me she doesn't feel safe with him out but he's telling me she won't stop calling him. I don't know who to believe."

Ben cupped his chin in his hand and wished he still had

some of those cookies from earlier. He'd thrown them away when they'd lost their taste and one of the orderly room clerks had already grabbed his trash. He was going to have to put a stop to that. He could take out his own damn trash.

"Wasn't her dad a first sergeant before he became a cop?" Ben asked. "She's supposed to be one of the well-adjusted ones."

"Not if Daddy was too busy fighting the war to be a daddy," Sorren said. There was a little too much bitterness in Sorren's words for Ben to ignore.

"Tell me about this daughter of yours." Ben asked abruptly. There was no wedding ring on Sorren's left hand. No faint mark where one had been recently, either.

"Been divorced since I was twenty-two," Sorren said roughly. "I've got a fifteen-year-old daughter." He reached into his wallet and flipped it open.

Ben leaned over and saw a beautiful girl with dark hair and her father's eyes.

"Man, she's beautiful." He glanced up at Sorren. "You sure she's yours? Cause you're ugly as all get out."

Sorren flipped Ben off as he leaned back. "Fuck you, sir."

"Seriously, she's beautiful."

"Thanks. I've already talked to her mother about getting a shotgun." It was almost funny watching the big man squirm talking about his daughter.

"Foster's right. She's already dating, isn't she?" Ben said with a grin.

"Don't say horrible things like that." Sorren visibly flinched, and shoved his wallet back into his pocket.

Ben's grin widened and he kicked his feet up onto the desk. "Dude, there is no way I would touch your daughter if I was a sixteen-year-old boy. You're terrifying."

"Especially not if I threatened that whatever you do to her, I do to you," Sorren said. His expression relaxed into a sad smile as he stared at the picture. "But I've been gone most of her life and I don't get that time back. I worry about what my not being around did to her."

Ben had no idea what to say. He knew what it felt like to have a parent be more soldier than parent. His mother wore her uniform like a shield. She'd never had time for him after his dad died—unless it involved interfering in his career where he didn't want her.

Finally, he broke the silence. "She looks like she's doing okay."

Sorren's eyes darkened and he rubbed his hand over his mouth. "We had her in a hospital last summer. She cuts herself."

Ben stilled. "What do you mean, cuts herself?"

"Like not trying to kill herself. She just…cuts. She hides it. Really well, actually."

"How did you find out?" Ben asked quietly. His heart hurt for his first sergeant's pain and the helplessness written on the big man's face.

"The school nurse called Melanie," he said. "Let me tell you, that was a shitty Red Cross message to get in the middle of Mosul."

"Were you able to go home?"

Sorren shook his head. There was nothing, nothing worse than being called in the war zone and not being able to go home.

Carmen had called Escoberra once. Just once. She'd been in a car accident. Escoberra had nearly lost his mind when the company commander had told him that he couldn't go home because there were no life-threatening injuries.

Sorren said, "Nah. We had major operations going in Tal Afar. And, to quote my battalion sergeant major, she didn't try to kill herself. I could deal with it when I got home."

Ben swore softly. "Are you fucking kidding me?"

Sorren shrugged. "That's the way it goes sometimes. She's better now."

"You have my permission to drop your retirement paperwork," Ben said. His throat wasn't working right all of a sudden. He'd never wanted kids, never figured he'd be the kind of dad who could raise stable, well-adjusted little humans. But if he did have them? What a terrible thing, to find out your kid was hurting herself.

Guilt damn near choked Ben, and she wasn't even his daughter. He looked over at Sorren and saw behind the rough exterior. For just a moment, Sorren's shields fell and he was just a man, a father who wasn't living up to his own expectations of what a dad should be.

Finally Sorren looked over at Ben.

"I'll see this deployment through," Sorren said. "But yeah, then I'm done. I think I'm going to go home. Try to be a dad to a kid who doesn't need me anymore."

"They always need you," Ben said. Maybe that was a lie but Sorren didn't need to know that Ben rarely called his own mother. He'd stopped needing her a long time ago.

His dad had died in the first Gulf War. Ben could still remember the day the phone call had come in. Because his mom had been a soldier, they'd done the notification differently.

It was the first and only time Ben had ever seen his mother cry. She'd buried his dad and thrown herself into work. Ben had been a kid but it hadn't taken him long to figure out he'd lost both parents that day.

Mom was a full bird colonel now on some staff in Washington.

And Ben? The only reason Ben was a soldier was because he'd wanted to feel closer to his dad.

Instead, it had driven the final wedge into his relationship with his mother.

Sorren cleared his throat roughly. "So what are we going to do about Foster?"

Ben sighed. "I have no fucking idea. But I know just who to ask."

Olivia's desk phone rang. She hung her head for a moment and counted to three. Damn it, it was always this way. Right before the end of the duty day, when she was planning on sneaking out and working on the rest of the files from home, the phone rang.

And it was going to be something that kept her at work for a very long time. She knew it. Because it always was.

It was never an easy call. Never something that could be answered in a five-minute conversation.

The phone continued to ring.

Olivia swallowed and picked it up. "Major Hale."

"Hey, it's Ben."

Something warm wrapped around her at the sound of his voice. "Hi." Even knowing this was most likely not a social call, just the sound of his voice eased some of the tension in her shoulders.

"So I've got a problem."

She smiled softly. "Why else would you be calling me on a Monday afternoon?"

Silence hung on the line a moment too long and Olivia wondered if she'd crossed into the wrong line. Or if she was on speakerphone. Now that would be terribly awkward.

He cleared his throat roughly. "Ah, yeah, so can we talk about that later?"

She laughed at the awkward heat in his voice. "There's someone in the office with you, isn't there?"

"Yep." He sounded strangled.

She relented but a slow smile spread across her mouth. There was a strange sort of power in knowing she could make him squirm. "What's up?"

"The woman who called the cops on Foster keeps calling

him and won't stop. Foster says he doesn't want to see her but she's told my first sergeant that she feels threatened."

Olivia sat down and started jotting down notes. "He can't see her. I need you to give him a no-contact order for the next fourteen days. After that, we'll need to reassess."

"What about the fact that she's calling him?"

"He needs to not answer and tell you or the first sergeant every time she calls him. No text messages, no answers from friends. He's completely forbidden from contacting her."

She heard his hand cover the mic and his muffled voice.

"Okay. That's all?"

"Does he live in the barracks or off post?"

"Barracks."

"Okay, he also needs to be restricted to post as well." She made another note. "All of this is to show the chain of command is doing due diligence to keep the victim safe."

Ben sighed roughly. "Okay, got it. Restricted to post, no-contact order. Am I missing anything?"

"No. Make sure you do it in writing on the appropriate form, okay?"

"Sure." He paused. "Thanks."

He sounded exhausted. Beaten down. "Are you okay?" she asked softly.

"Have to be, don't I?"

The phone went silent in her ear. She sat there for a moment, tapping the phone against her cheek absently, wishing there was some way to just stop the world for a little while. Just to take a breath and let everything fall away. Not forever. But long enough to really catch a breath.

Command was a marathon, not a sprint.

And Ben had a long time to go before he approached the finish line.

* * *

"Bring him in, Top," Ben said, tossing his phone onto his desk.

"What are we doing?" Sorren asked. The big first sergeant didn't move.

Ben straightened the chaos on his desk, needing to keep his hands occupied. "No-contact order and restricting him to post." Ben logged on to his computer and searched for the forms he needed.

"Let's see how he handles this," Sorren said. "But I have a feeling you're going to want to shackle him to the CQ desk after we're done with him."

Ben frowned as his fingers flew over the keyboard. "I take it Bell County doesn't agree with him?"

Sorren's smile was grim. "Not exactly. He's a little cranky."

"Lovely." Ben printed the forms. "Well, hopefully, he remembers that he's still a soldier and keeps his head out of his ass."

"Yeah, sure, and monkeys might fly out of mine," Sorren said flatly.

Ben laughed so hard his ribs hurt. "All right, stop that. You make me laugh and this whole thing is going to go to shit in a heartbeat."

Sorren offered a two-fingered salute. "Roger that, sir." He stuck his head out of the door. "Report to the commander."

Ben took a deep breath and focused on stuffing down the violent emotions twisting and churning inside him, trying to divorce himself from the situation. He wanted to pretend that this was someone else. Not Foster. Not the kid who had dragged him from a burning Humvee when he'd had his bell rung and couldn't figure out how to open the goddamned door.

Foster walked in and stopped three paces off the desk. He saluted sharply. "Sir, Sergeant Foster reporting as ordered."

No, this kid was not the same guy Ben had gone to war with. The kid Ben knew had been rough and ready. Rugged and always ready to scrap. Hands that had once been steady now twitched by his side.

Something was deeply, deeply wrong.

"Sergeant Foster, I am restricting you to post—"

"Oh, come on, Teague. That is such bullshit!"

Sorren reacted before Ben's brain had adjusted to the fact that his friend had just cussed him out. It was something Ben wouldn't have blinked at had they been out partying.

But Ben's first sergeant objected. Strenuously.

Sorren got an inch from Foster's face. The big man towered over Foster until Foster bent backward and had to take a step to keep from falling onto his ass.

"If you ever even think about talking to my commander that way again, I will make your life a living, breathing hell," Sorren whispered.

Shit, even Ben was intimidated.

And a boy dared date this man's daughter?

Foster, however, was not cowed. "Fuck you, First Sarn't. Put your hands on me and I'm calling the cops."

Sorren's smile was malicious and cold and dared him to do just that. "Please do. Because that worked out so well for you the last time you were involved with them, didn't it?"

"That's horse shit! Come on, Teague, you know me. It was just a stupid bar fight."

Ben swallowed the sudden dryness in his mouth. "I know but I don't have a choice. She's made the allegation that she doesn't feel safe around you. I've got to keep you away from her."

"Goddamn Monica," he mumbled. Foster had the decency to flush a deep, crimson red. "So I partied a little too hard, but she's just pissed."

Sorren damn near came unglued but Ben shook his head quickly.

Foster snorted. "You suck, you know that?"

"I don't have anything to say to that one," Ben said. And he didn't, because it was true. This was the ultimate violation of loyalty. He should have found a way to protect Foster. "As soon as the time period is up, you can go about your business. But in the mean time, you're restricted to post and you're under a no-contact order with Monica Glass. You can't call her, text her, nothing. Absolutely no contact."

Foster's shoulders slumped as Ben spoke.

"Don't make this any harder on yourself than it needs to be," Ben said. "Do what you're supposed to do and everything will shake out like it's supposed to."

Ben took a deep breath. And asked the question that physically *hurt* as it crossed his lips. "Foster, are you using?"

Foster looked up at him. The muscles in his neck quivered. Confusion blasted across his features as he searched for an answer to Ben's question.

His silence damned him before he ever spoke a word. "I plead the fifth," Foster said.

"I can command refer you," Ben said.

Foster looked between Ben and the first sergeant. "You haven't read me my rights," Foster said.

Ben looked at his first sergeant then back at Foster. "Which means that nothing you say can be used against you right now."

It was a risk, a terrible one. But he trusted Foster, had trusted him downrange, trusted him back home.

If Foster was honest with him, Ben would stand by him. He could do that. He could use the power of his position to make a difference instead of throwing everyone out of the army.

"I started using on the weekends," Foster whispered. "I just ... I just needed to not feel so tired all the time."

"What are you doing?" Sorren asked, his voice rough and quiet. Steady.

"Adderall."

Jessica Scott

"Jesus," Ben whispered. Meth—Adderall—was a fucking epidemic around Fort Hood these days.

"I...I don't want to use but I don't know how to stop," Foster said. "And since Sloban..."

Ben saw the confusion flicker across Sorren's face. "Sloban was addicted to meth. He killed himself a few weeks ago when the army denied his disability."

Reza had been there when it happened. No one had been unaffected by Sloban's death.

Foster, though, had taken it worse than most.

"Do you believe me?" Foster whispered.

Ben searched for an answer. Because he honestly didn't know. He wanted to believe him. He'd known Foster for too long. He knew what kind of soldier he was.

Sorren spoke up, cutting into whatever piss poor answer Ben could scrounge up. "It doesn't matter if he believes you or not, Foster," Sorren said. "He's got to uphold good order and discipline."

Foster looked back at Ben. "If I self-refer, can I go to rehab like Sarn't Ike?" There was hope, bleak and faint in his eyes.

Ben didn't look at his first sergeant. He knew what the right answer was. He knew what the smart, army answer was—throw the kid out and let him worry about it on his own.

But Ben had never been that kind of commander.

"Let me make some phone calls," he said quietly.

Relief washed over Foster and the shaking in his limbs was visible now. He approached the desk and took the pen Ben offered. His hands trembled as he signed the first of two documents—the no-contact order and the counseling statement.

Then he saluted weakly and left.

"We need NCOs checking on him all weekend, Top," Ben said softly.

"Already did the roster," Sorren said. He started to follow Foster out, then paused by the doorway. "That was a hell of a risk, sir."

"I know what you're going to say, Top," Ben said.

"No, I don't think you do," Sorren said. He closed the door behind him.

In the silence of his office, Ben felt the weight of command settle around his shoulders again, a little heavier and a lot, lot colder.

Chapter Seventeen

Y ou awake, sir?"

Ben blinked at the phone that was somehow still in his hand and squinted. He was slouched down on his couch, a half-empty beer tipping dangerously between his legs. He hadn't even changed out of his uniform before he'd fallen asleep.

But he'd been asleep. Actually asleep instead of floating in the dead space between sleeping and waking that usually left him more tired than anything. "What time is it?"

Sorren mumbled something that sounded like "god-damned sissy" but Ben couldn't be sure. "It's barely ten p.m. You need to get up and meet me at Ropers."

Ben frowned and sat up, rubbing his eyes with the heel of his hand. "Why?"

"Because Wookie just sent me a text and if we don't get our happy asses down there ASAP, we're going to have half a platoon in jail by morning."

Ben blinked as his first sergeant's words sank in. Then a slow smile spread across his lips. "So we're going to break up a bar fight?"

"That's the short answer. How long before you can meet me?"

"I'll be there in fifteen."

"Hurry up. I need you there to give out direct orders and shit."

"What, I don't get to get my hands dirty in the fight?" That wasn't any fun, and fun was in short supply in Ben's life these days.

"If I do my job, there won't be a goddamned fight," Sorren snapped.

Ben stretched and grinned at getting under Sorren's skin. "Don't get your panties in a bunch, Top. I'm on my way." He tossed the rest of the beer in the trash, glad he'd only had the little bit.

The night was definitely going to get interesting. He pulled on a pair of jeans and an old t-shirt and headed out, wondering just what he was going to have to explain to his battalion commander in the morning.

Olivia set the wine glass down on her coffee table and happened to catch a glimpse at her watch. Approaching midnight.

"Lovely," she said to the stacks of files next to the wine. The wine had failed to do its job of unwinding her, which meant that she was wide awake and looking with irritation at the state of the packets in front of her.

The fact that these were the packets deemed "closest to completion" by the new company commanders was annoying at best. Missing required documents. Counseling statements that looked like they'd been written by fourth graders.

Olivia wasn't sure what was worse: soldiers who were doing really stupid things or the fact that they thought they were smarter than their sergeants and getting away with the stupid things.

They hadn't counted on Olivia, however. She was halfway through the stack from Sean Nichols's company she'd brought home with her. Inside each file was a detailed note about what Nichols and his first sergeant needed to do to correct each packet.

She paused, taking a deep breath, and flipped open Escoberra's folder once more.

Two new counseling forms had been added to the file since the last time she'd looked at it. Both from First Sergeant Sorren. She frowned and looked at the dates.

Why did these stand out? There was nothing out of the ordinary with these two forms but something nagged at her. Something didn't feel right. Not at all. She jotted a note to herself to follow up with these the next day at work and set the folder aside. Once the final paperwork came through from Child Protective Services, she'd advise Ben on what he should do.

Sadly, she could guess. Without a formal charge against him, Ben was going to let the man walk. And the more she trusted Ben, the more she doubted her own convictions.

She'd been so sure about Escoberra, but Ben's loyalty was unwavering.

She sighed, wondering at the kind of loyalty that could make him overlook what happened to Escoberra's daughter. She couldn't shake the nagging feeling that there was something else she was missing.

She wished Ben didn't have to deal with all of this. She should have had a paralegal to do the bulk of this work for her, but the paralegal had popped hot for methamphetamines a week prior to Olivia being sent down to the unit. And because no one at division had been able to find her an under-utilized clerk and everyone else was short staffed at the moment, it meant Olivia was doing her own admin work.

She supposed she should sleep eventually. She lifted the glass of wine to her lips once more. Her cell phone lit up on the coffee table and she reached for it. It was never a good sign when the phone rang close to midnight. It didn't matter if it was the middle of the week or a weekend: midnight calls were never about someone delivering flowers or chocolate. They were always steaming piles of bad news and requests for legal opinions.

"Major Hale. How can I help you, sir or ma'am?"

"Major Hale, this is Captain Teague." He paused. "Why do you sound like you haven't been sleeping?"

She smiled at the sound of his voice. Her blood warmed at the memory of his mouth on her, the feel of his skin against hers. "Because I haven't," she said. She probably shouldn't be thinking about him naked when he was probably calling her for work. "I assume you wouldn't be calling in the middle of the night unless you had an issue?"

He made a sound and she narrowed her eyes, trying to figure out what was going on. "I was having trouble sleeping."

She sipped her wine, letting the cool liquid slide slowly down her throat. "And you assumed I would be having the same trouble?"

"I was kind of hoping that if you were asleep, your phone wouldn't ring and wake you up."

"I'm a lawyer. I get called in the middle of the night all the time. I hear my phone when it rings."

"Oh." He sounded vaguely disappointed.

She laughed quietly. "It's okay. What are you doing up?" She tucked her feet up beneath her.

"Calling you."

"Because?" It was strange, this quiet flirting in the middle of the night. She didn't know what was going on with him but it felt good. A peaceful balm to soothe the relentless fatigue that haunted her sleep and kept her working until she collapsed from exhaustion.

"Are you done working for the night?"

She looked at the pile of papers in front of her. She'd made a decent dent in them tonight. "I've done enough."

"Want to meet me for a drink?"

"I've already had a drink," she said. Her throat went dry, thinking of where this conversation was going.

"You're not driving?"

"Not tonight, no." She took a deep breath. "But I could use some company."

"I was hoping you'd say that." His voice turned husky.

"Yeah?"

"Does that make me the creepy guy you avoid in the ops office?"

She closed her eyes and slid down into the couch. "Only if you're actually parked outside my house right now. That would be creepy."

A long pause. "So is it okay if I just pulled in?"

She laughed, running her fingers through her hair and glancing toward her front door. "Seriously?"

"Maybe. You haven't answered the question."

A slow heat unfurled in her belly. Was he really outside her house?

"What happens if I say no?"

He cleared his throat and she imagined him dragging his hand through his hair. "No, me being in your driveway doesn't make me creepy or no, me being in your driveway does make me creepy?"

She tapped her bottom lip for a moment. "No, you being in my driveway right now does not make you creepy."

More silence.

"Good. Then you should really open your front door right now."

She licked her lips, looking at the closed front door. Her breath caught in her throat just then. "Really?"

She rolled off the couch and padded to the front door, then

paused. She was wearing a ratty t-shirt from Banana Republic and a pair of comfortably worn sweatpants. No bra.

He'd seen her in less. A lot less. But it felt incredibly daring and brazen to open her front door like this. Her nipples tightened with the idea that she had only to say the word and he could be in her space. Touching her. Chasing away the ugliness of her job with a few hours of dark, sensual pleasure.

She could open the door as is and let him see her exactly how she was right then.

Or she could keep him standing on her front step while she ran back into her bedroom and tried to find something that even remotely resembled sexy.

And then she remembered that the only thing she had that fit that description was a plain white tank top.

His voice from the phone distracted her, reminded her that he was waiting on her. "Holy crap, please don't tell me she hung up on me," he mumbled.

"No, I'm here," she said.

"Are you going to open the door?"

"I'm not really dressed for company."

"Neither am I."

Now *that* sparked her curiosity. She flipped on the outside light and opened the front door.

"Wow, you weren't kidding."

He *really* wasn't up for company. He was sporting a fat lip and holding a bloody tissue to it. There was blood splattered on his t-shirt and a hole ripped in the shoulder. His knuckles were scraped and bloody.

And he was grinning like he'd just had the time of his life.

"What in the world happened?" She ushered him into the house and closed the door behind him.

"Funny story," he said, wincing as the words split his lip again. Blood oozed from the cut and he dabbed it with the napkin. "Do you have some ice?"

* * *

"So there we were," he said, lifting the towel-wrapped ice away from his lip. A tiny speck of blood was the only hint that his lip was still bleeding.

Olivia sat against the edge of her couch, her feet curled beneath her. She balanced a fresh glass of wine on her knee and rested her head against her hand. "You look terrible," she said.

"Do you want to know what happened or not?" He tried to look disgruntled. He was pretty sure it didn't work because she laughed at him.

"Please enlighten me," she said. "I'm dying to know what happened."

"Really? Should I make some stuff up to make me sound heroic and sexy? Something that would get you to crawl over here instead of sitting over there?"

Her lips twitched as she sipped her wine. "Start with the truth and we'll go from there."

He grinned, then caught himself because the pain ripped through his bottom lip. "Ow. Don't make me smile."

She laughed quietly. "You're being a baby. It's just a fat lip."

Ben took a deep breath and tried to take a sip of his own wine from the unsplit side of his lip. It was awkward at best and he gave up rather than embarrass himself further. "Went to Ropers to try to get a bunch of our guys home before they got arrested. Couple of guys from the 3rd Armored Cavalry Regiment decided they didn't want to end the night peacefully." He looked at the towel again. "You should see the other guy."

"And no one got arrested?"

"Nope. I told the cops I was the company commander and was trying to get my guys out of there without causing any trouble. He gave me ten minutes. Needless to say, we got everyone into cabs and sent on their way in six minutes flat."

Olivia grinned, running her fingers through her hair and resting her head in her hand. "So you and your first sergeant kept everyone out of jail and all you have to show for your heroism is a fat lip?"

"Pretty much," he said. He lowered the towel. "Does it look really tough?"

"It looks like it hurts," she said. Her gaze dropped to his mouth and Ben's throat tightened. "If I kiss it, will that make it better?" One side of his mouth felt like it was the size of a golf ball and throbbed like a bastard. He'd eat his damn shorts if it made her crawl onto his lap. He touched his fingers to his lip gently, watching her watching him. "I think that would help," he murmured.

She didn't move for a long time. His entire body tightened as she leaned over and set her wine glass down. Ben went very still as she crawled across the couch. She nudged his leg over and slid up his body until she straddled him. "Such a hero tonight," she whispered.

She threaded her fingers through his hair. He framed her hips with his hands, wincing when his shoulder protested the movement.

"What happened?" Her fingers traced over the tear in his shirt.

"Collided with a soldier's head." Her touch was cool against his skin. His lungs were tight. "Your sympathy is making me feel so much better," he murmured.

He tipped his face, giving her access to his damaged lip. She brushed her lips gently near the swelling. He closed his eyes as she touched him, loving the feel of her fingers on his body.

"It doesn't look too bad," she whispered.

"Hurts."

She made a sound, something sultry in her throat, then pressed her lips gently to the side of his mouth. His pulse quickened beneath her touch.

He loved that she was wearing a t-shirt and sweatpants. There was something sexy about her comfort. The worn cotton shifted beneath his palms as he ran his hands over her thighs. She wiggled and pressed her body against his aching erection.

A groan escaped him before he could stop it. She leaned back. "Did that hurt?" she whispered.

He shook his head, meeting her gaze. "No." He gripped her hips, pulling her closer. Loving the pressure of her body against his erection. "You feel good," he whispered, pulling her down.

Her lips brushed against his. "I don't want to hurt you."

"Not kissing me is causing unimaginable pain," he said against her mouth.

She nipped his bottom lip at the farthest spot away from the swollen split. "We wouldn't want that."

She traced her tongue over the seam of his lips before kissing him, a gentle stroke of her tongue against his. She kept the pressure soft, her lips barely caressing the swollen bottom lip.

It was Ben who deepened the kiss. Who turned the moment from something light and teasing to something dark and sensual. He urged her closer, moved her hips against his cock, needing the friction, needing the connection blocked by their clothes.

Her fingers slid down his chest and danced beneath the torn t-shirt. They were cool against his fevered skin. He ached. Dear lord but he ached. He leaned up, still kissing her, twisting to yank his t-shirt over his head, breaking the kiss only when he absolutely had to.

She nestled close, the warm cotton of her t-shirt soft against his skin. "You're warm," she murmured, pressing a kiss to the side of his neck.

"You're not naked," he complained, tracing his fingers over the small of her back.

"We can fix that."

She leaned back to lift her shirt but Ben surprised her by pushing up onto his knees and lying her down on the couch. "Much better," he murmured.

He leaned down, lifting her shirt, pressing his lips to her belly. Dragging his tongue over her skin as he pushed the shirt higher.

Olivia was lost in sensation. She surrendered to the warmth of his touch, the heat that smoldered beneath his fingertips. His fingers traced over her ribs and tugged her sweats down.

She was naked.

Ben knelt between her thighs and urged them wider. She wanted to cover herself. To shield her body from his view.

This was too much. The brush of air on her skin. The dance of his fingertips over her stomach.

She closed her eyes. Ben smiled. She was beautiful. Strong. But spread before him just then, she was his. Nothing more. Nothing less.

His.

He slid between her thighs, loving the sensation of her wrapping them around his hips.

He kissed her then, slipping a hand between their bodies to touch her gently where she was open and swollen and so fucking beautiful. He captured her gasp in his mouth as he touched her. Felt her tremble when he slipped one finger inside her.

"Ben." His name was a plea on her lips. Something beautiful. A mark of possession. A need.

She could have watched him roll the condom in place.

But she didn't. She reached for it, sliding her hand over his erection. Stroking that soft, smooth satin steel before tearing open the small foil ring.

His stomach tensed beneath her touch.

She pressed her lips gently to the aching head. Felt him jump at the same time he sucked in a harsh breath. "Olivia."

Her name was pained. Tense.

She owned this. Wanted to claim him.

She traced her tongue over the tip of him. Felt his entire body tremble beneath her touch. She sucked him softly into her mouth, her tongue tracing the tip.

"Oh god."

He fisted his hands in her hair, his fingers tight and tense. His touch filled her with power. Raw. Ragged.

He wrenched her away and pulled the condom from her hand and rolled it into place.

"I want to be inside you when I come," he whispered right before he kissed her.

He filled her then, pushing deep, deep inside her. Touching the reserved center of her that ached for him.

Together they rode the wave of pleasure. Together they shattered. And when the world stopped spinning, together, they tumbled into sleep, twined in each other's arms.

Chapter Eighteen

Sir, I need a minute of your time." First Sarn't Sorren stood in Ben's doorway, his entire body radiating pissed off. But he was stiff and moving a little more slowly today than he had the night before.

"Age starting to catch up with you, big guy?" Ben asked, flipping his computer monitor the bird before closing out his e-mail.

"I'm too old to be getting into bar fights on the weekends. I took three Motrin eight hundreds when I got home and I'm still in fucking pain."

Ben smiled, glad the swelling had gone down in his lip. "I'm never getting as old and crusty as you."

Sorren flipped him off. "Your lip looks better than it did last night."

"I had it looked at."

"Uh huh. And the person who did the looking didn't happen to be the lawyer, did it?"

"Um…"

Sorren chuckled. It was the first time he'd ever heard his first sergeant laugh. "Sir, I could give a shit less what you do on your off time."

"Ah, thanks?" Ben said. He wasn't really certain of the direction of this conversation.

Sorren leaned forward, resting his elbows on both knees. "Look, the lawyer's got her head screwed on straight and she's helping move some of these packets along really fast." Sorren paused. "I like her."

Ben narrowed his eyes at his first sergeant. "Why do I feel like this conversation is about to get a whole lot more touchy feely?"

Sorren scrubbed his hand over his mouth. "Because despite yourself, I think you're a hell of a lot better at this than you give yourself credit for. There aren't too many officers who'll show up to a bar fight and then not report it higher."

Ben scrubbed his hand across his jaw. "Yeah, well, I've been in one too many incidents that weren't reported higher. The guys were just blowing off steam. They deserve to have a good time while they're home."

"Yeah, well, not in this day and age. We need to keep the good ones out of trouble and the shitbirds need to get the fuck out of my army." Sorren drummed his fingers on the back of the couch. "It pisses me off when these little assholes start running around, ruining what we stand for."

"By getting into bar fights? I thought that was a time-honored tradition of soldiers everywhere."

"It is." Sorren sighed deeply. "I'm talking about the assholes who go out robbing and stealing and wreaking havoc that bring discredit to our uniform." Sorren paused for a moment. "We have brothers and sisters who have died in these colors and if the soldiers don't recognize that, then they don't deserve the honor of wearing this uniform."

"Some of these guys have been through some bad shit downrange," Ben said quietly. The scar on his stomach itched.

"We've all been through some bad shit downrange, sir. We don't all come home and freak the hell out."

Ben pressed his lips together into a flat line, wincing when his still tender bottom lip protested the pressure. "Yeah. I know."

Sorren said nothing and Ben appreciated his not piling on right then. Finally Sorren spoke. "We'll do the Article Fifteens after lunch?"

Ben looked up sharply. "You already had them reviewed by legal?"

Sorren grinned. "I'm not above taking advantage of your relationship to fast-track certain things. I'd rather get this done early in the week so I don't have sergeants supervising them over two weekends."

Ben shook his head as his first sergeant left the office.

He needed to be careful. If Sorren had figured out something was going on between him and Olivia, someone else might, too. And while there were no rules against it, Sorren was right. He didn't need to give anyone any reason to start looking into either of them.

Olivia's blood was cold in her veins. She'd known this was coming. Had known for a few hours that the final paperwork on Escoberra was due in her inbox sometime that day.

Still, knowing it was coming was not the same thing as seeing it.

Two weeks of investigation came back with nothing. No ability to charge the man who'd put his daughter in the hospital. There was nothing she could do.

The scars on her sides ached with the absolute failure.

Another family was unprotected.

And there was nothing, *nothing* she could do about it. She'd thought she would be okay with it. That she trusted Ben's intuition. But right then, looking at the cold reality

in her hands, her emotions welled up, threatening to over-
whelm her.

She swallowed the bitter frustration and gathered her
paperwork before heading down to Gilliad's office.

Olivia clenched her fist around her pen, refusing to lose the
temper she held very tightly leashed as LTC Gilliad studied
her carefully. She could not lose her shit in front of the battalion commander.

It had been a long time since Olivia had needed to work
this hard to keep her temper in check. But not nearly long
enough.

She stood silently while Gilliad read the paperwork she'd
handed him.

Finally he looked up at her. "What does this mean, Major
Hale?"

"Sir, it means that Child Protective Services is closing the
case. Because his spouse refuses to testify against him and
the children won't either, I can't recommend we proceed."
Her words were tight. Clipped. Controlled.

Her hands shook by her sides. Rage was a live thing inside
her but it was the sadness that threatened to choke her. Her
throat closed off with frustration.

"I see." Gilliad steepled his fingers in front of him. "Is
there anything we can do?"

Olivia sucked in a deep, hard breath and held it for a moment.
"No, sir. We have to allow him to move on with his life."

The words tightened in her throat. The scars on her side
ached. She wanted to rail at the world and scream that it
wasn't fair.

But instead, she kept her composure. Breathed deeply
through her nose. In and out. Slow and steady.

Gilliad was silent. "Have the personnel officer draw up
the paperwork." He tossed his glasses onto his desk.

"Roger, sir."

Olivia turned to go, needing to get away from the office, from work, from the people around her who would shake their heads quietly and whisper that women shouldn't be in the army if they saw her cry.

No one had believed a little girl named Olivia when she'd tried to report what was happening at home.

She closed her eyes, hearing the police officer's hard words scraping against her once more. "You shouldn't make things up," he'd told her.

Her eyes filled with unshed tears. Frustration clawed at her. She got back to her office and shut the door behind her, needing her space, her solitude. Needed just a few minutes to keep herself from falling completely apart.

How could the case have fallen apart so badly? She'd made her peace with it. Damn it, it wasn't supposed to hurt like this.

She knew exactly. Everyone saw the war-weary soldier, the veteran begging apology, telling everyone he'd never hurt his daughter.

And *everyone* believed him, including the daughter he'd used his belt on.

She ground the heels of her palms into her eyes. No. No. No. Not again. Oh sweet Jesus not again.

There was a quiet tap on her door. Shit.

She swiped her fingers beneath her eyes and hoped they weren't red from the pressure. She scrambled to her feet and straightened her uniform before opening the door.

Ben stood on the other side, packets in one hand. She met his gaze and his expression instantly softened into concern.

He stepped into her office, closing the door behind him.

"What happened?" he asked softly.

She tried to back away. Tried to put a barrier between him and the wall of emotions threatening to crash over her. She held up her hand to keep him from approaching, trying to rein in her emotions. If he touched her, she was afraid she might shatter.

He collided with her palm and kept coming. He didn't force her into his arms. Her arm simply collapsed and he was there. His strong arms around her. His chest a solid wall of living, breathing support.

She tried to stay strong.

She failed.

"We're closing the Escoberra case," she whispered.

She couldn't fall apart. Not right then, no matter how good it felt to have his arms around her. To trust that she could lean against him and have someone stand with her.

"I'm sorry, Olivia."

"No you're not," she said.

"Olivia." His voice was thick. Tension radiated off him.

"Don't. Don't stand there and tell me you're sorry when you're not. You never believed he could do something like this." She took a single step backward. "You win. Your boy walks free and you get to sleep at night." She bit her lips together, needing the pain to keep the frustrated tears at bay. "Congratulations."

He took a single step toward her.

"Don't," she hissed.

But he didn't heed her warning. He took another step toward her until she was backed against her desk. The broken scale clanked loudly.

He rested his hands on her shoulders.

"I'm sorry, Olivia."

She covered her face with her hands and surrendered. She was so goddamned tired of fighting. She rested her forehead against his chest and let the emotions come. A gasp that was a mixture of sob and sorrow tore from her throat.

"I'm so sorry," he said. His voice rumbled beneath her

cheek. His arms tightened around her, his entire body stiff, radiating with anger. He rested his cheek on the top of her head and simply held her while she allowed the tears to leak out slowly. Because she still had to work the rest of the afternoon.

He'd never thought of her as vulnerable. Olivia had always been strong. Steadfast. He'd always admired her conviction, even if it terrified him and didn't match up with what he wanted out of life.

But feeling her trembling in his arms right then broke his fucking heart. He wanted to destroy something. Do something. Anything to keep her from hurting like this.

He knew that image of Hailey had stayed on her mind. Even when she was trying to focus on something else, he'd catch her looking at Hailey's picture in one of the files.

She believed protecting Hailey—girls like Hailey—was her purpose in life.

There wasn't a damn thing he could do to fix things for her.

He felt so fucking useless. He wanted to fix it. To make her laugh or do something to take her mind off the pain trembling through her body.

Instead, he didn't move. Didn't release his hold on her. He simply held her and let her lean on him and whispered soothing nothings into her hair.

It was an eternity before she moved, easing back gently from his arms. Her eyes were a little pink, the tip of her nose a little red. She sniffed and wiped her eyes.

"Thanks for letting me fall apart."

He didn't fight the urge to brush his fingers over her cheek and push a slip of hair out of her eyes. "That wasn't falling apart," he said gently.

Her smile was sad. "It was for me."

"I'd hate to show you what falling apart looks like for me then. It's not pretty."

Her smile spread a little. "Does it involve alcohol?"

"Mass quantities. And usually someone ends up throwing up."

"By someone you mean you?"

He stroked his thumb over her cheek. It smeared the wetness there. "Tell me why this is so personal," he whispered.

She looked away. "I can't."

He swallowed a bitter lump in his throat. "You can get naked with me but you can't tell me something so simple?"

She closed her eyes, her expression pained. "It's not that simple."

He leaned into her, capturing her face with both hands. He kissed her then because he needed to. Needed her to anchor him to the feelings of goodness and kindness that he felt leaving his soul with each decision he made.

He kissed her and poured everything he couldn't say, every comfort he wanted to give her, into that caress.

She leaned into him with a sigh, her fingers curling against the back of his neck. Her tongue slid against his and what was meant as a comfort turned abruptly passionate and hungry.

"It is that simple," he said, and the sound of the bitterness in his own voice surprised even him. Her eyes widened briefly as he took a step back.

"It's not a simple thing to take someone to bed, Olivia. And it's not a simple thing to spend the night with someone. And yet, we've done both those things." He breathed deeply. "I'll be in my office when you're ready to tell me what the fuck is going on."

He walked away, unwilling, unable to stand there while she reconstructed the walls between them.

He refused to be shut out when she was so clearly hurting.

"Mom"?

"Why are you still up, Benjamin?" Her voice was cold, no hint of the tears he knew he'd heard. *Even years after his father's death, he thought he heard her sometimes and it shocked him every single time.*

"Are you okay?" he asked from the doorway.

"I'm fine. You have your SATs tomorrow. Go to sleep."

His mother had locked him out of her life after his dad died and his life had been cold and empty since. Until Olivia had come into his life, it had stayed that way.

And now? Now she was closing off, too, pulling away.

If Olivia was going to shut him out, he wasn't going to stand there like a child, begging for her to open up to him.

No, he'd done that once before. Never again.

There was no victory in him for being right about Escoberra. It was tainted by the loss of something special with Olivia. Walking away was the hardest thing he'd ever done.

But he didn't look back.

Chapter Nineteen

Ben knocked on his battalion commander's door. It was almost eighteen hundred and the headquarters was empty for the day.

Hell, you wouldn't know there was a war going on, as quickly as the staff left the building by close of business each day. He paused for a moment, letting his hypocrisy sink in once more. He used to be one of those staff officers who'd be out the door before the end of the duty day.

Funny how things changed.

"You wanted to see me, sir?"

"Ben, come in. Close the door."

Ben did as he was directed. LTC Gilliad took his glasses off and tossed them on the desk before leaning forward, folding his hands together.

"Are you ready to take command tomorrow?"

Ben took a deep breath. "Whether I'm ready or not, I'm pretty sure we're having a ceremony, right, sir?"

Gilliad's expression was flat.

"Not funny, sir?" Ben asked.

His battalion commander sighed. "I suppose I've got to get used to your sense of humor. Are you ready for tomorrow or not?"

"Sir, we've submitted the paperwork about the missing property. I've signed the books. I'm as ready as I'm going to be." Ben released a heavy breath. The weight of the guidon had settled around his shoulders the moment he'd been directed to take command.

Tomorrow? Tomorrow was only a formality.

But it was an important one. Ben would assume the call sign Bandit Six.

The men of Bandit Company would officially be his. His to train. His to worry about.

His to take to war and, please God, bring them all home safely. His to court-martial and reprimand and send out of the army when they screwed up too badly.

No, he wasn't ready for this. Not by a long shot.

There was an aching hole in his chest from his encounter with Olivia earlier that day.

He hated himself for walking away from her but he couldn't deal with being shut out. She was too focused on Escoberra.

She'd taken the case way too personally. He'd hoped she'd call. That she would let him in to what made her break in her office.

But she hadn't and Ben could not get past that simple fact.

He wasn't demanding they get married and take long walks on the beach but damn it, he had a right to know what the fuck was driving her so hard after a man she didn't know.

A man that Ben did know. A man that Ben trusted.

There had to be some other explanation for Hailey's injuries. There had to be.

The bitter irony of it blocked his throat. But he deserved a damn answer from Olivia.

If she'd asked him about the scar on his body, he would have told her. But she'd never asked. Not about that. Not about the tattoos.

But he'd asked her about hers and while she'd told him some, he suspected there was more to the story. There was something she wasn't telling him and damn it, he had too much to do to worry about chasing down her secrets.

Like train his men for war. He wasn't naive enough to believe his men would come through unscathed. He could hope, but hope wasn't an approved technique the last time he'd checked.

He took a deep breath and released it because tomorrow would come just like every other day. And waited for his battalion commander to continue, counting the minutes before he could get out of his office and back to his own.

Hopefully without seeing Olivia. Because he wasn't really in the mood right then.

"How are things with your new first sergeant?"

Ben frowned. Now that was a random question. "Fine, sir. He's a steadfast NCO. Why?"

"There've been reports that he's been a little sandpapery with some of the soldiers."

A flush of anger crawled up Ben's neck. Sorren had put his ass on the line to keep soldiers out of jail last weekend and someone was bitching about him? "Sir, First Sergeant Sorren is one of the best NCOs I've ever worked with. He's top tier. Whatever you've heard..."

Gilliad held up his hand. "Relax, Ben. No one is in trouble. We're just all a little edgy after everything that happened with the previous commanders."

"Roger, sir, but going on a witch hunt when people are trying to clean house isn't the way to go." Ben's words were defiant. Angry. Damn it, he hadn't even wanted this job and they were going to hamstring him by taking away the only competent person around him? Not in Ben's fucking lifetime.

"There's no witch hunt," Gilliad said shortly, his tone carrying all the chastisement that Ben needed to get the damn point. Ben considered himself chastised.

Ben opened his mouth to argue then snapped it shut.

"That's what I thought you'd say," Gilliad said quietly. "Enjoy your last night of freedom."

Ben scoffed quietly. "Sir, I haven't had any freedom since you put in me charge."

"And you won't again until after you pass the guidon."

Ben walked out of his commander's office, unsure of the point of that conversation. He passed Major Denis in the hall. His former commander seemed beaten down. Tired.

Ben had dug in and battled the man every step of the way after that firefight years ago. It had gotten so bad that the battalion commander had pulled Ben out of Denis's company. Ben had hated leaving his boys but he'd had no choice. Not in the middle of the war.

He walked down the hallway, hoping he could make it back to his office without having to talk to anyone else. He was edgy and raw.

The sound of jangling keys made him look up and snapped him out of his wandering thoughts.

Olivia stood at the end of the hallway.

He hated his reaction to her. Hated that his body instantly stood up and took notice of the way her eyes drank him in. The way his skin puckered remembering her hands on him.

Her throat moved slowly. Her movements were wary. "Can I walk out with you?" she asked.

He thought about being a dick and then thought better of it. She didn't deserve that. "Sure."

Neither of them said anything until they were outside, away from the headquarters. The sun was still high in the late afternoon sky.

"You're right. This is personal to me," she said softly.

Ben held his tongue, barely. Somehow he didn't think she would appreciate any sarcastic remarks. He felt like his sense of humor had gone AWOL weeks ago.

"I figured that out all by myself, thanks."

"You're not making this any easier," she said quietly.

"Funny. I didn't think I was supposed to." He let some of the anger and frustration slip into his voice. He hated that she'd put this barrier between them. Maybe that made him weak and vulnerable but he'd felt something real with her. Something alive and warm and *needed*.

When she'd shut him out, that something went away. It was like a switch had been thrown inside him and everything was dark again.

"You want to know why this is important to me? Because it matters. It fucking matters that people with power and privilege get to get away with doing bad things." She stopped.

Ben shook his head slowly. "Nice try. This isn't about power and privilege. This is about one case. One NCO who matters a fucking ton to me." He jammed a finger toward her. "Why is *this* case so personal to you? Why this one? Why now?"

Olivia folded her arms over her chest and lifted her chin. He should have found her stubbornness sexy. But right then? It pissed him off.

And then she started talking.

"I knew a little girl who looked like Hailey once. She used to come into the division headquarters with her father." The memory rose up, bitter and sweet and sad. So goddamned sad.

"She was such a smiley little thing. She used to sit in the corner and do her homework while her dad worked."

She didn't look at Ben. She couldn't. Because no matter how many times she relived it, these memories *hurt*.

"I suppose I was too young to see what was happening to

the little girl. She never made a sound when her dad was in the room. She looked up at him with these huge brown eyes." She swallowed. "There were all these little warning signs that something wasn't quite what it seemed. The little girl never acted up in the office. Never said a word. Never asked to go to the bathroom. Nothing."

She sucked in a deep breath and held it until her lungs screamed in protest. "One day she was squirming in her chair." She could see Delia's little body in vivid color against a black and gray memory. "I asked her if she wanted me to take her to the bathroom because her father was in a briefing."

"She came out because she couldn't button her pants." She closed her eyes, not wanting to see again. Not wanting to relive the memories. "Her belly was covered in old bruises and new ones."

"Jesus, Olivia."

She barely registered that he'd spoken. "I reported it. What else could I do?" Deep breaths. Deep, deep breaths. "And because he was such a good NCO, the chain of command didn't believe the reports. His wife refused to leave him. Refused to press charges."

She bit her lips hard. She rubbed her hands down her arms. "But it was too late. The sergeant drank himself into a blackout rage the night after the new investigation started. He killed his wife. He killed himself. I think he would have killed the little girl if he'd found her but she was a smart little bugger. She hid." She breathed out again. Forced her lungs to work because she remembered being that little girl. Remembered all too clearly the disbelief directed at her, the absolute feelings of being utterly alone against the force of her father's addiction and abuse. "I still remember hiding in the closet from my dad." She couldn't look at him. "I remember the day I found my father. Dead from a drug overdose." Finally, finally she met his gaze. "I remember that little girl.

And I remember the chain of command that protected her father instead of protecting her."

"Olivia."

"Don't." She took a step back when he would have approached her. "You said I was keeping secrets and I was." She swallowed. "Because some things are just too shitty to talk about. I never told you about that little girl because it hurts too damn much. I can't separate her from the girl I was. I can't separate Hailey from the girl I was. I try, I try so fucking hard but I can't."

"I don't know what to say."

"You're not supposed to say anything," she said quietly. "But you wanted to know why this case mattered to me so much." She blinked rapidly. "And now you know."

"Olivia."

"Don't." She held up a hand, afraid that if he touched her, she would shatter into a million broken little pieces that she would never, ever put back together again.

"Olivia, please."

"Don't, Ben." She stood there, frozen. Unable to move. Unable to flee the crushing intensity storming inside her that threatened to tear her apart. "I can't do this with you," she whispered. "I thought I could but I can't. It's too personal." Torn between needing the comfort she knew she'd find with him and needing her solitude to put everything back in the box so that she could face the next day and the day after that.

She walked away, leaving him standing there. She didn't look back.

Because she was terrified of the pity she'd see looking back at her.

Ben wasn't alone in the office. His first sergeant was still there. Both of them were hunched over their computers, fighting the ever-rising tide of unrelenting e-mail and things to do.

There was a quiet knock on his door.

He half hoped it would be Olivia.

It had been hell watching her walk away but he'd had a feeling that if he'd touched her then, if he'd tried to follow her, she would have shattered.

As much as it had sucked to let her go, she'd needed that.

And Ben? Ben wasn't sure what he could say that would make things better. He'd drawn a blank when he'd tried to think of something funny. The only thing he'd felt was his heart breaking in his chest at the pain he'd seen written on her face and heard embedded in her voice.

He'd let her go. Until he could figure out what to say.

Because he had no idea how to fix this.

But he looked up and it wasn't Olivia at his office door.

It was Hailey Escoberra.

Ben stood. "Hailey." She'd grown up since the last time he'd seen her. Once he'd gone to her house with her dad but things...things had changed on that last deployment and he wasn't close to her dad anymore.

He should be.

But things didn't often turn out how they should.

"Hey, Ben."

"Is your dad with you?"

She nodded. "He's talking to First Sarn't."

Ben smiled at the way she blurred the words. Like she was an old soldier just like her dad. "You doing okay? How have you been?"

She was skittish now. More than she had been. Ben had no doubt that something had happened.

And as much as he prayed he was right about his old platoon sergeant, he couldn't help but worry that maybe, just maybe, he was wrong.

"We're good. My dad just needed to ride in and I figured I'd come with him." She hugged her arms to her chest.

Ben offered a hollow smile. It felt empty. "I'm glad you stopped by."

"Hailey—"

Escoberra stopped outside Ben's door.

The world froze as Ben stared at his old NCO. Escoberra had aged hard in the last week or so. There were lines on his face Ben didn't remember. Hard shadows under his eyes. "Sir," was all he said.

Things should not have been like this. They should not have been stilted and awkward, as if they were two strangers. But they were.

And it was Ben's fault.

"Hey, old man." Ben's joke fell flat but still Escoberra offered a token grin.

"I can still whip your ass," he said. There was forced lightness in his voice. "Come on, Hailey."

"Nice to see you, Ben."

"You too, Hailey."

And he was gone, leaving Ben feeling awkward and embarrassed and ashamed of everything he hadn't done.

"He's trying to get himself put on assignment. Maybe to Germany," Sorren said, stepping out of his office.

Ben pressed his mouth into a flat line. "I haven't said thank you yet." He glanced over at his first sergeant. "But thanks for taking care of everything with him. I lacked the ability to be objective."

"I know you did, sir." Sorren gripped his shoulder hard. "That's why I'm here."

"Ladies and gentlemen, the ceremony will begin in five minutes. Please take your seats and turn off all electronic devices."

Olivia scanned the stands on the edge of Cooper Field in front of the division headquarters, hoping to find a place to sit. Battalion-wide changes of command were unusual and it showed in the lack of space in the stands. Everyone who wasn't standing in formation on the field was jockeying for a spot to sit on the bleachers.

Reza melted out of the crowd, looking massive and intimidating in his black Stetson. Olivia sought him out, knowing he was a safe bet in the crowd of strangers.

"Emily didn't come?" she asked, moving to stand next to him.

Reza nodded in greeting but stood, arms folded over his chest, his gaze focused on the crowd of soldiers on the field. "She's on call at the clinic. She's upset she couldn't be here."

"When will it be your turn?" she asked, searching through the crowd of faces, trying to find the one person she was looking for.

Reza looked down at her. "I won't take command. I'm enlisted."

"I know. I meant for you to be the first sergeant," Olivia said, mirroring Reza's stance.

"I don't know," he admitted roughly.

She placed a palm on his upper arm. "You'll get your shot, Reza," she said quietly.

He grunted. There was disbelief in that sound. A rough, cutting disbelief that he'd ever get his feet fully back beneath him without the aid of the bottle that had sheltered him for so long.

She skimmed the field, looking for Ben, wishing she wasn't such a coward that she could call him. But the walls around her heart were too high, the shame that she had not been able to save Hailey from her father too heavy.

She saw him there, at the edge of the giant First Cavalry Division patch in the middle of the field. His expression was tight, the smile pasted on his mouth not reaching his eyes. His movements were tense, his shoulders stiff.

He looked over in her direction. And in a thousand years,

she never would have figured he'd spot her in the mass of soldiers.

But he did. His gaze locked with hers. Time hung suspended and the world fell away.

It was the pain, however, that overwhelmed her, tearing at her with a violent sense of loss.

And then he looked away, leaving emptiness. Leaving her alone, just like always.

Then there was nothing more to say as the ceremony started. She stood with Reza near the stands. Saluted when they played the national anthem. Bowed her head at the chaplain's invocation.

She did all the formal things in the ceremony but her eyes were focused on Ben at the front of that formation. He stood straight and tall. His Stetson made him appear larger than life.

A warrior stood on that field. A warrior with a sense of humor and a good heart. She folded her hands at the small of her back and wished that things hadn't gotten so utterly and completely screwed up.

She'd thought she could handle things with him. Thought she could keep things light and casual.

Things never worked out how she planned. And Ben wasn't a man that was used to being handled.

This was where things stood now. An abrupt ending to their casual thing.

She was going downrange with this unit so she needed to figure out how to fix things—or at least get them back to some semblance of professional. The men behind Ben would follow him into combat. He wanted to bring them all home. What commander didn't?

But there was something else that nagged at her. Ben had lost friends in battle. She knew that. But how would he react to losing men in a formation he *commanded*? Would that be different?

She didn't know.

If someone had asked her last week, she would have said she wanted to be that person he leaned on if he needed someone. Now? Now she was worried he would do what so many of them did, and stuff it down just to drive on with the mission.

The ceremony continued as LTC Gilliad walked in front of each command team. He took the guidon from each executive officer and handed it to the new commander.

And then he stopped in front of Ben.

Ben's hands closed over the staff, his movements sharp and stiff. Olivia felt a surge of pride as Ben accepted the guidon from LTC Gilliad.

The man sparked something inside her. Something she hadn't allowed herself to feel before.

He'd been there. Allowed her to lean when she'd thought she was going to tear apart. And she'd ruined it. Ruined everything by being too driven, too focused on the idea of justice rather than on the people involved.

The formation came to attention. The narrator informed them that this concluded the ceremony and they could join the new commanders in the battalion conference room for a reception.

Her phone buzzed violently in her pocket and she wove to the edge of the mass of people surging the field to congratulate the new commanders.

"Major Hale."

"Hi Major Hale, this is Sarah Childress with the high school."

Childress. The school nurse that had worked with CPS on the Escoberra case.

"Yes ma'am? How can I help you?"

"I'm not sure if you're the right person but someone told me today that the Escoberra case has been closed?"

Olivia's throat closed off. "Yes, I'm afraid that will be the case," she managed.

"Why?"

Olivia sighed heavily. "I can't really go into those details," she said softly.

That single word sliced at her, cut deeply at her sense of purpose, at her sense of what was right in the world.

Silence on the other end of the phone. "No one talked to me," Ms. Childress said.

Olivia's skin crawled. "Excuse me?"

"I gave a statement but there's more to this story than you know. And I can probably lose my job for telling you this, but someone needs to do something before that man does some permanent damage."

Olivia didn't stay for the reception.

Ben searched the faces in the crowd but no matter how many times he looked, he knew the truth. She wasn't there.

She had probably gone back to work but he'd hung on to the foolish hope that she would stay.

"She was here," Reza said, sneaking up behind him.

"I really hate it when you practice that ninja shit," Ben grumbled. "And how do you know who I'm looking for?"

"You're scanning the field like a lovesick puppy. It's pretty obvious," Reza said, folding his arms over his chest.

Ben sighed and rubbed his finger beneath the band of his Stetson. "Oh. Well."

"How did you already manage to screw things up with her?"

Ben stilled. The world fell away, his focus concentrated on Reza's next words. "How do you know things are screwed up?"

"Call it my finely tuned intuition," Reza said dryly.

"Not funny."

"Who's laughing?"

Ben sighed. "We had an argument. About Escoberra."

"And?"

"And I screwed up. What else is there to report?" Ben snapped.

Together they started walking toward the battalion headquarters and more congratulations. And cake. There would be cake at the reception.

Ben scoffed quietly. Cake was the only good thing coming out of this day.

As they rounded the corner of the pavilion and headed toward the conference room where the massive spread of food and cake was, Ben stopped short.

His mother stood there talking to his battalion commander.

A cold wave crashed into him and damn near drowned him in its wild, unrestrained intensity.

Five years since he'd seen her last. Five years since she'd shown up in that hospital in Baghdad and told him in no uncertain terms that he was not getting out of the army. That she was not going to let him ruin his life over some sentimental bullshit ideals.

His mouth went dry. His heart froze in his chest. He didn't know whether to stand his ground or turn and hide.

He didn't know what to say. What to do.

How to react. His heart skittered roughly in his chest.

She spotted him.

And her face spread into a warm smile that he would have killed for a decade or so ago.

Now?

Now his breath caught in his throat. Now a slick sweat broke over his skin. Now he straightened as she approached with his commander. He saluted because she was more Colonel Teague than Mother and because he honestly didn't know how else to react.

Falling back on rigid customs and courtesies seemed like as good a plan as any.

His hand trembled as he saluted.

"You don't salute your mother," she said. Her voice was warmer than he remembered. Her hair was steel gray, her face regal and polished. She was more beautiful than he remembered. Older. But still beautiful.

Still the mother that he remembered before Dad had left them both alone.

She would forever be frozen in his memory looking like she had the day his dad died.

"Sorry," he mumbled. "Wasn't sure."

LTC Gilliad offered a quick salute. "I'll let you catch up. Ma'am, it was nice seeing you again."

She returned his salute sharply. "You, too, Brian. Take care of my son."

"Will do, ma'am. I'm confident he'll make you proud."

Ben glanced over, realizing that Reza had stood fast by his side, not leaving him to face his mother alone.

God, but he loved that man for not leaving him alone right then. Ben wasn't sure he could have held his bearing. Old hurts wrestled with something new and unexpected.

Something he couldn't name.

"Mom, this is Sergeant First Class Iaconelli. He's a good friend," Ben said.

He waited for the flicker of disapproval but none came. She extended her hand and Reza shook it. "I've heard a lot about you, ma'am," Reza said.

"That's probably not a good thing," she said quietly. Ben didn't know how to react to this woman who was so much warmer than he remembered. "I know you weren't expecting me," she said to Ben. "But I didn't want what happened between us to keep me from seeing your big day." Her eyes glittered darkly. "Your father would be very, very proud of you, Ben."

Ben swallowed a hard lump. His eyes stung and he blinked rapidly. "Thanks, Mom," he said when he was certain he could speak without embarrassing himself.

She cleared her throat quietly. "I requested to be assigned here at Fort Hood." She paused and there was a flicker of uncertainty in her dark eyes.

"Oh." Again, Ben didn't know what to say. He stood there, rooted to the spot.

"I just wanted you to hear it from me," she said softly. "I'll let you get going to your reception."

She turned to go. Ben's throat locked up and she was a good fifty feet away before he could speak. "Mom?"

She stopped, turning back to look at him. In that moment, Ben realized that Dad would always stand between them. Dad had been the one they'd both loved but they'd been a family once. Once she'd laughed and loved him as much as she'd loved his father. But then Dad had died and at that moment, Ben knew it was grief, powerful grief that had torn his mother away from him. Because his mother had loved his father. With everything she had. Suddenly, he could no longer summon the energy to be angry with her for leaving him after his father had died.

Because she'd thought she had nothing left when his dad died. He'd hated her for so long for not loving him enough.

But grief was a powerful thing.

His throat closed off. He knew, in that instant, he knew that what he'd lost with Olivia could have been that kind of love.

He studied the woman who'd been so distant, so cold in her grief. The years of bitter cold that stood between them wouldn't fade in a day. But his mother had made a powerful leap of faith today.

It was Ben's turn to take the same leap and meet her halfway.

"Thanks for coming today," he said finally.

She nodded quickly and Ben suspected that her eyes were more than a little wet.

It wasn't like they were going to be having Sunday dinners or anything, but a little bit of the anger and the hurt faded in that moment.

He stood, keenly aware of Reza next to him. Finally Ben broke the silence. "Now how was that for a Hallmark moment?" he asked lightly.

Reza gripped his shoulder. "I see where you get your charming good looks. Your mother is a handsome woman."

Ben glanced over at his longtime friend. "I didn't know you had a thing for cougars," he said.

Reza laughed and slapped Ben hard on the shoulder. "Smart-ass."

Ben grinned but it didn't last. They walked into the headquarters and toward the crowded conference room, which was filled with soldiers from across the battalion, all coming to see the new commanders, and for a slice of free cake. Olivia was nowhere to be seen, and Reza's warning hung over his head like a shroud. Just then everything was piling on. He had not been prepared to see his mother at the ceremony today. It unhinged all the boxes he'd stuffed everything into and locked away.

Now it felt as if he had a hadron collider inside him. He was weighed down with responsibility now. The guidon. His soldiers.

Olivia.

They'd moved beyond something casual to something deeper and Ben had let stupid pride screw it up.

He needed to call her. To make the effort to bridge the chasm between them.

He smiled and nodded and made polite conversation but as the morning drew on, he couldn't shake the unsettled feeling that something big was coming.

Chapter Twenty

"You need to call the lawyer, sir."

His first night officially in command and he was standing on a street corner outside a shitty apartment complex on Rancier Avenue with his first sergeant because Zittoro had called and told them that Foster had broken restriction. This place was not exactly known for its family-friendly atmosphere.

Ben sighed and glanced over at his first sergeant. The streetlights overhead flickered and hummed. "Is it petulant and wrong if I don't?"

"Yes. Yes sir, it is."

Ben sighed and pulled out his government-issued cell phone that he'd taken ownership of when he'd taken the guidon. He was officially tied to his e-mail and phone now. He figured he at least had a chance of getting through to Olivia without her hanging up on him if he called from the official phone.

Goddamn it, he wished things hadn't gotten so screwed up between them.

He dialed her number, his heart tight in his throat while it rang.

"Major Hale. May I help you, sir or ma'am."

"Olivia, it's Ben."

Silence. He glanced at the phone. "Shit. I hope she didn't hang up on me."

"No. I'm still here."

Relief was a cold thing against his skin. "So I'm kind of hanging out near a crack house—"

"You're what?"

If he'd been kidding, he might have smiled, but considering it was nearly four in the morning, he wasn't exactly in the mood for jokes. "I'm at a crack house. One of my super troopers is in there. And I need some legal advice."

He heard the rustle of blankets as she sat up. His mouth went dry, wondering what she might have on.

Yeah, he couldn't exactly ask that question at the moment, now could he?

"Explain the situation to me."

"Well, I'm not one hundred percent sure. All I know is that Foster has violated restriction and the apartment isn't in his name so we can't go in and get him." He frowned. "I don't think."

She sighed heavily on the line. "Are the police there?"

"Yes."

"Let them arrest him."

"Again?"

"Yes, again. Then whenever he posts bail, you add all of this to his packet." She hesitated.

"I don't want to court-martial him," Ben said quietly. "I need to get him into rehab. If he gets arrested, what does that do to my chances of making that happen?" He leaned down, pinching the bridge of his nose.

"If he's arrested, there's no way the battalion commander will support rehab," she said finally. "Ben?"

"Yeah?"

"For what it's worth, I'm sorry."

An olive branch. A tentative peace offering extended after a shitty night.

"Thanks," he said softly. "Me, too."

The sun rose over Fort Hood as Ben sat in the cab of his truck with Sorren. Neither of them broke the silence, each lost in his own thoughts.

"He broke restriction, sir."

"That doesn't mean he's in there using," Ben said. "Maybe there's a really good reason for this?" His hands shook from lack of sleep and not nearly enough adrenaline. Ben shook his head and felt the powerlessness rise up inside him. The most powerful position in the army and he couldn't do a damn thing to help a friend.

Perfect.

"Well, the way I see it, we have two options," Sorren said after several seconds. "We can let the police arrest him."

"Or?"

"Or we go in and see what the hell is going on. And if there's even the slightest chance that you're right, we give the kid a second chance."

"And if I'm wrong?"

"Then he gets arrested and we deal with the consequences."

Ben looked at the shitty duplex. There were bars on the windows. A plastic chair with three legs was propped up against the dirty wall. "It might not really be a crack house, right?"

Sorren looked over at him. "Sure. I'll play your silly game."

"You and this unexpected sense of humor," Ben said. He sucked in a deep breath. "Well, here's hoping we don't get shot."

Sorren shot him a wry look and climbed out of the truck.

It was a long slow walk to the front door. There was no noise coming from the apartment.

Ben knocked on the door.

The sun slid a little higher in the sky. There was a muffled noise in the silence.

A lock clicked in the door.

The chain rattled and slid free.

Foster opened the door.

He was tired and worn out. But he didn't look high. "I don't suppose you want to hear a really good explanation for all this?" he said by way of greeting.

Ben folded his arms over his chest. "You better be one hell of a good storyteller."

"Monica was having a bad trip. She didn't have anyone else to call." Foster shrugged sheepishly. "I should have called you first but I didn't know what else to do."

"Is she okay?" Sorren asked.

"She is now," Foster said. He dragged his hands through his hair. "I'm in a lot of trouble, aren't I?"

Ben squeezed his shoulder. "Not nearly as much as you could be," Ben said. "I think this is about as good as this situation could possibly have ended."

An hour later, he pinched the bridge of his nose again as he walked into the headquarters. LTC Gilliad stood by the conference table in his office and was in the middle of strapping his reflective belt around his waist when Ben knocked on the door.

His gaze flickered down over Ben's civilian clothes. "Oh, I can't wait to hear this one," Gilliad said. "If you can beat Assassin Six's story, I'll give you the morning off."

Ben briefly wondered if his commander had been drinking. "Well, that depends on what Assassin Six's story was, sir."

Assassin Six was Alpha Company's commander, Captain Brint Martini.

Gilliad's expression was grim. "He spent the night running down the daughter of one of his sergeants. They found her down on Rancier in a hotel room, prostituting herself for heroin."

"Jesus, sir, I hope no one can beat that. Is the daughter okay?"

"They're at the hospital with her now. Getting her checked out for all the standard Really Bad Shit." Gilliad leaned against his table. "So what's your story?"

"I too spent the night on Rancier, getting one of my guys who broke restriction out of a crack house. But he didn't get arrested and he wasn't high when we found him. He was sitting with a friend who'd had a bad trip."

"I really wish I didn't know what any of that stuff was." Gilliad rubbed his hand over his jaw absently. Finally he released a heavy sigh. "I want a health and welfare before the weekend is over. I want the barracks cleared out, vehicles searched. The whole nine yards. We've got a goddamned drug problem in this battalion."

Ben frowned. "Sir, don't you need to talk to Major Hale about that?"

"I don't want anyone knowing about this but my commanders and my sergeant major. I want this kept quiet."

Ben considered his next words carefully before he spoke. "Sir, if we do the health and welfare and find anything, we're not going to be able to prosecute. We'll be stuck knowing we've got these guys in our formation and not be able to do anything to them." He breathed out slowly. "I recommend you talk to Major Hale before we do this. We need to do this right, sir."

Gilliad's eyes were sharp when he met Ben's gaze. "Are you trying to tell me how to run my battalion, Teague?"

"No sir. Just trying to make sure we're doing things the right way so we can clean it up." Ben straightened. "Major Hale's advice has been rock solid, sir. I trust her judgment."

Gilliad tugged on his bottom lip. "Major Denis doesn't

think much of her legal work. Says she's behind on almost everything."

Ben thought about parsing his words then said to hell with it. He wasn't exactly known for his tact. Why start now? "Sir, she's un-fucking what six of your previous commanders failed to do. I think she should have at least a month on the job before we stone her for incompetence."

Gilliad chuckled quietly. "Go get the damn lawyer." He jammed a finger in Ben's direction. "But keep this quiet. If we've got a drug problem in our formation, I want to catch the little fuckers and throw their asses out of the army."

"Roger, sir. I'll send her your way. I won't be at PT. I'm heading home to shower and change."

"Understood." Gilliad straightened, pausing near the door to place his hand on Ben's shoulder. "You're doing good work, Ben. Keep it up."

Ben looked down, unable to let the praise sink in. It didn't feel like he was doing a good job. It felt like he was barely keeping his head above water and that if he stopped and rested for even a minute, he was going to sink beneath the waves.

Ben glanced at his watch. "Sir, I've only been on the job two weeks, officially less than twenty-four hours. I recommend giving me at least a month on the job before we start assuming I'm capable of anything other than knock knock jokes."

The commander grinned and shoved him out the door. Ben stuffed his hands in his pockets and headed down the hall, planning on ducking into Olivia's office and letting her know the boss needed to see her.

But she wasn't in yet. She might still be at the gym. He shot her a quick text message, then tucked his phone back in his pocket.

He'd call her later if she didn't answer his text. He'd find her today and check on her. And see if maybe, just maybe, he could repair some of the strain in their relationship.

He did not expect to see Olivia sitting in front of his house.

She was nervous. Of all the ways she could have checked on him today, this was the most stupid. But she couldn't get the sound of his voice out of her head after he'd hung up the phone earlier and she didn't want to do this at the office in case it went horribly, horribly wrong.

Ben hesitated when he climbed out of his truck. "Am I in trouble?" he asked lightly.

Jokes. Jokes were a good sign.

"No. Not in trouble," she said. She wanted desperately to repair the damage between them before she brought Escoberra back between them. One thing at a time, though. And she wouldn't bring Escoberra up until Emily had checked something out for her first. If the school nurse was right…

Maybe it was wrong of her but she desperately wanted to rebuild the peace between them. Because if she was right about Escoberra, it was going to destroy Ben.

And she wanted to be standing with him when he found out.

Right now, though, she was worried about him and nothing more. He licked his lips, leaning against his truck. Not approaching. Not attempting to span the chasm between them.

"I wanted to see you," she said simply when she couldn't stand the silence anymore.

The muscles in his neck tightened as the quiet stretched on. "You could have seen me at work."

"I know." She breathed out deeply. "I wanted to check on you. You sounded like last night was a rough one."

"It was." It felt so good to just see him. Even the tired

lines on his face, the weary sag of his shoulders—even broken down with fatigue he was compelling. "Did anyone get arrested?"

"Worried you'd have to come visit me in prison? Prison sex is supposedly a new fad."

She coughed, grabbing her ribs as the laugh tore free. "There's something wrong with you," she said when she could speak.

"What? You didn't see it on *Dateline*?"

She lifted her face to look up at him and found his eyes warm and welcoming. Tired, but no longer cold and filled with unspoken hurt.

"Thanks, Ben," she said softly. "I needed a laugh."

"We all do now and again," he said. He didn't look away and she had the strongest urge to cross the space between them.

"You okay now?"

He nodded, folding his arms over his chest where he leaned against his truck. "Have to be, right?"

"Yeah."

She studied him then, her eyes warm and no longer red. "That doesn't actually make this any easier."

"I know." He sighed heavily "There are worse things than jail," he said quietly.

Finally, Olivia crossed the space between them. Olivia rested her hand over his heart, unable to resist touching him. "I know this is hard, what we do. But we've got to have limits on what we allow."

"But I've never gotten hemmed up for half the shit I've done. I can't tell you how many times I've gotten drunk downtown and gotten into fights. Shit, Iaconelli and I were on a six-week streak at one point."

She could easily picture him and Reza getting buck wild. Easily. "And what happened?"

"Sarn't Major threatened to court-martial Iaconelli and

the colonel told me if I didn't get my act together, he was going to put me on orders to Siberia."

Olivia traced her fingers over the muscles of his chest. "Do we have a base in Siberia?"

"Siberia, Alaska, same thing," Ben mumbled. He lowered his arms, his fingers dancing over her hips.

"Maybe you should have gotten in trouble. But you didn't. You recovered from this stuff. Maybe some of these guys can, too. That's what you want, right?"

"Yeah. I need them to get their heads out of their asses." The echo of Sarn't Major Giles ripping into Reza with Ben standing right next to him rang clearly in Ben's memory.

"Then hopefully, they will."

He folded his hand over hers. Her fingers were strong and soft beneath his. He caressed her knuckles with his thumb and then unexpectedly, lowered his forehead to hers. "I hate what this job is doing to me," he whispered.

She lifted her fingers to cup his face. He nuzzled her palm with his cheek. "You're still a good man, Ben."

"That's the crux of it, isn't it? How to wield this power and stay a good man."

"You're doing just fine, Ben." She brushed her lips against his. It was meant to offer comfort but it quickly turned sensual. "Command is hard because you care. Your soldiers are lucky to have you."

"Thanks for checking on me," he whispered.

"That's what people do when they care about each other," she said.

His hands slipped around her neck, dancing beneath the knot of hair at the base of her skull. She lifted her mouth, meeting him halfway in a kiss that was both urgent and needy. The fatigue, the worry—all of it evaporated, taking the fear and the strain with it. "Can I see you tonight?" he whispered against her mouth.

"I'd like that. I have no food, though."

"I'm not interested in food."

She smiled. "I didn't think you would be." She braced her palms against his chest. "But we need to talk shop before you head in to work."

"Let's get naked while you talk to me about legal packets," he said, his mouth curving into a wicked grin.

"Tempting," she said, nuzzling his top lip with hers. God, but it felt so good to touch him again.

"Had to try," he said with a warm smile. "What have you got for me?"

"You're not going to like this," she said quietly. "Major Denis hauled me into his office last night and asked for an update on the legal packets in every company. He singled out Zittoro's and wanted to know what was taking so long on getting it processed."

Ben glanced at his watch. "Just a few more days before Zittoro meets his thirty-six month mark. Brief him that I've got the packet. Tell him I'm dragging my feet."

She frowned. "But—"

He leaned forward, bracing his hands on either side of her against the car. His body was warm and hard against hers and she thought long and hard about reconsidering his plan for doing naked legal work. "I asked you not to tell the battalion commander. Telling Denis gives him the opportunity to take a shot at me and gets him off your back."

She tipped her chin and studied him quietly. "Okay."

He shrugged. "No reason to make his job easy," Ben said. "I damn sure hope I'm around to see karma stick it to him."

"One of these days you're going to have to tell me why you hate him so much," she said quietly. She stroked her fingers over his sides, well aware that they were still standing in his driveway as the sun crept over the hills into the early morning sky.

She had no desire to move. No desire to bring the real

world crashing in between them. She didn't have any official information from the school nurse. Not yet.

She could wait before she brought Escoberra between them again.

Ben breathed out deeply and she realized he was almost falling asleep where he leaned with her. "Can I see you tonight?"

"I thought we answered that question already."

"Just making sure." He brushed his lips against hers. "I missed you," he whispered.

Olivia smiled before she lost herself in his kiss. "Don't work too late," she said against his mouth.

"I wouldn't dream of it," he said.

"Are you still at work?" He called her at exactly 6:01. "Never mind, don't answer that. What's really important is what you're wearing."

Her laugh eased some of the ache around Ben's heart. He was dead on his feet but he wasn't going to skip a chance to see Olivia. "Dog tags and a smile?"

Ben froze, his body tightening instantly. "Really?"

"You'll have to find out. Don't get any speeding tickets."

The line went dead and it took Ben a moment to realize that he was standing in the middle of the parking lot, staring at his phone like a madman.

Ben dropped his phone back into his pocket and climbed into his truck, heading off post toward Olivia's house.

He'd survived the day. Barely. But he'd managed to get Foster's paperwork started for rehab so he had to take the win where he could. He rolled through a stop sign before turning down the road to Olivia's house.

He pulled into her driveway and sat for a long moment.

Maybe things weren't terrible. Foster was going to get help. Zittoro was going to get his college benefits.

Maybe this was why he was a commander. Maybe these few things were the only way to make a difference.

Maybe if he could do these few good things, command would be worth it.

He killed the truck's engine and walked to the front door. He was bone tired but every ounce of that fatigue dissipated when Olivia opened the door. Ben's gaze flicked down her body when she opened the door then darkened with disappointment when she answered in yoga pants and a bright orange tank top. He could see the outline of every curve in the tight-fitting clothing and he very much suddenly had the urge to see how flexible she might be.

"You didn't honestly expect me in dog tags and a smile, did you?" she said.

"A man could hope." He captured her against his body as soon as the door closed behind them.

She expected him to devour her, to crush her against him with a fierce desire that would end up with them naked on her living room floor.

Instead, Ben kissed her gently. Slowly. Nudged her lips apart. Coaxed a soft sigh from her throat as he made love to her mouth.

She leaned into him, enjoying the slow, subtle way his mouth relaxed her. His hands rested gently on her hips. One thumb stroked her hip bone beneath the soft cotton of her tank top.

It was a gentle kiss. Filled with desire, raw and hungry, that she could taste.

He nibbled on the corner of her lips before kissing the spot gently. "Hi," he murmured against her mouth.

"Hi."

He lowered his forehead to hers with a quiet sigh. "I'm so tired," he admitted.

"Yeah."

They stood that way for a long moment. She didn't want to move away from his embrace. The strength of his presence.

She wanted to stand there with him, holding him up, feeling his body against hers. Right there, in that moment, the world was steady. Stable.

Ben's lips brushed against her cheek. "You're thinking too hard," he whispered.

She closed her eyes, sliding her nose against his. "I've been trying to stop all day," she said.

"I know." His fingers tensed around her hips.

Then his fingers slid up the small of her back. She shivered, arching away from the gentle caress in a sensitive spot. "You're ticklish?"

She swallowed. "Maybe."

He smiled, a lazy, seductive smile that reminded her of warm caramel on a hot summer day. "Oh, now this is interesting," he murmured against her lips.

She narrowed her eyes and tried to slip from his grasp. His fingers tightened. "Let me rub your back."

She stilled. "This is an attempt to get me naked."

"What else would it be?" he said, grinning. He kissed her again, slow. Lazy. But beneath the sensual glide, a hunger. "Please?"

His hands on her hips guided her backward, past the kitchen and the uneaten pizza she'd ordered. Toward her bedroom and the unmade bed.

"When is the last time you had a massage?" he asked, slipping his fingers over her spine.

She trembled, her back spasming away from his teasing fingers. "It's been a while."

"Yeah? What's it going to take for me to get you to lie facedown on that bed?" he asked against her lips.

"Naked?"

"Completely naked."

"I'm not sure where you're going with this. I was only kidding that time I said you could bend me over and have your way with me."

Ben laughed and hugged her close. She nuzzled his neck, enjoying the connection of skin on skin. Wanting more. A slow need unfurled inside her. A spark of heat.

Ben took a step back and bent down to unlace his boots. He glanced up at her when she hadn't moved. "Completely. Naked."

Still she didn't move. Not when he kicked his own boots off and unbuckled his belt. Not when he slid the uniform pants down his narrow hips and revealed black boxer briefs.

Not when he lifted his shirt over his head and stood in her bedroom wearing dog tags and a wicked smile.

Her gaze dropped to his erection. "Is that for me?"

He shook his head. "You're not naked."

She hooked her thumbs into the waist of her yoga pants and slid them down over her hips.

A thrill of power shot through her when his throat moved. "Christ you're sexy," he whispered.

She stepped out of her pants, then reached for the tank top. She lifted it slowly, enjoying the power of making his gaze darken as she inched it higher, higher up her stomach.

Her nipples tightened as the cotton brushed over them.

The top fell to the floor, forgotten. Ben simply watched her for a long moment. He didn't move but his gaze...his gaze was a caress. Despite the scars. He looked at her like she was a precious thing, whole and undamaged.

He moistened his lips. "Lie down," he whispered. "Facedown."

The sheet was cold against her nipples but it warmed quickly from the heat of her body. Olivia stretched across her bed, the sheets rumpled at the bottom. She rested her cheek on the backs of her hands and closed her eyes.

Every sense was aroused, keyed in to the sounds Ben made as he moved around her bedroom.

He turned out the light but reappeared a moment later with a candle. She frowned, leaning up to look at him. "I'm not into candle wax," she said.

"Relax." He set the candle on the nightstand. "I just want to be able to see you."

He still wore his underwear. The outline of his erection was heavy and thick beneath the cotton. He knelt on the edge of her bed, his knee near her thigh.

The bed shifted again and warmth spread over her. His thighs framed hers where he knelt. She arched her hips toward his. He laughed quietly, then surprised her with a kiss above one buttock. "Not yet."

She made a throaty sound when his lips brushed her skin. He brushed her hair off her neck and back.

She closed her eyes as the ache inside her intensified with each passing moment that he didn't touch her. He shifted again and then both of his hands slid over her shoulders. His fingers were strong and warm, slipping over her skin. His thumbs pressed against the spot where her shoulders and her neck met.

She groaned when he found a sore spot. Then closed her eyes and surrendered to his touch.

Ben was out of his mind. There was no way he'd be able to do this long enough to brush aside the terrible memories of the day. He'd meant it as a game.

But then she'd lain on the bed and his blood had throbbed, hot and fierce in his veins. He ached to touch her. It was sweet, sweet torment to kneel over her, knowing he could do anything and she would let him.

There was something beautiful about the way she arched her hips when he touched her. Lifting them ever so slightly off the mattress, a tiny offering.

He traced the tip of his index finger down the centerline of her spine. Her gasp escaped before she could muffle it. His finger continued its easy glide down the center of her buttocks, stopping before he touched her most secret place.

She made a sexy sound deep in her throat and it might as well have been a fist around his cock. He leaned over her, tracing the path his finger had just taken with his tongue. Gently, barely touching her, he flicked his tongue down her spine, to the gentle part of her legs.

He wanted to taste her. To feel her moist slick heat against his tongue as she came.

But torturing her this way was infinitely more pleasurable. He nipped her buttock. Felt her breath catch in her throat. He smiled as he nipped her, tiny bites across her back, her shoulders. With each nip her body tensed, then released. She tried to part her thighs again.

He kept her there, lying on her belly, her back exposed to him. Her body supple and warm beneath his touch.

Moisture flecked her thighs each time she shifted. He was tormenting her, dragging out the promise of pleasure with each slide of his tongue, each gentle caress of his fingers.

He slid his fingers down the length of her back, his thumbs tracing her spine, sliding further down, down, over her buttocks, his thumbs parting her. Opening her. Barely brushing against her aching, swollen core.

He repeated his movements, each time coming closer to where she craved his touch. Each time denying her. Sliding his hands over her body, molding her hips. His thumbs flicked over the underside of her buttocks, the seam of her thighs. She arched a tiny bit, lifting.

Her body was taut. Tense. Ben had never been so fucking aroused by just touching a lover this way. Soft caresses, denying them both. His thumbs danced closer to her wet heat, closer to the spot where he wanted badly to slide his fingers through. He wanted to feel her coat him, feel her slick heat envelop him, pull him deeper.

His thumb brushed against the seam of her body. She jerked and cried out at the barest touch. He smiled and held her in place. "Shhh." He pressed his lips to her buttock. Gentling her. Loving every minute reaction. She whimpered.

He brushed his thumb over her seam once more. Slightly more pressure.

His touch came away wet. So fucking wet.

"Spread your thighs for me," he whispered. "Just a little."

Her eyes were closed. Her lips parted. Her breath coming in tiny little gasps.

He stroked her again, this time with his index finger, sliding the tip along her entire seam. He barely touched her. His finger was slick. Wet. Her body was soft. Swollen.

"Beautiful," he murmured.

He slipped his finger through her again, increasing his pressure slightly.

She fought to spread her thighs against his.

"Ben." His name, a plea on her lips. "Please."

"Please what?"

"Touch me." Her hips lifted from the sheet below her. He wanted her. Needed to tumble into the pleasure of sliding inside her.

He wanted her like this. Just like this.

He moved, lying against her, keeping his weight on his arms and his knees. Keeping her from spreading her legs any wider.

He slipped one hand beneath her belly, lifting her hips slightly. Her back arched beneath his touch, her skin scorching his.

* * *

Olivia's body was on fire. She'd never in her life imagined making love like this, her lover's thighs outside of hers, her body trapped beneath his. But she didn't feel vulnerable. She felt cherished. Erotic.

And then he was there, pressing inside her body, her thighs clenched tight, her hips lifted. A gasp of pleasure slipped from her lips as he slid into her body, filling her.

And then he began to move. The friction of her thighs made it impossible for her to do anything but receive him, take the pleasure he offered with each stroke. She surrendered, arching beneath him and urging him deeper. Her lungs refused to cooperate. The pressure built and built until she crashed into the wave, riding it until Ben tightened and tensed and then wrapped his arms around her and held her close. Her back to his chest. His arms holding her.

His palms folded over her heart.

His phone rang from someplace far away. Olivia sighed and stretched as he rolled over, searching for his phone in the pile of uniform on the floor by the bed.

She wrapped her arms around his waist as he answered the call. "Yeah."

Sorren's voice crashed through the haze of sleep. "Sir, we've got a problem."

Ben sat up, his blood pounding. "What kind of problem?"

"The kind of problem that involves you and me at Escoberra's house right now."

Chapter Twenty-One

They made it to the on-post housing area in record time. A small crowd was gathered outside. Several of the NCOs were keeping them from going inside. Sorren met Ben at the end of the driveway with Carmen and Hailey. He hadn't been able to keep Olivia from driving him.

He wished Olivia was anywhere but here.

"What's the status?" Ben asked his first sergeant even as he embraced Carmen. "Are you okay?" he asked.

She pushed away from his embrace. "Just scared. Ben, he's getting worse." Tears tumbled down her face. "I just want my Jose back and I don't know what to do. I called the police because he scared me."

"Where's Heath?" he asked, looking around for Carmen's son.

"At a friend's."

"Escoberra's destroying the place," Sorren said.

Ben's heart jammed in his throat.

A gunshot cracked through the silence. Ben froze, his heart slamming against his ribs as he fought the ingrained reaction to hit the ground.

His mouth went dry and panic and fear wrestled with rational thought for control.

He breathed deeply, looking between Carmen and Sorren. "Where the fuck did he get the gun?" Ben snapped.

Sorren folded his arms over his chest. "I have no idea," he said roughly.

Carmen held up her hands. "I don't allow guns in my house," she said. "I don't know." She squeezed Ben's arm. "Please help him, Ben. Please?"

Sorren looked over Ben's shoulder. "Ma'am, you probably shouldn't be here."

Ben turned to see Olivia next to him. "Any legal advice?" Ben asked, needing anything to distract himself from the shitstorm in the house.

"He needs to be taken straight to the hospital," she said quietly.

"I don't need to read him his rights?"

Olivia shook her head. "Not right now. He's a threat to himself and others. He needs to be contained." She folded her arms over her chest. Ben wished he didn't see how her hands shook. "Is there a reason why you're not letting the police go in?"

"Because I don't want him to get shot by some private who's played too much Call of Duty," Ben said simply. "Do we have a key?" Ben asked.

Sorren dangled it from one finger. "Already ahead of you, sir. You ready to do this?"

Ben breathed deeply. "Oh sure, why not." He looked at his first sergeant. Ben glanced at Olivia. He wanted to tell her to get back, to go somewhere else. He suddenly very much wanted to shield her from this side of the army.

He didn't want her to see him with blood on him. Or worse, bleeding.

She was determined not to wear that combat patch until she earned one. He'd just as soon she did not earn it today.

But he couldn't say that in front of the entire housing area. She met his gaze and offered a short nod. Her eyes were anxious but she kept her silence.

He walked toward the house, Sorren in step next to him. He stopped near the front door. "Well, here goes nothing. I'm really not in the mood to get stabbed, shot, or have any other holes poked in me," he said dryly.

"Not a good time for jokes, sir," Sorren said.

"When is it not a good time for jokes?" Ben said.

"Sir, one more fucking joke and I'm going to stab you," Sorren growled.

Ben took a deep breath and they went up to the house. He pushed open the front door.

"Escoberra?"

The silence in the house was eerie. There were no pets, no noise from the TV.

Just the silence of the damned. "Escoberra?" Carefully, they moved through each room.

Sorren peered into the kitchen. "First floor is clear," he murmured.

"Escoberra, we're coming upstairs, okay?" Ben tried to swallow but his mouth was dry. "Please don't shoot me. I haven't updated my insurance paperwork and all my money will go to my cat."

Sorren slapped him on the back of the head.

A sound like a booted foot banged against the floor. "We're coming up."

There was a fist-sized hole near the railing. The fallen plaster crunched under their feet on the stairs. A picture lay in a pile of broken glass and splintered wood.

Ben held his breath as they went up the stairs.

They found him in Hailey's room.

He was sitting on his daughter's bed. One hand was streaked with rust-colored blood. Blood mingled with the pink patchwork on the comforter. His eyes were red and filled with tears. A bottle of tequila sat lopsided between his thighs. "I don't know what's wrong with me," he whispered.

"Can I have the gun?" Ben asked quietly.

Escoberra dropped it limply onto the bed.

Ben cleared it and handed it to Sorren behind him.

Escoberra reached for a tiny white rabbit. Blood streaked its pilled fur. The tequila sloshed but didn't spill. "I got this for Hailey the day I adopted her." He looked up at Ben. "I put my little girl in the hospital."

Ben knelt on the edge of the bed. "This isn't going to help." He motioned to Escoberra's bleeding hand.

"I can't control it. It's like there's someone else running my body." He lifted the bottle to his lips, his hands shaking violently. There was a soft pop as he lowered it. "I can't keep doing this to them."

Ben moved slowly, easing the pillowcase off one of the pillows. He folded it into a long strip and reached for Escoberra's bleeding hand. The big NCO didn't fight him as he wrapped the injury, applying pressure to stop the bleeding. Ben's hands shook as he wrapped the wound.

"I think we need to head to the hospital," Ben said quietly. He reached for the tequila. Only then did Escoberra react, his good hand tightening on the neck of the bottle. "Come on, man. Let me take this. Let me get you checked out."

Escoberra's eyes were flat and dull when he looked up at him. "My career is pretty much fucked now, isn't it?"

Ben shook his head, fighting to speak past the lump in his throat. "One of the benefits of being in command. I get to make that decision." He reached up, squeezing his shoulder. "And I think the first order of business is to get you checked out."

"I'm a little bit drunk." Escoberra's eyes were glassy. Looked like that last shot of tequila had sent him over the edge.

"We'll help you out," Ben said. His stomach flipped beneath his ribs, filled with betrayal, fear.

But he shoved it down. He needed the rational part of his brain.

He could fall apart later.

"No cops?"

"No cops," Sorren said behind him.

Escoberra slid to the edge of the bed, swaying hard. He was a big man but between the two of them, they managed to get him down the stairs and outside.

Carmen pulled away from her daughter and rushed up, throwing her arms around his neck. Escoberra lowered his forehead to hers. "I'm sorry," he whispered. "I'm so sorry."

Ben reached out, gripping Carmen's shoulder gently. "We're going to take him to the hospital."

"I've got him, sir," Sorren said.

A chubby military police officer walked up. "Are you the commander?" he asked.

"Yeah," Ben said.

"You got this, sir?"

Ben nodded. "Yeah, we'll take care of it."

Ben and Sorren got Escoberra into the cab of Sorren's truck. Carmen and Hailey followed them in their car and slowly, the crowd dispersed, leaving Ben standing there, feeling useless and empty and angry.

And wrong. He'd been wrong. He'd placed his faith in a man who had let him down.

He needed...he just needed a few fucking minutes to pull himself back together.

He stood at the edge of the corner lot in the military housing unit and tried not to fall apart.

He should follow them to the hospital. He should get cleaned up and get the blood off his hands. Twisted, violent memories collided, coated in bright fucking blood red.

"Hey LT, you okay?"

"My guts hurt."

"No shit, Sherlock. You almost had a zipper self-installed."

Ben tried to lift his head.

"Lay down and stay fucking still."

He looked up at Escoberra. "What the hell are you doing to me?" he asked.

"Trying to keep your spleen from falling out," Escoberra said. "Now hold still. The MEDEVAC is on the ground."

Ben looked down at his hands. They were covered with blood. His heart slammed against his ribs. And then his hands started shaking again as the adrenaline rolled off him in waves, leaving him barely upright.

There were a million things he should be doing just then. A dozen other places he needed to be.

Instead, he stood, unable to move. Unable to stop his racing thoughts. His mind kept replaying the incident over and over and over in his head.

He bunched his hands into fists, breathing deeply, trying to get everything under control and failing badly.

There was movement out of the corner of his eye.

Olivia.

Chapter Twenty-Two

He was bruised. He was bloody.

He was shattered.

She looked into his eyes and did not see the man she'd come to know looking back at her. This man looked like Ben but in his bleak gaze, she did not see any trace of the man who laughed with her during sex. Or who'd struggled so much to hold on to his soul while executing the toughest of duties.

She took a single step forward. He flinched and the ingrained reaction hurt, cutting her deeply.

She stopped a breath away from him. His breathing was the only sound over the quiet that was falling over the now empty yard. Ragged. Rough.

She touched his shoulder gently. It was the same strong man she'd come to know beneath her fingers. The same solid man beneath her touch. "Ben," she whispered.

Slowly, he turned to look at her. His eyes were filled with unshed emotion. She ached for him. "Let me take you home," she whispered.

He shook his head. "I have to go to the hospital." His voice sounded like broken glass.

She glanced down at the blood. He shook his head, answering her unspoken question. "I'm fine," he said shortly.

"You're not fine."

"I don't have a choice." His smile was brittle and humorless, and he pressed his lips into a flat line. "I'm a big boy, Olivia."

She knew he'd just been through a traumatic event. But knowing it didn't make the pain of his harsh distancing any easier to bear.

Now was not the time to pick that fight.

"I'll drive you," she said, refusing to let him push her away.

"You'll get blood in your car."

If he was trying to piss her off, it worked. "Don't be an asshole, Ben. Get in the goddamned car."

When she could trust that he'd follow her down, she led him to her vehicle. Silence hung on between them on the short drive to the hospital. It hung on as he walked into the emergency room and caused a minor panic until he explained that the blood wasn't his.

They sent him to the back and let her go along. He disappeared into an exam room and when he didn't come out, she followed him.

She found him bent over the sink, scrubbing his hands furiously. Scrubbing, scrubbing. His face a mask of bitter concentration.

The water in the sink ran clear and still he scrubbed. He dragged paper towels from the dispenser and scoured his skin.

Her heart broke for him.

She approached him carefully. Slipped her hands into the water and captured his hands. The water nearly scalded her but she did not yank away.

Slowly she urged his hands out of the blazing hot water.

"Stop," she whispered. She held his hands to her chest, ignoring the water penetrating her jacket. She simply held them there, waiting, hoping she could break through the shell-shocked haze and see the man she cared so much about.

Finally, finally in the dim silence he met her gaze.

She could do nothing but wrap her arms around him. He stood there limp as she held him. Then slowly, he leaned into her and put his arms around her.

The only thing that mattered was the grief in his eyes. The blame and self-loathing that looked back at her.

Sorren walked in without knocking. He didn't even blink as Olivia took a step away from Ben's embrace.

Sorren held up his hand. "Don't worry about it, ma'am," he said roughly. "Sir, you're needed."

Ben frowned. "What's going on?"

"Escoberra's not cooperating. We need you to do that direct order thing."

He turned toward Olivia. She urged him toward the door. "Go. I'll wait for you out front."

He was gone, a shadow of himself. He was functioning purely on autopilot. She knew it. Sorren knew it.

But she wondered if Ben knew it.

And worse, she wondered what would happen when he finally surfaced from the haze.

It was nearly sunrise the next day when Ben finally stepped out of the emergency room. Hospital lights illuminated the gray pre-dawn and dark silence stretched out across the now deserted installation.

"It's quiet at dawn," he murmured, hiding his surprise that she was still there. That she hadn't left him.

Olivia stuffed her hands in her pockets and nodded. "Yeah."

He stopped walking and looked at her. "You've been here all night."

She lifted one shoulder. "Yeah?"

"Aren't you going to get in trouble?"

She shrugged again. "Had something more important to do," she said softly.

"Worry about me?"

"Maybe."

He swayed on his feet as fatigue finally conquered the adrenaline that had been keeping him upright.

Olivia was there, slipping an arm around his waist and pressing to his side. "Let me take you home," she said. Her voice was gentle but brokered no argument.

"I'm not going to be much company."

She lifted her chin to look up at him. "You shouldn't be alone."

He glanced down at his hands. Searched the shadows for signs of blood. They were still red and raw from the hot water and scrubbing he'd done earlier.

Olivia's hand slid over his. He looked at her. "I have to call my boss," he said quietly.

She waited near the car as he palmed his cell phone and called LTC Gilliad. "Sir, it's Captain Teague. They've got Escoberra stabilized. They're admitting him."

"Good work today, Ben. That NCO is alive because of you and your first sergeant."

Gilliad's words ran hollow. Ben tasted bile in his throat. "Roger, sir."

"Get some sleep."

Ben's first thought was to say something flippant about taking the party into next week, that sleep was a crutch. But he was too fucking worn down. "Roger, sir. Here's hoping I don't have to call you until Monday."

"We can only hope," Gilliad said.

Ben hung up the phone, too bone-dead tired to bother putting it back into his pocket. It sat, cradled limply in his hand. He leaned his head back on the seat and closed his eyes, fighting to keep the fatigue and soul-crushing sorrow from washing over him.

She drove him to her house and he simply closed his eyes and tried to stay awake. He wasn't sure if he dozed, if the sleep that pulled at him had actually managed to lure him into slumber but the next thing he knew, they were at her small home.

He tried to smile, he really did. But his bones felt just too fucking heavy. She silently closed the door behind him.

Then her arms slipped around his waist. Her palms folded over his heart. She simply stood there, pressed against his back, her body solid and soft against his when he wanted to crash to his fucking knees and collapse.

Her arms tightened around him then released him. "Go take a shower," she said, slipping around to his front. Her fingers were cool on his cheek. "I'll make breakfast."

Ben swallowed and lowered his forehead to hers. His fingers rested on the side of her neck and he simply stood, absorbing the heat of her skin against his. "Olivia," he whispered.

She brushed her lips against his. "Go. Shower."

He nodded and stripped off his bloodstained clothes. The shower seared his skin. Ben stepped beneath the water and let it scald his face and neck but he knew, knew that no matter what, the stain of Escoberra's blood would forever be on his hands.

His uniform was gone when he stepped out of the shower forty minutes later. He hooked a towel around his waist and padded into the kitchen to find Olivia chopping an onion on the center island.

She glanced up at him. She'd tied her hair up in a pony-tail, releasing it from her daily bun.

The fog in his head was clearing. The grief was fighting for release but still, Ben fought it. He wasn't ready to go there. Not yet.

Today was a win. No one had died.

Except for Ben's faith in the men around him. His blindness had nearly cost Escoberra's entire family everything.

She smiled up at him. "Omelets?" Her gaze flicked down at his towel.

He flushed. "It smells fantastic."

"I'm not much of a cook, but I do know how to do this much."

He leaned across the counter and kissed her. A gentle kiss. Nothing more. But loaded with all the things he couldn't say.

He wanted to tell her she was right; that he'd been a blind fool. But the words were lodged in his throat and he was terrified that if he started talking, everything would tear free.

And he wasn't ready to fall apart. Not yet.

Maybe not ever.

The crash would come soon. Olivia knew it from too much previous experience. Ben could have been a raging asshole tonight and she wouldn't have left him alone.

He padded back into the kitchen as she pulled the eggs off the stove. She set the pan in the sink and went to him then, wrapping her arms around his waist. She brushed her lips against his. "Eat. And here's hoping we don't end this horrific night with food poisoning."

His laugh surprised him. She saw the flicker in his eyes. As though it was wrong to crack a joke at that moment. "That's not very encouraging," he said, nudging the pile of eggs with his fork. "But I'll take my chances."

She picked at her own food while he ate, her stomach

twisted into too many knots to keep much down. "This is fantastic," he said, clearing his plate.

He sat there after he finished, his gaze a hundred years away, staring at memories only he could see.

"Hey." She padded over to him and slipped her fingers into his, urging him to his feet. He followed her down the hall to the bedroom. He sat on the edge of the bed, his shoulders slumped, his eyes bleak.

Then she crossed the space between them, kneeling in front of him. She slipped her arms around his waist, resting her head against his heart. Its beat was slow and steady and real beneath her cheek. His arms came around her effortlessly and held her tight. He rested his head against the top of hers. A simple, powerful embrace. "I'm so fucking tired," he whispered against her hair.

"Sleep is an excellent plan," she said, tipping her lips up to brush against his.

She crawled into bed next to him, shifting until they were both comfortable.

"I don't sleep well," he whispered when they were both settled. She rested her head on his shoulder, her palm over his heart.

"It started after I got blown up." His voice rumbled beneath her cheek. "That's how I got the tattoo. I was awake at all hours of the night. Tattoo parlors are open." He turned, brushing his lips across her forehead. "I started it because I wanted to feel again. I wanted to hide the scars." He shifted, his arm tightening around her.

"It's beautiful," she whispered.

He breathed in deeply. "It didn't help me sleep."

She curled her fingers into his chest. There was nothing for her to say. Nothing that could ease the pain or the fatigue in his voice. She simply stayed with him.

And waited until his breathing evened out, until sleep

pulled him under before she closed her own eyes, nestling closer. As she drifted down into troubled sleep, she couldn't help but worry about what tomorrow would bring.

In that space between sleeping and waking, his hand came up and covered hers. He threaded his fingers with hers, his grip warm. Solid.

Real.

Chapter Twenty-Three

The phone vibrated incessantly. Ben blinked at the solid weight pressed against his side. He angled his chin in the darkness and realized Olivia was curled against him. He groped and found his phone. He'd slept all day and into the night.

It was a goddamned miracle.

"Teague."

"Hey, sir."

Ben frowned and eased from the bed. "Top?"

"Yeah."

Ben didn't think it was possible to slur the word "yeah," a word without a single hard sound in it, but Sorren somehow managed. "Are you drunk?"

"Very much so."

"Are you alone?"

Sorren's laugh was caustic. "Don't worry, I'm not calling to tell you I'm cashing it in or anything. I just wanted to check on you. Today kind of sucked balls."

"What time is it?" Ben asked.

"Yeah, well, fuck you, too. That's the last time I worry about you."

Ben grinned and it felt real. Tired. But real. "I love you

too, Top." Ben braced his forehead on his palm. "Yeah, today really did suck."

"But Escoberra's gonna be okay."

Ben felt something sour in his guts. "Until we court-martial him."

"Nah," Sorren said. "Sarn't major is going to advise the colonel we just throw his ass out. No point in court-martialing him."

Ben frowned, rubbing his eyes with his hand, trying to clear the fog in his brain. "When did you talk to the sarn't major?"

"After I left the hospital. He came by with cigars." Ben heard the twist of a cap off a bottle. "We don't need to prove a point with Escoberra."

Ben snuck out of the bedroom, somewhat amazed that he was having this conversation. But what the hell.

Ben cradled his head in his palm. "Yeah, Top. I know." He took a deep breath. "Can we talk about it Monday? It's been a long fucking week."

"Yeah. Here's hoping I don't have to call you again."

"Here's hoping," Ben said. He clicked the phone off.

Ben's brain was fogged with sleep. He stared at the phone for a long moment. Sorren was half past hammered but for once it wasn't a middle of the night phone call about someone being in jail.

That was a good thing at least. He padded back into the bedroom and set his phone down quietly on the nightstand next to Olivia's bed.

Olivia was curled beneath the blanket, her body outlined by soft fabric. A searing tenderness ripped through him. There was no detachment toward this woman. No professional distance.

She'd stood with him when he'd fallen completely apart. He vaguely remembered it but still. Still, she'd stayed.

Ben brushed a strand of hair away from her temple and kissed her gently.

He slid into the bed with her and curled around her body until she was flush against him, her thighs cradled by his, her back pressed to his chest. He slipped his arm around her waist, his palm resting against her chest. She was everywhere against him. Soft and comforting. Warm and real.

He was tempted to wake her up. He had the sudden urge to lose himself in her, to find his pleasure with this woman.

But it had been a long day and even longer night. She needed sleep. God, but he'd wanted to keep her from living through the clusterfuck at Escoberra's. His hand trembled as he brushed her hair out of her face.

She'd already lived through it. Too many times. He should have been the one protecting her but instead, she'd kept him upright. She was so strong, so driven.

Damaged. The scars on her body hid the deeper scars, the scars that drove her to try and save the world.

But for now, she needed sleep. He wrapped her against his body, unaware of falling into sleep. Only that between one moment and the next he was awake and then he wasn't.

She found him outside as the sun rose in the eastern Texas sky. He sat with his feet on the porch railing, cradling a half-empty cup of coffee against his knee. A gentle breeze rustled his hair.

For a moment, Olivia considered leaving him in his solitude, unsure whether to interrupt. She considered going to take a shower and letting him be. But that wasn't in her nature. It was two days after they'd gotten Escoberra admitted to the hospital. They'd slept and eaten, made love and slept some more. But the shadow of the previous night hung over them.

Olivia stepped onto the porch. Ben glanced at her and

after a moment, offered her the coffee cup. She was tempted but instead shook her head gently. "I'm fine, thanks."

She moved to sit in one of the chairs on the porch, sliding close enough that she could slip her feet onto his chair near his thigh.

"Did you sleep?" she asked after a moment.

"Yeah."

She rested her cheek against her knees. "I didn't sleep for days after the Hellmans died." She shifted, locking her fingers in front of her legs. "Not sleeping happens a lot for me. Especially when something triggers the memories from finding my dad," she whispered.

"Jesus, Olivia. I'm so fucking sorry you went through that again."

"Thanks," she said quietly. She met his gaze. "But I can't keep hiding from it. It might have sucked but it's part of who I am." She bit her lip.

"That's why you stayed with me?" he asked.

She offered a half shrug. "I stayed because I care about you." She met his gaze in the midmorning light. "And I don't think anyone should be alone after something like that."

He lifted the cup again, then set it back down. "Are you hungry?"

"For food?" His eyes lit up a little at her weak attempt at a joke.

"Yeah," he said quietly. "Why don't we go to Talarico's for breakfast. I hear they have amazing crepes."

She cupped her chin in her palm. "Sounds like a good plan."

She stood then and moved between the table and his knees and sat on his lap. The chair groaned beneath their combined weight but she ignored it. She slipped her fingers into his hair, urging his mouth up where she could kiss him.

It was meant as a teasing kiss, something easy and light.

It quickly detoured into something searing and intense. It was harsh. It was fierce.

And it ended with both of them breathless. Ben's fingers cradled the back of her neck, stroking lightly. "Food?" he whispered against her lips.

"Food," she said. She lowered her forehead to his. "I worried about you last night," she admitted finally.

"It's nice to be worried about," he said softly.

He pulled her close then and she didn't protest. She buried her face in his neck, felt his breath on her shoulder as he held her. Or maybe he simply held on to her. She didn't know. She didn't care.

Something that had started as a casual escape from the darkness had morphed into something more. And now? Now she couldn't remember what her life had been like before Ben Teague had become a part of her day. Her morning. Her night.

He leaned his head back to look at her.

"What," he asked.

She kissed him gently. "Food." She brushed her thumb over his bottom lip. "We can talk shop later."

Breakfast was crepes and fresh fruit. Olivia couldn't remember the last time she'd had anything so delicious. They ate in relative silence, letting the morning go on around them.

Olivia had showered and tried to forget what Ben had looked like, covered in his soldier's blood and painted with his grief.

It was easy to let the warm Tuscan feel of the restaurant push away the harsh reality they were both attempting to avoid. When their waiter offered espresso, Olivia was tempted, but only for a moment, to say no.

Then a glance at her watch convinced her otherwise. It was past noon. "Breakfast is more like lunch," she murmured.

They sat on the patio to wait for espresso and canapés en route from the kitchen. Ben stared into his glass.

"It's been a hell of a week. I don't even know which way is up."

She brushed her thumb over his. "You'll find your stride, Ben. First few weeks in command are always rough."

He looked at her then. "Have you commanded?"

She shook her head. "There aren't a lot of command opportunities for lawyers." She sipped her wine. "But I've worked with a lot of commanders. First rule of command is that the first month is always the roughest."

"Really?"

"Yeah. You're like new parents, but figuring out someone else's kids."

He laughed softly then rested his head against the back of the chair. "Never really thought about it that way." He took a sip of his wine.

He stared out over the lake. A light breeze blew in from the water. "I keep thinking about Escoberra."

Olivia set her glass down as their waiter brought the espresso to the table. She unthreaded her fingers from his and tore open a couple of thin sugar packets then stirred her coffee slowly, trying to find the words to ease the guilt she heard in his voice.

She waited until he met her gaze. "You didn't drive him to this."

"I can't help but feel like the war changed something inside him. That's not an excuse. It's just…" His throat moved as he swallowed hard. He scrubbed his hand over his mouth.

"I know." She squeezed his hand. "I know. But you're not his keeper. You're not responsible for what he does or doesn't do."

Ben set his cup down roughly. "Do you know how much

we partied when we came back from Iraq the first time? Goddamn, we were so fucking happy to be home alive." He covered his mouth with his hand. "He was so fucking happy to be home." He rubbed the scar on his stomach. "It didn't matter that he'd nearly lost his career over the attack on our base." He sighed heavily. "I couldn't let it go. I couldn't be around him, knowing I was getting promoted and that the commander wouldn't even approve Escoberra for an award." He took a sip of his espresso. "I let the distance grow between us. Because I was ashamed to be an officer. I couldn't figure out how to be an officer and his friend."

There was nothing she could say to ease the guilt that tore at him.

She simply sat, her fingers twined with his. "I should have seen this coming," he said quietly.

"You can't blame yourself for this," she said quietly. "You can get him help." She slipped around the table, cradling his face. "You can't change the past, but you can make a difference now."

He tugged her until she came into his lap. Tucked her against him and simply sat.

And tried to find a way to face the day.

Chapter Twenty-Four

Ben walked into his company ops Monday morning and was greeted by the happiest thing he could possibly have seen. It was more than his first sergeant making coffee. It was *how* his first sergeant was making coffee.

Sorren slid his coffee cup beneath the espresso machine and waited for the water to heat up before he pressed the button that ground the beans and made magic happen.

Ben grinned at Sorren. "This is better than a puppy. You know that, right?"

"I figure we're going to have a lot of long days and nights. We might as well not have to suffer over shitty coffee." He pointed to the counter near the front door. "Cuss pot. Not that I expect any of us to actually stop cussing but it'll pay for the beans."

Ben grinned and shook his head, then went into his office for his own cup. "You know, I'm tempted to kiss you right now."

"Please don't," Sorren said.

Ben waited patiently for the machine to work its magic again and then sipped the espresso, straight up, and enjoyed the violent bolt of caffeine straight into his bloodstream. "Now that is a fabulous way to start a morning."

Sorren glared at him. "Did you just use the word 'fabulous'?"

Ben grinned. "Maybe."

Sorren shook his head and sighed heavily. "Some days, sir, some days."

"Happy Monday to you, too."

Sorren studied him quietly for a long moment. "You slept this weekend, didn't you?"

"Yeah." Ben sobered. "I take it by the fact that I didn't hear from you again over the weekend that there were no more incidents?"

Sorren shook his head. "Nope. Escoberra was a perfect saint with the nurses and his guards."

"Are they going to move him to the psych ward?"

"No. They're doing some CT scans, though, which is something I've never heard of before. They're keeping him for another day or so to make sure that he's stable."

Ben sank down into one of the chairs at the conference room table in the middle of his company ops. "So what do we do with him, Top?"

"Don't know. Spent all weekend thinking about it." Sorren made a second cup of coffee then joined Ben at the table. He took a long pull off his mug. "We've got major training events coming up in a month. We've got to get this formation under control. We need to send a message and send it fast." He pointed at Ben with his cup.

Ben sighed heavily. "I want to send him to rehab."

Sorren slammed his coffee cup down on the table. "Rehab isn't the answer here. Escoberra's not an alcoholic; there's something else going on. One minute he denies knowing what happened, the next he's thinking of killing himself because he remembers. I don't like this any more than you do but he's got bigger problems than we can fix in the fucking army. We're going back to war and we've got good soldiers out there who are waiting for us to lead them. We can't keep pussyfooting around with this guy who keeps drinking and beating up his family."

"He was a good soldier." Ben set his own cup down.

Sorren leaned toward him. "I got what you want to do here, sir. Believe me, I understand. But I don't want to bury any more kids because we were so busy chasing down these guys we didn't have time to train the rest of them right. We've got training we need to get to."

In the silence that followed, neither of them came up with a solution. Ben tipped his mug up and looked into the splash of coffee at the bottom of the mug. It was a hard, cold reality that some soldiers had bigger problems than the army could fix.

"Top, when's the last time anyone saw Zittoro? Tomorrow is his thirty-six month mark," Ben said quietly. "I'm kind of shocked he made it."

"He hasn't made it, sir." Sorren looked into his coffee and avoided Ben's gaze. "I've had NCOs go to his apartment twelve times over the last couple of weeks, dragging his ass to work."

Ben stilled, the implication of his first sergeant's words settling like a shroud over his shoulders. He'd made sure Zittoro got to work, made sure the kid did what he needed to do so that he could make his thirty-six month mark. He'd supported Ben's decision even though he disagreed with it.

"The NCOs are pissed off, aren't they?" Ben asked quietly.

Sorren shrugged, avoiding his gaze. "Not as much as you'd think. They're kind of impressed that you'd do this for one of the guys."

Ben's throat constricted and he took a drink of his coffee, hoping to break the lump. When he could talk without embarrassing himself, he said simply, "Thank you, Top. For taking care of Zittoro."

Sorren grunted. "Like you said, he was a good soldier. We can't save him but maybe he'll be able to do it on his own someday." He sniffed. "Sometimes the right thing to do isn't the easy thing to do."

"Sometimes it's not the legal thing to do, either." He sighed. "If the colonel finds out about this, he could have my ass for it."

Sorren shrugged. "What's he going to do, yell at you some more?" He lifted his coffee in mock salute. "What's going on with you and the lawyer?" Sorren asked.

"I don't know what to call it," Ben said. "She's—" Steady. Amazing. Funny. Smart. Sexy. He settled on amazing. "She's pretty amazing."

"She's terrifying," Sorren said. "I mean that in a good way."

Ben drummed his fingers on the table, needing to change the subject away from whatever this thing between him and Olivia was. Because it was a strange thing, this feeling of being needed, wanted. Of knowing someone was there, waiting for him at the end of the day.

He didn't have the words for it.

But it felt good. That much, he knew.

And he wasn't ready to pour his heart out to his first sergeant and start writing poetry. He cleared his throat roughly. "The LTs have a wager on the shoot house next week."

Sorren lifted one eyebrow. "Oh, really?"

"They think they can take you and me out."

Sorren snorted rudely. "They're dreaming."

Ben shrugged. "Three against two."

"The day I get taken out by three lieutenants is the day I need to retire," Sorren said. "What's the wager?"

"A fifth of black label Crown Royal." Ben pointed at him with his mug. "You know we can't lose this, right?"

Sorren shot him a baleful look. "Excuse my language but are you high, sir? I've seen the LTs do PT. I'll wipe them off the floor in three minutes and that's if we take our time."

Ben grinned. "Glad to hear you're up for it. I'd really hate to have to watch them drink that in front of us. That stuff is expensive."

Olivia's hands trembled as she looked at the file in front of her, then looked up at her friend. The news was no easier to swallow hearing it from a friend than from a complete stranger in a white lab coat. "You're sure, Emily?"

This was going to devastate Ben. But it was an answer. Not a good one but the mystery was no longer hidden.

They knew what was wrong with Escoberra.

"I'm positive. There's no mistake in the results from the CT scans we just did. Classic symptoms."

Her breath shook as she tried to inhale, then she looked over at her friend, sitting across from her in Olivia's office.

Olivia looked at the scales on her desk. The broken scale heavier than the intact plate.

But this? This was so much worse than what she suspected. Because it was a permanent thing. Maybe even a thing that they couldn't fix.

"If the nurse at the school hadn't told you what Hailey's little brother had said, we might not have looked into this until it was too late," Emily said.

Olivia rubbed her hand over her mouth, her heart lodged in her throat. She had been wrong about Escoberra.

For once, she was glad.

But it didn't make the diagnosis any easier to deal with. Because it meant that Escoberra might never get better.

It could mean that things were only going to get worse for him.

She had to tell Ben. She had to be the one to tell him what was going on with his sergeant. He needed to hear it from her.

She owed him that much.

Olivia ran her fingers over the broken plate on the scales of justice. And with a slight flick of her wrist, the unbroken plate tipped lower. For once, maybe just this time, justice wasn't the most important thing. Maybe this time, jail wasn't the answer.

The lump in her throat was solid, making it hard to breathe.

"Are you okay?" Emily asked quietly. "I know you were pretty hard up on putting this guy in jail."

Olivia shook her head, smiling flatly. "For once, I'm glad to be wrong." Her voice cracked as she spoke. "But I wish this wasn't the reason." She studied the paperwork and tried to swallow the lump blocking her throat. "It's going to crush Ben," she whispered.

"They've got some good treatment programs," Emily said. "It'll take the division commander to sign off on it but it's worth a shot to try."

Olivia nodded then stood. "I guess I need to go. This shouldn't wait," she said.

She didn't resist when Emily pulled her into a quick hug. "You did the right thing," she whispered.

"It doesn't feel like it," Olivia said.

She picked up the folder and sent Ben a text, asking him to meet her.

"What's so important that I had to meet you here?" Ben walked up to Olivia outside the First Cav headquarters. To their left, the memorial rose out of the parade field. Polished black granite gleamed in the midafternoon sun.

"I have something to tell you." She swallowed, her voice thick. "You're not going to like it."

His expression shuttered closed. He stuffed his hands in his pockets. The muscles in his neck tensed. "Are you secretly a man?"

She smiled and wished she could laugh at the joke. "No."
Deep breaths did nothing to dislodge the knot in her chest.
"This is about Escoberra."

"Damn it, Olivia…"

"Hear me out." She reached for the folder she'd cradled
beneath her arm. "I wanted to be the one to tell you.

"About a week ago, the school nurse called me. She said
Hailey's little brother had been talking to her about his dad."
She wished she didn't see his hand shake as he took the
folder. "I asked Emily to see about some extra tests while
he was in the hospital." Olivia swallowed. "It's a confirmed
diagnosis."

She held her silence while Ben read through the paperwork. A shadow darkened his expression. His eyes were
bleak and sad and empty when he finally looked back up
at her.

"Severe traumatic brain injury?" His voice broke. "What
does that even mean?"

"In his case? Blackout rages. Memory loss. Severe head-
aches." She sucked in a deep breath. "He's been in at least
five documented explosions. He's lost consciousness at least
six times that the docs know about."

"How do we fix this?" Ben whispered. His eyes were
nothing but sad now. "There's got to be something we
can do?"

Olivia took a step closer, afraid that he would break with
the reality that Escoberra might be lost forever. TBI was a
life-altering injury. "There's an experimental program down
at Fort Sam in San Antonio." She took a step toward him,
turning a page in the folder. "I've called in a favor with the
division commander."

Ben looked at her sharply. "You did that?"

She nodded. "You believed in this man. And I was wrong
about him." She lifted her palm to cover his heart. "I'm so

fucking glad I was wrong." She breathed out slowly. "This paperwork will get him admitted. No red tape. No waiting months for the packet to be approved." She hesitated and a long silence stretched between them. "Just have your commander sign off on it and I can get it signed by division."

Ben stared at the packet, his heart pounding in his temples. Severe TBI. Evidence of brain damage. The world beneath his feet tilted and rocked. Everything clicked all at once. The anger. The feeling that things had changed.

That Escoberra was no longer the man who'd kept Ben from bleeding out all those years ago.

He *had* changed. Everything had changed.

He blinked rapidly, staring down at his brave, fierce lawyer. "That means he really beat the hell out of Hailey, didn't he?"

He finally lifted his gaze to hers. She nodded slowly and his heart broke a little more. "But you were right. There was some other reason," she whispered.

He shook his head, denying the reality of her words. "I don't want to be right. Not like this. Not if it means he can't get better."

She rested her hands on his shoulders. His skin burned where she touched him. His soul ached with the truth of her words.

He stopped then. Clenched his fists by his sides and breathed deeply, staring at the packet in his hand that held Escoberra's fate on a single sheet of paper. "Thank you," he said quietly. "For doing this for him."

He bit his lips together, needing space before he broke. Before the weight of the war and the weariness threatening to destroy him succeeded and he fell apart in front of her. "I have to go brief the boss," he said.

"Are you okay?"

He looked down at the file. "I don't have a choice," he said quietly.

If there was a word for the misery simmering in Olivia's chest, she didn't know what it was. It physically hurt to breathe but there was nothing she could do but trust that Ben would be okay. She trusted him. It was a leap of faith, one that hurt her to take. She'd hurt him. She'd known it would hurt him when she told him about Escoberra.

Her heart was tight in her chest and there was a solid lump in her throat. Grief for him was a physical thing sitting on her lungs, pressing down. But she held on to the trust in him.

There was a sharp rap on her door.

Hope soared inside her, only to die in a fiery crash on the cold polished floor. Captain Marshall stood in her doorway. "LTC Gilliad wants to see you."

She could see at that moment why Ben hated this greasy prick. He wore a self-satisfied smirk that made her want to slap him. But she refused to give him the satisfaction. "Thank you," was all she said.

"Do you always shack up with the guys you work with?"

She stopped and briefly reconsidered her stance on workplace violence.

She turned and smiled coldly. "Funny, I wouldn't think you'd be casting too many stones considering you were relieved from command for malfeasance, Captain."

Marshall's smile could have cut glass. Marshall shrugged. "I figured since you're blowing Teague, you've sacrificed any right to be called by your rank."

Olivia's smile didn't budge. "I'm sorry, Captain, but when exactly did I grant you permission to talk to me that way?"

"Marshall!" Marshall stiffened as Gilliad came out of his office. "Get your fucking ass outside my office, Captain.

You're in enough goddamned trouble without adding cursing at my staff to your file."

Olivia stepped out of his way as he stomped down the hallway.

She wisely kept her mouth shut as she walked into Gilliad's office. She'd never seen Gilliad so furious. His breathing was labored and rough. His fists clenched by his sides.

"How many packets is Ben Teague sitting on?"

"Sir?"

He slammed his hand on his desk. "Don't fucking lie to me, Major Hale. I am not in the fucking mood to be lied to." He sucked in a hard, ugly breath. "Now then. How many packets."

Olivia lifted her chin. "Sir, you will not talk to me that way."

Gilliad came around the desk. He didn't approach her. He didn't have to. She could feel the rage radiating off him like a physical thing. "I'm going to ask you one more time, Major."

"Sir, if you're accusing me of something, say it. But I'm not going to stand here and be threatened."

He yanked a file off his desk and thrust it at her. "Late packets. Teague's. And yet you never briefed me on any of them."

"Sir, they were not outside the window requiring your direct involvement. If you want to command each individual company, you don't need the captains."

His jaw twitched. There was violence in his eyes. The muscle in one cheek spasmed. "Sergeant Major!"

She felt the blast from his shout. Still she did not move, not when Sergeant Major Cox walked in. Not when he closed the door behind him.

"I want every first sergeant and commander in this office in the next twenty minutes. We're going to go line by line over every single packet in this battalion."

"Roger, sir." Beside her, Cox sniffed. "Teague is outside."

"By all means, send him in and let's see what he's got to say for himself."

She held her breath when Ben walked in and stood at the position of attention beside her. His expression was still raw, still aching. It was too soon for any attempt to talk to him. He needed time. She could do that. He was reeling from the news about Escoberra.

That didn't make standing next to him, unable to offer any comfort, any easier.

"Teague, how many packets have you processed?"

Beside her, he stiffened. "Twelve, sir."

Gilliad looked down at his list. "What about Zittoro?"

"Zittoro is on emergency leave, sir."

Gilliad's cheek twitched again. "Who gave you permission to put him on leave?"

She heard his quick intake of breath and held her own. Shit, this was going to be bad.

Ben's words were carefully measured. "Sir, I wasn't aware that you were the approving authority for leaves and passes. I thought that was well within the scope of my duties."

Gilliad's nostrils flared violently. "Don't get fucking smart with me, Teague. Now is not the fucking time."

Beside her, Ben stiffened. "As opposed to a more appropriate time? When would that be, sir?"

"I want Zittoro out of the army today, do you understand me?"

"He's on leave, sir. He'll be back tomorrow."

"Today."

Ben shook his head, looking straight ahead. "I can't do that, sir."

Gilliad pinned him with a hard look. Olivia held her breath. "Are you telling me you're going to disobey a lawful order?"

"Sir, I'm telling you I can't comply with that order."

Gilliad said nothing for an impossible space of time.

Olivia felt sweat running down her spine but she didn't dare move. Gilliad sank down into his chair.

Ben couldn't remember his commander ever looking so worn down. Ben had a new appreciation for what his commander was going through. After last week, Ben wanted to keep a flask in his desk. "When were you going to tell me about Escoberra?" Gilliad asked quietly.

"Sir, I informed you that he was admitted over the weekend."

"You did not tell me that he'd been beating his daughter and threatening his family," Gilliad said quietly. "How am I supposed to trust you if you can't tell me the truth?"

"Sir, I never lied to you."

Gilliad pinned him with a cold, hard look. "If I have to give you a class on lying by omissions still being lying, Captain Teague, I don't think I need you as a commander," Gilliad said quietly.

Ben sighed quietly. "Sir, the hospital diagnosed Escoberra with severe traumatic brain injury. I've got the paperwork to send him to San Antonio for a treatment program."

"This is the man we just said was beating on his family?" Gilliad said. "Is that what we're doing with domestic abusers now? Rewarding them with treatment?"

"Sir, I have to agree with Bandit Six," Sergeant Major Cox said. "Escoberra needs treatment, not punishment."

"You've never agreed with me a day in your life." Ben glanced at the sergeant major. "Who are you and what have you done with Sergeant Major Cox?"

But the joke fell flat, coated in the barely restrained fury in Ben's voice.

"Now isn't the time, Teague," Sergeant Major said out of the side of his mouth.

"I'm not sending Escoberra to a treatment program. I want that son of a bitch out of my army immediately."

Sergeant Major Cox moved to stand next to Ben. "Sir, I think it's time you and I had a long talk."

Gilliad glared at both of them. "Everyone get the fuck out of my office. If those packets aren't processed by close of business today, Teague, you're out of a fucking job."

Ben started to speak but Olivia grabbed him, dragging him out of the office before he could stick his foot into his mouth any further.

"What the hell are you doing?" she hissed.

"I don't need you to save me from myself. He wants to fire me over Escoberra, fine. Fucking fine. I quit. I never wanted the goddamned job in the first place."

"You don't mean that."

He ripped the rank off the center of his chest and threw it at her feet. "Try me."

Ben stalked out of the headquarters. His lungs ached; his shoulders were tight and tense with unspent anger and frustration. This was what completely losing his shit felt like.

He knew it all too well.

It had been a good five years since he'd last taken his rank off and thrown it at someone's feet.

"You keep quitting, one of these days someone is going to take you seriously."

"I'm not in the mood, Iaconelli," Ben snapped.

"I can see that," Reza said mildly, falling into step next to him as Ben stalked furiously away from the headquarters. Away from work. Away from the noise and the chaos and the burning betrayal of the leaders around him.

Ben rounded on his longtime friend. "I never wanted this fucking job. You, Gilliad, everyone pushed me to take it. I should have fucking resigned my goddamned commission."

"So why didn't you?" Reza stepped right into his face, shoving him backward. "Why the fuck did you take the goddamned job? You could have refused. You could have walked away just like you did. But you picked up the fucking guidon and you ran with it." He shoved Ben back a little bit. "Don't blame this on anyone but yourself. You could have refused. You didn't."

"Don't get on your high fucking horse right now, Reza."

Reza jammed his index finger into Ben's chest. "I'm tired of you running and acting like a scared little boy every time something gets a little rough."

"That's really rich, coming from you. You've been out of the bottle for what, sixty days this time?"

Reza ground his teeth, the muscles in his jaw pulsing violently. "This isn't about me. This is one hundred percent about you."

"No, it's not. It's about them." He motioned behind him toward the wall of names, etched forever into the cold, black granite memorial. "It's about all of them," he whispered.

"No." Reza moved to stand next to him. "It's about you. You can't bring them back. Fighting with your battalion commander doesn't bring a single one of them back." Reza gripped his shoulder. "And getting yourself fired doesn't help guys like Escoberra and Foster and Zittoro. Those are the boys you can still help. But not if you get yourself fired. Or quit."

"What's the point, Reza? What's the point of this job if I can't even do anything to help my guys? Nothing I do is going to make a goddamned difference and the battalion commander is flipping his shit about these packets."

Reza scoffed quietly. "He's a little tense right now. The brigade commander threatened to relieve him this morning."

Ben looked over at Reza. "How do you know that?"

"Overheard the conversation at PT."

Ben couldn't summon a single emotion. Not outrage. Not sympathy. "Not sure I really care," he said after a moment.

"You can't bring any of them back," Reza said. "But you can make a difference now." He paused, letting the silence hang heavy between them. "But it starts with putting that rank on your chest and being a goddamned leader. Standing up for your men is the most important thing you can do," Reza said quietly.

"Escoberra needs to be transferred to Fort Sam and there's no fucking way the boss is going to let that happen now." He shoved his hands in his pockets. The sense of defeat was crushing. But beneath the defeat was a faint seed of hope.

Faint but there.

"Wait until tomorrow. Talk to the boss then." Beside him, Reza sighed. "But don't quit. You're better than that."

It was a long time before Ben walked back into his company ops.

Sorren was waiting for him. Near his hand on the conference room table sat Ben's rank.

And Sorren looked ready to whip Ben's ass.

"You quitting on me, sir?" Sorren said.

"I haven't decided yet," Ben said.

Sorren tossed the rank at him, slamming Escoberra's packet onto the table in front of him. "You need to make a decision and stick with it. I'm not going to deal with you getting PMS once a week and quitting on me every time the commander chews your ass."

Ben let the rank fall to his feet. He stood there and stared at it for a long moment.

"Pick the fucking rank up."

Ben didn't move for a long time. Then he picked up the rank and pressed it back to his chest.

"I'll be right back," Ben said softly, picking up Escoberra's file.

It was a long walk to battalion.

Reza was probably right. He should probably wait until tomorrow when the commander wasn't still pissed.

But this couldn't wait until tomorrow. Every day they waited on Escoberra was a day that he got worse. It was a day that Escoberra spent not getting help.

He knocked on Gilliad's door.

The commander looked up, his eyes dark and furious.

Ben stepped into his office, closing the door behind him. "Sir, we need to talk."

"I'm not in the mood right now, Teague," Gilliad said.

It was too soon. Ben didn't care.

"Sir, I need you to sign this."

"I thought I was clear," Gilliad said quietly.

"Sir, command isn't about being a hard-ass for the sake of being a hard-ass. Sometimes, the hardest thing in the world is to be kind. To be merciful." He sucked in a deep breath. "You can do the army thing right now." He released it slowly. "Or you can do the right thing." Another breath. "Sign the paperwork, sir. Do the right thing."

Gilliad studied him. The silence stretched on, the ticking of the wall clock behind Ben the only sound in the dead empty quiet. "This doesn't guarantee he'll get better," Gilliad said quietly. "We'll be wasting time and money."

"It might be, sir," Ben acknowledged. "But it's a chance. And right now, hope is the most powerful thing Escoberra has going for him."

It was a long time before Gilliad moved.

It was late. The company ops was long since deserted but Ben and Sorren sat at the table in the middle of their orderly room. It was a comfortable silence. Silence that didn't need to be filled.

There was a quiet knock on the door.

Ben looked up to see Escoberra standing in the doorway. His throat closed off and just like that, the anxiety was back. Tighter. Making it harder to breathe.

"Hey, sir." Escoberra looked tired. "Sorry I'm late, Top."

Sorren pushed a chair away from the table. "Don't worry about it. You're here. Have a seat."

Ben glanced at his first sergeant over the top of Escoberra's head.

Sorren nodded once, tacit acknowledgment that they were on the same page. Ben had always heard about command teams that could read each other's minds, but this was the first time it had ever happened to him personally.

The scar on Ben's stomach ached as he sat across from Escoberra. "So listen," he said. His voice broke. He cleared his throat then tried again. "We got some paperwork back from the docs."

Escoberra's eyes went wide. Ben had never seen the man more afraid than he was at that moment. "It's not…"

Ben reached across the table, gripping his old platoon sergeant's forearm. "You're sick. You're not dying. And we're going to get you some help."

There it was, all of it. No beating around the bush. No empty platitudes. The rank on his chest was a lead weight. The facts were hard and ugly. But if the rank on his chest was worth anything at all, it was for this.

It was to make a difference. To give someone hope.

"What's wrong with me?"

Ben slid him the folder that Olivia had given him earlier that day. He said nothing while Escoberra read the paperwork.

He was not prepared for Escoberra's eyes to fill. "I really did it." He covered his mouth with his hands. "I really beat up my baby girl?"

It was Sorren who spoke. He gripped Escoberra's shoulder tightly. "You didn't do it on purpose. We can get you help."

"But it involves you taking a knee for a while," Ben said. "You need to move to San Antonio. They've got a real intense treatment program."

As long as he'd known him, Ben had never seen the big man at a loss for words. Not when Ben had gotten blown up. Not when the world had gone to shit around them.

But sitting there, facing the reality of what he'd done, Ben felt the weight of command heavy around his shoulders.

Escoberra looked at him then. "I'm going to have to get out of the army, aren't I?"

Ben swallowed, the knot heavy and thick in his chest. "I don't know. But right now, I think the best thing you can do is try to take some time for you. To try and get healthy." He couldn't save his friend. He didn't even know if treatment would help. But it was something. A tiny ray of hope.

It wasn't enough to make up for the distance between them.

Escoberra nodded, saying nothing for a long, long time. "Thank you." He met Ben's eyes. "For not giving up on me."

Ben didn't tell him he almost had. But instead, Ben remained silent, keeping his doubt, his shame to himself.

Escoberra left. Sorren walked him out.

Ben sat for a long, long time at the table. It should have felt good, getting his commander to sign the paperwork. It should feel good, knowing he'd been right about Escoberra.

But it didn't feel good.

It was a relief but it was heavy. There was no happily ever after.

But it was hope.

And for now, it was enough.

Chapter Twenty-Five

Private First Class Zittoro, Anthony."

Ben looked up at Zittoro as he read through the rest of the packet that would formally end Zittoro's army career.

Zittoro's hands were steady today. His eyes a little more clear.

And Ben felt that tiny seed of hope bloom inside him into something deeper. Something with roots.

"I already signed up for a class at Central Texas College," Zittoro said after he signed the paperwork.

Ben closed the folder. "Yeah? You're staying around here then?"

Zittoro nodded. "No point in going home," he said. "This is the closest thing I've got." He cleared his throat. "I'm moving in with Foster. Figure the two of us can maybe try to help each other stay clean."

Ben smiled. "You two are going to be nothing but trouble." But trouble in a good way, Ben hoped.

"Yeah, well, maybe." Zittoro looked at Ben then. "Thank you, sir. For doing this for me."

A lump blocked Ben's throat. He nodded. "It was the right thing to do," he said when he could speak.

* * *

Olivia found him sitting in his office. The lights were out; the only illumination came from his computer monitor. The light from his computer screen saver slid over his features. Smoke from a cigar wafted through the dim light, glittering darkly with dust.

Fatigue was carved into every shadow on his face.

"All the paperwork is signed," she said quietly, nudging the door closed behind her.

He looked up at her then stood. Emotion slowly filled his eyes once more and he offered a tired smile before opening his arms. She crossed the tiny space between them and slid into his embrace.

Slipped between his thighs and wrapped her arms around his waist. It was a simple embrace. Nothing erotic. Nothing sexual. Just an offer of support after an emotionally draining week. An offer of warmth in the cold turbulence that had raged around them both.

He sat again, drawing her close until she was in his lap, her legs draped over his. He tugged her until her face was buried in his neck. The harsh scrape of his beard stubble abraded her skin but she didn't mind. The warmth of his skin against hers pushed away the cold. His arms around her were tight. Strong. Steady.

She needed nothing more at that moment than to hold him, to be strong as she felt him breaking in her arms. They sat in silence, the connection of their bodies saying more than any words could.

"Thank you," he whispered finally. "For believing in me."

She pressed her lips to the pulse in his throat. "I'm sorry I didn't trust you sooner," she said.

He kissed her forehead gently. "It happens. We all let the scars of our past color our present."

He shifted then. A brush of his lips against her forehead.

The stroke of her thumb against his neck. Tiny actions that drew on the tension, that claimed it and made it something more.

She lifted her mouth to his, opening for his kiss. His breath tangled with hers a moment before he kissed her. Something soft. Fierce. A gentle bite of pleasure that drew her deeper into the vortex of his touch.

She tugged at his shirt. He yanked hers over her head. She pulled open his pants. Passion spiraled wide to pull them both in, deeper. Closer to the center of this thing that was growing between them. Something stronger than either of them could have imagined.

A stapler crashed to the floor as he stood, laying her back on his desk, everything urgent and fierce and needy. He kissed her, hard and deep, while his tongue made love to her mouth. He slipped his fingers lower. Down over the slick edge of her panties to find her core, wet and swollen. He stroked her through her panties then, savoring the arch of her back, the sweet gasp that she made when he slipped a finger beneath the edge of the moist fabric to stroke her sensitive skin.

He wanted her mindless. Needed to lose himself in her passion, her drive, the blinding pleasure of her orgasm. He straightened between her knees, parting her, loving the way she looked spread on his desk. Wanton and wild and with complete abandon. He stood for a moment, his hands framing her hips, looking down at this woman who'd believed in him when he'd wanted to give up.

This woman who had pushed and prodded until he'd believed that he could do the right thing.

Who'd stood by him when he'd made the hardest decisions of his career—and the decision to fight for his men instead of abandoning the field.

He traced his tongue down her belly, overwhelmed by

desire. He paused, placing a gentle kiss above the sweetest, swollen core. He kissed her then, a gentle kiss right at the heart of her. Her hips arched at the sharp, aching pleasure. He dragged his tongue over her, flicking that tiny swollen knot beneath the damp cotton of her panties. And then he stroked her, making love to her with his fingers and his mouth while she writhed on his desk. She was fucking primal. Gorgeous.

His.

Her body tightened on his fingers, her stomach tense beneath the hand he'd placed there to hold her captive.

And then she trembled. Exploded. Shattered. And still trembling, she shimmied her panties over her hips and opened her arms, urging him where he fit most perfectly.

He slid inside her then in a single, hard thrust. Savored the trembling, shaking remains of her orgasm as the remnants of her pleasure rocked through her, over him.

And when she was still, he met her eyes. Twined her fingers with his. And started to move. Slowly. Filling her, touching something deep, deep inside her. Something deep. Something primitive. Something pure.

She hooked her legs around his hips as he rocked against her. Slid her arms around his neck and drew him down. He never looked away from the promise held in her eyes.

From the genuine emotions looking back at him. The care. The concern.

The faith.

The love.

Ben shattered. In the darkness, in the center of her embrace, he lost a piece of himself he'd been clinging to.

And found something new, something he hadn't realized he'd lost so long ago. He held her there, whispering her name in the darkness.

With Olivia. Tangled in her arms, they moved from the desk to the narrow sofa.

And in the sweet, lingering silence, she heard words she'd feared once upon a time. For so long, love had meant pain and betrayal. But right then, whispered across Ben's lips, they were the sweetest sound she'd ever heard.

"I love you," he whispered.

She curled into him. Draped her thigh over his and tangled her arms and legs with his. Pressed her lips to his throat. "I love you."

It was the only response she could manage before tumbling over the edge and into something she'd never dared hope for herself.

Into love.

Epilogue

Three months later

Olivia stepped out of her shower and shrieked.

Ben was sitting on her bathroom sink.

"That is seriously not funny, Ben!" She tugged the towel tight around her body, her hands shaking from the scare.

She hadn't heard him sneak into her home. She should be used to having him in her space now but every so often, he surprised her.

He grinned at her and held out a tiny gold Godiva box. "I brought you a resupply."

She glared at him, not at all mollified by the sudden appearance of emergency chocolate. He'd stopped by her office last week after a particularly draining legal briefing and they'd curled up on her office floor long after the rest of the staff had gone home, eating chocolate and laughing about the day.

"I'm quite positive that did not need to involve stalking me in the bathroom," she said dryly.

"You don't want it?" He held it up over her head, out of her reach.

She tipped her chin, refusing to surrender her dignity by reaching for it.

"I don't want it in the bathroom while I'm naked," she said.

Ben hopped off the counter and wrapped his arms around her shoulders. He was warm and dry where she was wet. Her skin chilled as the moisture evaporated. "Beautiful naked woman and decadent chocolate," he murmured, leaning down to claim her mouth. "What could be more perfect?"

She leaned back to look up at him, tasting crisp white wine on his lips. "Have you been drinking?"

His grin was purely Ben. It was good to see him smiling more. To see the weariness fading. He still had trouble sleeping but it was better than it had been. He was always there when she woke up in the morning.

It was a good way to wake up.

"There may or may not be an open bottle of wine on the kitchen counter."

"Really? The night is looking up." She slipped her arms around his waist. "I thought I was meeting you for dinner."

He shrugged. "I wanted to see you." He nibbled on her bottom lip. "I don't get to see you enough."

It was true. They were a few months out from the deployment and they were busier than ever—and because Ben and Sorren had made a concerted effort to clean up their company, Ben saw less of Olivia during the day.

He regularly threatened to give out random Article Fifteens so he had an excuse to stop into her office more.

She relaxed into his touch, opening for his kiss. Her tongue traced his, sliding against his in erotic friction. "Hmmm. Dinner doesn't sound nearly as good right now as this does," she murmured, arching against him.

"You really should open the chocolate," he whispered, nipping her earlobe.

There was a suspicious note in his voice. She leaned back, looking up at him through narrowed eyes. "What did you do to it?"

"Nothing." His voice was pure innocence but she'd known him long enough to know he was lying.

"Ben."

"Just open the box." He left her standing there, wrapped in a towel.

For a moment, she was unable to move. Fear skittered down her spine as she rubbed her thumb along the edge of the tiny box. Nerves fluttered in her belly as she looked at the small container in her palm. Her breath caught in her throat as she slipped the pretty brown ribbon off and lifted the top.

A tiny black velvet pouch was nestled between four pieces of dark chocolate.

She looked up at him. His expression betrayed raw nerves; his eyes glittered darkly in the steamy bathroom. After a few seconds he left her alone.

Her fingers shook. He wouldn't do this to her, would he? They hadn't talked about this. Not at all. They were deploying in a few weeks.

She fumbled with the pouch. A tiny card slipped out.

She smiled then as her eyes burned. She blinked rapidly and kept reading.

Come into the kitchen.

She was far too curious to get dressed. Wrapped in her towel, she padded down the hall, stopping just before she entered the kitchen. Ben stood at the counter, fiddling with the cork in the top of the bottle of wine. His thumb flicked over the edge, a nervous tick.

"Shit," he mumbled, then turned toward her.

He froze, his gaze dropping down her body in an intimate, dark caress.

She'd stopped at the edge of the carpet.

"What happens if I come into the kitchen?" she whispered.

His throat moved as he swallowed. "You'll have to come to find out." His voice was thick. Nervous.

Olivia didn't move as she sought to control the violent emotions rioting inside her. Questions. Fears.

Fears she saw looking back at her from his dark eyes.

Finally she took a single step. The tile was cold on her bare foot but only for an instant before Ben met her halfway. He sucked in a deep breath, lifting her against him. Holding her close as though he was afraid she wouldn't take that step.

"I'm not really good on big gestures and all that," he whispered. He set her down gently. He captured her left hand. "But I was hoping you'd marry me." He stroked his thumb over her ring finger.

"I know we didn't talk about it…" He looked down at her.

She didn't move, watching the emotion play out over his face. Disbelief. Amazement.

And finally she gave a single nod. He cradled her face in his palms. She laughed then lost herself in his kiss, his touch. He set her on the counter. "You said yes."

"Yeah," she whispered. "Maybe I like having you around."

"You did that on purpose, didn't you," he growled against her mouth.

"What, made you wait?" She threaded her arms around his shoulders. "Maybe."

"That was a really, really screwed up thing to do, toying with my emotions that way." His thumb brushed over her cheek and he lowered his forehead to hers. "I'm not sure how this whole going-to-war-together thing is going to work," he whispered. Deployment was looming closer and closer.

"Does it worry you? Me being there with you?"

"I'd be lying if I told you no," he said quietly. "I'm not sure I won't completely lose my shit if you get yourself hurt."

She kissed him gently, moved by his concern. "I'll do my best not to get blown up."

He wasn't kidding. His eyes were darkly serious. His fingers tensed on her cheeks.

She lifted his face until he looked at her. "Ben, I was kidding."

She knew the look on his face. Serious Ben was always such a stark change from how he was normally. "I don't know how guys do this," he said. "I can go. I can lead patrols and do what I do. But I don't know how I'm going to deal with you being out in sector with the colonel. I don't know how I'm going to deal with you being out there, at risk."

"Just like you deal when your soldiers go out. You train them to be the best you can, then you have to let go."

He lowered his forehead back to hers. "It's not the same. I don't want to spend the rest of my life with one of my soldiers. I want to spend it with you," he whispered. "And I'd like that to be a really long time." He kissed her gently. "So no getting blown up, okay?"

She brushed her lips against his. "Same goes for you, too."

She didn't know how to answer his fear. Didn't know how to assuage it or help him face it. Instead, she did the only thing she knew how to do.

She dropped the towel from her body. Wrapped her legs around his hips. And made love to the man she wanted to spend her life with.

Traumatized by combat and alienated
from his family, army captain Trent
Davila deploys again and again. When he
faces a court-martial, only his wife
Laura can save him. But as her act of
kindness inflames a desire she thought
long buried, can Laura trust that this time
he's back to stay?

**Please see the next page for
an excerpt from**

Back to You.

Prologue

Fort Hood, 2007

I put your checkbook in the front pocket of your rucksack. Did you find the sleep medication? You'll need to sleep on the plane so that you're rested when you land. And I put your calling card—"

Captain Trent Davila looked up from where he sat on the edge of their bathtub. He held a tiny folded flag in his hands. For a moment, he'd been somewhere else. Sulfur scorched the inside of his nose. The thunder of the fifty cal reverberated off his breastbone.

"What's that?" she asked softly, watching him from the bathroom door.

He held out his palm so she could see the little flag. "Good luck charm. I can't deploy without it."

A thousand questions flickered over her face as her gaze fell onto that tiny flag. She bit her lip and turned away, but not before he saw the naked fear looking back at him.

He moved, stepping in front of his wife and capturing her face in his palms. Her skin was smooth and soft and achingly familiar, and a deep part of his soul missed her already.

But that part of his soul wasn't in control right now. The moment she touched him, his soul recoiled, refusing to let him take even the simplest pleasure in her touch.

He'd cheated death and he knew, *knew* he didn't deserve to be there with his wife when so many of his men had died.

That's why he had to leave. Again. It didn't matter to where. It didn't matter if it was the war in Iraq or a transition team somewhere in the mountains of Afghanistan. He needed to get away. To get back into the fight.

And pray that his wife would understand why he had to go.

"Laura." He whispered her name, capturing her attention.

She tried to look away, to pretend that today was just another day. But Trent knew her too well. He saw the doubt and the fear that she tried to hide. Her eyes, though, her eyes always gave her away. He stroked an errant strand of copper hair away from her forehead, meeting her golden eyes, unable to speak any words of comfort. He knew they'd just be more empty lies.

She offered a watery smile. "I'm terrified of losing you again," she whispered.

"I've deployed since I got hurt. This time is no different."

"You didn't get hurt." She refused to meet his gaze. "You died. Your heart actually stopped beating. And this time is worse. This is the Surge." Her voice broke. "I can't lose you again," she whispered. Her voice cracked as the tears tumbled down her cheeks.

He hated to see her cry. Worse, he knew he could prevent those tears.

He pulled her close and simply held her, wishing he could feel as alive with his wife and family as he did when he was at war. Maybe someday, when the war was over, he could figure out what had broken inside him and how to fix it.

He stroked his thumbs over her cheeks as the kids

shrieked in Ethan's bedroom. The sound sent a spike of anxiety through Trent's heart, but he smiled, hoping to cheer her up. "Sounds like someone just lost a Lego."

"Daddy!"

"He's probably going to beg you for a hamster again," she said. Laura swiped at her eyes, blinking rapidly. "Can't let them see me like this."

He slid from her embrace, regret sealing the walls that four deployments had erected around his heart. Trent tried not to notice how intently Laura watched him, her gaze sweeping over the scars on his body as he finished getting dressed. His dog tags banged against his ribs as he dragged his t-shirt over his head and pulled on the rest of his uniform and then his boots.

"Well, you could get one," Trent said, needing the distraction of simple conversation.

"Or," Laura said with a smile that didn't reach her eyes, "you could promise him one when you get home. It'll give him something to look forward to."

Trent frowned at the odd note in Laura's voice and focused on tying his boots and tucking the laces beneath the cuffs of his pants. "He won't even notice I'm gone. They're both too little."

Trent straightened as Laura approached, placing her palm over the scar on his heart. It burned where she touched him. It took everything he had not to flinch away from the gentleness in that touch. "Keep telling yourself that," she said with a soft kiss. "They miss you when you're gone. We all do."

He sighed quietly and glanced at her, resting his hands gently on her hips. "Laura, you know I have to go."

He couldn't explain it. Didn't have the words to explain the emptiness inside him that consumed every waking moment when he wasn't over there. And worse, he didn't ever want her to see the emptiness he tried so hard to hide from her.

She believed he'd come home. As long as she continued to believe that, his world would continue to exist.

She brushed her thumb over his bottom lip. She blinked rapidly and the sight of her tears almost penetrated the cold empty space where his heart had been. "I just wish it got a little easier waiting for you, that's all." Her fingers wrapped around his dog tags, her thumb sliding along the chain. "But we'll be here when you get back. We always are."

He ran his fingers lightly over her face. The lie he'd told his wife so often sat like a concrete wall between them. She didn't know that he'd volunteered for this deployment, for so many others, and he had no way of killing the lie without killing their marriage. "Don't go getting a deployment boyfriend while I'm gone."

"I don't think you have to worry about that." Laura wrapped her arms around him, nuzzling his neck. They stood for a long moment before Laura eased away.

Trent swallowed and let her go. Again.

Five hours later, Trent kissed his wife good-bye for the fourth time in six years. His four-year-old son and two-year-old daughter were getting antsy, climbing up and down the bleachers nonstop. As he walked away from the gym where he and the rest of his unit had checked in for the deployment, he glanced up at her in the stands. She was steady. Stoic. Trying valiantly not to join the ranks of the wives and children who were crying as their soldiers left them, assault packs and weapons in hand. God but he wished he didn't have to go. That he was man enough to stay home and fix whatever was broken inside him. Wished that he was man enough to need her more than the heady, uncertain terror of war.

"You ready, sir?"

Trent glanced over at First Sarn't Roy Story, a man who'd taught Trent the right way to kick in doors and the difference between knowing when to wipe a nose or whip an ass. The war was lined into Story's leathery face. Fifteen years as an infantryman that had started in Mogadishu and continued with the long slog through Iraq.

"Are we ever really ready for this?" Trent asked, taking one more long look at his wife and kids. And then he turned away, needing to harden his heart for the battles to come.

Outside, Trent climbed aboard the bus that would take them to the airfield. Spouses filed out from the gym along the sidewalk. In the seat behind him, Sergeant Vic Carponti was harassing one of Trent's platoon sergeants, Sergeant First Class Shane Garrison. He almost smiled. With those two around, things would never be dull.

He scanned the crowd, searching for his wife amongst the blurry faces of other people's spouses lining the sidewalk. There. She held her vigil in front of a light pole, a tiny hand in each of hers. Beside her, Ethan stood bravely, tears streaming down his face. He held a tiny salute, his mouth pressed into a flat line as he tried to be a tough little man. Emma waved brightly at the bus, still too little to fully understand that Daddy was leaving for longer than a trip to the grocery store.

He looked away but it was far, far too late. When he closed his eyes, the image of his small family was seared onto his retinas as the bus pulled out of the parking lot and headed for the airfield.

"Never gets any easier, does it?" Story asked quietly, sucking on the end of an unlit cigar while he fiddled with a light on his helmet. There was little love left between Story and his wife. Story deployed to avoid his wife.

But Trent deployed to avoid his *life*. Because life back in the rear was too complicated, too loud, too chaotic. War was simpler.

The scar on his chest ached and he rubbed it, wishing

he could forget the way his family looked as the bus pulled away.

He closed his eyes, trying to put them out of his mind. He didn't want to remember his wife with her cheeks streaked with tears or the raw grief in her eyes. He wanted to remember her face as she slept curled into his side. Or laughing with their kids. He needed to carry those memories into war with him. Because that was all that would steel him against the long hours and bone-crushing fatigue to come.

He had soldiers to command. His family would be there when he came home.

He hoped.

Chapter One

Fort Irwin, California, 2008

One year later...

Trent walked out of the ops tent, needing a few minutes to himself. They'd just sent word that the wife of a kid in one of the companies was in the hospital. She was going into labor while her husband was enjoying the fun and sun of the National Training Center.

At least the kid wasn't deployed. He'd be able to get home quickly. Sure, not as quickly as if he was back at Fort Hood, but still. It beat the hell out of trying to get home from Iraq.

The notification was something simple, and yet it had struck Trent that yet another soldier was going to miss the birth of his child because of the army.

He knew exactly how that felt, and right then a thousand bitter memories rose up, reminding him of everything he'd willingly squandered. The resurrected hurt was so raw, the regret so powerful, he nearly choked on it.

He should have been used to the hurt by now, but lately it seemed to be getting worse. It overwhelmed the dead space inside him, forcing him to feel things he didn't want—and wasn't ready to feel.

He didn't know *how* to feel them, how to deal with them. So for the moment he sat outside the ops tent and let the raging emotions storm inside him. Until he could get them under control. Until he could function again.

It had been happening more and more this year. The things he'd stuffed away had started having a nasty habit of reappearing when he least expected them.

He was starting to get comfortable with the crazy, but at least now he was starting to recognize the warning signs. Which was why he was sitting outside the ops tent.

"So your BFF Marshall is looking for you." Story walked out of the ops tent, a smirk on his face that only meant bad things for Trent. It was so strange calling him "master sergeant" instead of "first sergeant," but Story wasn't a first sergeant anymore. Just like Trent was no longer a commander.

Trent sat on the hood of a Humvee, smoking a cigar and contemplating his sixth cup of coffee since he'd come on shift twelve hours ago. He pushed his glasses up higher on his nose then glanced over as Story hopped up next to him.

Since they'd both been fired more than a year ago, they'd been hanging out on the staff together, responsible for nothing but PowerPoint slides. Funny how getting fired meant giving up the hard jobs in the army. You still got to stay in the army, but you just weren't trusted with taking care of soldiers anymore. It was a punishment, being put in the easy jobs. Trent would have given anything to get his old job as a company commander back, but that wasn't going to happen so he and Story and Iaconelli kept each other sane and avoided the new commander. Captain James T. Marshall the Third drove everyone fucking crazy.

"Should I be worried?" Trent asked dryly, adjusting his glasses again. He'd long ago given up getting upset when

Marshall attempted to piss in his cornflakes. Marshall had been tapped to take over Trent's company when he'd gotten himself fired and Marshall took great pleasure in reminding everyone that he was fixing all the things that Trent had screwed up. It grated on Trent's last nerve every time the words, "Well sir, I'm still fixing the mess I was left when I took over" came out of Marshall's mouth at staff meetings, but what could Trent say? He *had* gotten fired. It didn't matter why. He supposed part of his penance for being a shitty commander was having to listen to Marshall without knocking his teeth out. He'd leave that for Story and a few of the captains like Ben Teague who were leading the insurgency on the staff. Trent had other things on his mind.

Like his wife. His two kids. The house that was no longer his.

He cleared his throat and tried to listen to Story.

"I don't know," Story said. "Marshall wasn't screaming so I think maybe you should be okay?"

Sergeant First Class Reza Iaconelli, one of Trent's former platoon sergeants, stepped out of the ops tent. "No, you should definitely hide," he said, interrupting the conversation. "He's bitching about having to transport you back to the rear early and he's pretty cranky."

Iaconelli was a big man: broad shoulders and built like an ox. He was steadfast and solid downrange but when they got home? Yeah, that's when things went to shit for Iaconelli. He'd never met a bottle of alcohol that he didn't like. He was lucky he still had a career but the sergeant major liked him. Trent respected his ability in combat enough to overlook any personal failings. Trent was the last one to judge someone's personal failings.

He reined his thoughts back to the present and the feeling that flittered in the dead space around his heart. "I'm getting sent back?"

Iaconelli shrugged. "Maybe they're finally going to court-martial your sorry ass," he said lightly.

Trent flipped him off. "That would be nice, actually. If they'd at least get the damn thing over with. If I never see Lieutenant Jason Randall ever again, it will be too soon."

"He is a special little fuckstick, that is for certain," Iaconelli said, staring at the end of his cigar for a moment.

Iaconelli may or may not have threatened to kill LT Randall downrange. Twice. But all of Randall's interpersonal hostility had been a sideshow, a distraction to keep Trent or anyone else from figuring out that he had been selling sensitive items and funneling the money to bribe the Iraqis to stop blowing their boys up. Randall had finally gotten caught and now was determined to take down Trent and anyone else he could with him. Iaconelli chopped the tip off his cigar and sucked on the end while he tried to light it.

"Too bad I won't be around for his court-martial," Story said.

"Did you get reassigned?" Iaconelli asked Story.

"Yeah. I'm deploying again in about two weeks. As soon as we get back from here," he said.

"Your wife isn't going to be happy," Trent said quietly.

"Actually, she's going to be thrilled. It'll give her a chance to find her some twenty-year-old boy toy to keep her busy while I'm gone." Story spat into the dust.

"So you're still married because ... ?" Iaconelli sucked on the end of his cigar.

"Because it's too fucking expensive to get divorced," Story said. "I'll take care of it after this next deployment. I'll save up some money first, though."

"Sure you will," Trent said. "You've been saying that since '04."

It was Story's turn to flip Trent off. "At least I'm willing to accept my marriage is over."

Trent rubbed his heart, knowing his first sergeant hadn't meant to score such a direct hit. At least not with malice. "Yeah well, my divorce is complicated."

"These things always are." Iaconelli leaned against the truck. "Which is why I've never gotten married."

Trent snorted and was going to make a crack but Marshall took that opportunity to step into the darkness outside the ops tent. "Davila, you're going back to Fort Hood."

Trent glanced at his watch. "It's four-thirty in the morning."

"And you're going to be on a plane in three hours. Pack your shit." Marshall turned to stalk off, mumbling about pain in the ass captains and not having enough time for this shit.

Iaconelli blew a smoke ring into the darkness. "God but he is such a charmer."

Trent sat there long after Story and Iaconelli went back into the ops tent.

He wanted to go home. But now that it was happening, fear slithered down his spine.

It had started slow. One day he'd wake up, dreaming about Laura. Other times, he'd be in the mess tent and he'd think he heard her laugh. He'd hear a kid giggling on the TV and he'd look up, expecting to see Ethan or Emma.

Always, though, he was alone. He'd wanted it that way for so long. He'd wanted quiet when they'd been running around his feet, shrieking and bickering like kids did. He'd craved silence at the end of the day when someone would get out of bed for a glass of water.

He'd certainly gotten the silence and the solitude.

And the oppressive emptiness of it all ate away at him. He'd thrown himself into work here in the California desert. He'd pulled eighteen hour days gladly. The longer he spent away from the war, the less he felt its siren call, luring him back. And somehow, work wasn't enough anymore. Nothing he did pushed away the aching need to get to the one place he simply didn't belong: home.

He was back in the States but he couldn't go home. Not with an investigation hanging over his head and the potential for a very long jail sentence standing in front of him. And the worst part about the entire court-martial was that his brigade commander was changing command soon. If Colonel Richter left before the case was resolved, Trent would be at the mercy of the new commander—a new man with no loyalty to the soldiers he'd put in leadership positions.

It was not a comfortable place to be. The power plays between the senior officers never ended well for junior officers, and Trent? Trent was caught right now. He had to trust that Colonel Richter would take care of this before he left.

But a year after Trent had been sent home, Trent was running low on trust and patience.

Patience had never been his strong suit. Every other time he'd been home, he'd been prepping to go back to war. This time, the year had stretched in front of him like an unending slog.

It was the longest time he'd spent in the States since he'd gotten shot. It had taken him almost that long to realize just how badly he'd fucked up everything in his life that was supposed to be important.

His marriage. His kids. His family.

If there was a grade lower than an F at being a husband or a dad, he'd earned it. He'd come home from Iraq nearly a year ago—pending a court-martial and a divorce. And since then, nothing had happened. The case had been stuck in investigation mode forever. And the divorce? He just wasn't able to sign the papers. His life had been frozen in carbonite on all counts.

The investigation had moved slower than molasses in winter. And he was glad.

Because standing out here in the California desert, he'd come to a conclusion. He wanted his family back. He wanted his *wife* back. When she'd slapped him with divorce papers last year, he'd refused to sign them, hoping that the investigation would go away and that he could fix things with her. But that hope had proved futile. The distance between them was too much. The warmth he remembered was gone, but still, he'd been unable to let her go. He couldn't. Sure, they spoke on the phone or when he saw her at the office, but they were a few stolen minutes here, a quick chat about the kids. There was nothing there to give him hope that he could fix things with her.

He'd volunteered to train soldiers anywhere he could so that he didn't have to face the cold emptiness of the reality that he was no longer welcome in his own home. And if he volunteered, someone else wouldn't have to.

Now? Now he sat in the middle of the California desert and thought about the new dad who wouldn't be there for the birth of his child. He looked down at his wedding ring and thought of all the time he'd willingly given up.

He was a goddamned fool. He wanted her back. Damn it, he wanted his *life* back. The life with this woman who had once smiled and laughed with him and wrapped herself around him while she slept. Who was as beautiful changing Emma's diaper as she was dressed up in an evening gown for the Cav ball. This woman who used to ask about his day when he called home at two in the morning, even after she'd been up half the night with one of the kids.

He sobered, his hands trembling at the thought of his children and the tiny family that had grown while he'd been away. The tiny family that overwhelmed him and terrified him and dropped him to his knees with a need so strong, it crushed his lungs until he could not breathe. He didn't know how to feel good, but he knew he'd never figure it out without them.

He had no clue where to start. He had no idea how to be a father to his kids. Or a husband to a wife who could barely look at him.

Trent hopped off the top of the truck. He had a phone call to make.

Because it looked like he was getting exactly what he wanted.

And it was time to figure out how to be the man his family needed him to be.

Fort Hood

"Son of a bi-iscuit!"

"Bad Mommy!"

Laura Davila wrapped her scraped and bleeding knuckles in a paper towel and prayed to the patron saint of army wives for patience. Her six-year-old dishwasher was currently spread in carefully laid out pieces across the kitchen floor and counters. And now the cavernous white interior was splattered with her blood. Awesome.

Her son Ethan looked up at her with disapproval in his dark brown eyes, and Laura flinched. "Sorry, honey. Mommy just hurt herself."

"You said a bad word." This from her daughter, Emma. "Agent Chaos said you're not allowed to say those words."

Laura glared at the fat brown hamster that was clutched in her daughter's hands. Agent Chaos looked up at her with disapproving beady brown eyes. Sitting there, silently judging her.

She had joked with Trent that he should buy the kids a hamster when he returned from his latest deployment. By the time he came back, things between them had already crumbled but he still remembered the damn hamster. He'd bought not one, but two of the stinking, smelly creatures.

The hamster cuteness factor did not override the pain in the ass factor of having to clean their cages every other day to keep the smell from overpowering the entire house.

Maybe if Trent had been around more over the last year, she wouldn't have minded them so much. But instead of sitting at Fort Hood and working in an office like any other officer who was under investigation, he'd volunteered for several rotations at the National Training Center in Fort Irwin. He'd spent more time there than at Fort Hood over the last year. He might as well have just moved there.

She took a deep breath and pressed on her throbbing knuckles, focusing on the pain so that she wouldn't feel the tension that squeezed her heart every time she thought about her husband. She regretted sending him the divorce papers. She could admit that now, but she'd done the only thing she could at the time.

She could still remember that stupid flare of hope when he'd stood in her office that day. Hope that maybe, finally, he had come home to her.

But he hadn't.

And as time had ticked by and he'd refused to sign the papers and let her go, she'd moved beyond regret. Now, she wanted to move on with her life. Maybe someday she'd be able to think of Trent without the hurt and frustration that kept reminding her of everything she'd lost.

"You have to pay us each a quarter," Ethan said, stroking the fat orange hamster in his hands. Laura was seriously thinking about buying a cat—that would solve the hamster problem quickly enough. But it would be just one more thing to clean up after.

And she wasn't really up for the trauma of finding a dead hamster under the bed.

She could only imagine the therapy bills.

She pursed her lips and counted to ten…thousand. "Okay

guys, why don't you go play in the garage or something? Mommy has too many parts in here, and I don't want you to get hurt."

Or move anything. But she didn't say that out loud, because that would only encourage them to run off with some vital component that would take her three days to identify and two more days to find online and order. A new dishwasher was not in the budget at the moment. Besides, she wanted to see if she could actually fix the thing herself.

She shooed the kids and their accompanying hamsters out of the kitchen and made her way through the master bedroom to the cache of Band-Aids she hid in her bathroom. The kids were all too eager to use every bandage in the house if she let them, which always meant that she couldn't find a Band-Aid when she really needed one. She'd resorted to hiding them like they were some kind of precious commodity. In her house, they were.

Laura pulled down the shoebox that held the first aid kit. She held her breath as she cleaned the cuts on her knuckles with iodine, then wrapped gauze halfway down her fingers, covering the empty space where her wedding and engagement rings had once been.

She paused, staring at her ring finger. Blood pooled on the pale band of skin there, as if her finger refused to forget the rings that had been there since forever.

Her finger might not forget the rings but that didn't mean it was a marriage worth waiting for. No amount of waiting or wishful thinking was going to change that. Trent had seen to that. And broken her heart all over again.

She knew in her heart that they were finished. He had lied to her so many times about his deployments. That alone had destroyed her trust in him. And then there was the rest of it...

She was ready for the pain to stop. Ready for her heart to

stop waiting for the phone to ring. Waiting, so desperately for her heart to stop beating for a man who was never coming home.

A spike of melancholy pressed on her lungs. Damn it, what was wrong with her today? She was past mourning the death of her marriage. At least she kept telling herself that. So when was it going to stop hurting?

She briefly considered a shot of vodka to numb the pain, but that wasn't really a good idea since she was alone with the kids. She barely ever had a drink these days. She sighed and glanced wistfully at the discreet box on the top shelf in the bathroom closet. Droughts were not limited to alcohol.

She had gotten used to it, this new normal. While the kids were vibrant chaos, full of life and joy, the married part of her life was...well, it simply was. There was nothing there anymore. No joy. No hatred. Just silence and cold detachment overlying a dull aching sadness.

She simply wanted it to be over. And damn Trent to hell for dragging it out when he wasn't even willing to fight for them. And the silence between them? Between her and the man she'd thought she'd love for the rest of her life?

She sat on the edge of their bed, one finger rubbing absently over the bruised knuckles and her empty ring finger. She could hear the kids shrieking in the garage. One of the hamsters had gotten away. She smiled. She really didn't mind them, not when the kids loved the judgmental little beasts so much. It was a gesture of kindness from a man who couldn't be a father. She knew that.

It didn't make it hurt any less. She'd married him knowing what she was getting into, thinking her love for him was strong enough to withstand whatever the army could throw at them. Knowing that the army was a demanding job, that he'd be gone a lot. But that first deployment had done something to him, something deeper than just the visible scars on his body.

Once she never would have thought the silence would grow too loud or that his empty side of the bed would become too heavy to bear. Once she would have waited forever for him to come home to her.

But forever was a long time.

And her faith in their love had died long ago on some distant battlefield.

Fall in Love with Forever Romance

A HOPE REMEMBERED
by Stacy Henrie

The final book in Stacy Henrie's sweeping Of Love and War trilogy brings to life the drama of WWI England with emotion and romance. As the Great War comes to a close, American Nora Lewis finds herself starting over on an English estate. But it's the battle-scarred British pilot Colin Ashby she meets there who might just be able to convince her to believe in love again.

SCANDALOUSLY YOURS
by Cara Elliott

Secret passions are wont to lead a lady into trouble... Meet the rebellious Sloane sisters in the first book of the Hellions of High Street series from bestselling author Cara Elliott.

Fall in Love with Forever Romance

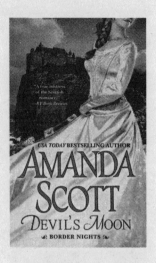

DEVIL'S MOON
by Amanda Scott

In a flawless blend of history and romance, *USA Today* bestselling author Amanda Scott transports readers again to the Scottish Borders with the second book in her Border Nights series.

THE SCANDALOUS SECRET OF ABIGAIL MacGREGOR
by Paula Quinn

Abigail MacGregor has a secret: her mother is the true heir to the English crown. But if the wrong people find out, it will mean war for her beloved Scotland. There's only one way to keep the peace—journey to London, escorted by her enemy, the wickedly handsome Captain Daniel Marlow. Fans of Karen Hawkins and Monica McCarty will love this book!

Fall in Love with Forever Romance

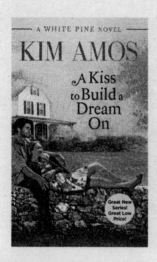

A KISS TO BUILD
A DREAM ON
by Kim Amos

Spoiled and headstrong, Willa Masterson left her hometown—and her first love, Burk Olmstead—in the rearview twelve years ago. But the woman who returns is determined to rebuild: first her family house, then her relationships with everyone in town...starting with a certain tall, dark, and sexy contractor. Fans of Kristan Higgins, Jill Shalvis, and Lori Wilde will flip for Kim Amos's Forever debut!

IT'S ALWAYS BEEN YOU
by Jessica Scott

Captain Ben Teague is mad as hell when his trusted mentor is brought up on charges that can't possibly be true. And the lawyer leading the charge, Major Olivia Hale, drives him crazy. But something is simmering beneath her icy reserve—and Ben can't resist turning up the heat! Fans of Robyn Carr and JoAnn Ross will love this poignant and emotional military romance.

Fall in Love with Forever Romance

TOTAL SURRENDER
by Rebecca Zanetti

Piper Oliver knows she can't trust tall, dark, and sexy black-ops soldier Jory Dean. All she has to do, though, is save his life and he'll be gone for good. But something isn't adding up...and she won't rest until she uncovers the truth—even if it's buried in his dangerous kiss. Fans of Maya Banks and Lora Leigh will love this last book in Rebecca Zanetti's Sin Brothers series!